"In *Blood Hollow*, Krueger delivers his superb sense of atmosphere in a solidly plotted tale of betrayal, bigotry and mysticism. *Blood Hollow*'s twists continue to surprise even to the last line."

—*Sun-Sentinel* (Fort Lauderdale, FL)

"The first ten pages . . . are so heart-stopping you'll feel as though you're riding on the snowmobile with Cork when he becomes lost in a blizzard. . . . Krueger is at the top of his form."

—*St. Paul Pioneer Press*

PURGATORY RIDGE

"The kind of work that is all too rare in the suspense genre, a book that combines a first-class plot with excellent writing. . . . The result is a story that pulls the reader in on the first page and holds him fast until the satisfyingly correct wrap-up on the last."

—*The Denver Post*

"Mr. Krueger shows sensitive insight into the conflicts between ancient culture and contemporary economic needs. He has developed a cast with deep feelings and intelligent responses to their surroundings and their fellow humans. Suspenseful, compelling and highly readable, *Purgatory Ridge* is a page-turner."

—*Dallas Morning News*

BOUNDARY WATERS

"Krueger's writing, strong and bold yet with the mature mark of restraint, pulls this exciting search-and-rescue mission through with a hard yank."

—*Publishers Weekly*

ALSO BY WILLIAM KENT KRUEGER

Blood Hollow
The Devil's Bed
Purgatory Ridge
Boundary Waters
Iron Lake

MERCY FALLS

WILLIAM KENT KRUEGER

POCKET BOOKS

New York   London   Toronto   Sydney

POCKET BOOKS, a division of Simon & Schuster, Inc.
1230 Avenue of the Americas, New York, NY 10020

This book is a work of fiction. Names, characters, places and incidents are products of the author's imagination or are used fictitiously. Any resemblance to actual events or locales or persons, living or dead, is entirely coincidental.

Copyright © 2005 by William Kent Krueger

Originally published in hardcover in 2005 by Atria Books

ISBN-13: 978-0-7434-4589-4
ISBN-10:   0-7434-4589-9

This Pocket Books paperback edition July 2006

10 9 8 7 6 5 4 3 2

POCKET and colophon are registered trademarks of Simon & Schuster, Inc.

Cover design by John Vairo, Jr.
Cover photo by Jupiter Images

Manufactured in the United States of America

For information regarding special discounts for bulk purchases, please contact Simon & Schuster Special Sales at 1-800-456-6798 or business@simonandschuster.com

In memory of
Marilynne Miracle Krueger
and
Jane Jordan Browne,
two great women who have passed.

ACKNOWLEDGMENTS

First, a hearty thanks to all my cohorts in Crème de la Crime who, for a dozen years, have offered me the best in comradeship and critique.

I am so very thankful for Danielle Egan-Miller's decision to return to the business of being an agent, which she does so well.

For their editorial guidance and strong voices on my behalf, I owe a deep debt of gratitude to my editors, Emily Bestler and Sarah Branham. Thanks also to Anne Harris and Holly Bemiss of Atria, who have worked so hard with me to get the word out.

There are people who live the reality the rest of us draw on for our fiction. We are fortunate that they tend to be generous with their expertise and experience. Thanks to: former Pine County sheriff Steve Haavisto; Sergeant Jane Laurence of the St. Paul Police Department; Ramsey County Assistant Attorney Tami McConkey; and Connie Carlson and all her gang (cops and otherwise) in Prior Lake, Minnesota.

Finally, a big hug to Jim Theros and my friends at the St. Clair Broiler, staff and regulars, who make the place feel so much like home.

MERCY
FALLS

HOW IT ENDS

SHE WOKE NAKED on the bed, in a room she didn't recognize, her mind as clear of memory as the sky outside her window was of clouds. A huge pillow that smelled faintly of lavender cradled her head. She was too warm and drew back the covers so that she lay exposed on the white sheet like a delicacy on a china plate.

She tried to sit up, far too quickly, and the room spun. A minute later, she tried again, this time rising gradually until she could see the whole of the great bedroom. The bed itself was a four-poster with a canopy. The armoire a few feet distant was the color of maple syrup and carved with ornate scrolling. On the walls, in elegant, gilt-edged frames, hung oil paintings of Mediterranean scenes, mostly with boats and angry, blue-black seas. The magnificent red of the Persian rug matched the thick drapes drawn back to let in the morning light. None of this was familiar to her. But there was one detail that struck a welcome chord: an explosion of daisies in a yellow vase on the vanity. Daisies, she remembered, had always been her favorite flowers.

A clean, white terry cloth robe had been neatly laid out at the foot of the bed, but she ignored it. She walked to the daisies and touched one of the blossoms. Something about the fragility of the petals touched her in return and made her sad in a way that felt like grieving.

For whom? she wondered, trying to nudge aside the veil that, at the moment, hung between her perception and all her understanding. Then a thought occurred to her. The birds. Maybe that was it. She was grieving for all the dead birds.

Her eyes lifted to the vanity mirror. In the reflection there, she saw the bruises on her body. One on her left breast above her nipple, another on the inside of her right thigh, oval-shaped, both of them, looking very much like the blue ghosts of tooth marks.

As she reached down and gingerly touched the tender skin, she heard firecrackers go off outside her window, two of them. Only two? she thought. What kind of celebration was that?

She put on the robe, went to the door, and opened it. Stepping out, she found herself in a long hallway with closed doors on either side, her only companions several tall standing plants that were spaced between the rooms like mute guardians. At each end of the hall, leaded windows with beveled glass let in enough daylight to give the emptiness a sense of benign well-being that she somehow knew was false. She crept down the hallway, listening for the slightest sound, feeling the deep nap of the carpet crush under the soles of her bare feet. At last she reached a staircase that wound to the lower level. She followed the lazy spiral unsteadily, her hand holding to the railing for balance, leaving moist fingerprints on the polished wood that vanished a moment after her passing.

She stood at the bottom of the stairway, uncertain which way to turn. To her right, a large room with a baby grand piano at its center, a brick fireplace, a sofa and loveseat of chocolate brown leather. To her left, a dining room with a huge crystal chandelier and a table large enough for a banquet. Sunlight from a long window cleaved the table, and in the bright gleam sat another vase full of daisies. Drawn by the smell of freshly brewed coffee, she moved through the dining room to the opened door of the kitchen beyond.

A carafe of orange juice sat on the counter near the sink, and next to it a glass, poured and waiting. The smell of the coffee came from a French-press coffee-maker that sat on a large butcher-block island. An empty cup and saucer had been placed on the block, as if she were expected. A book lay there, too, opened to a page that began, *I couldn't sleep all night; a fog-horn was groaning incessantly in the Sound, and I tossed half-sick between grotesque reality and savage, frightening dreams.*

The sliding glass door that overlooked the veranda was drawn back, letting in the morning air, and she walked across the cool black and white kitchen tiles to the doorway. From there, she could see the back of the estate with its pool set into the lawn like a piece of cut turquoise. Beyond was the blue-gray sweep of a great body of water that collided at the horizon with a cornflower sky. Beside the pool stood a man in a yellow windbreaker with the hood pulled up. Although she couldn't see his face, there was something familiar in his stance. She stepped outside, not bothering to slide the door closed behind her.

It was a chilly morning. The cold marble of the veranda made her feet ache, but she paid no attention, because something else had caught her eye. A crimson billow staining the blue water. She descended the steps and followed a limestone walk to the apron of the pool.

The body lay on the bottom, except for the arms, which floated free, lifted slightly as if in supplication. The swimming trunks were white, the skin tanned. She couldn't see the wounds, only the blood that leaked from somewhere underneath, gradually tinting the turquoise water a deep rose.

The standing man turned his head slowly, as if it were difficult, painful even, for him to look away from death. The sun was at his back, his face shadowed, a gun in his hand.

She recognized him, and the thought of what he'd just done pulled her heart out of her chest.

"Oh, Cork, no," she whispered.

When he heard his name, his hard, dark eyes grew soft. Corcoran O'Connor stared at his wife, at her clean robe, her bare feet, her hair still mussed from a night she barely remembered.

"Jo," he said, "I came to bring you home."

1

THEY HIT THE skunk just outside of town, and after that, they drove with the windows down. It didn't help much.

"I know what you're thinking," Deputy Marsha Dross said.

"How could you know what I'm thinking?" Cork replied.

"Because it's what I'd be thinking if I were you."

"And what's that?"

"That if I'd let you drive, this wouldn't have happened."

"You're not me," Cork said. "And that's not what I'm thinking."

"What are you thinking?"

"Just wondering if there's enough money in the budget for a new Land Cruiser." He put his head out the window and let the air clear his nose.

The road they were traveling had been traveled before by generations of Ojibwe and Voyageurs. It connected the Blueberry River with Iron Lake and had been an important passage in the days of the fur trade. The French had called it Portage du Myrtille,

Blueberry Portage. To the Ojibwe, whom the white men often called Chippewa but who preferred the name Anishinaabe, which meant Original People, it was known as Maanadamon—Bad Trail—because it was a long portage with stretches of marsh and deep mud. And skunks. To the engineers who, in the mid twentieth century, had widened and graded it and laid down asphalt, it was called simply County Road 23. They'd killed the beauty of the names, but they hadn't been able to destroy the stunning grandeur of the land through which it ran, the great Northwoods of Minnesota.

The asphalt ended at the beginning of the Iron Lake Reservation. On the rez, the wide shoulders disappeared and the road became a narrow gravel track following a clear stream that threaded its way through vast stands of pine and rugged hills topped with birch trees and spruce.

As Dross slowed down, the skunk smell grew worse.

"Maybe I should take it through a creek or something," she suggested.

"With skunk, I think you just have to let it wear off. Maybe we'll put this unit out to pasture for a while." He scanned the road in front of them, looking for the turn he knew was coming up.

Autumn had started out cold that year. The sugar maples and sumac had turned early, a deep crimson. At sunrise, the eastern sky was often the color of an open wound and sometimes on crisp mornings the frost that lay over everything reflected the sky, and the whole land appeared to bleed. Warm weather returned in the first week of October, and for the past few days it had felt almost like June again.

"I love Indian summer." Marsha Dross smiled, as if hoping for a pleasant change of subject.

She was a tall woman, nearly six feet, and slender. Her hair was coarse and brown and she kept it short. She had a broad face, large nose. In her uniform and without makeup—something she never wore on the job—she was sometimes mistaken for a man. Off duty, she knew what to do with mascara and eyeliner and lip gloss. She preferred tight dresses with high hemlines, gold jewelry, and line dancing.

"Don't you love Indian summer, Cork?"

"Know where the term *Indian summer* comes from?" he asked.

"No."

"A white man's phrase. They didn't trust Indians, so when the warm days returned in late fall and it felt like summer but everyone knew it was a lie, they gave it a name they deemed appropriate."

"I didn't know."

"Yes."

"Yes, what?"

"I do love Indian summer." He pointed to the right. "Turn here."

"I know."

Dross pulled onto a side road even smaller and rougher than the one they'd just followed, and they slipped into the blue shadow of a high ridge where a cool darkness had settled among the pine trees. The red-orange rays of the setting sun fell across the birches that crowned the hilltops, and the white trunks seemed consumed by a raging fire.

"I wish you had let me take the call alone," Dross said.

"As soon as you hit that skunk, so did I." He smiled briefly. "You know my policy."

"I responded to a lot of calls on the rez when Wally was sheriff, and Soderberg."

"I'm sheriff now. Domestic disturbances can turn ugly, even between people as harmless as Eli and Lucy."

"Then send another deputy with me. You don't always have to go on the rez calls."

"When you're sheriff, you can do things your way."

Life, Cork knew, was odder than a paisley duck. Three months before he'd been a private citizen, proud proprietor of Sam's Place, a small burger joint on a lovely spot along the shore of Iron Lake. Flipping burgers was a vocation many people probably considered only slightly less humble than, say, rounding up shopping carts in a Wal-Mart parking lot, but Cork had grown fond of his independence. When a scandal forced the duly elected sheriff, a man named Arne Soderberg, from office, the Board of County Commissioners had offered Cork the job. He had the experience; he had the trust of the people of Tamarack County; and the commissioners happened to catch him in a weak moment.

Dross slowed the Land Cruiser. "The truth is, you love going out like this."

The truth was, he did.

"There," Cork said.

It was a small, shabby cabin set against the base of the ridge, with a horseshoe of poplar trees around the back and sides. There was an old shed to the right, just large enough for a pickup truck, but Cork knew it was so full of junk there was no way a pickup could fit. A metal washtub sat in the yard, full of potting soil and the browning stalks of mums that had frozen days before. A big propane tank lay like a fat, white hyphen between the cabin and the shed. Behind the shed stood an old outhouse.

Dross parked off the road in the dirt of what passed for a drive. "Looks deserted," she said.

The curtains were open and behind each window was deep black.

"Eli's pickup's gone," she noted. "Maybe they patched things up and went off to celebrate."

The call had come from Lucy Tibodeau who lived with her husband Eli in the little cabin. These two had a long history of domestic disputes that, more often than not, arose from the fact that Eli liked to drink and Lucy liked to bully. When Eli drank, he tended to forget that he weighed 140 pounds compared to Lucy's 200-plus. In their altercations, it was generally Eli who took it on the chin. They always made up and never actually brought a formal complaint against one another. Patsy, the dispatcher, had taken the call and reported that Lucy was threatening to beat the crap out of Eli if someone didn't get out there to stop her. Which was a little odd. Generally, it was Eli who called asking for protection.

Cork looked at the cabin a moment, and listened to the stillness in the hollow.

"Where are the dogs?" he said.

"Dogs?" Dross replied. Then she understood. "Yeah."

Everybody on the rez had dogs. Eli and Lucy had two. They were an early-warning system of sorts, barking up a storm when visitors came. At the moment, however, everything around the Tibodeau cabin was deathly still.

"Maybe they took the dogs with them."

"Maybe," Cork said. "I'm going to see if Patsy's heard anything more."

Dross put on her cap and opened her door. She stepped out, slid her baton into her belt.

Cork reached for the radio mike. "Unit Three to Dispatch. Over."

"This is Dispatch. Go ahead, Cork."

"Patsy, we're at the Tibodeau place. Looks like nobody's home. Have you had any additional word from Lucy?"

"That's a negative, Cork. Nothing since her initial call."

"And you're sure it came from her?"

"She ID'd herself as Lucy Tibodeau. Things have been quiet out there lately, so I figured we were due for a call."

Marsha Dross circled around the front of the vehicle and took a few steps toward the cabin. In the shadow cast by the ridge, everything had taken on a somber look. She stopped, glanced at the ground near her feet, bent down, and put a finger in the dirt.

"There's blood here," she called out to Cork. "A lot of it."

She stood up, turned to the cabin again, her hand moving toward her holster. Then she stumbled, as if she'd been shoved from behind, and collapsed face-down. In the same instant, Cork heard the report from a rifle.

"Shots fired!" he screamed into the microphone. "Officer down!"

The windshield popped and a small hole surrounded by a spiderweb of cracks appeared like magic in front of Cork. The bullet chunked into the padding on the door an inch from his arm. Cork scrambled from the Land Cruiser and crouched low against the vehicle.

Dross wasn't moving. He could see a dark red patch that looked like a maple leaf spread over the khaki blouse of her uniform.

The reports had come from the other side of the road, from the hill to the east. Where Cork hunkered, the Land Cruiser acted as a shield and protected him, but Dross was still vulnerable. He sprinted to her, hooked his hands under her arms, and dug his heels into the dirt, preparing to drag her to safety. As he rocked his weight back, something stung his left ear. A fraction of a second later another report came from the hill. Cork kept moving, his hands never losing their grip as he hauled his fallen deputy to the cover of the Land Cruiser.

A shot slammed through the hood, clanged off the engine block, and thudded into the dirt next to the left front tire.

Cork drew his revolver and tried to think. The shots had hit an instant before he'd heard the sound of them being fired, so the shooter was at some distance. But was there only one? Or were others moving in, positioning themselves for the kill?

He could hear the traffic on the radio, Patsy communicating with the other units, the units responding. He tried to remember how many cruisers were out, where they were patrolling, and how long it would take them to reach that cabin in the middle of nowhere, but he couldn't quite put it all together.

Dross lay on her back staring up with dazed eyes. The front of her blouse was soaked nearly black. Cork undid the buttons and looked at the exit wound in her abdomen. A lot of blood had leaked out, but the wound wasn't as large as he'd feared. It was a single neat hole, which probably meant that the bullet had maintained its shape, hadn't mushroomed as it passed through her body. A round with a full metal jacket, Cork guessed. Jacketed rounds were generally used in order to penetrate body armor, which Dross wasn't wearing.

Cork had choices to make and he had to make them quickly. If he tended to Dross's wounds, he ignored the threat of an advance from the shooter—or shooters—and risked both their lives. But if he spent time securing their position, the delay could mean his deputy's life.

He weighed the possibility of more than one assailant. The shots had come one at a time, from a distance. When he considered how Dross had fallen, the trajectory of the bullet that had pierced the windshield, and where the final round had hit the engine, he calculated they'd all come from approximately the same direction: from somewhere high on the hill across the road. The shooter was above them and a little forward of their position, with a good view of the driver's side but blind to where Cork crouched. If there'd been more than one assailant involved, a crossfire would have made the most sense, but so far that hadn't happened.

So many elements to consider. So little time. So much at stake.

He chose.

He holstered his revolver and leaned toward the deputy. "Marsha, can you hear me?"

Her eyes drifted to his face, but she didn't answer.

"Hang on, kiddo, I'll be right back."

In the back of the Land Cruiser was a medical kit

that contained, among other things, rolls of gauze, sterile pads, and adhesive tape. Cork crept toward the rear of the vehicle. If he was right about the shooter's location, he should be able to grab the medical kit without exposing himself significantly to gunfire. *If he was right*. It was a big gamble. Dross gave a low moan. The blood had spread across the whole of her uniform, seeped below the belt line of her trousers. Still she looked at him and shook her head, trying to warn him against anything rash. Cork drew a breath and moved.

He reached around the back end of the Land Cruiser, grasped the handle, and swung the rear door open. He stood exposed for only a moment as he snatched the medical kit and the blanket, then he spun away and fell to the ground just as another round punched a hole in the vehicle and drilled through the spare tire, which deflated with a prolonged hiss. He rolled into the cover of the Land Cruiser.

While he put a compress over Dross's wounds, the radio crackled again.

"Dispatch to Unit Three. Over."

Cork glanced up from the bloody work of his hands. At the moment, there was no way to reach the mike. He tore another strip of tape with his teeth.

"Unit Three, do you copy?"

He finished tending to both wounds, then turned Marsha gently and tucked the blanket underneath her along the length of her body. He crawled to the other side, pulled the blanket under her, and wrapped her in it tightly like a cocoon.

"Unit Three, backup is on the way. ETA is twenty minutes. Are you still taking fire?"

Despite the blanket, Dross was shivering. Cork knew that shock could be as deadly as the bullet itself. In addition to keeping her warm, he had to elevate her feet. He opened the front passenger door and wormed his arm along the floor until his hand touched a fat thermos full of coffee he'd brought along. He hauled the thermos out and put it under the deputy's ankles. It elevated her feet only a few inches, but he hoped that would be enough.

Then he turned his attention to the son of a bitch on the hill.

He drew again his .38, a Smith & Wesson Police Special that had been his father's. It was chrome-plated with a six-inch barrel and a walnut grip. The familiar heft of it, and even the history of the weapon itself, gave him a measure of confidence. He crawled under the Land Cruiser, grateful for the high clearance of the undercarriage, inching his way to the front tire on the driver's side. From the shadow there, he peered up at the wooded hill across the road. The crown still caught the last direct rays of the sun and the birch trees dripped with a color like melting brass. After a moment, he saw a flash of reflected sunlight that could have come off the high polish of a rifle stock plate or perhaps the glass of a scope. If it was indeed from the shooter, Cork's target was 250, maybe 300 yards away, uphill. He thought about the twelve-gauge Remington cradled on the rack inside the Land Cruiser. Should he make an attempt, risk getting himself killed in the process? No, at that distance, the shotgun would be useless, and if he were hit trying for it, there'd be nothing to prevent the goddamn bastard from coming down the hill and finishing the job he'd begun. Better to stay put and wait for backup.

But his backup, too, would come under fire. Cork knew he had to advise them of the situation. And that meant exposing himself one more time to the sniper.

He took aim at the place where he'd seen the flash of sunlight, which was far beyond the effective range of his .38, but he squeezed off a couple of rounds anyway to encourage the sniper to reconsider, should he be thinking about coming down.

He shoved himself backward over the cold earth and came up on all fours beside the front passenger door. He gripped the handle and tried to take a breath, but he was so tense that he could only manage a quick, shallow gasp. He willed himself to move and flung the door open. Lunging toward the radio unit attached to the dash, he wrapped his fingers around the mike dangling on the accordion cord and fell back just as a sniper round slammed through the passenger seat back.

"Unit Three to Unit One. Over."

"Unit One. Go ahead, Sheriff."

"We're still taking fire, Duane. A single shooter, I think, up on a hill due east of our position, directly in front of the cabin. Which way you coming from?"

"South," Deputy Duane Pender said.

"Approach with extreme caution."

"Ten-four, Cork."

"Unit Two to Unit Three. Over."

"I read you, Cy."

"I'm coming in from the north. I'll be a couple of minutes behind Pender."

"Ten-four. Listen, I want you guys coming with your sirens blasting. Maybe we can scare this guy."

"We might lose him, Sheriff," Pender said.

"Right now our job is to get an ambulance in here for Marsha."

"Dispatch to Unit Three."

"Go ahead, Patsy."

"Ambulance estimates another twelve to fifteen minutes, Sheriff. They want to know Marsha's situation."

"Single bullet, entry and exit wounds. I've got compresses on both. I've put a blanket around her and elevated her feet. She's still losing blood."

"Ten-four. Also, State Patrol's responding. They've got two cruisers dispatched to assist."

"I copy that. Out."

Cork crawled toward Dross. Her face was pale, bloodless.

"A few more minutes, Marsha. Help's on the way."

She seemed focused on the sky above them both. She whispered something.

"What?" Cork leaned close.

"Star light, star bright . . ."

Cork lifted his eyes. The sun had finally set and the eastern sky was turning inky. He saw the evening star, a glowing ember caught against the rising wall of night.

From a distance came the thin, welcome howl of a siren.

Cork looked down at his deputy and remembered what she'd said: that he loved this work. At the moment, she couldn't have been more wrong. Her eyes had closed. He felt at her neck and found the pulse so faint he could barely detect it.

Then her eyes opened slowly. Her lips moved. Cork bent to her again.

"Next time," she whispered, "you drive."

2

"HE MUST'VE SPLIT when he heard the sirens."

Cy Borkmann looked across the road at the hill, which was a dark giant at the threshold of night. Cork, Deputy Duane Pender, and a state trooper named Fitzhugh had just come down from reconnoitering the top. They hadn't encountered the shooter, but they had found a couple of shell casings in a jumble of rocks overlooking the road and the Tibodeau cabin, in the area where Cork had seen the flash of reflected light off the sniper's rifle.

"Got word from the ambulance," Borkmann went on. They were standing beside his cruiser, a Crown Victoria parked a few yards back of the shot-up vehicle Cork had come in. At sixty, Borkmann was the oldest member of the Sheriff's Department. He was also the most overweight. He'd offered to climb the hill with the others, but Cork had left him behind to monitor the radio transmissions. "Marsha was rushed into surgery as soon as they wheeled her into the hospital."

"How's she doing?" Cork asked.

"She was still alive, that's all they said."

"Keep on top of it, Cy. Let me know when you hear anything."

Pender walked over from where he'd been conversing with the state troopers. He was young and brash, and Cork suspected not even experience would moderate his more irksome tendencies. "Christ, what's that smell? Skunk?"

Cork noticed it again, too, and realized that during the sniper's attack, he'd forgotten the odor entirely. "It's from the Land Cruiser," he said. "Marsha hit it on the way out."

Pender opened his mouth, probably to make a crack about women drivers, but wisely thought better of it.

Borkmann said to Cork, "I looked around while you were up on the hill. The two dogs you were wondering about? Dead, both of 'em. Rifle shot, looks like. They were carted around back and dumped out of sight. I'm thinking it's their blood Marsha was looking at."

"You check the cabin?"

"Quick look."

"Any sign of Eli or Lucy?"

"No."

"Let's hope that blood is from the dogs."

"Patsy located Larson. He was having dinner with Alice at the Broiler. He's on his way."

Borkmann was speaking of Captain Ed Larson, who headed the major-crimes investigations for the Tamarack County Sheriff's Department.

"I want to keep the scene clean until he gets here."

"You going to call BCA?" Borkmann asked.

"Soon as I'm back at the office."

It had been an assault on officers. Bringing in the

state's Bureau of Criminal Apprehension was standard procedure, not only because of the organization's expertise and superior resources, but also to ensure that no local prejudice might warp the investigation.

Pender eyed the empty cabin. "Eli can get mean when he's drunk. Maybe that was him up there on the hill."

Cork had already considered that possibility. The call that had brought him and Marsha Dross out there had been made by Lucy to keep her from beating Eli ragged. Maybe Eli had retaliated in a big way. Anything was possible when love and hate became a heated jumble. But if Eli had been up there, if he had lashed out at his wife in a deadly way, where was Lucy?

Night was falling fast, flooding into the hollow from a sky salted with stars. Two more cruisers from the Sheriff's Department pulled up and several deputies got out wearing Kevlar vests and carrying assault rifles. The emergency response team. It had been fifty minutes since Cork's call for help had first gone out.

"Got here as quick as we could, Sheriff," Deputy John Singer said. "Took a few minutes to assemble the whole team." He was apologizing for what probably seemed to him like an inexcusable delay.

"That's okay, John. I think we're secure now, but why don't you post a couple people on the crown of that hill." Cork pointed toward the rocks where the sniper had taken his position. "I'd hate to have somebody start shooting at us again from up there."

"Done." Singer turned to his team and gave the order.

Fitzhugh, the state patrolman, left his vehicle and crossed the road to where the others stood.

"You need us anymore?"

"No," Cork said. "Appreciate the assistance."

"Any time, Sheriff. Hope you get the bastard."

"Thanks."

Cork watched Fitzhugh walk away.

"Get on the radio, Duane," Cork said to Deputy Pender. "Have Patsy round up Clay and tell him to bring out a generator and floodlights. He can get them from the fire department."

Pender nodded and moved away.

"What did you see in the cabin?" Cork said to Borkmann.

"No bodies."

"You have to break in?"

"It was open."

"Figures. On the rez, nobody locks their doors. Any sign of violence?"

"Nope. Not the neatest housekeepers, but I'd say the mess in there looks pretty organic."

"Organic?"

"You know, rising naturally out of the elements of the environment."

"Organic." Cork shook his head.

"See for yourself," Borkmann said.

"I will. I want you to keep everyone away from the scene for now. When Ed Larson gets here, and the generator and lights, we'll go over the ground carefully. Where'd you say the dogs were, Cy?"

"Behind the woodpile in back."

"Okay." Cork turned toward the cabin. He knew he risked contaminating the scene, but he needed to know if there were dead or injured people somewhere.

He lifted a pair of latex gloves from the box Borkmann had in his cruiser. He also borrowed the deputy's Maglite. Carefully, he skirted the area where blood had turned the dirt to a muddy consistency. He hoped it was only the mutts who'd bled. He made his way around the side of the cabin to the back. Behind a cord of split hardwood stacked between the trunks of a couple of young poplars, he found the dogs. They lay one on top of the other, thrown there, it seemed, with no more thought than tossing out garbage. They'd been shot through the head, both of them, straight on and at close range. Cork wondered if they'd come at their assailant and been killed in their attack, or if they'd sat there bewildered by their fate because whoever shot them was someone they'd trusted. He considered Eli again. Had the man finally gone over the edge, gone into a drunken rage as a result of Lucy's bullying, done away with his wife, and then killed his dogs? If so, why hide them like this? And where was Lucy?

It didn't feel right. A man like Eli might get drunk and riled up enough to kill his wife, but he'd never shoot his dogs. A sad statement, but Cork knew it to be true.

He returned to the front of the cabin and pushed the door open. Inside was dark. He located the switch on the wall and turned on the lights.

Eli's first wife had been a small, quiet woman named Deborah, a true-blood Iron Lake Ojibwe. She'd been good to her husband, had kept a clean house, and when ovarian cancer took her, Eli had grieved long and hard. His second wife was nothing like Deborah. As Cork stood in the doorway, he could see what Borkmann had meant about organic mess. The room was cluttered with magazines and newspapers, dirty glasses and plates, clothing left lying where it had been shed. The place had a sour, soiled-laundry smell to it.

He wove through the clutter to the kitchen, where he found a sink full of unwashed dishes. On the kitchen table lay a half loaf of dark rye and a butcher knife with a residue of butter on the blade. Next to the bread was a small pile of scratched tickets for the state lottery.

Cork checked the bedroom. It looked as though a struggle had taken place, the bed unmade, clothes tossed everywhere, but he suspected that was probably the norm. A few empty Pabst Blue Ribbon cans lay on the floor on the right side of the bed. Eli's side, he guessed.

The bathroom was in desperate need of a good scrubbing, but nothing struck Cork as particularly noteworthy.

He stood in the main room.

A sniper on the hill across the road. Two dead dogs behind the woodpile. No indication of violence inside the cabin, but no sign of Lucy or Eli, either. What the hell was going on?

"What happened to your ear?"

Cork turned and found Ed Larson standing in the doorway.

Larson wore gold wire-rims, little ovals that made him look bookish. His silver hair was bristle short, his face clean shaven, still a little pink, in fact, from the recent draw of a razor over his long jaw. He was dressed in a blue suit, white shirt, burgundy tie. His shoes were Florsheims, polished oxblood. During the brief tenure of the previous sheriff, Arne Soderberg, who'd managed to stay in office only six months, Larson had quit the department and taken a job teaching criminal justice studies at the community college. When the county Board of Commissioners tapped Cork to fill out Soderberg's term, he'd asked Larson to return, which the man had done in a heartbeat.

Cork touched the gauze he'd taped over his left earlobe to stanch the flow of blood where a sizable chunk of flesh was missing.

"Sniper round."

"Lucky," Larson said.

"Luckier than Marsha." Cork noted the man's clothing. "Awfully well dressed."

"Anniversary dinner. Thirty-fifth."

"Alice mad you had to leave?"

"She knows how it goes."

"You could've taken a few minutes to change clothes."

"The suit will clean." Larson looked at the room. "Struggle?"

"I get the feeling this is a natural state."

Larson walked cautiously into the cabin, watching where he stepped. "I talked to Cy outside, got a thumbnail of what's going on. I radioed Patsy to double-check the location of the call. Thought maybe it didn't actually come from here."

"Did it?"

"From right there." He pointed toward a phone on a low table next to the sofa, half hidden by a soiled, gray sweatshirt. "You didn't touch it?"

"Didn't even see it," Cork said.

"Door unlocked?"

"Yes."

Larson didn't seem surprised. "You check out the other rooms?"

"Yeah."

"Anything?"

"Not that leaped out at me."

Larson looked over his shoulder toward one of the windows. "It's getting pretty dark out there. What do you want to do about the hill?"

Two shell casings. Six, maybe seven shots fired. More casings to locate. Maybe other evidence as well.

Larson went on. "Cy says you've got floodlights coming. I hope you're not thinking of dragging them up that slope tonight."

Cork didn't answer. He didn't want to decide anything until he had an idea of what had become of Eli and Lucy.

"It's going to be a long night" was all he would say.

Larson turned back toward the front door. "I'll get my things and get started."

They both heard the screaming, and they went outside quickly.

An old puke-colored pickup was parked behind Borkmann's Crown Victoria, and Lucy Tibodeau had climbed out. She was trying to swing at Cy Borkmann while Pender did his best to restrain her. Cork hurried over.

"What's going on?"

"She wanted to go inside," Borkmann said.

"It's my damn house," Lucy hollered. She kicked at Cy but Pender pulled her back just in time. "What the hell's going on?" she demanded.

Eli's first wife had been like a fawn, small, soft, quiet. For his second bride, Eli had chosen a different animal altogether, huge and fierce. Lucy Tibodeau came from Fargo and, when Eli met her, had been dealing blackjack at the casino in Mille Lacs. She was short but big boned, with a lot of meat on those bones. Her hair was copper-colored, wiry like a Brillo pad. Her skin was splashed with huge brown freckles. Her eyes were green fire.

"Take your hands off me," she warned Pender, "or I'll bite your thumb off."

"Take it easy, Lucy," Cork said.

"Don't tell me to take it easy. You're crawling all over my place like a bunch of maggots and this son of a bitch has got his hands everywhere except up my dress. And he looks like he wouldn't mind going there next."

"Let her go, Pender."

The deputy did and stepped back quickly.

"What's going on?" Lucy asked, only slightly more civil.

"Where's Eli?" Cork said.

"I left him at Bunyan's. Last I saw of the little shit, he was kissing the lip of a whiskey glass."

"When was that?"

"Half an hour ago. What? Did he do something?"

"You've got the truck, Lucy. How's he getting home?"

"He can walk for all I care."

"Pender, drive over to Bunyan's. Round up Eli if he's there."

"Sure thing, Sheriff."

"What's going on?" Lucy said again, only this time with genuine concern in her voice.

"I was hoping you could tell me." It was hard to see the woman's face clearly. Cork opened the front door of Borkmann's cruiser and motioned Lucy to where the dome light would illuminate them both. "I'd love to know what happened after you called the Sheriff's Department."

"Called you?"

"At six-twenty, a call came from this location from a woman claiming to be you."

"At six-twenty me and Eli were playing pinochle at Bunyan's, like we do every Tuesday night. Hell, everybody knows that. We go for the walleye fish fry, then play a couple hours of pinochle."

A dark blue pickup rolled up and maneuvered alongside the other vehicles that crowded the narrow road. In the back sat a generator and some floodlights.

"You didn't call?" Cork said.

"Hell no." Something dawned on her, and she tried to pierce the dark with her eyes. "Where's our dogs?"

Cork didn't relish what he had to do, and when he spoke his voice sounded tired. "Somebody shot them, Lucy. I'm sorry."

All her spit and fire vanished in an instant, and devastation poured in to replace it.

Cork looked to Cy. "Would you see to Ms. Tibodeau. We'll need a full statement, but go easy." He turned and walked away.

Larson followed him. "Think she's lying?"

"Too simple to check. And why would she?"

Larson paused and looked up at the hill that was now a towering black shape hard against a soft night sky. "What's going on, Cork?"

"I'd say it was a trap."

"You guys got pulled out here to be shot at?"

"No," Cork said. "To be shot."

3

CORK LEFT ED LARSON in charge with Borkmann backing him up. He intended to drive himself to the Aurora community hospital so that he could check on Marsha and have his ear tended to, but Larson stopped him.

"You shouldn't drive."

"It's just my damn earlobe," Cork said.

"It's a bullet wound and your body knows it and any minute may decide to overrule your stubborn brain. If that happens, I'd just as soon you weren't behind the wheel. Collins," he called to a deputy who was taking digital photos of the bullet-riddled Land Cruiser, "take the sheriff to the hospital. Radio ahead and let them know he's coming." He turned back to Cork. "You want us to call Jo?"

"No, I'll do that from the hospital. And I'll take care of contacting the BCA, too."

At the hospital, Cork told the deputy not to wait, that he'd have Jo give him a lift from there. Collins headed back to the rez.

In the emergency room, Cork ignored the admitting clerk and walked directly to the main hallway. As he approached the reception desk to ask about Marsha, he ran into his dispatcher Patsy Gilman, who was asking the same question.

Cork had hired Patsy during his first stint as sheriff. She was not quite forty, bright and funny, with deep laugh lines on either side of her mouth, and small intense eyes that noticed everything. She was good in Dispatch because she kept her head and her humor. As two of the only three women in the department, she and Marsha Dross had formed a tight friendship, so much so that Patsy was to be the bridesmaid at Marsha's wedding, which was scheduled for the day after Halloween. Marsha was engaged to a big Finn named Charlie Annala.

"As soon as I knew they were bringing Marsha in, I called Charlie." She walked with Cork toward the surgery waiting area. "Then I called Bos and asked her to relieve me early. I didn't want Charlie to have to wait alone. You mind?"

She was still wearing her uniform, and there were dark stains under the arms. It had been a tough evening all around.

"Makes good sense," he said.

Cork knew he shouldn't feel this way, but he hated hospitals. They were places that did people good, that cured the sick and healed the injured, but it was also a place completely outside his control. He'd watched both his parents die in hospital rooms, and there hadn't been a damn thing he could do about it. Rationally, he knew that hospitals weren't about death, but whenever he entered the glass doors and caught the unnatural, antiseptic smell in the corridors, his heart told him differently.

They found Charlie Annala in the waiting room. He

was sandy-haired, heavy, with a face made babylike from soft fat. He wore a forest green work shirt, dirty jeans, and scuffed boots. Cork figured he'd come straight from his job at the DNR's Pine Lake Fish Hatchery. He stood with his big, fat hands stuffed in his jean pockets, his head down, staring at the beige carpeting. There was a television on a shelf in a corner, tuned to one of the new reality shows. Cork figured Annala wouldn't have minded dealing with somebody else's reality at that moment. When he heard them coming, Annala looked up, not a happy man.

Charlie Annala was the protective type. Marsha didn't need that, but apparently she didn't mind, either. Maybe she appreciated that Charlie saw her in a different way than her male colleagues: saw the woman who liked, off duty, to show a little leg, line dance, and wear jewelry and cologne. Cork knew that her job was a sore point with Charlie, who was worried about her safety, a worry that, until this evening, Cork hadn't particularly shared.

Patsy rushed forward and threw her arms around the big man. "Oh, Charlie, I'm so sorry."

"Yeah," he said. He looked over her shoulder at Cork.

"Any word?" Cork said.

"Nothing since she went in. I haven't called her dad yet. I won't until I know how it's gone. What happened?" Charlie's eyes were full of unspoken accusations.

Patsy stood back, and let the two men talk.

"We're still trying to piece it together."

"What do you mean, 'piece it together'? You were there."

"At the moment, all I know is somebody shot her."

"Who?" He'd leaned closer with each exchange, putting his face very near to Cork's. There were deep pits across his cheeks from adolescent acne.

"I don't know," Cork said.

"Why not?"

"He was too far away, hidden in some rocks."

"Why her?"

Cork figured what he really meant was *Why not you?*

"When I understand that, Charlie, I'll let you know. I honestly will."

Patsy put her arm around Annala just as a nurse entered the waiting area. "There you are," the nurse said to Cork. "We've been expecting you in the ER." When he turned to her, she said with surprise, "Oh, my."

The shot that grazed his ear had opened a spigot of blood that had poured all over his shirt, and he looked like hell, as if he'd sustained an injury far worse.

"Keep me posted," he said to Patsy.

"You know I will."

Cork followed the nurse. He was beginning to feel his strength ebbing, and thought about what Larson had said. Maybe his wounded body was finally overtaking his stubborn brain. He hoped not. There was still so much to do.

He called Jo from a phone in the ER and asked her to pick him up, then he let them sew his earlobe closed.

She was waiting for him when he came out. She looked with alarm and sympathy at the gauze and tape on his ear. "What happened?"

"I'll tell you on the way."

Two blocks from the hospital, Jo pulled her Camry

to the side of the street, parked in front of a fire hydrant, and listened. He told it calmly, almost blandly, but her face registered the horror of the scene.

"Oh God, Cork. How's Marsha?"

"She's still in surgery. We won't know for a while."

She gently lifted a hand toward the side of his face. "How's your poor ear?"

"Smaller."

"Does it hurt?"

"They gave it a shot. Can't feel much now."

She stared through the windshield. It was night and quiet and they sat in the warm glow of a street lamp. She put a hand to her forehead as if pressing some thought into her brain. "Why, Cork?"

"I don't know."

She leaned to him suddenly and held him tightly, and the good smell of spaghetti came to him from her hair and clothing. It was a quick dinner and a favorite of their children.

"Oh, sweetheart," she said. "I'll get you home and you can relax."

"No. I need to go to the department. I want to listen to the tape of Lucy's call."

It was a little before nine on a Tuesday night. Aurora, Minnesota, was winding down. Many of the shops had already closed. A good crowd was still visible through the windows of Johnny's Pinewood Broiler, and the air on Center Street was full of the tantalizing aroma of fried food. In front of the display window of Lost Lake Outfitters, against the buttery glow of a neon sign, stood old Alf Pedersen, who'd started the outfitting company fifty years earlier. Alf knew the most beautiful and fragile parts of the Boundary Waters, the great wilderness area north of

Aurora, and although he'd guided hundreds of tourists in, he kept those places secret. In the next block, the door of Wolf Den Books and Gifts opened and a plank of light fell across the sidewalk as Naomi Pierce stepped out to close up. He couldn't hear it, but Cork knew that the opening of the door had caused a small bell above the threshold to jingle. He thought about the show that had been on television at the hospital. He didn't know whose reality that was, but his own reality lay in the details of this place, his hometown, details an outsider might not even notice. A tinkling bell, a familiar silhouette, the comfortable and alluring smell of deep-fry.

There was another reality for him as well. It was grounded in a maple leaf of blood on Marsha's uniform, the sound of glass shattered by a bullet capable of exploding his head like a melon, and the long, terrifying moments when he'd scrambled desperately to make sense of the absolutely senseless.

"You okay?" Jo asked.

"Yeah, I guess," he answered.

She accompanied him into the Tamarack County Sheriff's Department. Bos Swain, who'd relieved Patsy as dispatcher, buzzed them through the security door.

Bos was short for Boston, which was the name by which Henrietta Swain was known. As a young woman, she'd dreamed of going to college, specifically to Boston College, for reasons which she'd never divulged. Instead, she'd married her high school sweetheart, who went off to Vietnam and came back messed up psychologically. Bos had worked to support them and the two girls who were born to them, and although she never went to college herself, she sent both girls east, one to Barnard and the other to

Boston College. When the girls were gone, she divorced her first husband and remarried, a good man named Tim Johnson who had a solid job stringing wire for the phone company. Although she didn't need to work to support herself anymore, she kept on as a dispatcher, drawing a county paycheck every two weeks, which she deposited in trust funds for her grandchildren's education. She was a fleshy woman, unusually good-humored, but the events of that evening had put her in a somber mood.

"I thought you were going to the hospital," she said to Cork in a scolding tone.

"I just came from there."

"How's Marsha?"

"Still in surgery when I left. Thanks for coming early so Patsy could be there."

"She seemed to be holding up real good, but I know it's tough for her. How's Charlie taking it?"

"Hard."

"Well, sure." She eyed his uniform and shook her head. "Jo, you ought to take him home so he can change those clothes. He's not exactly a walking advertisement for law enforcement."

Cork said, "I want to listen to the recording of the call that came from the Tibodeau cabin."

"Lucy's call?"

"That's what I want to know. Lucy claims it wasn't her."

Bos went to the Dispatch area, where the radio, at the moment, was silent. The public contact phone was linked to two different recording systems. The first recorded date, time, and the number of the phone from which the call had been made. The other system was a Sony automatic telephone tape recorder. It wasn't top-of-the-line—it had actually been donated to the department by the Chippewa Grand Casino when they'd upgraded to a digital recorder voice bank that fed directly into a computer—but it was a work-horse of a unit. Bos rewound the tape to the call that had purportedly come from Lucy. She played it, and they all listened. Then she played it again.

Patsy: *Tamarack County Sheriff's Department.*

The caller: *I'm telling you, if you don't get somebody out here, I'm going to kill the son of a bitch.*

Patsy: *Who is this?*

The caller: *Lucy Tibodeau.*

Patsy: *Where are you, Lucy?*

The caller: *At my goddamn cabin. And I'm telling you, you better get someone out here pronto, or I swear I'll kill him.*

Patsy: *Kill who?*

The caller: *That son of a bitch husband of mine.*

Patsy: *Eli?*

The caller: *You think I got another husband stashed in the woodpile, sweetie? Well, I wish to god I did, 'cuz the one I got ain't worth a bucket of warm spit.*

Patsy: *Where is Eli?*

The caller: *Outside, pounding on the door, hollering to let him in.*

Patsy: *You just stay put, Lucy. Take a few deep breaths. We'll have someone out there right away.*

The caller: *I'm warning you, the sheriff better get here real fast, he wants to avoid bloodshed.*

Patsy: *He's on his way, Lucy. You just relax, and don't you let that husband of yours rankle you, under-stand?*

The caller: *I ain't making any promises.*

The caller hung up.

Jo was the first to respond. "If someone's trying to sound like Lucy, they did a pretty fair job."

Bos nodded. "If I hadn't been leery, I'd have been fooled. I can see why Patsy didn't give it a second thought. Whoever it is, she's got Lucy's speech down pat. But it's someone younger, I'd say."

Cork had Bos play the tape once more. "Hear that?" he said, midway through.

"What?"

"Rewind it a bit." He waited. "Listen." He held up a finger, then dropped it suddenly. "Now. Did you hear it? A door closing in the background."

"Somebody came in?" Bos said.

"Or went out." Jo looked at Cork. "Either way, she wasn't alone."

"Pull that tape, Bos. We'll give it to BCA to analyze."

He went into his office and made the call to the Bureau of Criminal Apprehension office in Bemidji, explained the situation to the voice mail, then pulled out the clean uniform he kept in the closet. When he stepped back into the department common area, Jo looked at the uniform.

"You're not coming home," she said.

"No. I'll shower downstairs, change, and then I'm going back out to the rez."

"I wish you'd come home. You've got people who can handle the investigation."

"I need to be there. Don't wait up."

She kissed him and he could feel her restraint, her irritation.

"Be careful," she said, and left.

As he showered, he was conscious of his wound. The local anesthetic was wearing off, and a dull ache crept in behind it. He put on the clean uniform and went back upstairs.

"I'm taking my Bronco," he told Bos. "Let Ed know I'm on my way."

"You really ought to get a radio in that vehicle."

He started for the door, but Bos called him back.

"Sheriff?"

He turned around.

"Somebody lured you out there."

"It looks that way."

"They wanted you dead. Or maybe Marsha."

"That's generally the reason they use bullets."

"My point is this," she said. "They didn't succeed. Does that mean they'll try again?"

4

*F*LOODLIGHTS LIT THE hollow with an unnatural glare, and the poplar trees around the Tibodeau cabin looked like a crowd of gawkers gone white with shock. Cork pulled up behind Cy Borkmann's cruiser and got out.

Ed Larson stood in the doorway of the cabin. He wasn't wearing the latex gloves anymore and looked as if he'd gathered evidence and was weighing the meaning. Or at least, that's what Cork hoped his look meant.

"Where's Lucy?" Cork asked.

"She and Eli went into Allouette to stay with his uncle. We took statements from both of them. They were pretty broken up over the dogs."

Cork glanced inside the cabin. "So, what did you find?"

Larson adjusted his wire-rims, not a good sign. Then he said, "Well," which nailed the coffin shut.

"Nothing?" Cork said.

"Not down here. Whoever it was, they actually wiped out the tracks leading back to the woodpile where they threw the dogs. Looks like they used a pine branch or something. I took prints off the phone, but I'm betting they're just latents from Eli and Lucy. Nothing on the shell casings you found earlier. We pulled the slugs out of the Land Cruiser but they're too mashed up to be of any use for ballistics. We're still looking for the round that went through Marsha. Doing a quadrant search of the ground surface right now, then I'll have the guys start digging. Come morning, we'll go over every inch of the hilltop where the shooter was. We bagged the dogs. If you think it'll be of any value, we can have them autopsied."

Duane Pender, who was working on the search of the ground, hollered.

"What is it?" Larson said.

Pender picked up something and held it up in the light. "It's a bell. A little jingly Christmas bell."

Larson walked carefully to the deputy and took the bell from him. It was a silver ball with a little metal bead inside that jingled when the ball moved. "It's new. Not dirty, so it hasn't been on the ground long. What do you make of it, Cork?"

Cork walked over. "Could be from a Christmas ornament."

"In October?"

"Or maybe from a jingle dress."

"A what?"

"For ceremonial dances. It may be nothing, but make a note of where you found it, Duane, and put it in a bag."

Larson followed him back to the cabin door. "Any word on Marsha?"

"She was still in surgery when I left the hospital."

"You don't look too good yourself."

Cork slumped against the door frame. The lights

for the search were bright in his eyes, and he turned his face from them. "I keep trying to figure all this."

"I've been thinking," Larson said quietly. "Someone went to a lot of trouble to get you out here. Think about it, Cork. The call comes from the rez. Since you've taken over as sheriff, the old policy of you responding to most of the calls from out here is back in place. Marsha's driving the Land Cruiser. She's your height, more or less. She's wearing a cap. The sun's down, the whole hollow here is in shade. The shooter assumes it's you who gets out and he fires."

"Or she fires," Cork said.

"She?"

"I listened to the tape of the call when I was back at the department. It was a woman doing a pretty good job of sounding like Lucy."

Larson considered it while he scratched the silver bristle of his hair. "Whoever, they knew what they were doing. Two dead dogs, tracks erased, a well-chosen vantage point from which to fire."

"Why didn't he . . . she . . . set up a crossfire?" Cork said.

"That probably means the number of people involved is limited. Maybe just the shooter. Or the shooter and the woman he used to get you out here."

"A lot of speculation," Cork said.

"Without a lot of hard evidence to go on, you've got to begin your thinking somewhere. I'm guessing it's someone who knows the rez. They knew that Lucy and Eli would be gone, anyway. They were pretty sure it would be you who'd respond. Cork, this wasn't some sort of random violence. It was well planned and you were the target."

Borkmann strolled over. In the glare, his bulk cast a huge shadow before him. "We still got two men on that hill."

The moon wasn't up yet, but it was on the rise. "Might as well bring them down," Cork said. "I don't think we'll have to worry any more tonight. Maybe we should all call it a night. What do you think, Ed? Come back in the morning? BCA'll be here then. In the meantime, we can post a couple of men to keep the scene secure, and we'll send everyone else home. That bullet you're hoping to dig out of the ground'll still be there tomorrow."

"Cork?" Borkmann called from his cruiser. "Just got word from Patsy via Bos. Marsha's out of surgery and doing well."

Cork felt something begin to break inside him, a wall behind which an ocean of emotion was at risk of flooding through.

Ed put a hand on his shoulder. "I'll take care of getting things packed up here. You go on home and get some rest. We'll have a go at it again tomorrow."

He went back to the department and filled out an incident report, then stopped by the hospital one last time. Patsy had gone, but he found Charlie Annala asleep on the sofa in the waiting area of the recovery room. Someone had put a thin blanket over him. Shortly after midnight, Cork headed home.

By the time he turned onto Gooseberry Lane, the moon had risen high in the sky, a waxing gibbous moon, a silver teardrop on the cheek of night. His home was an old two-story frame affair with a wonderful front porch and a big elm in the yard. The whole town knew it as the O'Connor place. With the exception of college and a few years when he was a cop in Chicago, he'd lived in that house his whole life. In a way, it contained his life. He stood on the lawn a few moments, in the shadow the elm cast in the moonlight, trying to draw to himself the feel of all that was familiar. A light in his bedroom upstairs told him Jo had waited up for him. A soft glow drizzled through the window of his son's room, Stevie's night-light. His daughters' rooms were on the backside of the house, but it was late and a school night and he figured they would be asleep by now. He listened to the creak of the chains on their metal hooks as the porch swing rocked slowly in the breeze. He put his hand against the rough bark of the big tree that was as old as he and took in the dry smell of autumn.

Jo had left a light on in the living room so that he wouldn't walk into a dark house. He turned it off and headed upstairs, where he checked the children's rooms. Stevie was snoring softly. Jenny lay asleep with the headphones of her Discman still over her ears. Annie's pillow was over her head, and her right leg was off the bed. Cork took a moment and carefully settled her back in.

In his own room, he found Jo sitting up but asleep, a manila file folder open on her lap; her reading glasses had slipped to the end of her nose. She was a lawyer and she often brought her work to bed, one way or another. Cork decided not to wake her. He wasn't quite ready for sleep yet, anyway. Too much going on inside.

He went back downstairs and stood in the dark living room, feeling oddly alien in the quiet of the house, as if he'd been gone a long time and had lost touch with the details that created the mosaic of a normal day. He felt adrift, stranded in a place he didn't quite know or understand.

In the kitchen, he latched onto the cookie jar, an icon of familiarity. It was Ernie from *Sesame Street,* and it had been in the O'Connor house for more than a decade. Cork dipped into Ernie's head and brought out a chocolate chip cookie, which he put on the kitchen table while he took a glass tumbler from the cupboard next to the sink. From the refrigerator, he grabbed a plastic gallon jug of milk and filled the tumbler halfway.

As he turned back to the refrigerator, the shatter of glass exploded the quiet of the kitchen. He hit the floor, let go of the jug, reached automatically for his .38. He scrambled across the linoleum and pressed his back to the cabinet doors below the sink, clutching his gun. *One of the windows?* he wondered. But a quick glance told him no bullet had come through any of the panes.

Then he saw the broken tumbler on the floor, the puddle of milk around the shards, and he realized he'd knocked the glass off the table. A simple accident due to his own carelessness, a small incident in a day full of enormous event. Still, it felt as if something had finally snapped inside him, the cord that had kept him from taking a long fall.

Finally alone, he drew his legs up, laid his arms across his knees, cradled his head, and with a violent quaking gave himself up to the dark emotions—terror, rage, regret—that had stalked him all night.

5

BOSTON WAS STILL on duty when Cork rolled in at first light.

She glanced at her watch. "You didn't sleep much," she said. "And you don't mind me saying so, you still look like hell."

"What's the word from Morgan and Schilling?" he asked, referring to the two deputies who'd been posted overnight at the Tibodeau cabin.

"Checked in every hour; nothing to report."

Cork poured himself some coffee from the pot in the common area before going to his office. He spent a few minutes typing a memo on his computer, printed thirty copies, and handed them to the dispatcher. Bos lifted the top copy, read it, and looked up.

"Everybody wears armor on duty now?"

"No exceptions," Cork said. "I want this memo posted on the board and I want every deputy to check off with initials so I know they've read it." He handed her another sheet on which he'd printed some instructions. "Give this to Cy when he comes in. I want him to brief everyone about last night. Duty assignments remain the same except for Larson's evidence team, who'll be out at the cabin. I'm taking a cruiser and heading to the rez."

She eyed him with maternal concern but said nothing.

He drove a Pathfinder that had been confiscated in a raid on a meth lab near Yellow Lake in August. It had since been fitted with a radio and was now an official part of the vehicle pool. He'd taken only a couple of sips of the coffee he'd poured himself earlier, so he stopped at the all night Food 'N Fuel and bought three coffees and several granola bars.

As he headed north out of town, a red sun inched above the ragged tree line on the far side of Iron Lake. In an autumn in which the whole earth had seemed the color of a raw wound, the water itself appeared to be a well of blood. Cork couldn't look at it without thinking of all the blood that had soaked the blouse of Marsha Dross's uniform. As much as possible he kept his eyes on the road and considered the question of who might want him dead.

He'd been sheriff of Tamarack County before, for a period of seven years. Things had happened near the end of that tenure, terrible things that had torn him apart and nearly shattered his family as well. His badge had been taken from him. He'd spent the next three years running Sam's Place and putting himself back together. Over time he'd begun to feel whole again and to believe that his life still had promise. In those first seven years as sheriff, he'd been responsible for a lot of people going to jail. On many occasions, he'd been threatened with reprisal, idle threats for the most part. Or so he'd thought.

Still, that was old business. Retribution was usually born of rage, and rage generally lost its heat over time. So an old grudge, while possible, didn't feel like a solid thread.

It was a chilly morning. In protected coves, the surface of Iron Lake was covered with a languorous mist. Russet leaves hung on the branches of the oaks. The tamaracks, brilliant yellow, seemed like plumes of fire exploding from the dark ground that edged the marshes. Normally, Cork would have reveled in the beauty of the woods, but as he sipped his coffee he was deep in thought, not only baffled over who'd want him dead, but wondering if Ed Larson would find anything useful at the Tibodeau cabin.

The deputies, Howard Morgan and Nate Schilling, knew he was coming, and they both stepped from the cruiser as he drew up and parked behind them. They looked tired, as though they'd had enough of sitting all night trying to fight sleep, as though they'd probably had enough of each other, too. He hauled out the other coffees he'd bought and the granola bars and offered them to his men.

"The java's probably a little cool by now, but it's pure caffeine. And take your pick of the bars."

"Thanks," Morgan said. He was the older of the two deputies, a seven-year veteran of the force and of Duluth PD before that. He was an easygoing sort, and Cork liked him.

The hill cast a shadow across the road. The sun would be a long time in reaching the hollow, hours before it drove out the cold that lay along the bottom. When the men breathed and when they spoke, clouds of vapor escaped their lips.

"Bos said everything was quiet last night."

"That's right, Sheriff." Schilling took a bite of a peanut butter–chocolate chip granola bar and followed it with a slug of coffee. Although he'd completed his schooling and training almost two years before, he was still considered a rookie. Usually, he had a little rose in his cheeks, but he looked pretty sallow at the moment.

"Nobody curious drop by?"

"Nobody we could see anyway," Schilling said. "After the floodlights got packed up, it was pretty dark. Could have been someone watching from the trees, I suppose."

"You suppose?" Morgan laughed so hard coffee dribbled out his nostrils.

"What's that all about?" Cork said.

"Nothing, Sheriff. Not a thing," Schilling said.

"Like hell. Cork, he was so scared somebody was taking a bead on us that he spent the whole night on the floor of the cruiser." Morgan wiped his nose with the sleeve of his uniform.

"Morgan, you asshole. It wasn't like that, Sheriff."

"You both wore your armor the entire watch?"

"Absolutely," Schilling said.

Cork figured it was a good thing Morgan was sporting his Kevlar vest, because if Schilling's eyes had been bullets they'd have blown holes all the way through him.

He stared at the dark side of the hill, where snakes of mist coiled and uncoiled among the pine trees along the base. "I'm going up, see what things look like on top."

"You're not waiting for Captain Larson?" Schilling said. When he saw Cork's face, he added, "I just meant that he's on his way. We got word from Bos just before you came."

"Hey, Einstein, the sheriff's got a radio," Morgan said.

"Oh, right."

"Just let him know where I am," Cork said.

He walked fifty yards down the road to the place where, the day before, he and Pender and the state trooper named Fitzhugh had begun maneuvering up the hill, moving under the cover of trees and exposed outcroppings, working their way carefully toward the rocks where the sniper had been. He wasn't wearing his uniform now. He'd put on old jeans, a forest green wool shirt with a quilted lining, and his Timberland boots. His badge was pinned on his gun belt next to his .38. And he wore a Kevlar vest.

The night had not been cold enough for frost, but the hillside was covered with dew, and his boots slipped on the wet rocks and wild grass. The top of the hill was maybe two hundred feet above the road. He was breathing hard by the time he reached the crown, puffing out clouds like an old steam engine. He hoped this was due mostly to the lack of sleep, but he was concerned that his age might also be an issue. He wasn't far from turning the corner on half a century, and although he was an avid jogger, he knew that age eventually caught up with everyone, even the swiftest runner.

Cork walked along the spine of the hill a hundred yards south to the jumble of rocks where they'd found the shell casings. The thin topsoil there had completely eroded away, exposing gray gneiss beneath that had been fractured by aeons of freeze and thaw. There were sharp edges to the rocks, and the shooter had covered his position with a bedding of pine needles. It was among the needles that Cork had found the shell casings the night before.

The road down the hollow took a right turn and

followed a deep furrow just to the south where a thread of water called Tick Creek ran. North, the narrow access to the Tibodeau cabin was clear all the way to where it branched off the main road. Wooded hills stretched away in every direction. Pressing down above it all was the great blue palm of the sky. The shooter had chosen well, a vantage from which he could clearly see not just the cabin but also the approach of anyone traveling the road from the north or south.

He looked down at the pine-needle bed in the rocks and was puzzled.

The shooter had been careful in so many respects. Knowing Lucy and Eli's schedule. Calling from the cabin, then wiping away all traces of his or her presence. Choosing a position that was excellent not only because of its vantage but also because it lay on solid rock where no footprints would be left. So why did he ignore the shell casings? They were crumbs on an otherwise empty plate, impossible to miss. Had the shooter simply overlooked them? Or been suddenly rushed, worried by the sound of the sirens as Pender and Borkmann approached, and fled without taking the time for the last details?

Cork considered the dead dogs. He thought it likely they were killed first, then the shooter or the accomplice made the call and climbed the hill, probably the same way he'd come. Did the accomplice come, too? How did they leave? Cork walked toward the back side of the hill where the night before it had been too dark to go. The slope was gentler there, with more soil and long tufts of wild oats beneath the aspen trees. About fifty yards from the shooter's rocks, Cork found a spot where the incline increased suddenly and where some of the ground cover had

been disturbed by a sliding shoe or boot. A few feet
farther down was a scar in the soil where a whole
bunch of oat stalks had been pulled completely out, as
if someone had grabbed them in an attempt to prevent
a fall. Below that, the bushes had been broken by the
weight of a large object, perhaps a tumbling body.
The shooter, or someone with the shooter, had taken a
nasty spill.

Cork picked his way down the back side of the hill
and reached the bed of Tick Creek. Fall had been dry,
and this late in the season there was only a small
trickle of water crawling along the bottom. A couple
of hundred yards to the south, the creek crossed the
road. That was the direction from which Pender had
come the day before with his lights flashing and his
siren screaming. Cork didn't think the shooter would
have fled that way. North was different. Before it
intersected County 23 a half mile distant, Tick Creek
curved sharply away from the turnoff to the Tibodeau
cabin, so that a cop coming from that direction would
see nothing of the creek. Cork turned north. The
banks were high and formidably steep from the cut of
floodwaters that came with the snowmelt each spring,
and they were crowned with a thick growth of brush
and popple. Someone on foot could have climbed out,
but not a vehicle. In a few minutes, Cork reached the
bridge at County Road 23. The structure was made of
creosote-soaked wood with a web of rusted iron railing along either side and decorated with painted graf-
fiti. In the soft dirt of the narrow shoulder at the east
end of the bridge, Cork found recent tire tracks.

Larson watched Cork approach on foot. "I thought
you were up there." He pointed toward the hilltop.

Cork said, "I walked down the other side and around the hill."

"You needed the exercise?" came a voice behind him.

Cork smiled and turned as BCA agent Simon Rutledge stepped from the cabin.

Rutledge spoke like Jimmy Stewart, with a little catch in his throat and a naively honest tone that you had to love. He was in his midforties, an unimposing man with thinning red hair and a hopelessly boyish smile, but his appearance and demeanor belied a tough spirit. Cork had watched Rutledge question suspects. He never browbeat, never bullied. He offered them his sympathy, bestowed on them his neighborly smile, opened his arms to them, and, after he got their trust, almost always got their confession. Simon Rutledge was so good that whenever he interviewed a suspect, other agents referred to it as "Simonizing."

"How's it hanging, Cork?" Rutledge said. The two men shook hands.

"I've had better days."

"Bet you have. Where you been?"

Cork nodded toward the hilltop. "Our shooter left the back way. I found tire tracks at the bridge over Tick Creek on County Twenty-three. They'll photograph well, and I'll bet if we're careful we can get a good cast made."

"Mack," Rutledge called to one of his BCA evidence team who was digging in the ground in front of the Tibodeau cabin. He gave the agent directions to the bridge over Tick Creek. "Check out the tire tracks . . ." He glanced at Cork.

"East side, south shoulder."

"You heard him. Get good photos, and I'll be there in a bit to help with casting."

"On my way." Mack put his shovel down and headed for his state car.

"You take a look at the cabin?" Cork asked Rutledge.

"Yeah. But I know Ed did a good job on it, so I wasn't expecting much. I was just thinking of going up top to have a look where our shooter camped out. You see anything while you were up there?"

"I didn't look hard. Mostly I was thinking."

"Wondering who wants you dead?" Rutledge flashed a slightly diminished version of his smile but it still produced dimples. "I had a talk with Ed, and he's got a point about you being the target. You need to be thinking seriously about who'd want you in their gun sight."

"Any time you bust someone, deep down they want to bust you back," Cork said.

"Not everybody's got the balls for that. The question for you is who does?"

Two of Cork's deputies were helping the BCA people dig in front of the cabin. They put a shovelful into a metal sieve, sifted, tossed out rocks and other detritus, then repeated the process. They were looking for the round that hit Marsha Dross. Cork hoped they'd find it and that it would prove good for a ballistics analysis.

Rutledge walked to his car, an unremarkable blue Cavalier, and brought back an evidence bag that held the two shell casings Cork had found the night before. "Remington .357, packed with a hundred fifty grains, I'd say. Probably fired from something like a Savage One-ten. That would be my firearm of choice, anyway."

"Why? That's a game rifle," Cork said.

"With a good scope, one of those babies could make Barney Fife into an effective assassin. And up here, a Savage One-ten is as common as a snowmobile. Wouldn't raise any eyebrows like a more sophisticated sniper weapon might."

"You're saying it could be anyone," Cork said.

"Those tracks you found at the bridge might help narrow things a bit." Rutledge looked at Cork wistfully. "So?"

"So what?"

"Who wants you dead?"

6

CORK DROVE THE Pathfinder back to Aurora and parked in the lot of the community hospital. He checked at the reception desk, then walked to Intensive Care, where Marsha Dross had been moved. It was breakfast time for the patients, and the smell of institutional food that filled the hallways reminded Cork that he hadn't eaten that morning. He should have been hungry, but he wasn't.

He found Frank Dross sitting in a chair outside Marsha's room. Marsha's father, a widower, was a retired cop from Rochester, Minnesota. Like his daughter, he was tall and not what you would call good looking. He had a long nose, gray eyes, and gray hair neatly parted on the right side. He wore a black knit shirt and tan Haggar slacks with an expandable waist that was, in fact, expanded over a small paunch. Cork had met him several times and liked the man.

Dross stood. "Sheriff." He shook Cork's hand.

"How're you doing, Frank?"

"Better, now that I know Marsha's out of danger. They tell me you saved her life."

Saved her life? Maybe he'd kept her from dying in

the dirt in front of the Tibodeau cabin, but he'd also been responsible, in a way, for the bullet that put her there.

"Do you know why yet?" Frank asked.

"We're working on that. How is she this morning?"

"Officially, she's listed in guarded condition. They got her hooked up to all kinds of monitors, but she'll be fine."

"Fine?" Charlie Annala came from Marsha's room. He didn't appear to be any happier with Cork this morning than he'd been last night. "Because of that bullet, she may never be able to have kids. We may never have kids. You call that fine?" He wore the same clothing as the night before. He hadn't shaved, and from his smell it was clear he hadn't showered, either. The skin seemed to hang on his face like heavy dough, and his bloodshot eyes looked fractured. "And the hell of it is, nobody can tell me why."

"Sometimes, Charlie, just being a cop is reason enough for people to hate you." Frank put a hand on his shoulder. "In the sixties, seventies, they called us pigs. It's not a job that gets a lot of respect. I told Marsha it wouldn't be easy, but it was what she wanted to do. It was always what she wanted to do." Frank gave Charlie a gentle pat. "It can be tough, being in love with a cop."

"Is she allowed visitors?" Cork asked.

"One at a time," Frank said.

"Mind if I go in?"

Charlie opened his mouth, about to object, but Frank said, "Sure. Keep it short, though, okay?"

The curtain was partially drawn. Cork walked to the end of the bed. An IV needle plugged into Marsha's right forearm fed a clear liquid into her body.

She was hooked to a heart monitor and a machine that tracked her respiration as well. She lay with her head deeply imbedded in a pillow, the skin of her cheeks a bloodless white. Even so, she managed a smile when she saw Cork.

"Hi," she said.

"How are you feeling?"

She beckoned him nearer. He walked along the side and took the hand she offered.

"Drugged," she said. "Not feeling much." She squeezed his hand. "Thanks."

"Any time."

She shifted a little, tried to rise, but gave up. "The investigation?"

Cork looked out the window, which faced east. The hospital was on a small rise at the edge of town, and Iron Lake was visible beyond a line of birch trees that were like white scratches against the blue water.

"We're getting somewhere," he said. "We've got shell casings, and I'm sure we'll get a bullet for ballistics. We've got tire tracks, too."

"A suspect?"

"We're working on that."

"Eli and Lucy?"

"They weren't anywhere near the cabin last night."

She nodded faintly. "I've been thinking. You and me in our uniforms, in bad light, we probably don't look all that different. I think somebody knew you'd answer that call."

"I've been thinking that, too," Cork said. "We'll get him, Marsha."

"*Him*? A woman called in the complaint."

She was a good, smart cop. Even in her drugged state, she'd been putting the pieces together.

"Him, her, them. We're going to do our jobs and we're going to get them."

"You better." She smiled weakly and gave his fingers another squeeze.

"Rest," he said.

She nodded, closed her eyes, and let go of his hand.

It was clear to everyone—even Marsha, full of drugs—that Cork was the one the sniper had meant to take out. As he drove away from the hospital with the sunlight sliding off his windshield, he thought about the question Simon Rutledge had posed: *Who wants you dead?*

They'd talked about it for a bit at the Tibodeau cabin, gone over a few possibilities. Only one seemed plausible. The raid on the meth lab outside Yellow Lake had gone down in July, just two weeks after Cork took over as sheriff. He'd had very little to do with the investigation, but the bust resulted in a tragic afternoon for a family of criminals. Two men, brothers, Lydell and Axel Cramer, were inside an old Airstream trailer parked next to their rural home when Cork's people arrived and pounded on the door. The chemicals used to make methamphetamine were volatile. It was dangerous business. The two brothers had panicked. There was an explosion, and flames engulfed the trailer. One man stumbled out, his clothing on fire. Cy Borkmann wrestled him down and rolled him in the grass until the flames were extinguished. The man was Lydell Cramer. His little brother Axel never made it out. Lydell was airlifted to St. Joseph's Hospital in St. Paul, where he awaited trial while recovering from third-degree burns over most of his body. He didn't talk much, but when he did it was all about getting even with "the pig-fucking cops" who'd killed his brother.

They'd kicked around the idea of Lydell Cramer and decided it was worth looking into.

Patsy, who was on duty in Dispatch, radioed Cork and told him Jo had requested he call her at her office. Instead of calling, he drove straight over.

The Aurora Professional Building was a newer, single-story brick construction on the west side of town. Cork pulled into the lot and went inside. He passed the offices of David Spender, DDS, and Francis Kennilworth, CPA. He came to Jo's office and went inside. The anteroom was empty, and the door to Jo's inner office was closed. A sign sat propped on the desk: BACK IN 5 MINUTES. HAVE A SEAT. Which probably meant that Jo's secretary had gone for coffee, and Jo was with a client. Cork was just about to sit down and wait when the inner office door swung open and a man stepped out. Cork had met him only once before, and he hadn't liked him.

Edward Jacoby was the kind of guy who smiled broadly and often but without a trace of goodwill. It was hard to know what was really behind that flash of teeth, but as it was, Jacoby's smile reminded Cork of a wound that showed white bone. Jacoby was in his early thirties, good-looking in a dark way. He had thick black hair, heavy-lidded eyes, the shadow of a beard across his jaw. He was small, but with a large upper body and thick neck, a man who worked out seriously.

When they shook hands, Jacoby's grip, like his smile, was not about being cordial. A class ring dwarfed the knuckle on his right pinkie. The pinkie of his left hand sported a chunk of gold set with a diamond. Cork had always thought a pinkie an odd finger on which to wear a ring, especially for a man.

"Good to see you again, Sheriff," Jacoby said.

"I hope I'm not interrupting anything."

Jacoby magnanimously waved off Cork's concern. "Not at all. I was just leaving. Heard you had some trouble last night. Everything okay?"

"Under control."

"I'm sure it is." Jacoby eyed him with a shade of concern. "Say, you look like you could use a good night's sleep. Want some advice? Melatonin before you go to bed. It's one of those hormones older people's bodies don't regulate very well."

"I'll keep it in mind."

Jacoby reached back and squeezed Jo's hand. "Always a pleasure, Counselor. Give me a call—you have my cell phone number, right?—after you've spoken with the RBC. I'm staying at the Four Seasons. You should have my number there, too. If you don't get me, just leave a message. Ciao," he said, and left.

Inside Jo's office with the door closed, Cork said, "I've met rabid badgers I liked better."

"You don't have to like him." Jo picked up a document and scanned it.

Cork sat down at her desk and began to rub the back of his neck, which had developed a slight crick. "Do you?"

"I've dealt with him for six months now. I'm almost used to him."

Starlight Enterprises, the company that employed Jacoby, provided management for casinos all over the lower Midwest and was eager to expand into Minnesota. Jacoby had been working hard for the past half year to make the Iron Lake Ojibwe one of the company's clients. Because Jo had often represented the interests of the rez and had worked on the casino from its inception, Oliver Bledsoe, who headed the tribal legal affairs office, had retained her to handle the negotiations. The Reservation Business Committee, which oversaw all financial dealings the rez conducted as an entity, had initially rejected the idea. The casino was just about to lose its fourth manager in as many years, however, and several members of the RBC had become vocal advocates for using Starlight to supply consistent, qualified management. They'd finally authorized Jo to come up with a contract that the RBC could put to a vote.

As light as a butterfly, she touched Cork's wounded ear. "How are you doing?"

"Holding up."

"You didn't sleep much."

"A lot on my mind."

"You left this morning before the girls were up. They were disappointed they didn't see you."

"There were things I needed to do."

She pressed her palm gently to his chest. "I understand, Cork, but they're scared. Their father could have been killed last night."

"I wasn't."

"And thank God for that. But they need some reassurance and it needs to come from you."

When he'd agreed to step in again as sheriff, Cork had promised himself and Jo that, as much as possible, his job wouldn't affect his family, especially the children. Deep down he knew it was a futile pledge. He was the son of a sheriff himself, and he understood what the job demanded. He'd said yes for the most selfish of reasons. He missed the badge. He missed the camaraderie that came with it, the challenge, the feeling that he was doing something that mattered. It was also satisfying to have the Board of Commissioners come to him, hat in hand, after the people of Tamarack County elected Arne Soderberg, a man as near to being a cop as a duck was to being an eagle. They'd screwed themselves royally, and they needed Cork. That felt good. Damn good. So he'd said yes knowing full well the sacrifices it would require of his family.

He took her hand and kissed it. "I'll be home for dinner, promise. I'll talk to them then. Was that all you wanted?"

"And this." She kissed him softly. "Take care of yourself out there, cowboy."

In the early afternoon, he drove out to Allouette on the Iron Lake Reservation to meet with the tribal council. Simon Rutledge followed in his state car.

Allouette was the largest of the communities on the reservation. Even so, there wasn't a lot to it. From one end of town to the other was just over half a mile. A few years before, the housing had been mostly trailers and HUD homes in desperate need of repair, but lately things had improved considerably thanks to the Chippewa Grand Casino that was owned and operated by the Iron Lake Band of Ojibwe. Typically, the tribal council met in the new community center, which had been built with casino money. In addition to the large room where the tribal council gathered and where meetings open to the reservation at large were held, the center housed the offices of a number of tribal organizations, a health clinic, a day care center, and a gymnasium. Cork had spoken earlier in the day with

George LeDuc, chairman of the tribal council, and had arranged to meet with that body to discuss the incident at the Tibodeau cabin.

In 1953, Congress passed Public Law 280, which allowed responsibility for law enforcement on Minnesota Indian reservations to be transferred from federal jurisdiction to the state, if that's what the enrolled members wanted. The Iron Lake Ojibwe had chosen to be policed by the state's local authority, which was the Tamarack County Sheriff's Department. As sheriff and as a man part Ojibwe, Cork had always tried to be a judicious presence on the rez. For the most part, he'd succeeded. But this time he was bringing Simon Rutledge of the BCA with him, and he wasn't hopeful about how well that would go over.

Seven of the eight members of the council had managed to be there and were waiting in the meeting room. Seated at the conference table with George LeDuc were Judy Bruneau, Albert Boshey, Roy Stillday, Edgar Gillespie, Heidi Baudette, and Thomas Whitefeather.

"Anin," Cork said as he entered, offering the traditional Ojibwe greeting.

He shook hands with LeDuc and the others and introduced Simon Rutledge all around. When everyone was seated again, he explained what had occurred at the Tibodeau cabin the night before. He also explained why Rutledge would be in charge of the investigation. He was pretty sure they'd all heard about the shooting—heard some version of what had gone down, anyway—but it was impossible to tell from their faces, which showed little expression. They simply nodded now and then as he spoke. He'd been to lots of meetings on the rez, tribal council and otherwise. When there were only Ojibwe—or Shinnobs, as they often referred to themselves—present, discussions were almost always heated, with long digressions and references to obscure relatives and old incidents that had little if any bearing on the issue at hand. With Rutledge there, an outsider and a white law officer to boot, the council's silence didn't surprise Cork in the least.

When he was finished, there was a long silence, then George LeDuc spoke. In the dark, LeDuc might have been mistaken for a bear, an old bear, because he was seventy and huge. Although his long hair was streaked with silver, he still had a powerful look and feel about him. Only two years before, he'd fathered a child with his third wife, Francie. He and Cork had been friends for a lot of years.

"First of all," LeDuc said in a gentle growl, "we're all real sorry about Marsha Dross. We sure hope she'll be fine." He paused a long time, looking implacably at Cork. "As for that chunk of ear you're missing, well . . ." He glanced at the woman on the far side of the conference table. "Heidi, there, told me a little while ago she thinks a few scars on a man is sexy, so maybe it'll prove a blessing in the end." He almost smiled. "We'll do everything we can to help Agent Rutledge with his investigation."

"George, it would help most if you could encourage anyone on the rez who might know something to step forward. Talk to Agent Rutledge, or give me a call at my office, if they'd rather."

"We'll get the word out," LeDuc promised.

Thomas Whitefeather, an old man who was not an elected member of the council but was a part of it because he was a hereditary chief, spoke up. "Should we be afraid for the safety of the people on the rez?"

Rutledge fielded that one. "Until we know for sure the reason for the attack on Sheriff O'Connor and his deputy, I'd advise that any suspicious activity you observe warrants concern. However, at the moment we're operating on the belief that this was an isolated incident. I'll be spending time here today, and later in the general vicinity of the shooting. I'll be available to speak with anyone who might be able to shed some light on what's happened."

Rutledge stayed after, but Cork left and walked to the Pathfinder with George LeDuc.

"You must've really pissed somebody off," LeDuc said.

"Looks like."

"Folks on the rez, we've been glad to see you back in that uniform. Most of us. We hear anything, Cork, you'll know. But don't count on anyone talking to your BCA friend."

"I already told him that, George."

LeDuc shook his head and his long white hair shivered. "Out here, you can always tell a white man, but you can't tell him much."

7

A LITTLE BEFORE three that afternoon, Larson strode into Cork's office. The sun was bright and cast a long blade of light with a sharp edge that cut across Larson's thighs as he sat down.

"What have you got?" Cork asked.

"A good cast of the tire tracks," Larson said. "Excellent casting, actually. Rutledge's people are going to do a pattern match and then we can start checking sales around here. We dug the bullet from the ground, and that's on its way to the BCA lab. We didn't find any more shell casings, or anything else on the hilltop."

"You saw the tracks down the back side of the hill?"

"There were definite signs someone had gone that way, but we didn't find a good boot print. You took Rutledge out to the rez?"

"Yeah. He's there now, interviewing, hoping he'll find somebody who noticed something unusual. Problem is, there's nobody for a couple of miles in any direction from the Tibodeaus' place," Cork said. "And even if they'd seen something, they're not going to tell Simon."

"He's good. Let's wait to see what he comes up with." Larson's mouth went into a tight line, as if he were trying to keep something from slipping through his lips. "Cork," he finally said, "you need to see Faith Gray."

Faith Gray, MSW, PhD, was the consulting psychologist retained by the county for a variety of purposes. She did psychological testing for certain positions and was also responsible for counseling any sheriff's personnel involved in an officer-related shooting until she was ready to certify that they were fit for duty.

"I didn't shoot anybody," Cork said.

Cork had been toying with the silver pen he'd used to work on the duty roster. The pen slipped from his hands. He bent to retrieve it and, when he came up, realized that Larson's dark eyes had followed every move.

"You were shot," Larson said. "I can get you the policy statement, but you ought to know what it says. You wrote it."

"All right." Cork put up his hand as if to stop an argument. "I'll do it."

"It would be a mistake to put it off."

"I said I'd do it."

Larson nodded, rose from his chair, and left.

Cork sat for a while, eyeing the telephone. Finally he lifted the receiver to call Faith Gray and noted, a little distantly, that his hand was shaking.

As he'd promised, he was home for dinner. Jenny had put in a meat loaf, Annie had done potatoes and a tossed salad, and Stevie had set the table. His children weren't always this organized or cooperative, but whenever the foundation of the family seemed threatened, they pulled together admirably. They greeted him with prolonged hugs, as if he'd been away on a long trip.

He stowed his gun belt on the top shelf of his bedroom closet and put his revolver in the lockbox there. He took off his uniform, donned jeans and a yellow chamois shirt, and came down to dinner looking like a man who might be doing anything for a living. Except that he had stitches closing the lobe of his left ear where a bullet had narrowly missed piercing his skull. They talked about what happened. The children asked about Marsha, whom they all liked, and they were glad she would recover. As soon as he could, Cork moved them on to other topics.

"Get any great college offers today?" he said to Jenny as he wedged off a piece of the meat loaf with his fork.

She'd taken her SATs early and had done extremely well, scoring in the ninety-fifth percentile. For several months, she'd been considering the schools to which she would make application, and had narrowed her choices to Northwestern, Stanford, and Columbia, none of which the O'Connors could afford outright. They'd filed a statement of financial need, and knew that much of the final decision of a college would rest on what kind of aid Jenny was offered. She was a straight-A student with a lot of extracurricular activities and honors. Through a state-sponsored program, she'd already taken a number of college-level courses at Aurora Community College and aced every one. On top of it all, she was part Ojibwe. According to her high school counselor, all of these things made her an attractive candidate.

It was Northwestern that Jenny talked about most.

"No, but Mom and I talked some more about going to Evanston to check out Northwestern's campus."

"Sounds like a wise idea." Then he said, "'Some more'?"

Jo said, "We've been talking about a short trip to Evanston for a while."

Cork paused with his fork halfway to his mouth. "Really?"

"We told you, Dad. Don't you remember?"

"Sure." Although at the moment, he didn't. "When?"

"That's one of the things we need to discuss," Jo said.

Stevie, who was seven, put down his glass of milk. He had a white mustache on his upper lip. "I told Roger Turppa that I had a sister in the twelfth grade and he said I was a liar 'cuz school doesn't go that high."

"It might not for Roger Turppa, if he's anything like his dad," Cork said.

"Evanston's not that far from South Bend," Annie said.

Everyone knew Annie wanted to go to Notre Dame. There'd never been any doubt. Although only a sophomore, she was already determined to secure an athletic scholarship in softball, and when Annie set her mind on something it usually came to pass.

"We'll talk about Northwestern—and Notre Dame—later," Jo said. "When your father's not so tired."

After dinner, Jo washed the dishes, Cork dried. He was just hanging up the dish towel when the front doorbell rang.

"Dad," Annie called from the living room. "It's for you."

Simon Rutledge stood at the door, his hands folded patiently in front of him, smiling as he watched Cork come from the kitchen.

"Smells good," Rutledge said.

"The kids fixed meat loaf."

"The kids?" Rutledge laughed. "Mine can't even follow a recipe for ice water. Let's talk outside, okay?"

Cork stepped onto the porch and closed the door. It was a blue twilight with a few clouds in the west lit with a faint rose glow. The air was cooling rapidly, and by morning, Cork figured, there'd be frost. Gooseberry Lane was empty, but the houses along the street were lit by warm lights from within. During summer, when the evenings seemed to stretch into forever, he loved to sit with Jo in the porch swing and watch Stevie play with the other kids on the block, their laughter a perfect ending to the day. He didn't have that feeling now.

"I didn't get a lot on the rez," Rutledge said.

"I figured."

"People seem pretty well split in how they think of you."

"They always have been." Cork put his hands on the porch railing and leaned against it lightly. "You know anything about my family, Simon?"

"Nope. Only know you."

"My grandfather was a teacher, opened a school on the reservation in a time when most Ojibwe kids got sent away to government schools. The BIA's approach was to do its best to rub out the Indian in Indians. My grandfather had friends on the rez and also in politics and he was able to keep a lot of children from being taken from their families. Know why he did that?"

"He appreciated the culture?"

"He was in love. With my Grandma Dilsey, who convinced him to do the right thing. He was a decent man, but it was my grandmother who guided his heart. People on the rez respected my grandfather but they loved Grandma Dilsey.

"My mother chose to marry a white man, too. And a law enforcement officer, to boot. My father was a man of strong beliefs. He tried to be fair, and I think he did a pretty good job of it, but not everybody saw it that way. A lot of white folks called him a squaw man behind his back, like they did my grandfather. The Anishinaabeg called him *odeimin*. Know what that means?"

Rutledge shook his head.

"Strawberry."

"Because of his sweet disposition?"

"His ruddy Irish complexion. Now here I am, a little Indian and a lot of Irish. When folks, white or Shinnob, don't like what I'm doing, often as not they blame it on my blood." Cork glanced at Rutledge who was looking at the sky. "You find anyone who seemed pissed enough to shoot me dead?"

"You know the Ojibwe. For all the emotion they showed, I might as well have been talking to sticks. Nothing they told me was very useful." He yawned. It had been a long day for him, too. "We've got an agent in St. Paul who's going to St. Joseph's Hospital tomorrow to interview Lydell Cramer. We'll see what he has to say for himself."

Cork heard the dismissive tone of his voice. "But?"

"I've got to tell you, the Indian connection seems pretty strong. Whoever the shooter was, he knew the territory, knew the Tibodeaus' schedule, and knew it would most likely be you who responded to the call."

"Could mean it's just someone who's a good strategist."

"You make it sound like a war."

"I don't think it's over. Do you?" Cork said.

Rutledge put his hands in his pockets, hunched his shoulders. "He went to a lot of trouble and didn't get what he wanted. No, I don't think it's over."

Cork looked up and down the empty street. "Then it *is* a war. What do we do in the meantime?"

"Follow up on the tire castings and see what ballistics can tell us about the weapon." He saw Cork scrutinizing the neighborhood. "Worried?"

"He drew me out where there wouldn't be witnesses. I don't think he'll try anything here."

"Even so, it might be best to confine yourself to your office for a while. No rural calls."

"I'm not going to hide, Simon."

"That's not what I meant."

"I won't be stupid."

"All right." Rutledge started down the porch steps. "I'll be in touch."

Cork watched the agent get into his car and drive away. Night was pressing hard against the last stubborn light of day. He stood a few minutes longer on the front porch, peering deeply into the places where night and shadow already met. He turned his back to the street, felt a prickle run the length of his spine, the brief anticipation of a bullet, then he stepped inside.

8

*H*E WAS FOLLOWING his father through a stretch of pine woods he didn't recognize, following him at a distance. Liam O'Connor loped ahead, a giant of a man, putting more and more distance between himself and his son with each stride. He broke through shafts of sunlight, flashing brilliant for a moment, all gold. In the next instant he dropped into shadow. Cork tried to call out to him, to bring him back, but his jaw felt rusted shut, and all he could push through his lips was a desperate, incoherent moan. He struggled to run faster, to catch up so that he could throw his arms around his father and hold him forever. From somewhere in the pine boughs above came the harsh taunts of crows. He realized that everything around him had been perfectly still until the birds shattered the silence, and he became afraid. The cawing turned into the rattle of gunfire, and he saw that it was not his father he was chasing but Marsha Dross. As he watched, blood bloomed on the blouse of her uniform and she fell. Cork fought to free his legs, which had sunk deep into a bed of pine needles that held him like quicksand. The gunfire again became the cawing of the birds, and the cawing became the ringing of the phone in his bedroom as he pulled himself awake.

"Sheriff?"

"Yeah."

"Sheriff, it's Bos."

Cork registered that it was Boston Swain, the night dispatcher.

"You awake?"

"I'm here. What time is it?"

"Three A.M. You're sure you're awake."

Cork wiped away tears but was quite sure he was awake. "What is it, Bos?"

"Sheriff." She paused a moment, perhaps waiting for Cork to affirm that his eyes were open. "It looks like we've got a homicide."

He'd gone to bed to a clear sky and a moon heading toward full, and he'd thought by morning there would be frost. Clouds had moved in during the night, however, and kept the temperature up. As Cork headed away from home, a light precipitation began to fall, more mist than rain, coating everything with a wet sheen. The wipers of his old Bronco groaned intermittently across the windshield, the headlights shimmered off glazed asphalt, and the tires hissed as they rolled. The road to the overlook at Mercy Falls wound through dripping forests that, in the dark morning hours, seemed primordial and menacing.

There were two parking lots for the overlook at Mercy Falls. The first lot was for the picnic shelter and the restroom blockhouse. The second lot, a hundred yards up the hill and hidden by a thick stand of aspen, was nearer to the falls but had no facilities. The lower lot was empty; in the upper parking lot Cork found three vehicles. Two were department cruisers. The other was a silver Lexus SUV with an Avis sticker on the bumper. Nearby, heard but unseen, Mercy Creek gushed through a narrows in slate-gray bedrock before tumbling one hundred feet into a small pool. The falls overlook was a favorite place for sightseers during the day. Officially, it closed at sunset, but at night it was a popular spot for couples to do what couples in parked cars had always done in dark, beautiful places. The deputies on night patrol would swing by occasionally, often enough to keep the local kids guessing.

The two cruisers had been positioned so that their headlights blasted over the SUV from either side. Cork parked in back of the Lexus and left the Bronco's headlights on. Morgan and Schilling stood in the mist, their jackets zipped against the damp chill.

"Watch your step," Morgan said as Cork approached.

Cork looked down and skirted a small puddle of vomit, yellow-white on the wet pavement.

Schilling looked pale and shaken. "On the ground, in front." He nodded toward the Lexus.

The man lay on his back. A Cubs ball cap was pulled down over the top half of his face, obscuring his eyes. His mouth was open in an unending yawn. Long splashes of blood, almost black now from clotting, clung to his cheeks like leeches. His shirt, a button-down light-blue oxford, was a stained, shredded mess, getting damp from the mist. His pants and black briefs had been yanked down around his ankles. His knees were spread wide, and his crotch and inner thighs looked as if someone had taken a big brush, dipped it in a bucket of blood, and painted his skin.

Schilling said behind him, "They didn't just kill him, Cork. They castrated him, too."

"You found him?"

"Yeah." Schilling blew into his hands and shifted on his feet as if he were freezing.

"You touch anything?"

"I checked him for a pulse, that's it."

Cork looked back at the puddle of vomit. "His?"

"Mine," Schilling said. "Sorry."

"How're you feeling now?"

"I've been better."

"Okay. Nothing gets touched until Ed gets here. In the meantime, Howard," he said to Morgan, "I want you to get on the radio and run the plate, make sure it's a rental. Then let's contact Avis and find out who rented it."

Morgan nodded and headed to his cruiser.

"What about me?" Schilling said.

Cork considered the body and the ground around it becoming wet as the mist grew heavy, turning to a light rain. He didn't want to disturb the scene, but he also didn't want the rain to wash away evidence.

"Pull your cruiser around in front, Nate, and park with your grille facing the grille of the SUV. Stay back from the body a good ten feet. Leave your head-lights on."

While Schilling maneuvered his vehicle, Cork grabbed a ground cloth and length of nylon rope from his Bronco. With his pocketknife, he cut four cords from the rope, each a couple feet long. When Schilling got out of his cruiser, Cork handed him one end of the ground cloth.

"Tie the corners to your grille. I'll tie the other end to the SUV."

When they were done, the ground cloth provided a shelter that kept the rain from falling directly on the crime scene.

"Now what?" Schilling asked.

"Wait for me in my Bronco. I'll be there in a minute."

Cork went to Morgan's cruiser and spoke to his deputy through the open window. "How's it going?"

"Bos is making the call now. Captain Larson's on his way. Should be here pretty quick."

"Stay with it. I'm going to talk to Schilling."

"How's he doing?"

"Still a little pale."

Cork returned to his Bronco, where Schilling sat hunched on the passenger side up front. Cork killed his headlights, and the two men sat for a moment in silence.

"Ever seen someone dead before?" Cork asked.

"Only in a casket. Never like that."

"Tough, huh?"

"You've got that right."

"You want to smoke, go ahead."

"Thanks." Schilling pulled a pack of Marlboros and a silver lighter from the inside pocket of his jacket. He tapped out a cigarette, wedged it into the corner of his mouth, flipped the lid on the lighter, put the flame to the tip of the Marlboro. He shot a cloud of smoke with a grateful sigh.

Cork opened his window a crack.

"Didn't touch the body, right?"

"Like I said, only to check the pulse."

"When did you throw up?"

"Right after that. It hit me real sudden."

"Sure. So you threw up and radioed the call in immediately?"

"Yes, sir."

"What time was that?"

"I don't know exactly. A little before three, I'd guess."

Cork had given up smoking a couple of years earlier, but he still found the smell of the cigarette enticing. "Tell me about your night up to that point."

"Nothing to tell. Real quiet up till then."

"Routine check of the park? That's why you were here?"

"I ran Arlo Knuth out earlier. I just wanted to be sure he didn't come back."

Arlo Knuth was an itinerant who spent his nights sleeping in parks or on back roads or wherever he could get away with parking the old pickup that was his home.

"What time?"

"Maybe midnight. Maybe a little before."

"You always do that after you've run Arlo off? Come back later to check?"

"Sometimes, not always."

"What made tonight different?"

"I don't know. Just a feeling."

"Why the hard-on for Arlo? He's harmless."

"Park closes at sunset. He's not supposed to be here at night. No one is."

"Most deputies cut Arlo some slack."

"I figure it's the law. Park's closed, everybody should stay out. Hell, I run kids off all the time who are making out here. Why should Arlo be any different?"

"When you came back, did you check behind the restroom blockhouse down in the lower parking lot?"

"No, sir."

"Sometimes Arlo uses the blockhouse for cover. That way he can wash up first thing in the morning."

"I know. And I would have checked it out, but when I got here I found a dead man. Pretty well ended my patrol."

"Think Arlo could've been involved in this?"

The deputy looked down at his cigarette, which hadn't touched his lips since his first drag. "No, sir, I don't expect so. Like you say, he's harmless."

Headlights flashed through the trees as several vehicles pulled off the main road and came up the winding access.

"All right, tell you what," Cork said. "Finish that cigarette, then take a hike down the path to the lower lot, check the blockhouse, see if Arlo's still around."

Ed Larson pulled up in his Blazer and parked. Cork left Schilling and headed to the Blazer just as Larson got out.

"Early start to your day, Ed."

"Same for you," Larson said. "What have we got?"

"Male Caucasian. Multiple stab wounds to the chest. And castrated. That's it so far."

"ID?"

"Not yet. I didn't want to disturb anything until after you'd had a chance to go over the scene. Looks like a rental vehicle. We're running the plates, so we may get something soon."

"All right. Who found him?"

"Schilling."

"Where is he?"

"In my Bronco. He's pretty shook. When you see the vic, you'll understand why. Oh, and watch your step as you approach the Lexus."

Larson looked at the SUV. "I called Simon Rutledge. I figured as long as he was in the neighborhood. He'll be here in a bit."

"Good," Cork said.

Morgan stood beside his cruiser, arms folded, water dripping from the bill of his uniform cap. Cork went over, and together they watched as Larson's team arrived and set about their work. Morgan had started his engine and left it idling so that the battery wouldn't wear down while his headlights lit the scene. The exhaust gathered in a ghostly white cloud that crawled around and under the vehicle. A minute later, Schilling left the Bronco and started down the path to the lower parking lot.

"Where's he going?" Morgan asked.

"I told him to check behind the blockhouse for Arlo Knuth."

"Think Arlo's still around?"

"Worth checking out. And gives Nate something to do."

"Good idea. I still remember the first body I saw on duty." Morgan's face was lit from the reflection of all the light in front of him. His mouth was in a grim set. "Traffic accident. Guy went through the windshield, ended up on the other side in pieces. I lost my lunch that day."

Ed Larson was kneeling under the ground cloth Cork and Schilling had tied above the body. "Cork," he called.

Cork wasn't in uniform. He'd thrown on a pair of wrinkled jeans and a green sweatshirt with MACKINAC ISLAND across the front, slapped a stocking cap on his head, and shrugged into his bombardier's jacket that was so old and worn it looked like the hide of a diseased deer. The jacket was soaked dark from the mist and his face dripped as he walked to Larson.

"What is it?"

"You told me his balls were missing," Larson said.

"They are."

Larson held his flashlight out to Cork. "Look in there."

Cork knelt beside Larson and shined the light into the cavern of the dead man's mouth, which Larson held open with gloved fingers.

"Jesus."

"They're not missing," Larson said. "They were fed to him as a last meal." He straightened up. "We'll move him in a little while to see if we can locate a wallet for an ID."

Cork had had a good look at the face. He swung the beam of his flashlight down to the dead man's right hand, where a big gold ring adorned the pinkie—an odd finger, Cork had always thought, for a man to put a ring on.

"No need," he said quietly. "I know who it is."

9

Jo WAS SLEEPING soundly, and Cork hated to wake her. For a little while, he sat in a chair in the corner, a maple rocker they'd bought when Jenny was a baby. Over the years, they'd taken turns rocking one child or another back to sleep during long nights of illness or restlessness or bad dreams, and Cork had often drifted off himself with a small body nestled against his chest. He hadn't always been the father he wanted to be, but somehow his children had clung to their love for him, and he felt blessed. Blessed, too, with Jo, although they'd had their problems. The point was, he thought, looking at his wife's face half lost in her pillow, to do your best as a man—father, husband, sheriff—and hope that your mistakes weren't fatal and they would be forgiven.

He moved to the bed, sat down beside Jo, and touched her shoulder gently.

She made an effort to roll over. "You're back?"

"Just for a bit."

Her eyes struggled to stay open. "Who was it?"

When he'd left, all he knew was that there appeared to have been a homicide at the overlook for Mercy Falls. He had told her to go back to sleep.

"You awake?" he asked now.

"Almost."

"I need you awake for this."

His tone brought her eyes fully open. "What is it?"

"I have to ask you a couple of questions."

She sat up, her back against the headboard, her blond hair a little wild. She pulled the covers up to keep warm. "Go ahead."

"How well do you know Edward Jacoby?"

"I've met with him half a dozen times over the past few months. Why?"

"How much do you know about him personally?"

"Almost nothing. What's going on, Cork?"

"The homicide at Mercy Falls. It was Jacoby."

"Oh my God."

The mist had developed into a steady rain that ran down the windowpanes. Outside, the street lamp on the curb pushed a yellow light through the window, and shadows from the streaked glass lay over the whole room like gray stains.

"Jo, do you have any contact information we can use to notify someone?"

"Downstairs in my office."

She threw back the covers. She wore a sleep shirt, her usual attire in bed. This one was black. She went barefoot ahead of Cork.

Downstairs, she turned on the light in the office she maintained at home, sat down at her desk, and reached for her Rolodex.

"Do you know who did it?" she asked.

"No."

"Any idea why?"

"No." Cork sat in the chair Jo's clients used. "Do you want to know how?"

Jo glanced up, her blue eyes guarded. "Do I?"

"Pretty brutal."

"Then no." She flipped a couple of cards on the Rolodex, then looked across the desk at him. "All right. How?"

"Multiple stab wounds. And he was castrated."

"Oh Jesus."

"Still had his wallet with him, stuffed with cash, so robbery doesn't seem a likely reason. Did he ever say anything to you, Jo, that might be helpful here?"

"Like what?"

"There's a lot of feeling on the rez that runs both ways about Starlight taking over management of the casino."

"Cork, you can't think somebody on the rez would do this. Over a business issue?"

"I don't know, Jo. That's why I'm asking questions."

She found the card she was looking for and took it off the Rolodex.

"All right," Cork said. "What about his personal life?"

"I don't know much."

"Married?"

"I believe so."

"Happily?"

"I have no idea."

"Does he gamble?"

"I don't know."

"Has he ever talked about people here, what he might do when he's not meeting with you?"

"Not really, but . . ."

"What?"

"I have my suspicions." She sat back. "He had a

pretty high opinion of himself, and he appeared to
have a libido the size of Jupiter."

"Yeah? Why do you say that?"

"He hit on me every time we met."

Now Cork sat back. "You never told me."

"It wasn't important. I dealt with it."

"You think he messed around?"

"I think he was the type."

"He ever mention any names?"

"Not to me. Here." She leaned across the desk and
handed him the card. It contained Jacoby's office
number, his cell phone number, the number for his
home phone and a mailing address at Starlight Enterprises in Elmhurst, Illinois.

"Mind if I keep this?"

"No, go ahead." She studied him with concern.
"You look so tired. Any chance you can lie down for a
while?"

"I'm going to the office."

"At least let me fix you some breakfast."

He shook his head and stood up. "I'll hit the
Broiler when it opens. You go on back to bed."

"There's no way I can sleep now." She came around
the desk and took him in her arms. "Marsha, you,
now this. What's going on, Cork? Didn't we leave
Chicago to get away from this kind of thing?"

He took her in his arms and savored the feel, the only
solid hold he had on anything at the moment. "Damned
if I know, Jo, but I'm doing my best to find out."

He waited until 7:00 A.M. to make the call to
Jacoby's home phone. After five rings, the line went
to voice messaging, Jacoby's own oily voice saying he
and Gabriella weren't home, leave a message.

Cork did, asking Ms. Jacoby to call him as soon as possible. It concerned her husband.

He stepped out of his office. The day shift had checked in, and the deputies were waiting for him in the briefing area. He gave them the lowdown on Mercy Falls, told them about a few changes to the duty roster, and reminded them to wear their vests.

At eight, he tried Jacoby's number again. This time someone answered, a woman with a slight Latino accent. Puerto Rican, maybe.

"Yes?"

"I'd like to speak with Ms. Jacoby, please."

"She is not here." Her *is* came out *ees*.

"Do you know how I might reach her?"

"Who is this?"

"Sheriff Corcoran O'Connor. I'm calling from Aurora, Minnesota."

"Mrs. Jacoby is gone. She will be back tomorrow."

"Does she have a cell phone number?"

"I can't give that out."

"Who am I speaking to?"

"I'm Carmelita."

"Carmelita, this is an emergency."

Carmelita breathed a couple of times before replying, "Mr. Edward?"

"Yes. Mr. Edward."

"Sometheen happen?"

"I need to speak to his wife."

She paused again, again considering. "Just a moment." Her end of the line went quiet. Then: "She is on a boat on the lake. I do not know if you can reach her. Her cell phone number is . . ." Cork wrote it down. Then she said, "His father. You should call him."

"His name?"

"Mr. Louis Jacoby. You want his telephone number?"

"Thank you."

He tried the cell phone that belonged to the dead man's wife, but it was "currently unavailable." He punched in the number Carmelita had given him for the father. It was the same area code as Edward Jacoby's home phone. The call was picked up on the first ring.

"Jacoby residence." A man's voice, modulated and proper.

"I'd like to speak with Louis Jacoby, please. This is Sheriff Corcoran O'Connor."

"Just one moment, please." The elegance of his voice seemed to lend a formality to the silence that followed. Half a minute later: "May I ask what this is in regard to, sir?"

"His son Edward."

A very proper silence again, then: "This is Lou Jacoby. What is it, Sheriff?"

"Mr. Jacoby, I'm calling from Aurora, Minnesota. It's about Edward."

"What's he done now?"

"It's not that, sir. I'm sorry, but I have some very bad news. Are you alone?"

"Just tell me, Sheriff."

"There's no way for this to be easy. The body of your son was discovered this morning in a park not far from here."

"His *body*?"

"Yes, sir. Mr. Jacoby, your son is dead."

Cork hated delivering this kind of news and hated doing it in this way.

"How?" Jacoby finally managed to ask.

"At the moment, we're treating it as a homicide."

"Somebody killed my son?" It was not a question but a hard reality settling in.

A silence that was only emptiness filled the line.

Then Jacoby rasped, "Eddie, Eddie. You stupid little shit."

10

A LITTLE BEFORE ten, Cork visited Marsha at the hospital. Charlie Annala had taken time off from his job at the fish hatchery and was a constant companion. Marsha's father, Frank, was there, too. Marsha looked better, with more color in her face, and she was sitting up. She'd heard about Mercy Falls and asked for details. Cork told her what they had. Then he had to tell her that as far as her own shooting was concerned, he knew nothing more than he did yesterday. But Rutledge was waiting for results from the BCA lab that he was sure would be helpful.

A few minutes after noon, he met with Simon Rutledge and Ed Larson in his office.

Larson explained that they'd completed their investigation of the crime scene at Mercy Falls after daybreak when they had more light to work with. They'd gone over the interior of the Lexus, taken hair samples from the upholstery that didn't appear to match that of the dead man, and had found in the ashtray two cigarette butts with lipstick on them. They'd fingerprinted everything; it was a rental, so there was a shitload of prints to process, and that would take a while. The door handles, however, had been wiped clean.

"Tom got right on the autopsy. He completed it about an hour ago. He's working on the official report right now, but basically this is what he found," Larson said, reading from his notepad. "There were fourteen stab wounds, all in the upper torso. Death was the direct result of a single stab wound to the heart. The mutilation came after Jacoby was deceased. The stab wounds were all delivered by a sharp, slender blade seven inches in length. The same instrument was probably used in the castration."

"Sounds like a fillet knife," Cork said.

"That's exactly what Tom thought."

In addition to being a physician and the county medical examiner, Tom Conklin was an avid angler.

"Was he robbed?" Cork asked.

"Nearly five hundred in his wallet, along with half a dozen credit cards."

"What was he doing out at Mercy Falls late at night?"

"Good question," Larson said.

"No indication of a struggle?"

"No lacerations on his arms or hands that would indicate he tried to defend himself."

"So Jacoby was taken completely by surprise?" Cork said.

"I'm guessing the final autopsy report will show a high blood alcohol level. There was a nearly empty bottle of tequila in the Lexus. Probably it'll show other drugs as well. We found a stash in the glove box. Cocaine, Ecstasy, marijuana, and Rohypnol."

The date-rape drug. Also known as Roofies, Ruffies, Roche, and by a dozen other names.

"It's entirely possible that Jacoby was too high to put up a struggle," Larson said.

Rutledge picked it up from there. "Jacoby had some receipts from the Four Seasons Lodge in his wallet. While Ed and his people finished at the scene, I dropped by and spoke with the lodge staff. Jacoby was staying there. He was a big tipper, flamboyant guy, and it wasn't unusual for him to be seen returning to his cabin at night in the company of a woman."

"Description?" Cork said.

"Not any particular woman anyone could describe. But we'll do more checking. Also we'll try to put together a complete history of his activities prior to his death."

"We'll be going over his room as soon as we leave here," Larson said. "See what turns up there."

"The drugs in the SUV," Cork said. "How'd he get those? Did he bring them with him? Risk a search of his luggage or person at airport security? Or did he buy them here?"

Rutledge nodded thoughtfully. "The castration might point toward a drug connection. Not uncommon to see something like that in drug deals gone bad. It could be the drugs were the reason he was at Mercy Falls."

"Anyone around here would know we patrol the park," Cork said.

Larson made a note on his pad. "Still worth checking out."

"Jacoby worked for Starlight. Casino management, right?" Rutledge said.

"That's right. He's made half a dozen trips over the last six months trying to convince the Iron Lake

Ojibwe to become clients. The RBC is going to vote on it pretty soon."

"RBC?"

"Reservation Business Committee."

"But it's been Jo who's dealt with him mostly, right?" Larson said. "Have you talked with her, Cork?"

"Some. About all she could offer was that he was probably a skirt chaser." Cork rubbed his eyes, which were so tired they seemed full of sand. "Fourteen stab wounds, castration, and drugs. Cigarette butts with lipstick. Could it be we're dealing with a woman? Considering all the drugs, maybe a woman in an altered state?"

"What about an angry husband?" Larson threw in. "Maybe he followed them to Mercy Falls?"

Rutledge said, "I've requested the phone records for his room at the Four Seasons. Also his cell phone records since he arrived in Aurora. That might tell us who he's been seeing here for pleasure."

"The casino's something we should take a hard look at, though," Cork said. "Starlight's not a popular notion with everyone on the rez."

"Unpopular enough for someone to kill Jacoby over it?"

"Jo doesn't think so."

"What about you?"

What he thought was that, in the end, the rez was simply a community of people, and people—white, red, brown, black, yellow—were all subject to the same human weaknesses, more or less. He would like to have believed that the heritage of the Anishinaabeg, the culture and its values, made them strong enough to resist the temptations that accompanied the new wealth the casino brought, but he knew it was wishful thinking.

"I honestly don't know," he finally said. "Let's do a background check on Jacoby, make sure he didn't simply bring trouble with him when he came."

"Here's something that's kind of interesting we found in his wallet," Larson said.

He handed Cork a business card. The logo was the Hollywood sign of legend, the one perched atop the Hollywood Hills. Beneath was printed *Blue Smoke Productions* with Edward Jacoby listed as a producer and an address on Wilshire Boulevard in Los Angeles. No telephone number.

"Jacoby made movies?"

"Or wanted people to think he did."

"Women?"

"He certainly seemed to like them."

Cork handed it back. "Something more to check on." He addressed Rutledge. "How're we coming on the rez shooting?"

"My guy in St. Paul went out to St. Joseph's Hospital first thing this morning and talked with Lydell Cramer. Says Cramer was so full of shit, his eyeballs were brown. Cramer claimed that although he was happy to hear about your difficulties, he had nothing to do with them."

Cork nodded. "Cramer would have trouble just figuring how to put butter on bread. I don't think he could pull off a hit like this."

"Let me finish," Rutledge said. "My guy does a routine check of the visitors Cramer's had since incarceration. Only one: A sister. Address is in Carlton County. She visited Cramer the day before the sniper attack on the rez."

"Could be just a coincidence," Cork said.

"Could be. But I think it's worth checking out. Carlton County's only an hour south, so I'm going down today to have a talk with her."

"All right. Anything from the lab on the shell casings we found?"

"They haven't run them yet for markings, but they've identified them as oversized Remingtons. Hundred and fifty grain. Could have come from almost anywhere. The shooter could even have packed the loads himself. We'll check out the local hunting and sporting-goods stores, but unless we get very lucky, I'm not hoping for much."

"What about the tires?" Cork said.

"Better luck there. They're Goodyear Wrangler MT/Rs. High-end off-road tires, almost new. If they came from around here, we have a good chance at finding out who bought them. I've got one of my team on that, but I'd like to give him some help. Can you spare anyone?"

"I'll swing Deputy Pender your way. He can be abrasive but he's also thorough," Cork said.

"Two odd occurrences in two days." Larson raised his eyebrows. "Any way they might be related?"

Rutledge shook his head. "I don't see anything that would connect them. One shows a lot of planning, the other has the look of impulse. Of course, at this point, I suppose anything is possible." He eyed Cork. "I imagine you've been racking your brain pretty hard. Anything rattle loose?"

"Not yet," he said.

"All right, then."

Rutledge stood up and Larson followed him out the door.

Cork sat for a while, trying to muster some energy. Beyond the window of his office, the gray rain continued to fall. Across the street was a small park. All summer, the Lion's Club had raised money for new playground equipment and had spent several days volunteering their own time to install it, heavy plastic in bright colors. The playground was deserted. Beyond the park rose the white steeple of Zion Lutheran Church, almost lost in the rain.

Cork went out in the common area to pour himself some coffee. Two men stood on the other side of the security window that separated the waiting area from the contact desk. Deputy Pender was listening to them and nodding. When he became aware that Cork was behind him, he said, "Just a moment, folks," and turned to Cork. "Sheriff, there are some people here to see you. They say their name is Jacoby."

11

HE SEATED THE two men in his office. The elder man had white hair, a healthy shock of it that looked freshly barbered. He was tanned, in good condition, and dressed in a dark blue suit and red tie, as if he'd come to chair a board meeting. His eyes were like olive pits, hard and dark. If there was sadness in him, they didn't show it.

"Louis Jacoby," he'd said in the common area when he shook Cork's hand. "Edward's father. We spoke on the phone."

He'd introduced the second man as his son Ben. Ben remained quiet as his father talked.

"You arrived sooner than I'd expected," Cork said when he sat at his desk.

"I have a private jet, Sheriff O'Connor. Tell me what happened to Eddie."

Cork explained the events of the preceding night and where the investigation stood. "I have some questions I'd like to ask."

"Later," the old man said with a wave of his hand. "I want to see my son."

"That's not a good idea, Mr. Jacoby."

"I'm sure he's right, Dad," Ben Jacoby said. He appeared to be roughly Cork's age, maybe fifty. There was a lot of his father visible in his features, but his eyes were different, not so dark or so hard.

"I want to see my son." Jacoby didn't raise his voice in the least, but his tone was cold and sharp, cutting off any objection.

Still, Ben tried again. "Dad—"

"I've told you what I want. I want to see Eddie."

Ben sat back and gave Cork a look that asked for help.

"I can't prevent you from seeing your son, but the autopsy's only just been completed. If you could wait—"

"Now," the old man said.

"I don't understand—"

"I'm not asking you to understand, Sheriff. I'm telling you to show me my boy."

Cork gave up. "All right."

He took the Pathfinder. They followed in a rented black DeVille driven by a man they called Tony.

In a few minutes, Cork pulled up in front of Nelson's Mortuary on Pine Street. It was a grand old structure with a lovely wraparound front porch. It had once been a two-story home and was still one of the nicest buildings in town. When the Jacobys met Cork in the drive, Lou Jacoby stood in the rain, looking the place over dourly.

"I thought we were going to the morgue," he said.

"The morgue's at the community hospital, and it isn't set up for autopsies."

For a long time, the mortician Sigurd Nelson had been the coroner in Tamarack County. That position didn't exist anymore. Most of Cork's officers had become deputy medical examiners qualified to certify death. The autopsies were now contracted to be done by Dr. Tom Conklin, a pathologist who'd retired to a home on Iron Lake. For years prior, he'd been with the Ramsey County ME's office in St. Paul. He still used Sigurd's facility.

Cork rang the bell and the mortician answered. He was a small man with a big belly and a bald head, in his early sixties. He greeted Cork, then glanced at the other people on the porch.

"These are the Jacobys, Sigurd. Family of the man Tom autopsied today. They'd like to see the body."

"That's not a good idea," Nelson said. "Tom's finished the autopsy, but he hasn't repaired the body yet."

"Is Tom downstairs?"

"No. He went out for a bite to eat. He was going to finish up when he came back."

"We'll come back," Cork said.

"We're here," Jacoby said. "We'll see him now."

"Lou Jacoby," Cork said by way of introduction. "Edward Jacoby's father."

Sigurd Nelson addressed the man firmly but civilly. "With all due respect, you don't want to see your son's body right now."

"If you try telling me again what I want, I'll shove one of your coffins up your ass. Take me to my boy."

It wasn't so much that Nelson was cowed by Jacoby. Cork figured he probably decided a man with that attitude and those manners deserved to get exactly what he asked for. The mortician allowed them inside. Ben Jacoby signaled for Tony to accompany them, and the tall driver followed.

Nelson led them down a hallway. He lived upstairs

with his wife, Grace, but the first floor was all business and included a large room used for memorial services, several viewing rooms, and a display room for
coffins. At the end of the hall, he opened a door and
they followed down a flight of stairs to the basement,
which was divided into a number of rooms, all with
closed doors. Nelson went to the last room, swung the
door wide, turned on the light.

"Wait here just a minute," he said and disappeared
inside. Shortly, Cork heard the flap of a sheet snapped
open and the rustle of linen being arranged, then Nelson reappeared at the door. "All right."

Cork had seen the room many times before. It
always reminded him of a laboratory. The walls were
sterile white, the floor shiny red tile. There were cabi-
nets with glass fronts through which shelves of plastic
jars and jugs and glass bottles were visible. In the
middle of the room stood a white porcelain prep table.
It was old. Cork knew most prep tables were stainless
steel now. Near the table was a flush tank and a pump
for the embalming fluids. Beneath the table, the red
tile sloped to a large floor drain.

The body lay on the table fully covered by the
sheet the mortician had just positioned. Dark stains
spread slowly across the white fabric.

"It won't be pleasant," Nelson said.

Jacoby paid him no heed. He walked forward
stiffly, reached out, and drew the sheet back from
Eddie's head. His son's face was bloodless, chalk
white, but relaxed as if he were only sleeping. Which
might have been a perfectly acceptable sight had
Edward Jacoby still had a whole head. In his autopsy,
Tom Conklin had slit the skin along the back of
Jacoby's head from ear to ear, pulled the scalp forward

over the face, opened up the skull as neatly as a tin can, and removed the brain.

"Oh God," Ben Jacoby said, and looked away.

Cork had been present at a lot of autopsies, and the sight didn't bother him. He figured it would be plenty to turn Lou Jacoby away, but the man surprised him. He drew the sheet back completely, exposing the raw, open, empty body cavity.

"Dad." Ben reached to steady his father.

"Leave me be." Jacoby stepped back, faltering. A tremor passed through him like a quake along a fault line. His hands shook and his jaw quivered. He squinted as if a bright light had struck his eyes, but he uttered not a word as he walked from the room.

The driver had not come in but had hung back, waiting in the corridor.

"Stay with him, Tony," Ben said. He turned to Cork and Sigurd Nelson. "I'm sorry. He's a man who gets his way."

"We need to talk," Cork said.

"How about not here," Nelson suggested, and ushered them out.

In the hallway, Lou Jacoby stood staring down the basement corridor with its false light and its dead end. Tony leaned against a wall nearby. He appeared to be in excellent condition, with long black hair and an olive cast to his skin. He watched the elder Jacoby carefully, ready to help should he be needed.

"Take him to the hotel," Ben said to him. "I'll be along."

Tony said gently and with a soft Spanish accent, "Let's go, Lou."

"I'm sure the sheriff has questions."

"I'll take care of them, Dad."

Jacoby nodded. Despite all his earlier posturing, all his effort at control, he seemed suddenly weak and uncertain. He didn't move toward the stairway until Tony urged him forward with a hand on his arm.

"We'll be right up, Sigurd," Cork said.

The mortician turned off the light in the prep room, closed the door, and left them alone.

"I have some questions about your brother, Mr. Jacoby."

"Of course. And call me Ben."

Jacoby was a handsome man, a little taller than Cork and, like his father, tanned and in good physical condition. He had his father's thick hair. It was still mostly brown, but there was a hint of gray at the temples. His face was smooth, the bones prominent. When he spoke, it was with quiet authority, a man accustomed to being listened to, who didn't need to flaunt his power. Sometimes the rich were like that, Cork had learned long ago. A profound sense of the responsibility that went along with wealth and position.

"Edward was here on business, is that correct?" Cork said.

"As far as I know, that's the only reason he came to Aurora."

"For Starlight Enterprises?"

"I assume so, yes."

"What does he do for Starlight?"

"I'm not entirely certain, but a lot of it has to do with bringing in new business."

"What do you do?"

"I run an investment firm with my father."

"You and your father but not Eddie?"

"Eddie had other ideas about what he wanted to do with his life."

"Did he talk about his visits to Aurora?"

"Eddie talked a lot. It was hard to know what to listen to, so I usually didn't. In terms of his business here, there's an attorney you ought to talk to. Eddie dealt with her a lot, I believe. Someone named Jo O'Connor." He stopped and gave Cork a quizzical look. "O'Connor?"

"My wife."

"Convenient."

Cork shrugged. "Small town."

"I assume you've spoken with her."

"I have."

"Would you mind if I did also?"

"Why?"

"My father is a little numb at the moment, but he'll be expecting answers soon. I'd like to be able to offer a few. Is there a reason I shouldn't speak with her?"

"No," Cork replied. "In fact, if you'd like, I'll drive you there."

"I could take a taxi."

"Ben, this isn't Chicago. We don't have taxis. I'll be happy to take you."

Jo was busy with a client, and they waited a few minutes in the anteroom of her office. Her secretary, Fran Cooper, asked if they'd like something to drink. They both declined.

Jo's door opened and Amanda Horton stepped out. Amanda was a transplant from Des Moines who, Cork knew, was trying to buy lake property currently tied up in probate.

"Hello, Cork," she said.

"Afternoon, Amanda."

She gave Ben Jacoby an appreciative look as she left.

Cork watched her go. When his eyes swung back, he found his wife standing in the doorway of her office, her eyes huge, her mouth open in an oval of surprise.

"Ben?"

"My God," Jacoby replied with equal wonder. "Jo McKenzie."

12

JACOBY ACCEPTED THE coffee she offered him and sat in one of the chairs available for clients.

Cork took the other client chair. "So," he said. "Law school together."

"My second year." Jo put the coffee server back on the tray with the mugs she kept on hand, went behind the desk, and sat down.

"My last," Jacoby said. "But you still practice, Jo."

"You don't?"

"I never did. I do investments."

"In Chicago?"

"We're in the Sears Tower." He shook his head and smiled. "You look wonderful. You haven't changed at all."

"What are you doing here?" She furrowed her brow. "Jacoby. Eddie?"

"He was my brother. My half brother."

She folded her hands on her desk, then unfolded them. "I never made the connection. I'm sorry, Ben."

Jacoby looked at his coffee mug but didn't take a sip. "No reason you should be. You and I, we knew one another a very long time ago. And Jacoby's not that unusual a surname."

"I mean I'm sorry about Eddie."

"Ah, yes. You dealt with him, with the business he had here?"

"That's right."

"Then maybe you can help me."

"In what way?"

"Before Eddie left for Aurora, he told me this visit would be different, that I'd understand when he got back. I got a call from him yesterday, late in the afternoon. He said he was going to celebrate. He sounded as if he was already two sheets to the wind, so I didn't know how much more celebrating he planned on doing. I wonder if you have any idea what that might have been about? Business?"

Cork looked at her, too.

Jo chewed on her lower lip, something she only did when she was very nervous. "It's possible. He'd been working for months to get the Iron Lake Ojibwe as clients for his company. He presented me with the contract yesterday. The RBC won't vote on it for a while, but they're certainly favorably disposed at the moment. So maybe that was it."

Jacoby thought it over and nodded slightly. "Maybe. Nothing Eddie touched ever turned out right. I think he was in trouble with Starlight and needed this casino deal." He glanced at Cork. "Does that help you at all?"

"We'll be looking into the possibility that his murder is related to his stay in Aurora, certainly, but is it possible this was something tied to his life in Chicago?"

"You mean somebody came out here to kill him?" The skepticism in his voice was obvious.

"I'm just asking are you aware of any circumstances in his life that ought to be considered."

"Did you know Eddie at all?"

"I'd met him a couple of times."

"Did he strike you as a gentle soul?"

"I'd appreciate it if you'd just answer my question."

"Look, Eddie and trouble were old friends, but I'm not aware of anything at the moment that I would connect with this. I can easily believe, however, that while he was here he pissed off somebody enough to want him dead."

Cork was making notations in a small notepad he kept in his shirt pocket. While he wrote, Jacoby turned suddenly toward Jo.

"Kids?" he asked.

Jo hesitated. "Three."

"I have a son. His name's Phillip. He's in his senior year at Northwestern." He waited, as if expecting Jo to reply in kind.

There was an uncomfortable silence, and Cork finally said, "We have two girls and a boy. Jenny's a senior in high school. Annie's a sophomore. Our son Stephen is in second grade."

Jacoby spoke toward Jo. "Sounds like a nice family."

"We think it is," Cork replied. "Interesting that your son's at Northwestern. That's Jenny's first choice for college."

"She couldn't choose better as far as I'm concerned. It's my undergraduate alma mater." He set his coffee mug on Jo's desk. "Sheriff, do you need anything more from me right now? I'd like to go to the hotel and check on my father."

"Where are you staying?"

"The Quetico Inn."

"I'll take you there."

The two men stood up, and Jo after them. Jacoby reached across her desk and warmly took her hand. "It's good to see you again, Jo. I'm just sorry it couldn't have been under more pleasant circumstances."

"I'm sorry, too, Ben." She drew her hand back, and addressed Cork. "Will you be home for dinner?"

"I'll try."

"I'd like you there. For the kids."

"Like I said, I'll try." He kissed her briefly and followed Jacoby out the door.

In the Pathfinder, as Cork pulled out of the parking lot of the Aurora Professional Building, Jacoby said, "Do you believe in synchronicity, Sheriff?"

Cork made a left onto Alder Street and headed toward the lake. "If that's anything like coincidence, no."

"I prefer to think of it as the convergence of circumstances for a particular purpose." He looked out the window. They were passing the old firehouse that had been converted into a suite of chic offices. "Nice town," he said, and sounded as if he meant it. "Aurora. The goddess of dawn."

Cork said, "What kind of man was your brother?"

Jacoby looked at him. "You'll get a prejudiced answer."

"I'll work around the prejudice."

"He was the kind of man I'd rather have working for Starlight than for me."

"Why?"

"He had a style I strongly disagreed with. What's that wonderful smell?"

"It's Thursday, barbecued rib night at the Broiler."

Jacoby smiled vaguely. "What was last night?"

"Homemade meat loaf and gravy."

Jacoby gave his head a faint shake. "Must be comforting."

"To live in a small town and like it, you have to appreciate routine."

"Routine. There are days when I'd sell my soul for a little of that." The sentiment seemed sincere.

The main lodge at the Quetico Inn was a grand log construction that stood on the shore of Iron Lake a couple of miles south of town. Cork pulled up to the front entrance and put the Pathfinder in park. Jacoby reached for the door handle.

"I'd like to talk more with your family," Cork said.

"We'll be in town a couple of days." He gave the handle a pull, opened the door, and stepped out. He tossed Cork a bemused look. "Nancy Jo McKenzie. Who would've thought it? Good afternoon, Sheriff."

He meant to get home for dinner as Jo had asked, but when he returned to his office, he found the department besieged by the media, and he arranged for a press conference at the courthouse at five o'clock. He contacted Simon Rutledge, who agreed to be there, but Rutledge was delayed and the conference began twenty minutes late. Cork had prepared an official statement that included the first public announcement of the identity of the murdered man, and he dispensed the statement to all the reporters. News cameras had also been sent by network affiliates in Duluth and the Twin Cities. Simon Rutledge deferred to Cork on most questions, and Cork answered honestly what he could, indicating that evidence had been gathered and that they had leads which he declined to go into.

After the press conference, he met with Rutledge and Larson in his office. They didn't feel either of the investigations had made much headway.

"I'm expecting to have a fax of Jacoby's phone records by tomorrow. I'm hoping that'll give us some direction," Rutledge said.

Larson chimed in. "In the meantime, we've pulled prints from his room at the Four Seasons. The linen gets changed daily, and it appears he didn't sleep in his bed last night, but we've taken the bedspread and maybe we'll get something from that—hair samples, for example, that match those from the SUV."

"How about the cigarette butts?"

"Still being analyzed," Rutledge said, with a note of apology.

Cork knew that the resources of the state BCA crime lab were in great demand, and whatever was sent from Aurora would have to wait its turn.

"One thing, though," Larson said. "When I talked with the Four Seasons staff, they told me that in the past Jacoby stayed for only two or three days. This time, he'd been there more than a week."

"And this time," Cork said, "the RBC is getting ready to vote on a contract proposal for Starlight's services."

"A lot of heavy lobbying on Jacoby's part?" Rutledge said.

"We should find out. I'll head out to the rez first thing tomorrow and talk to LeDuc and some of the other members of the RBC," Cork said.

"Another thing to think about is Jacoby's libido,"

Larson said. "I talked to the staff at the Boundary Waters Room." He was speaking of the restaurant at the Four Seasons. "Jacoby ate late, usually after a couple of drinks at the bar, then he generally left the inn. He sometimes came back with company."

"He got lucky?"

"Or he was the kind who didn't want to be alone, even if it cost him."

"I talked with Newsome," Larson said. Then, for Rutledge's benefit he added, "The night bartender at the Four Seasons. Newsome said Jacoby had asked him once where a guy with cash could find himself a little company."

"What did Newsome tell him?" Cork asked.

"Claims he said he didn't know."

"How hard did you lean on him?"

Larson said, "There are a lot of people to talk to, Cork."

"I know there are, Ed." He took a moment, shifted his thinking to the incident on the rez. "Did your man or Pender come up with anything on those Goodyear tires?"

"Nothing. They'll widen their area of inquiry tomorrow."

"How about the ammo?"

"Nothing there, either. But we'll keep on that, too."

"Simon, anything from your talk with Lydell Cramer's sister?"

"I never got to her. She lives on a farm. The road's gated and locked. I wanted to get back here for the press conference, so I'll try again tomorrow, talk to the local cops, see what they can tell me."

They ended their meeting. As he was leaving, Larson said quietly to Cork, "How're you doing?"

"Tired. I imagine you are, too. But if you're worrying about my mental state, don't. And by the way, I have an appointment to see Faith Gray tomorrow."

"I wasn't worried, Cork," Larson said. "Just concerned."

13

CORK HAD CALLED to say he wouldn't be home for dinner. Jo wasn't angry. She understood his situation. But she wasn't happy, either. The children helped with dishes, then turned to their homework.

Jo went into her office at the back of the house to do some work of her own. She was going over the file of Amanda Horton when the phone rang.

"I was hoping you would answer." The voice was low and certain, and she knew it instantly. "I need to see you."

"What for?"

"To talk."

"That's not a good idea."

"Please. Just to talk."

"We can talk on the phone."

"There are things you need to know. For your own good. Please."

She closed her eyes and knew even as she made her decision that it held all the potential for disaster. "All right. My office in the Aurora Professional Building. In fifteen minutes."

"Thank you."

She went to the living room, where the children sat among their scattered books and notebooks and pencils.

"I have to go to my office for a while. You guys okay?"

"Sure, Mom," Jenny said. "A client?"

"Yes." The lie felt like something piercing her heart.

The rain had ended in the afternoon, but a dreary wetness lingered. It was after seven, the sky a dismal gray that was sliding into early dark. The radio in her Camry was on, tuned to NPR, *All Things Considered*, but she wasn't listening. She turned onto Oak Street, pulled to the curb, and stopped half a block from her office. She sat with her hands tight on the steering wheel, staring through the windshield at an old tennis shoe abandoned in the street. It looked like a small animal cringing in the beam of her headlights.

She closed her eyes and whispered, "Christ, what am I doing?"

She heard the car approaching, the whish of the tires on wet pavement. A black Cadillac passed and half a block farther turned into the parking lot of the Aurora Professional Building. She took a deep breath and followed.

When she parked beside the Cadillac, he stepped out.

"This way," she said, and went to a side door where she used her key.

The hallway was quiet and dimly lit, but from somewhere she couldn't see came the sound of a buffer going over a floor.

"Cleaning staff," she said, more to herself than to him.

She led the way to her office, unlocked the door, stood aside to let him pass. Closing the door behind her, she walked to her inner office and flipped on the light. She turned around. He stood close to her, smelling of the wet autumn air.

"What do you want, Ben?"

He wore a light-brown turtleneck that perfectly matched his eyes and hair and pressed against his chest and shoulders in a way that made it seem as if the muscles beneath it were about to burst through.

He said, "A very long time ago I built a wall across my life. There was everything before you and everything after."

"Very poetic," she said. "And what? The wall crumbles now, our lives suddenly merge again? Ben, you left me, remember? How's your wife, by the way?"

"She's dead, Jo."

"Oh." She felt the knot of her anger loosen just a little. "I'm sorry."

"I've been a widower for a year. But even before that we were . . ." He shrugged in his tight, expensive sweater. "The marriage was over years ago. It was never much of a marriage to begin with."

She slipped behind her desk, put the big piece of polished oak between her and Benjamin Jacoby. "I'm sorry your life didn't work out the way you'd hoped, but I put you behind me a long time ago. I went on with my own life. I've been very happy."

He came to the desk. "You never thought of me?"

She didn't answer.

"It's a big world, Jo. It's unthinkable to me that fate would bring us together again without a reason."

"Fate?" She laughed. "Ben, you never left anything to chance. How long have you known I was here?"

He looked deeply into her eyes. "I always knew it. I just never did anything about it. Then one night, we're having dinner at my father's house, the whole family. Eddie's talking about this casino deal he's working on in Minnesota, going on about the gorgeous lawyer he was dealing with. I ask him where this casino is. And bingo—Aurora. I don't know. With Eddie coming here, it made a difference somehow, connected us. Since then I've often thought about using him as an excuse to contact you, but I'm not egocentric or stupid enough to believe there could ever be anything between us again. I wouldn't be here now if it weren't for what happened to Eddie. I don't have any desire to complicate your life."

"You can't complicate it, Ben. You're not even a part of it."

"I'm not looking for that, Jo. My life hasn't been perfect, but it was the one I chose, and it's had its advantages." He moved his hand across the desk but stopped far short of touching her. "You haven't asked why I left you."

"It was pretty obvious. You were married within six months."

"The roads we take aren't always of our own choosing."

"What? She was pregnant?"

"There are other compelling reasons to marry."

"Love?"

"In my whole life, Jo, I've loved one woman. I didn't marry her."

"I don't want to go on with this conversation. But I do want to know why the charade? Why pretend that my being here was such a surprise?"

"I was afraid that I'd scare you. I know how crazy all this must seem."

Jo shook her head. "I haven't heard you say one thing so far that sounded real to me."

He looked genuinely hurt. "The wall, Jo, that was real. You did divide my life. For a while, you absolutely defined it. I'm not saying that I've thought of you every day for the last twenty years, but whenever I think about a time when I was happy, I think about the summer with you." He seemed to be at the edge of defeat. "Look, I'm in town for only a couple of days. Could I . . ." He faltered. "Could I ask a favor? A small one, I promise."

"What is it?"

"I'd like to meet your family."

"Why?"

"I'd love to see the life you've made for yourself."

"I don't think that's a good idea."

"Only you and I know the truth about us. It wouldn't be awkward, I promise. And maybe it would help with closure."

"After twenty years you need closure?"

"All right. Then just to satisfy my own damn curiosity. An hour of your time and your family's. Is it really so much to ask?"

"Yes, it is. I can't believe you don't understand that."

"There's so much you don't understand. So much you never will." He put up his empty hands. "I guess that's it."

"You said there were things I needed to know, for my own good."

"I was mistaken. They were things I needed to know, and now I do."

He turned and walked to the anteroom. At the door that opened onto the hallway, he turned back, his hand on the knob. He took a look around him, at the ordinary room where Fran Cooper worked and Jo's clients waited. "Do you like this?"

"I love it," she said.

His eyes held a look of wistful sadness. "I wish I could say that about what I do. I wish I could have said it, ever. Good night, Jo." He went out and closed the door behind him.

She waited until the sound of his footsteps in the corridor had faded to nothing, then went back into her office, sat down, and put her hands over her face as if she were trying to hide behind a small, fragile fence.

14

THE BAR AT the Four Seasons was a big room with a stone fireplace and wide windows that overlooked Iron Lake. On sunny days, the view of the marina and beyond was stellar, row after row of boats at rest on blue water, framed by the sawtooth outline of pines. But at night there was only darkness outside the window glass, and what people saw then was the reflection of the fire and themselves, and the room seemed much smaller.

Cork caught Augie Newsome in an idle moment, wiping down the bar. Newsome was a rubbery-looking man with a willowy body, long arms, and face like stretched putty. He wore Elvis Costello glasses and combed his hair in a gelled wave. He usually appeared to be on the brink of smiling, as if all the ironies of life were right in front of him and always amusing. Cork had known him a dozen years, ever since Newsome migrated up from the Twin Cities for reasons that only Cork and a very few others knew. During his first stint as sheriff, he'd given Newsome a break that had meant a difference in the kind of bars behind which the man spent his time.

"Sheriff," Newsome said brightly, wiping his way down the bar toward Cork. "What can I do you for?"

Except for a couple seated at one of the tables near the fireplace, the bar was deserted. It was Thursday, the night before the weekenders descended. The locals called them 612ers, because the vast majority of the tourists and the nonresident landholders came from the Twin Cities where for years those three numbers had formed the prominent telephone area code.

Cork said, "Ed Larson talked to you today."

"That he did. Asked about the dead guy out at Mercy Falls. Man, is that crazy or what? Right here in Aurora. Say, I understand Marsha Dross is doing fine. Glad to hear it. Her and Charlie Annala are pretty regular customers. Can I get you something?"

"I just need a few answers, Augie. You told Larson that Edward Jacoby asked you where he might find a prostitute around here. Is that correct?"

"He didn't use the word *prostitute*, but that's what he wanted."

"What did you tell him?"

"I told him the lake was all the entertainment most folks needed up here. If it was a boat he was looking to rent, or fishing gear, I could point him in the right direction."

"Augie," Cork said, leaning close so that his voice wouldn't carry to the couple near the fireplace. "I've got a dead man on my hands. I need you to cut out the bullshit and help me here. Whose name did you give him?"

Newsome looked pained that Cork didn't believe him. "Sheriff, I—"

"Augie, do I have to remind you about the incident in Yellow Lake?"

"All right. I gave him one name and that was a few months ago. Krisane Olsen."

"Where's she working these days?"

"She hangs out at the casino."

"One name, last year, that's it?"

"That's it."

"He never asked again?"

"He asked. I played dumb."

"Why?"

"Talk to Krisane, you'll understand."

"All right, Augie. Thanks."

"Guys like him, Sheriff, when they end up with their balls cut off, it's not hard to figure why."

Cork gave him a puzzled look.

"Talk to Krisane."

Augie Newsome walked down the bar to where a man in a Minnesota Twins T-shirt had just sat down on a stool.

The Chippewa Grand Casino was a blaze of lights among the pine trees a quarter mile south of the town limits just off State Highway 1. Before the Iron Lake Ojibwe purchased the land and built the casino a few years earlier, the area had been a county park. The lot was packed with cars when Cork arrived. Even in the worst winter weather or in the black hours of morning when the rest of the county slept, the casino lot was never less than half full. That so many people felt compelled to empty their pockets, blithely or in desperation, had always baffled Cork. He'd been among the most skeptical when the casino had first been proposed, and while he knew that its success was a blessing both to the Anishinaabeg and to the economy of Tamarack County, there was something about the enterprise that felt like wolves feeding on sheep.

He found Krisane Olsen sitting at the bar, smoking a cigarette, a glass of red wine on a napkin in front of her. She chatted with the bartender, Daniel Medina, a Shinnob from Leech Lake. Krisane wore a shiny lime-green dress with a hemline that barely covered her ass. There was gold, or more likely imitation gold, around her neck and wrists and dangling in big hoops from her earlobes. She was a small woman, nicely built, with cranberry-colored hair and a face done brightly to mask her fatigue. Days, she worked as a dog groomer. Nights, she worked even harder.

Cork had changed out of his uniform before leaving his office, put on a blue flannel shirt, brown cords, a yellow windbreaker. When he wanted information, the uniform often presented a barrier. People would talk to Cork, but they clammed up in the official presence of the sheriff.

"Evening, Krisane." He took the stool beside her.

"Oh Jesus." She sent a cloud of cigarette smoke heavenward.

"What's she drinking, Dan?" Cork asked.

"Merlot."

Cork pulled out his wallet. "Give her another on me and then give us some space, okay?"

"Sure thing, Cork."

"What do you want?" Krisane said.

"Information, that's all."

"Right."

"Know a guy named Eddie Jacoby?"

"Never heard of him."

"A little shorter than me, dark hair, nice physique. From Chicago. Wears a gold ring on both of his pinkies."

"Never laid eyes on him."

Medina brought the glass of merlot. Cork laid a ten on the bar, told him to keep the change.

When they were alone again, he said, "I've always been square with you, Kris. I know how it is when you're a single parent trying to make ends meet, and as long as you've done business quietly and safely and no one complained, I haven't bothered you. Isn't that right?"

"Whatever," Krisane said. She ashed her cigarette in a star-shaped tray.

"This is the deal. You play straight with me now or I'll arrange to have an undercover vice officer follow every move you make."

"You'd do that?"

"I just said I would."

"I've got a kid to worry about."

"Right now your biggest worry is me. Understand?" He turned on his stool and faced her directly. "Did you ever hook up with Edward Jacoby?"

She stubbed out her cigarette, dug out a pack of Salems from the small beaded purse she carried, and fished out another smoke.

"Well?"

She lit the cigarette and exhaled with a sigh. "Only once. Four months ago."

"Only once? He didn't look you up again?"

"He came looking all right. I didn't want to have anything to do with him."

"Why?"

"The guy was psycho. He liked to hurt people. Women, anyway."

"What did he do?"

"Come on, Sheriff."

"I need to know."

She rubbed her thigh nervously with her free hand. "He was into a rape thing. He wanted me to fight him—you know, struggle. But he got rough for real. I tried to stop him for real. He just beat me up and did what he wanted. When he was done, he threw the money on the floor. Is that what you wanted to hear?"

"Why didn't you come to the department and make a complaint?"

She gave him a withering look.

"Anything like that ever happens again, Kris, you come to me directly. Okay?"

She was twenty-seven years old. Cork figured that by the time she was forty, the dye would ruin her hair, the smoking would make her voice like the growl of a bad engine, and the hard life would burn her out, leave her with no more substance than the ash at the end of her cigarette.

"All right," she said.

"Where were you last night?"

"Here. Danny'll tell you." She nodded toward the bartender, who was laughing with a man farther down the bar.

"You were here all night?"

"I left at ten."

"Alone?"

She hesitated a moment. "No."

"But not with Jacoby."

"No way. You can ask Danny about that, too. He knows who Jacoby is."

"What time did you go home?"

"Around one."

"I may have to talk to the john you were with."

"Jesus, Cork."

"I didn't say it was for sure. But you'd better know who he was, or how to find out who he was."

"He had a room at the hotel here. I can give you the number."

"All right."

She seemed to think she'd given him everything she could and turned away.

"Krisane, is it possible he went to another working girl?"

She smoked her cigarette and didn't look at him, like they were lovers who'd just had a quarrel. "There aren't that many around here, and I made sure they all knew about him."

"Okay." He slid off his stool. "I meant it."

"What?"

"You ever have any trouble again like you had with Jacoby, I want to hear about it."

She studied the glowing end of her cigarette, finally gave a slight nod.

15

CORK CAME HOME LATE. Jo pretended to be asleep as he undressed for bed. He had to be exhausted, with so little rest since the shooting on the rez; but he lay for a long time, and although he was quiet, she knew his eyes were open and he was staring at the ceiling in the way he always did when he was worried. When he finally nodded off, she was certain his dreams would be troubled.

She couldn't sleep, either, but she didn't want to talk to him. Pretending sleep was easier than pretending other things. Like pretending she had never loved Benjamin Jacoby, loved him desperately.

Cork rolled over, his face, so familiar even in the dark, close to hers. She could feel the strong grip of his love around her, her own love covering him like a blanket.

So what was this unsettled feeling, this rumble of fear? Ben Jacoby was twenty years ago. She'd lived a whole life since then, a full life with Cork and her children at the center.

Oh God. Was it possible that even after all this time, after all her experience, there was still some ember alive in her heart, burning for Ben Jacoby? Could she still feel something for the man who'd abandoned her on a cold rainy autumn night twenty years before—abandoned her without explanation?

She'd met him at law school, the final semester of her second year. He was older, funny, brilliant, gorgeous. They'd become lovers.

She was living in a small apartment in a run-down building on South Harper in Hyde Park, an easy walk to the University of Chicago Law School. Ben worried that it was not a good neighborhood, but Jo, a military brat, assured him she knew how to take care of herself.

Although they often ate out, he had come to her place for dinner that evening. She was a horrible cook, but she knew how to make spaghetti and that's what she'd prepared. He brought a good Chianti. He looked tired when he stepped in, and when she kissed him, he seemed to hold back.

She took his wet overcoat. Cashmere. He always dressed well, as if he had money, or his family did, although he never talked about it. In fact, he never talked about his family at all. He claimed he was a man of the moment. He didn't discuss his past, never speculated on the future, his or theirs together. Jo had a brief glimpse into his life, however. Ben had a younger sister, Rae, a student at Bennington, an art major, a fine artist already from the things Jo was allowed to see. Rae worshipped her older brother. In the long summer of Jo's affair with Ben, Rae, home from college, had joined them on some of their outings. She'd once taken them through the Art Institute and proved to be a knowledgeable guide. Jo liked her immensely. Rae was under strict orders not to talk about family, and although she tried to hold to that, once in a while she let something slip. Often it was something harsh about "Daddy." In September, she returned to Bennington.

Jo wasn't reluctant to talk to Ben about her own life, her own past. About the rootlessness that went with being raised by a single parent, an army nurse. About her teenage rebellions, her drive to excel in everything she did so she could escape the alcoholic mother whom she referred to as The Captain. She'd confessed her fear that, like her mother, she drank too much, was too harsh in her judgments of people. Ben Jacoby had been a marvelous listener, something new to her in a man, and although his intellect was towering, she never felt it was a shadow he cast over her or anyone else. He was, in her experience, a rare, good man. And she loved him powerfully.

"Are you all right?" she asked that rainy October night.

"Just a little tired," he said.

On graduation from the U of C Law School, he'd taken a prestigious clerkship with a state supreme court justice, a demanding position, and he worked long hours.

"I have something for you." He handed her a cardboard tube.

"What is it?"

"Open it."

She popped out the metal cap and from inside pulled a rolled canvas. She moved to good light under a standing lamp.

It was a portrait of her. She sat on the green grass of Grant Park, in a white dress, looking at something to her right that must have pleased her because she was smiling. Behind her, Michigan Avenue was an impressionistic mist of suggested buildings and pedestrians. It was a beautiful painting, and she fell in love with it immediately.

"Oh, Ben, where did you get this?"

"I asked Rae to do it. I gave her a photograph."

"I love it. I absolutely love it."

She kissed him passionately, but again felt his reserve.

Often they made love before dinner. That night they simply ate, seated at her small kitchen table in the glow of candlelight, with the sound of rain against the windows.

"You're quiet," she finally said. "And you keep looking at me like I've just left on a train out of town. What's going on?"

He said, "Jo." One word, but oh, it was like a funeral bell.

She sat back in her chair as if he'd hit her. "It's over, isn't it?"

In the candlelight, she saw that his eyes were filled with tears. Men never cried when they said good-bye. They found some way to make it not their fault, to feel justified. They left behind a foul sense that somehow it was all wrong from the beginning, a mistake everyone was better off forgetting.

But not Ben Jacoby.

"You're the best thing that ever happened to me," he said.

"Then why?"

He shook his head and looked truly bewildered. "I wish I could say the thing that would make it all clear, but it's so complicated. It has nothing to do with you or with what I feel for you."

"Right," she said, not bothering to hide her bitterness.

He reached across the table and took her hands. "If I had a choice, I would stay with you forever."

"You always have a choice. It's clear you've made it."

"Not being with you will just about kill me." He gripped her hands so powerfully that he'd begun to hurt her a little.

"Just go," she said. "And here. Take this with you."

She gave him back the painting.

"That's yours," he said.

"I don't want it. I don't want anything to remind me of you. Take it. Take it, goddamn it."

He didn't argue, didn't try to wheedle from her one last time in the sack, didn't suggest a last glass of wine or a final kiss. But he didn't hurry, either. He left with an air of profound sadness, and when she was able to think about it later through the filter of time, without anger or hurt, she realized that he'd left with a sense of dignity, his and hers, somehow intact. And for that she loved him, too.

They hadn't made promises, but they'd been in love, and there had never been a clear reason for the ending. Time had helped put him behind her. Time and her marriage. She hadn't thought of Ben Jacoby in years.

That something inside her still responded to him—his presence, his voice, even the scent of him, the same after all these years—surprised her. There was something going on with her emotions over which she seemed to have no control. She knew she would never act on what she felt, but it still frightened her.

She studied her husband, sleeping restlessly beside her. There had been rough periods in their marriage, but they were in the past. And the truth was, she loved Cork, as much for all he'd committed to working through with her and forgiving as for all that had been effortless and good between them.

He stirred, moaned softly. She lifted herself, leaned to him, and gently kissed his lips. Although she knew his sleep was troubled, for a moment in his dreaming he smiled.

16

FIRST THING IN the morning, before the day watch came on, Cork met with Ed Larson and Simon Rutledge so they would have time to alter duty assignments for the deputies if necessary. Cork related his conversation with Krisane Olsen and suggested it would be a good idea to interview the other women in Tamarack County who were known to take money, even occasionally, for sex. He and Larson came up with the list, and Larson said he'd see to it. Rutledge expected the records for Eddie Jacoby's cell phone any moment. He hoped they might offer more leads. Cork wanted to talk with the Jacoby family, find out if Eddie might have said anything to them that would be enlightening about his activities in Aurora. Rutledge thought he would try again to interview Lydell Cramer's sister. The possibility of Cramer being involved in the rez shooting was thin, but until they got more lab results there weren't any other threads to follow. They agreed to stay in touch and to meet again around noon.

The overcast of the day before was gone, and the morning was bright and crisp as Cork drove to the Quetico Inn. For the last quarter mile, the road ran alongside the resort's Jack Nicklaus–designed golf course, where the grass sparkled with dew. All the holes appeared to be empty, but Cork spotted a lone figure jogging in the green apron between the thirteenth fairway and the road. He recognized Tony, Lou Jacoby's driver. He passed, slowed, pulled over, and stopped. As the man approached the Pathfinder, Cork got out to meet him.

"Good morning, Sheriff," he said brightly. His face was flushed and his long black hair was damp with sweat, but he seemed barely winded. He wore tight black Lycra pants and a light-blue windbreaker. "Paying a call on the Jacoby family?" He glanced toward the lodge in the distance, then down at his sports watch. "You'll find Lou eating breakfast. He has breakfast every day sharply at nine. Ben's probably with him. Or playing golf." Now Cork could hear very definitely the Spanish accent he thought he'd caught the day before.

"Golf?" Cork said, thinking the man's brother had just died.

Tony smiled. "It's a strange family, Sheriff."

"I didn't get your full name."

"Tony Salguero."

"You do something for the Jacobys besides chauffeur?"

"I almost never chauffeur. Mostly I'm a pilot."

"You flew the Jacobys out here?"

"Yes." He rubbed his thighs vigorously. "My muscles are getting a little stiff, Sheriff. Do you mind if I return to my run?"

"Maybe you could help clear up a couple of things first. You got here awfully fast yesterday. Lou must've called you right away."

"He did. I was sailing. I got the call on my boat."

"Sailing where?"

"I was returning from an outing to Mackinac Island."

"And you still made it back to Chicago to fly the Jacobys?"

"I had docked at a marina in Kenosha, Wisconsin, for the night. When Lou called, I arranged for a helicopter to O'Hare where we keep the jet."

"Couldn't he have used a different pilot?"

"He prefers me. And I told him I could get him here."

"When Eddie Jacoby came out, did you fly him?"

"Not usually. That was for his business, so his company took care of that."

"Commercial flights?"

He shrugged. "I guess so."

"What about this last time?"

"I flew him. He asked me as a favor. I don't know why this time was different. But I told him he was on his own coming home. I would be sailing."

That probably answered the question of how Edward Jacoby had come by the drugs in his SUV. He'd brought them with him.

"Look, Sheriff, if I don't start running again, I'll pull something. Okay?"

"'Preciate your time."

"By the way," he said as he stretched down, grabbed his calves, and put his forehead against his shins, "when you get to the lodge, you're in for a surprise." He came up smiling enigmatically and took off at a run.

Cork parked in the lot and went into the main lodge. The Quetico Inn was on the national register of historic buildings. It had been constructed in 1928 by a consortium of celebrities that included, among others, Babe Ruth, and was intended to be a getaway for the rich and famous. The Depression pretty much quashed that idea, but the beauty and integrity of the lodge had been maintained, and during the crazy economic boom of the 1990s, the resort had been expanded into a conference center that included tennis courts, the golf course, an Olympic-size indoor pool, a marina, and a restaurant with the best wood roast in all the north country.

The restaurant, a large, sunny room with a million-dollar view of Iron Lake, had few diners. It was Friday morning; on Saturday, however, and again on Sunday, the place would be packed. The Jacobys sat at a table near one of the windows overlooking the lake. They weren't alone. A woman sat with them, listening intently to Lou Jacoby as he talked. When Cork approached, Jacoby looked up, and the talking ceased. A moment of cold silence, then Ben Jacoby spoke up.

"Sheriff, won't you join us?"

From the residue on the elder Jacoby's plate, Cork guessed he'd had the renowned eggs Benedict. Ben Jacoby had a bowl, nearly empty now, of fresh fruit and yogurt. The woman had eaten oatmeal. They all were drinking coffee.

Cork took the chair on the empty side of the table. The sun was at his back, and his upper body cast a shadow over the white tablecloth.

"Dina, this is Sheriff Cork O'Connor," Ben Jacoby said to the woman. "Sheriff, Dina Willner."

The woman, who was seated to the right of Cork, extended her hand. "How do you do?"

Her eyes were green and smart in a face that was easy to look at. She had brown hair with highlights, cut sensibly short. She was slender and probably stood no more than five feet three or four, but Cork felt an undeniable power in her the moment he shook her hand.

"Fine, thanks," Cork said.

"Would you like something to eat?" Ben Jacoby said.

"I've had breakfast, thanks."

"How about coffee?"

The woman said, "You look like you could use some."

"You look only half-awake yourself," Cork replied.

"Red-eye from Chicago last night. I drove up from the Twin Cities this morning. Just got here. I'm a little shy on sleep."

"Dina is a consultant on security issues. I've asked her here to give you a hand with your investigation of Eddie's death."

"A hand?"

The waiter returned. He was young and blond, with a healthy blush to his cheeks. He wore a name tag that read *Jan* and below that *Finland*. For years, the Quetico Inn had hired staff from all over the world to help during high season. He asked, in English that sounded very British, if everything was to their liking and whether Cork would care to order something.

"Coffee," Cork said.

"Try the blintzes," Ben Jacoby said. "They're marvelous."

"Just coffee," Cork said.

When Jan from Finland had gone, Dina said, "Sheriff, I headed the Organized Crime Section for the

FBI's Chicago office for seven years. Before that, I was with the Money Laundering Unit out of DC. And before that, I spent several years as an investigator for the Cook County prosecutor's office."

"Impressive," Cork said. "But we don't need another hand."

"My experience with rural law enforcement is that resources are always scarce. It's my understanding that at the moment you're conducting two major investigations."

"The BCA is helping."

"Let me ask you something. When you send evidence to the BCA, how long before they process it?"

"Depends."

"A week? Three? I have access to private laboratories that guarantee results within twenty-four to forty-eight hours."

"We can't afford—"

"I can," Lou Jacoby broke in.

"With all due respect, sir—"

"I'm going to cut through the crap." The old man pointed his fork at Cork. "I want to know who killed my son, and I want to be sure that no hayseed with a badge fucks things up."

"Dad," Ben Jacoby said.

"Am I clear, Sheriff?"

Cork felt heat rising, his face flushing, his stomach drawing taut. His anger must have been apparent because the younger Jacoby said quickly, "We're all a little tired and upset, Sheriff. I hope you can understand."

It took a moment, but Cork finally swallowed the words that had been ready to leap from his throat. Ben was right. They'd lost a member of their family. That kind of loss was confusing, and people often responded in ways that were, in the end, understandable and forgivable.

"I'm not here to interfere with your investigation, Sheriff," Dina said. "I'm here to offer resources that might not otherwise be available. Honestly, wouldn't you appreciate getting answers faster than they've been coming?"

"I'll consider it," Cork finally said.

The patriarch looked as if he were about to speak again, perhaps to shove something more down Cork's throat, but his son said, "Dad, why don't we give Dina and Sheriff O'Connor a few minutes alone to talk."

Lou Jacoby cast a look toward Dina that was clear in its message: *don't fuck up*. He stood up.

"Ben," Cork said. "Would you stay for just a moment?"

Lou Jacoby glanced at his son, seemed to weigh the request, and nodded. He turned and walked from the room.

Cork folded his hands on the table. "I won't tolerate any interference. Your father might have influence in Chicago, but here he's just another guest at the Quetico Inn."

"I understand," Jacoby replied. "And please accept my apology. As I said, he's upset. That's part of the reason I asked Dina here. Dad was insistent that he was going to stay through the end of your investigation. Believe me, he would make life hell. Dina not only has the background to be of service, but she's also infinitely easier to work with. If you decline her help, you'll find yourself dealing directly with my father. Do you really want that?"

"Like I said, I'll consider it."

Dina Willner listened impassively but smiled pleasantly whenever Cork looked her way.

"I'm wondering if you could clarify something for me, Ben. Eddie's your half brother, correct?"

"Yes. After my mother died, my father married Eddie's mother, Gwen. She passed away two years ago."

"Were they married long?"

"Nineteen years."

"Nineteen years? Eddie was what, thirty-five?"

"If you're wondering about the math, Sheriff, Eddie was a bastard child. Lou and Gwen didn't get married until he was fourteen."

"How did you feel about him?"

"What do you mean?"

"He was a half brother, born to what, your father's mistress? Was there any resentment?"

"For better or worse, he was part of the family. My father loved him. I love my father. So I tried to be a brother to Eddie. I admit that wasn't always easy."

"Why?"

"We saw the world in different ways."

"What was his way?"

"He saw everything in terms of Eddie. A rather limited view."

"So, he was a difficult sibling. How was he as a husband?"

"You should probably ask his wife."

"She's not here. And I'm sure you have an opinion."

"I thought the police dealt in facts."

"Here's a fact. Eddie was a womanizer. More than that, he liked to hurt women."

Jacoby didn't appear at all surprised. "Is that why he's dead?"

"It's certainly one of the possibilities. You say your father loved him. Did they talk about things?"

"What things?"

"Eddie's work, his life, his hobbies, his treatment of women."

"I don't know. I'll be happy to ask him."

"How about if I ask him?"

"You've seen him, Sheriff. You'd get nothing helpful from him right now."

"Mind if I ask you where you were the night Edward was killed?"

"You think I resented Eddie enough to kill him?"

"I'm just asking where you were."

"I was working on a business deal until very late, with several associates. I can give you their names."

"Not necessary at the moment."

Jan from Finland finally arrived with the coffee Cork had ordered. Cork ignored it and turned his attention to Dina, who'd been listening patiently to the conversation. "We have evidence taken from the SUV in which Eddie Jacoby was murdered. A couple of cigarette butts with lipstick prints. If we came up with other samples that we'd like to compare against, DNA or the lip prints, how long would that take?"

"Depending on the kind of samples, if we shipped them overnight express, we could have results within forty-eight hours of their arrival."

"Results that would stand up in court?"

"Absolutely."

"Meet me at the Sheriff's Department at noon. I'll introduce you to the other investigators. Remember, you're with us only so long as you're useful and stay out of the way."

Dina Willner gave a serious nod. "Understood."

17

*H*IS MEETING WITH the psychologist was scheduled for 10:00 A.M. and he was already five minutes late.

He said, "Thanks, Margaret," into the phone and hung up.

Cork had worked with Special Agent Margaret Kay of the FBI's Minneapolis field office on an important case over a year ago, one that had put both Jo and Stevie in mortal jeopardy. He'd called to ask a favor of her: would she be willing to check on Dina to verify the woman's claim about her background with the Bureau, and to supply any other background information to which she might have access? Kay had agreed to help.

Cork left his office and headed to the converted Old Firehouse where Dr. Faith Gray had her practice. The psychologist smiled pleasantly when Cork hurried in, and she offered him herbal tea. They sat in green stuffed chairs in a room with a big dieffenbachia in a corner and a lush Swedish ivy in a brown jute macramé hanger at the window. Filled bookshelves lined the walls, a garden of knowledge. Faith Gray's long hair flowed white like fast water down the middle of her back. Her eyes were bright blue and kind. She wore a long denim skirt, a white turtleneck, and an oval of turquoise on a long silver chain around her neck.

"How's that ear?" she asked.

"Itchy. I'll be glad when the stitches come out."

They chatted awhile, then she lifted her cup to her lips. "How have you been sleeping?"

"I sleep."

"Not well, I'd wager, from the look of you. Trouble going to sleep? Staying asleep?"

"Both," Cork said.

"Do you dream?"

"Yes."

"Any disturbing dreams?"

He related the recurring dream in which his father transformed into a wounded Marsha Dross and he couldn't save either of them.

She listened, nodded, then said, "Tell me about the shooting."

Cork said, "You know about that. I had Pender drop off the incident report, as you asked."

"Tell me about it anyway."

Cork went through it from the time the call came in from the Tibodeau cabin to the moment the EMTs rushed Marsha Dross away in the ambulance.

"Look at your hands," she said when he'd finished.

"What?"

The light changed as clouds passed across the sun and the room took on a gloomy cast.

"Look at your hands, Cork."

Her eyes drifted gently to his fingers, which were dug into the padded arms of the easy chair so hard, his fingernails had turned red and his knuckles white. He loosened his grip.

Her eyes moved next to the pendulum clock on the wall behind Cork. "Our time's up," she said. "I'd like to see you again."

"Faith, I'm pressed for time these days."

"Let me rephrase that. If you want to continue performing your duties, you need to come until I tell you not to. It's in the regulation, Cork, the one you and I wrote together."

Cork, Larson, and Rutledge met before Dina Willner arrived. He told them what FBI Special Agent Margaret Kay had reported to him, confirming Willner's background and excellent record. They discussed her involvement. Neither Rutledge nor Larson liked the idea of an outsider being a part of the team, but the speed with which she might be able to get evidence analyzed was very appealing. They'd dealt with law enforcement agencies at all levels, and working with a consultant, they decided, wouldn't be significantly different. They wanted to meet her in person before they agreed.

Promptly at noon, Willner entered Cork's office. After shaking hands all around, she said, "You have the look of probation officers. Honestly, I'm here to help in any way I can, to offer anything you need that might facilitate your investigation. I'm also here as an intermediary. Sheriff O'Connor's already dealt with Lou Jacoby, so he knows that Lou prefers a cattle prod to diplomacy. He'd make your lives miserable, believe me."

She looked refreshed, as if she'd managed a nap or taken a shower. She wore jeans, a yellow cable knit sweater, and hiking boots. Cork noted again that although she was modest in size, there was a surety in her manner that made her seem substantial, someone you could trust watching your back. That she was attractive didn't hurt in the least.

"Questions, gentlemen?"

"My only concern is maintaining the integrity of the investigation," Larson said. "I'd like you to agree not to pass along any information to Mr. Jacoby or anyone else without explicit permission from us."

"Agreed," Dina said.

"Anything else?" Cork waited a moment. "If not, then could you step outside for a minute, Dina?"

"Of course." She left the room and closed the door behind her.

"Well?"

"Her credentials seem all right," Rutledge said. "And the chance of getting faster lab results is attractive."

"As long as she doesn't interfere, I don't see a problem," Larson said.

"Simon?"

"Goes for me, too."

When Dina returned, she took a chair to the left of Larson and Rutledge.

The day had warmed. A few minutes earlier Cork had opened a window, and the smell of fall drifted into the room. In the park across the street, children too young for school filled the playground, and their small high squeals provided an odd background music to the grim discussion taking place.

Larson reported that he'd talked to most of the women on the list of known prostitutes. They all knew about Eddie Jacoby's penchant for cruelty and claimed they'd refused to have anything to do with him. They were all able to account for their whereabouts the night he was killed.

"I haven't followed up on the alibis yet," Larson said. "But if we get anything that points us in that direction, I'll hop right on it."

Dina gestured at the accordion folder Larson held. "Is that Eddie's case file?"

"Yes."

"May I see it?"

Larson looked to Cork, who nodded, then handed it over.

Rutledge had finally received the fax of the records for Jacoby's cell phone. He'd made copies, which he supplied to everyone present. In the week Eddie had been in Aurora, he'd called a lot of folks on the rez, and had received calls from them. All the names listed with the phone numbers were members of the Reservation Business Committee. Some calls had also come from a pay phone located at the North Star Bar. Rutledge asked about it, and Cork told him it was an Indian bar in the middle of nowhere. Several calls had been made to the Chicago area, mostly to Starlight Enterprises, and one to Ben Jacoby's cell phone the afternoon Eddie died.

Cork said, "Jacoby told me about his brother's call. I'd like to know what they talked about, exactly what was said. Ed, you mind taking that one? I want to follow up on some of these calls to the rez."

"Sure. You want to come?" Larson asked Dina.

"I'd rather work the rez."

Cork said, "You go anywhere, it's with Ed."

She didn't argue.

Cork turned to Rutledge. "Any word from the BCA lab?"

Simon looked a little chagrined. "I called. They're backlogged. We probably won't get anything for another week at least."

"Do you have any of the cigarette butts left that you found in the SUV?"

"One."

Dina said, "I'd be happy to send it to our lab in Chicago. We could have a DNA analysis by this time day after tomorrow, guaranteed."

"I'll consider it."

She looked as if there was something more on her mind.

"Yes?" Cork said.

"I'm just wondering." She'd taken the autopsy report from the file and she tapped it with a polished nail the color of pearl. "I've been looking at this. Death was the result of a stab wound directly to the heart."

"Yes," Larson said.

"And it appeared that Eddie put up no struggle, right?"

"That's right. High blood alcohol content in his blood and traces of Ecstasy. He was probably pretty high."

"Hmmmm," she said.

"What is it?" Larson asked.

"Eddie Jacoby was in terrific physical condition. All the Jacobys are. Even drunk, even high on Ecstasy, even surprised, he'd fight, believe me. Unless . . ."

She put a finger to her lips and the men waited.

"The very first knife wound was the fatal one."

Larson thought it over. "That would require a lot of luck on the assailant's part."

"Wouldn't it," she said.

"Or someone who knew where to stick the knife, knew what would kill a man instantly." He rolled that over in his mind. "Maybe somebody put more thought into this than it might appear at first glance."

The men looked at one another, then at Dina.

"Of course, it could be a jealous husband, as you've speculated," she said. "But he'd have to be one cold, calculating son of a bitch with more restraint than most jealous husbands, in my experience, are capable of."

Larson nodded slowly. "So scratch jealous husband."

She waited a moment, then offered, "According to the autopsy, the wounds on the body came from a long, slender blade approximately seven inches in length," she said.

"Like a fillet knife," Larson suggested.

"Or a stiletto," she said. "So. An isolated rendezvous, prints wiped clean, a postmortem castration. I think we can scratch hysterical woman, even a lucky hysterical woman."

"For the moment, let's assume that Jacoby brought his own drugs and his murder had nothing to do with that," Cork said. "He'd been working to secure a contract with the RBC. It's a controversial issue on the rez." He paused as he realized something, and he looked at Dina. "You already decided this was about Starlight. That's why you wanted to go with me to the rez."

"Given everything we know at the moment, it seemed the best prospect," she replied.

Larson said, "What about those cigarette butts and his need for female companionship? Are we going to ignore that?"

"Maybe he was lured to Mercy Falls," Dina said.

Larson nodded. "It would be good to know if he was seen with anybody that night. I'll check his hotel again and the bars in town. Maybe somebody remembers something."

"Sounds good," Cork said. He moved on to the other investigation. "Anything more on the shooting, Simon?"

Rutledge shook his head. "We blanked on the tires. But I've been thinking. It's possible we're dealing with somebody who has a military background. A lot of strategy in the planning and setup. A good position to shoot from. The hardware to do the job. An escape route chosen to keep the shooter away from traffic at the cabin."

Cork said, "What about the shell casings he left behind? Not great planning there."

"I don't know. That is puzzling. It's as if the shooter was distracted from his mission."

"The shooter may not have been alone," Cork said. "The woman who imitated Lucy Tibodeau on the phone may have been with him. Maybe she panicked, and that was the distraction."

"I think we'd do well to look for someone with a good knowledge of the Iron Lake Reservation who has a military background and a grudge against you, Cork," Rutledge said. "Do you know anyone who fits that description?"

"I could name a few Shinnobs who were Vietnam vets and weren't happy when I arrested them, but I can't imagine any of them wanting to kill me for it."

"What about a hunter rather than a soldier?" Dina said. "From what I understand reading the incident report, the sniper was two hundred and fifty, maybe three hundred yards from his target. That's not a difficult distance for a good hunter, especially one with a reasonable rifle and scope. I would imagine hunters in this area are quite used to having to adjust for upslope and downslope shots. And they probably have a good understanding of where to position themselves for maximum effect. Plus," she went on, "I think there's a fundamental problem with the military scenario."

"What's that?"

"Again, just from what I understand reading the report, the sheriff saw a flash of light off the rifle, maybe from the scope, maybe a plate on the rifle stock. A trained sniper would never let that happen. The scope would be hooded and any metal on the stock that might reflect light would be covered. It also seems to me that a trained sniper would have chosen a position on the west side of the hollow, in the shadow of the hill behind the cabin where sunlight in his eyes or on his weapon wouldn't have been an issue."

"A hunter," Rutledge said, and gave a slight nod. "The problem there is that this is a county full of hunters."

She tilted her head. "That is a problem."

There was a knock at the door. "Come in," Cork said.

It was the dispatcher Patsy Gilman. "I've got the flowers, Cork. I'm heading to the hospital."

"I'll be right with you."

"I'll wait," she said, and closed the door as she left.

The department had taken up a collection to buy flowers for Marsha Dross. Patsy wanted to deliver them before she had to report for her shift at three o'clock that afternoon. Cork had asked to go along.

He took his copy of Jacoby's cell phone records. "After the hospital, I'll head out to the rez and have a talk with the members of the RBC."

"I'd still like to petition mildly that I come with you," Dina said.

Cork shook his head. "People on the rez will be reluctant to talk to me as it is. With you along, they wouldn't say a word."

"If you're going rural, Cork," Ed Larson said, "wear your vest."

Cork wasn't sure he would. He didn't want to sit down and talk with people if it appeared that he was dressed for battle. And this trip to the rez would be different from the one he'd made with Marsha Dross. This time, no one knew he was coming.

18

THE TOWN OF Allouette was the political and social center of the Iron Lake Reservation. That didn't mean there was much to it. A grid of a dozen streets, several still not fully paved. A new community center that housed the tribal offices and a health center. A Mobil gas station and garage owned by Les Standing. The Nanaboozhoo Café. And George LeDuc's store.

LeDuc's was a small general store in a clapboard building with scratched wood floors. The shelves held a little of everything, from bread to Band-Aids to bait and tackle. It was also the post office for the rez.

When Cork stepped in, LeDuc was behind the counter.

"Boozhoo," LeDuc called out in greeting.

"Boozhoo," Cork called back. "Good to see you, George." He walked to the counter where LeDuc was preparing the day's mail for pickup.

"Good to see you, too. Still alive." LeDuc grinned. The lines of his face deepened, but there was a vigor in his dark eyes much younger than his seventy years. "How's your deputy?"

"She'll be fine."

"Everyone on the rez is talking about that shooting."

"Anything come up I ought to know about?"

"Nope. Got us all scratching our heads. Eli Tibodeau, he's still real broke up over those dogs of his. Seems to me it had to be somebody just plain mean to do that to a couple of dogs. And to shoot Marsha Dross. She's a good person. Like I said before, I hear anything, I'll let you know."

"I'm here about Eddie Jacoby, George."

LeDuc bound the mail in a bundle. It was all letters today—a lot of bills being paid, from the look of it. "That guy, he was bad news. Whenever I shook hands with him, I counted my fingers after to make sure I still had 'em all."

"From what I'm hearing, the rest of the RBC didn't feel the same way."

"You don't have to like a man to like what he's selling."

"You think a contract with Starlight Enterprises is a good idea?"

"Not necessarily with Starlight. But we sure been having trouble with the managers we've hired. Russell Blackwater, he stole us blind. Daniel Wadena couldn't stomach the politics. That guy come up from Mystic Lake, he was just plain incompetent. And now Kirby Hanes has just about everybody at the casino threatening to quit. We could use some good management."

"The RBC's been dragging its feet for months. Suddenly you're all hot for Starlight. Why the change of heart?"

"Lots of ways to change a person's thinking. A sound argument, for one."

"Jacoby put one forward?"

"It was sound. Like I said, we been desperate for good management for a while. But the man himself . . ." LeDuc shook his head. He reached under the counter and brought out a small canvas bag labeled U.S. MAIL. He put the bundled envelopes inside.

"Lots of ways to change someone's thinking, you said. Was money one?" Cork asked.

"When you're dealing with a weak person, sure. And there are people on the RBC who might bend pretty easy that way."

"Did he try to bribe you?"

"I don't bend easy, and everybody out here knows it."

"Hear of any arm-twisting?"

"I heard he tried with Edgar Gillespie."

"How?"

"I don't know. Edgar wouldn't say. But with his past, hell, you wouldn't have to dig too deep to find a little buried garbage."

"Jacoby's been working on this deal for six months. Why all the sudden pressure? Did he lose patience?"

"He was an impatient man to begin with. Doing things on Indian time really burned him. I was surprised he waited so long to get tough. Edgar probably wasn't the only one he leaned on."

"Where would he get the information he'd need for that kind of leverage? I'm thinking a white man, especially a white man like Jacoby, asking questions on the rez, that would get around."

LeDuc's face was unreadable, but the fact that he didn't reply was an indication that it was an area he wasn't willing to explore with Cork.

"Well someone talked to him." Cork opened a jar of jerky that sat near the register, pulled out a piece, laid money on the counter, and began to chew. "Going with Starlight or not going with Starlight. You think someone would kill over that?"

LeDuc took the money, put it in the till. "I had me an uncle who was murdered during the Depression, stabbed to death by a man who wanted his shoes. That tell you anything?"

Cork had left the records for Jacoby's cell phone calls in his vehicle. What LeDuc had just said made him want to look at them.

"*Migwech,* George," he said as he turned to leave. *Thanks.* "Give my best to Francie."

"Tell Jo hello."

In the Pathfinder, Cork put his half-eaten jerky strip on the seat and checked the phone records. Several calls had been made to Eddie Jacoby from the North Star Bar. It was the kind of place where men who would kill for a pair of shoes did their drinking.

The bar stood at a crossroads just south of the rez, surrounded by thick woods and nothing else for miles. The regulars were mostly Shinnobs, although members of other tribal affiliations felt at home there. The common denominator was heritage and hard luck. Occasionally white folks stumbled in, hunters or snowmobilers who didn't know the lay of the land, but they didn't stay long. It was an old wood structure, the paint faded, walls spattered with mud churned up by tires spinning in the unpaved lot. The windows were small and crowded with signs advertising the booze inside. Not much light squeezed through, and the North Star was notoriously dark. When Cork opened the door, the smell of liquor greeted him. It wasn't the kind of place that served food, except for pickled pig's feet in a big glass jar and fried pork rinds and chips that hung on a rack. If it wasn't beer or straight whiskey or at most a boilermaker you wanted, you were better off going somewhere else. Coming in from the sunny afternoon outside, Cork had to wait a minute for his eyes to adjust to the dark. It was deadly quiet, which surprised him because there were several pickups in the lot. When he could see again, he realized the silence wasn't because the place was empty. All eyes were on him and all mouths were shut.

On the way to the North Star, he'd pulled over and taken a few minutes to change into his uniform, including his Kevlar vest. His .38 was holstered on his belt. He walked to the bar where Will Fineday, who owned the place, leaned a couple of beefy arms on a surface badly in need of refinishing.

Fineday had a face straight out of a nightmare. Twenty years earlier, an accident with a hockey stick had nearly cleaved it in half. Although doctors in Canada where the incident occurred repaired the bone and stitched the skin back together, the wound left a jagged scar like a huge fault line across his left cheek, nose, and right eye before it ended halfway up his forehead. He didn't see at all out of the damaged eye. That was the part of the accident that ended a promising NHL career as a forward with the Maple Leafs. Fineday came back to the rez, used the money from the settlement to buy the bar, and for two decades his freakish face had added a certain timbre to the place. He'd managed to secure the stick that had done the deed, and it hung above the bottles at his back. He'd been known to snatch it down and use the threat of it to end a disturbance or roust an unruly customer.

"I don't suppose you want a beer," Fineday said. His voice was soft for such a hard-looking man.

"Got somebody to watch the bar, Will?"

"Why? Arresting me?"

"We're going in back to talk for a while."

The crack across Fineday's face lightened as the skin around it grew an irritated red. After a moment, he straightened up and called, "Lizzie!"

A door in the corner behind him opened and his daughter stepped out.

Lizzie Fineday was twenty, pretty in a surly way, with long black hair and anger in her eyes. Growing up, she'd been a Walt Disney dream of Pocahontas, a pure beauty. She had a lovely voice, sang at school, at pow-wows. She'd always wanted to be an actress, but Lizzie had a problem, and the problem was drugs. Cork had begun picking her up when she was barely thirteen. At sixteen, she'd run away, headed for Hollywood. She got as far as Denver, where she was arrested in a raid on a crack house. Her father went to fetch her and he put her in rehab. In the four years since, her record had been better, but Cork knew from the things he heard on the rez that she wasn't clean, just careful. She was still pretty, but in a damaged, brooding way. At the moment, a large bruise marred her face, a purple shadow along the high bone of her right cheek. Her upper lip was puffy, too. She moved behind her father, and she didn't look directly at Cork.

Fineday started toward the open door, but Cork held back.

"What happened to your face, Lizzie?"

Her hand went automatically toward the bruise but stopped before she touched it. "Nothing."

"Just woke up and there it was?"

"I fell," she said, looking at the floor.

"You fall again, how about letting me know."

She didn't answer, just turned to the sink where beer glasses waited to be washed.

In the office, with the door closed, Will Fineday sat down at an old desk that was covered with the sports section of several newspapers. He didn't bother to clear them away.

"What do you want?" Fineday said. "Someone complain I water down the whiskey?"

Cork hadn't been invited to sit, and although there was an empty chair, he remained standing.

"The name Eddie Jacoby mean anything to you?"

"The guy who got himself killed at Mercy Falls, right?"

"You ever see him out here?"

"Can't recall."

"A pain-in-the-ass white man, Will. You'd recall."

"Then I guess I never saw him."

"Somebody called him from here several times, from your pay phone."

"The pay phone's outside. I don't see who calls."

"How'd Lizzie's face get bruised?"

"Like she said, she fell."

"Bullshit. You hit her?"

"I never hit Lizzie. And I'd kill anyone who did."

Cork knew this was true. Will Fineday's wife had died young, and the man had raised his daughter alone. He'd made mistakes, but hitting Lizzie hadn't been one of them. Although Fineday had a harsh face, his heart, at least where his daughter was concerned, was something else. Cork had accused him only in the hope of jarring something loose.

"Stone hit her?"

Cork was referring to a man with whom Lizzie was known to keep company. They slept together—everyone knew it—but no one thought of it as love. Stone wasn't that kind of man.

"Like I said, if he hit her, he'd be dead."

Cork thought about Lizzie's weakness for getting high and about the drugs that had been found in Jacoby's SUV. "Did Eddie Jacoby hit her?"

"I didn't kill that man, if that's where you're headed. I didn't even know him."

"Mind if I talk to Lizzie?"

"Yeah. In fact," Fineday said, pushing himself up, "you've done all the talking you're gonna do here. I don't want you bothering Lizzie or my customers. You got a warrant or something, fine. Otherwise, I want you out."

"Bother your customers?" Cork laughed. "Hell, Will, nothing short of a bazooka's going to bother them."

Fineday went ahead of him out the office door and put himself between Cork and Lizzie. Cork thanked him for his time, gave Lizzie a nod, and started out.

Just as he reached the exit, someone gave a high squeal behind him and said, "The other white meat."

Cork kept right on walking, glad for the feel of the Kevlar against his back.

19

CORK HAD CALLED early in the afternoon to tell Jo he'd be late and not to hold dinner for him. She didn't feel up to making anything when she got home. When she suggested to the children that they all eat at Johnny's Pinewood Broiler, she got no argument.

Jo was fond of the Broiler, of how it was the center of much that went on in the community. A big bulletin board hung near the entrance, crowded with notices of local events. Everyone knew everyone else and warm hellos were thrown across the dining room. The aroma always made her mouth water the moment she stepped in, the smell of grease on the griddle, of deep-fry.

They took a booth near a front window overlooking Center Street. After they ordered, Jo and Jenny talked about college applications while Annie helped Stevie with the maze and puzzles on the children's place mat. Several people stopped by to tell Jo how awful it was, what had happened on the rez, and to ask did Cork have a clue who was responsible.

They were near the end of the meal. The waitress was clearing their dishes when Ben Jacoby appeared at the table looking tremendously pleased to see them.

"Hello, Jo. What a nice surprise."

She wasn't sure it was.

"I drove by with your husband yesterday. Smelled delicious. I wanted to stop in before I left. Is this your family?"

She introduced the children. "This is Mr. Jacoby."

"How do you do?" he said, addressing them all at once with a charming smile. He studied Stevie's place mat. "Looks like you solved everything. Good for you."

"Annie helped."

"That was nice of her." He turned to Jenny. "I understand you're interested in Northwestern. That's my alma mater."

"Really?" Jenny's eyes danced.

"My son's a senior there this year."

"Sweet," Jenny said.

"Sweet?"

"She means way cool," Jo interpreted.

"I'd be happy to talk to you, tell you anything you want to know. The only problem is that I'm leaving first thing in the morning."

"Oh." Jenny's disappointment showed. Then she brightened. "We're having pie at home. Maybe you could join us?"

"I'm sure Mr. Jacoby has other pressing matters," Jo said.

"Actually, no. I'd love some pie. That is, if it's all right with you."

She wasn't pleased, but there didn't seem an easy way out.

"All right," she said, reaching for her purse.

"I'll just follow in my car," Ben suggested. "How's that?"

He sat at the kitchen table with Jenny. Jo made coffee while Annie dished up the apple pie, which, she explained, she'd made herself from a recipe her aunt Rose had given her. Ben declared it delicious, the best he'd ever tasted. Annie blushed deeply under the compliment.

Stevie went out to play, and Ben told Jenny all about Northwestern. She asked about the writing program.

"I'm not familiar with it," he said. "You want to be a writer?"

"Doesn't everybody?" She laughed.

"Who are your favorite authors?"

"Anaïs Nin, Virginia Woolf, Louise Erdrich. And I absolutely love *To Kill a Mockingbird*."

"Doesn't everybody?" It was his turn to laugh. "Do you know Tillie Olsen?"

"Should I?"

"Read *Tell Me a Riddle*. I think you'll find it to your liking. Have you ever visited Northwestern, toured the campus?"

"No, but Mom and I have been talking about it."

"I'd be glad to show you around sometime. If you and your mom decide to come down."

"Really? That would be terrific."

Ben looked at Annie. "And you, I've heard, are an athlete. Softball, right?"

"That's my favorite, but I like all sports."

"Notre Dame fan?"

"Go Irish."

"It's not that far from Evanston to South Bend. You

could probably talk your mom into visiting both campuses the same trip." He gave her a conspiratorial wink.

The back door opened and Cork stepped into the kitchen. His surprise at finding Ben Jacoby at the table with his family was obvious.

"Good evening," he said.

Jo rose to greet him, kissed his cheek. "We ran into Ben at the Broiler. When Jenny found out he graduated from Northwestern, she had to give him the third degree."

"Informative?" he asked Jenny.

"I've learned tons, Dad."

Jo said, "Have you eaten?"

"Grabbed a sandwich."

"How about some pie, then?"

Cork shook his head. "Looks like everybody's finished. Maybe later."

"Dad," Jenny said. "I'm going canoeing with Alexandra Cunningham tomorrow on Higman Lake. You said I could borrow the Bronco, remember?"

Cork said, "I'll leave the keys on the counter for you."

"Thanks."

"It's a beautiful evening out. Why don't we have our coffee on the front porch?" Jo suggested.

"I'd like that," Ben said.

"Can you stay, Cork? Or do you have to get back?"

"I'll stay."

The children cleared the table while the adults stepped out onto the porch.

"A porch swing." Ben smiled. "I've never actually seen one except in movies. May I?"

"Be our guest," Jo said.

He sat down and began swinging gently. Cork leaned against the porch railing. Jo joined him there.

"I hate to bring up an unpleasant topic, Cork, but did you make any headway on Eddie's murder today?" Ben said.

"Maybe. I need to follow up a couple of things before I know for sure."

"Promising leads?"

"Leads often look promising but end up nowhere."

"You must have a lot of patience."

"What he has," Jo said, "is obsession. Once he starts on an investigation, he can't stop until he's solved it."

"Bulldog Drummond, eh?" Ben laughed.

It was Friday evening, the sun had just set, and Gooseberry Lane was cradled in quiet and a soft amber light. In the O'Loughlin house across the street, someone played easy blues on a guitar. Stevie stood in the yard tossing a baseball into the air. It fell back into his glove with a little slap of leather.

"This is nice," Ben said. "All so very nice." He sipped his coffee. "I understand you were a cop in Chicago for a while, Cork. You ever miss the big city?"

"Never. This is my hometown."

"Mine is Chicago. I love it, but this is pretty damn fine, I have to admit. What about you, Jo? Miss Chicago?"

"No, but I would love to get down there soon. My sister lives in Evanston."

"Rose?"

"Yes. With her husband Mal."

"Convenient. Especially if Jenny decides to attend Northwestern." Ben scanned the street, the yards in late shadow, and gave a satisfied sigh. "All the arrangements have been made to fly Eddie's body home. We'll be leaving first thing in the morning. Jo, it's been a pleasure seeing you again. Cork, you're a lucky man."

The front door opened and Annie said, "Dad, there's a phone call for you. She said it's important."

"I'll be right there." He glanced at Ben. "Excuse me."

"Of course."

When Cork left, they fell into silence, but Ben didn't take his eyes off Jo. She wanted to say something but wasn't sure what, and was relieved when Cork returned.

"I need to go," he said.

"Business?" Ben asked.

"It was Dina."

"Dina?" Jo hadn't heard the name before.

"A consultant the Jacobys have brought in to help with the investigation."

Ben drank the last of his coffee. "What did she want?"

"She was a little circumspect, but she seems to think it's important."

"Should I come?"

"You're leaving tomorrow, Ben. I'll be consulting with Dina when you're not here, so I might as well start now. Anything important, she can fill you in."

"Of course."

Cork started toward the steps. "I might hit the office afterward, Jo. Don't wait up. Ben, I wish I could say it's been a pleasure, but this hasn't been pleasant business." He shook Jacoby's hand. "We're going to solve your brother's murder."

"I'm sure you will."

On the way to his Bronco, Cork said something to

Stevie, who giggled. A minute later he'd backed out of the drive and was gone.

Jo glanced at her watch, then at the sky, where the light was fading rapidly. "I should bring Stevie in. It's time to begin winding down for bed."

As if he knew what was coming, Stevie suddenly bolted across the street and disappeared behind the O'Loughlins' garage. Jo guessed that he'd spotted Rochester, the O'Loughlins' cat, for whom he had a great affection.

"Winding down?" Ben asked.

"He gets into his pajamas, we have a cookie and milk together, then I read to him—or sometimes these days he reads to me. The kind of bedtime stuff you probably did with your son."

He stared into his empty cup. "Unfortunately, no. We'd probably have a better relationship if I had." He looked up, smiled a little sadly. "Thank you, Jo."

"For what?"

"I know my being here isn't your choice, but I appreciate that you let me come. It's good to see how happy you are."

"You're not?" she said.

"The last time I remember being truly happy was when I was with you. But that's the past. Or maybe just the nature of the past. Everything seems better in retrospect."

"You were the one who left," she reminded him.

"That I was." He stood up suddenly and put his cup on the porch railing. "I'd best be off. We leave early tomorrow. Good night, Jo."

"Good-bye, Ben."

He took her hand briefly, then left the porch. He glanced back once and waved. A minute later, he was in his car, heading down Gooseberry Lane in the same direction Cork had gone.

Jo stood for a little while, alone, aware of a feeling like loss, but a small one, in her heart. Then she turned on the porch lamp and called, "Stevie, time to come in."

Almost immediately her son appeared, loping through the growing dark toward the light of home.

20

CORK HAD NOT been happy to find Jacoby in his house, at his table, eating with his family. The man was an acquaintance from Jo's law school days, and what was the harm in offering him a little hospitality, particularly considering the circumstances that had brought him to Aurora? Still, it gnawed at him. Maybe it was just the surprise, because Jacoby's presence had been so unexpected. Maybe it was territorial, because his wife and children seemed to enjoy the man. Or maybe it was because he still didn't know what to make of Ben Jacoby. With rich people, Cork was always on the lookout for the power play. In his experience, people with money held the belief, however veiled, that there was nothing that was beyond the influence of their wealth. In Lou Jacoby, it was as obvious as if he'd worn a suit made of hundred-dollar bills. The old man was used to getting his way. It was possible the same skewed thinking existed on some level in Ben, but he was better at hiding it.

Cork met Dina at the bar in the Quetico Inn, where the Jacobys were staying. He could have invited Ben Jacoby along, but he didn't see any reason. Dina could report to her employers if they really wanted to know what was going on.

She sat next to a window with a view. A small candle burned in the center of the table. Dina was looking at the lake, which, as night crept in from the east, had turned a dark, velvety blue. A drink in one hand, she didn't turn when Cork's image loomed behind her own in the glass.

"Is it always this pretty?" she said.

"To me it is."

Cork took the seat across from her at the table, but she still didn't look at him. She had a nice profile; a small nose with a little squaring of the tip; soft, full lips; good bone structure. Her eyes, he'd noticed, seemed to change color with the light. They were now a dark, intense green.

"Pretty even in winter?" Those full lips formed a smile and she finally looked at him. She wore the sweater she'd had on in Cork's office earlier that day, but she'd done something to her face, defined the features with makeup that made her seem a different kind of woman from what he'd imagined at first, a little less business. He put that information in the Wait and See file in his mind.

"It has a different beauty in winter," he said.

"I guess I'll have to take your word for that. Buy you a drink?"

"Sure."

She signaled the cocktail waitress. Cork ordered whatever Dina was having. It turned out to be Glenfiddich on the rocks.

While he waited for his Scotch, he said, "So what have you got?"

"Who is Harmon LaRusse?"

"LaRusse? Why do you want to know about him?"

"Because a Chevy pickup registered to one Harmon LaRusse followed you all over the reservation this afternoon. Loved the sticker on the rear bumper. 'If this is tourist season, why can't I shoot 'em?'"

"How do you know he followed me?"

"He was parked down the block from the Sheriff's Department and he pulled out after you when you left this morning. I happened to observe him do this, and I tailed him."

"'Happened'?"

When she smiled, her green eyes danced. "I intended to follow you, too, but he beat me to it."

"I thought you were going to work with Ed Larson."

"A misconception on your part. Who is LaRusse?"

"A Shinnob, used to live on the rez. Big guy, goes by the nickname Moose. I busted him five, six years ago for a string of burglaries. He did a nickel at Stillwater. Must be out by now."

"A Shinnob?"

"Short for Anishinaabe. LaRusse is full-blood Ojibwe."

The Glenfiddich came. The waitress asked if Dina wanted another. "Later, maybe," Dina replied.

"He followed me everywhere?"

"The hospital, the store in Allouette, the bar."

"Son of a bitch."

"I can't imagine it has anything to do with Eddie Jacoby's murder, but it might have something to do with the shooting on the rez, and so it's really not my concern. But that bar you went to is."

"The bar?"

"I just came from there."

"You went to the North Star alone?"

"I wanted to ask a few questions."

"That wasn't smart."

"I got answers."

"You got answers at the North Star?" He didn't try to hide his skepticism.

"Here, let me show you a trick." She reached down, grasped the bottom of her sweater, and in one quick, fluid movement, pulled it off over her head. Underneath she wore a low-cut top of some thin scarlet material that hugged her body like a surgical glove. Under that was a push-up bra that offered up her breasts with enough cleavage to swallow the *Titanic*.

Cork dragged his eyes from her chest. "They teach you that at Quantico?"

"I learned that one in the field." She made no move to put her sweater back on.

"Going in alone was a dangerous thing to do."

"I wasn't alone." She reached down and lifted the right cuff of her jeans, exposing an ankle holster fitted with a small Beretta Tomcat. She let the cuff drop.

"Eddie Jacoby sometimes met a man named Stone at the North Star. You know him?" she asked.

Cork said, "I know him."

"What would Eddie want with him?"

"Stone's the kind of guy who'd traffic in anything. Drugs, guns, information. I'm guessing it's that last one he was selling to Jacoby."

"What kind of information would Eddie buy?"

"The kind that might be used to influence a vote of the RBC on whether to sign a contract with Starlight."

"How would Eddie know of him?"

"I don't know. Slime finds slime. It's entirely possible Stone was the one who made the approach."

She sipped the last of her Scotch and the ice clinked against the glass. The sound seemed to intrigue her and she stared for a few moments at the cubes, whose hard edges had been rounded by the Glenfiddich. Cork caught himself glancing again at her breasts.

"Did you see the girl behind the bar?" she asked.

"Lizzie Fineday."

"Somebody hit her."

"Will, that's her father, says it wasn't him. Probably wasn't."

"She have a boyfriend?"

"Stone has a claim on her. I wouldn't call it love. He's a hard man, but I don't think he'd hit Lizzie. Fineday would kill him. But get this. In the bar today, when I tossed Jacoby's name out there as a possibility, Fineday tossed me out."

"That so? It might be interesting to talk to her."

"I've been thinking the same thing," Cork said. He took a long, burning swallow of the Scotch. "Want to be there when I do?"

21

THAT NIGHT Cork woke, looked at the clock on the stand beside the bed—1:47 A.M.—and realized he was alone. He got up, stepped into the hallway. Downstairs a dim flow of light came from the direction of Jo's office.

He found her sitting at her desk, staring across the room at a window where the blind had not been lowered. There was nothing to see but the empty glass, the vague reflection of the room on the pane.

"You okay?" he asked.

"Couldn't sleep," she said.

"Something bothering you?"

She tilted her head back and laughed, not a mirthful sound. "Now, why would you think that? Someone shoots Marsha but they probably meant to shoot you. My client Edward Jacoby is brutally murdered. And you've stopped sleeping. What's to worry about?"

He walked to her desk, sat in the client's chair. "Anything else?"

"That covers it pretty well, I'd say."

"Tell me about Ben Jacoby."

She'd been asleep when he came home, or had seemed to be. He'd been thinking about Jacoby a lot and wanted to talk to her about him, but he hadn't wanted to disturb her rest.

"There's nothing to tell."

"Jo, I'm sleep deprived, not blind."

"Ben was a long time ago."

"Not from the way he looks at you."

She sat back. Her eyes went toward the window again, as if seeking some focus that was not her husband's face. "I knew him before I met you."

"So I gathered. Knew him well, I'd say. Better than just law school acquaintances."

She took a breath. "We had a relationship for several months."

"What happened?"

"He left. Married someone else."

He leaned forward. His body was tired and it was hard to sit up straight. "Why didn't you tell me about him?"

"He was in the past."

"You told me about others."

"I don't know, Cork."

"So tell me now."

She shook her head. "You're angry."

"No, I'm tired."

"Either way, it's not a good time to talk about this."

"I'd rather we did."

"He was twenty years ago. He'll be gone tomorrow."

"Were you happy to see him again?"

"I was surprised."

"You must have loved him a lot to be so afraid to talk about him," Cork went on.

He thought she was going to put him off again. Instead, her blue eyes settled on his face and she said, "I loved him very much. And he hurt me very badly."

Cork mulled that over. "Did you marry me on the rebound?"

"Has it ever felt like that?"

"No."

"When you became my life, I put Ben Jacoby away, far away."

"And now he's back."

"Not because I wanted him." She stood up, intending to take Cork into her reassuring arms, but her attention was drawn to something behind him, something that put fear in her eyes. "Someone's at the window."

He turned in his chair. The pane at his back still showed only the reflection of the office. Beyond that, only night.

"He's gone," Jo said.

"Wait here."

Cork ran from the room, down the hallway, and into the kitchen. He flipped the dead bolt, flung open the door and the screen, then plunged into the dark outside. He charged along the side of the house toward the backyard and stopped at the corner. Except for the oblong of light that fell from Jo's window onto the grass, there appeared to be nothing to see. He stood listening intently, peering at the hidden recesses of the yard. Nothing moved or made a sound.

He heard a sudden rustle behind him in the lilac bushes that edged the driveway, and he pivoted and crouched, thinking what an easy target he was in his boxers and barefoot. He tensed as if he could feel the night scope on him, and he imagined the chambered round, the finger squeezing. The bushes shivered again; he forced himself to be still, to wait. It was dark and his eyes were useless. He cocked his head, trying to catch the slightest sound, the slide of a rifle bolt or the shallow intake of the steadying breath before firing.

A small rocket launched itself from the lilacs. It stayed low to the ground, and Cork stumbled back, startled. The shape made a sudden right-angle turn and scrambled down the driveway. Cork leaped to where he could see the drive all the way down to the street. As the shape passed into the light of the street lamp, it was clearly defined: the O'Loughlins' cat, Rochester. Cork's legs went weak, and he leaned against the Bronco, which he'd left parked in the driveway.

Jo stepped out the kitchen door. "Are you all right?"

"Yeah. You didn't happen to get a good look at who it was in the window?"

"No. He was there and then he wasn't."

"He? You're sure it was a he?"

She thought a moment. "No."

He took her arm. "Let's get back inside."

He threw the dead bolt on the kitchen door and checked the lock on the front door. He made sure the blinds over all the windows were down and the curtains drawn. Upstairs, he took his .38 from the lockbox in his bedroom closet.

"Are you going to sleep with that?" Jo asked.

"Yes, but downstairs, on the sofa."

She eyed the gun with concern. "Do you think that's necessary?"

"I don't know what's necessary, and I don't want to take chances."

"All right," she said. "Want company?"

"I'll be fine."

He put on sweatpants and slippers, took his pillow and a blanket, and stretched out on the sofa in the living room. He put the revolver under his pillow, then lay for a long time listening and thinking.

He'd believed he was safe in town, but maybe he was wrong. And if he was wrong, it meant that his home wasn't safe. Not for him, not for his family. He would have to do something about that. Whatever it was, he'd figure it out in the morning.

His father stood at the top of a hill, facing the setting sun, his back toward Cork. Cork tried to call out, but his jaw was paralyzed and nothing escaped his mouth but a low, helpless groan. His father began to walk away, disappearing down the other side of the hill, as if the ground were swallowing him. Cork fought desperately to follow, clawing at a slope that lay in deep shadow. He came at last to a place where pine needles had been laid as bedding in a jumble of black rocks that were embedded with gold nuggets glittering in the sun. Then he realized they weren't nuggets but brass shell casings. He started to run down the other side of the hill, but shots were already being fired and he saw his father tumble. And then it was not his father on the ground but Marsha Dross with her eyes wide open in terror, her lips rapidly moving, whispering words that were like the soft slipping of feet over a rug. In the next instant he was awake, hearing someone come down the stairs in his house.

Jenny shuffled across the carpet to where Cork lay on the sofa.

"Daddy?"

"Morning, sweetheart."

She seemed surprised to find him there. "What happened?"

"Trouble sleeping."

"Again?"

He ignored her remark, saw that she was dressed in jeans, a green sweatshirt, a billed cap, and her hiking boots, and he remembered. "All set for your canoe outing?"

"Yeah. Thanks for letting me borrow the Bronco."

"Got the keys?"

"Right here." She held out her hand to show him.

"Have a good time."

"We will."

"When should we expect you home?"

"After dinner. We're going to eat at the Sawmill when we come off the lake."

"Got money?"

"Plenty."

She kissed his cheek, went into the kitchen, and a moment later he heard the door open and close.

Morning sunlight fired the curtain. He looked at the grandfather clock in the hallway. Seven-ten. He thought about getting up, but was so tired that he could barely move. Every muscle of his body ached. His head felt thick and fuzzy. But the dream he'd been having when Jenny woke him was still vivid.

Although he hadn't had a cigarette in a couple of years, he wanted one now.

He heard the kitchen door open and Jenny came back in.

"Dad?"

"What is it, Jen?"

"I can't get the car started. It won't even turn over. I think the battery's dead."

"More likely a loose cable. Let's take a look." He slowly rolled off the sofa.

Outside, the morning was bright and crisp. The day had a peaceful feel. Cork loved this kind of morning, the light in the sky gold and promising, the smell in the air sharp with evergreen.

The night hadn't been cold enough for frost, but there was a thick layer of dew on the Bronco's windshield. "Give me the keys," Cork said.

He got into the vehicle and turned the ignition. Nothing happened. He popped the hood latch and got out.

"Hop in," he told his daughter. "When I tell you to, try to start it."

Jenny slipped behind the wheel. Cork walked around to the front of the Bronco and lifted the hood. What he saw froze him.

"Jenny," he said.

"Try it now?" she called.

"No," he ordered harshly. "Don't turn the key. Just get out of the car."

"What?"

"Just get out, sweetheart," he said, trying to keep his voice even.

Jenny did as she was told, then joined her father and saw what he saw.

"Oh, Jesus. What do we do, Dad?" She whispered, as if afraid that speaking too loudly might be dangerous.

"We're going inside," he told her. "I'm going to call the Department and then we're going to wake everyone up and get them out of here."

22

THE BOMB SQUAD from the Duluth Police Department advised that everyone within fifteen hundred feet of the O'Connor house be evacuated. Standard procedure. The Tamarack County Sheriff's Department barricaded the streets, and two yellow pumpers from the Aurora Volunteer Fire Department stood ready. The bomb squad indicated they would be there in ninety minutes. In the meantime, all there was to do was keep the crowd back and wait.

The deputies reported that most folks who evacuated had been cooperative. Cork himself encountered only one instance of outright hostility, this from Gunther Doktor, an old widower who'd lived on Gooseberry Lane forever. Doktor had turned his good ear toward Cork, an ear that sprouted hair like corn tassel, and said, "You O'Connors. Always been trouble." Still, he'd abandoned his house as requested, muttering as he shuffled to the end of the block.

Most other neighbors made it a point to tell Cork they were outraged by this personal attack, and if there was anything they could do to help, then just, by God, let them know. The Women's Guild from St. Agnes

Catholic Church somehow got word of the situation and had very quickly set up tables outside the secured perimeter to offer coffee and juice, doughnuts, and banana bread to those for whom breakfast was now a long way off.

Jo and Stevie stood with the O'Loughlins in the street under the shade of an oak with russet leaves. Jenny and Annie mingled with the crowd and Cork wasn't always able to see them. He would have preferred to keep his whole family in sight, but he had his hands full.

He stood beside a cruiser parked beyond the barricades at the west end of the block, and he talked with Cy Borkmann, Ed Larson, and Simon Rutledge.

Borkmann said, "Duluth bomb squad radioed their twenty. They just passed the casino. Maybe five minutes now."

Rutledge had been in such a hurry that he hadn't combed his hair, and he'd put his sweater on inside out. "Jo told me the guy wore a ski mask, that she couldn't see anything that might ID him."

"That's right."

"And you saw no one when you went outside to check?"

"Like I told you, Simon, only the cat. Rochester's smart, but I don't think he planted that dynamite."

Rutledge was the only one who smiled. "We'll want your Bronco for a while, so we can go over it carefully for evidence."

"If it's still in one piece when this is over, you're welcome to it."

The bomb detail arrived in a Duluth Police van with a trailer in tow. On the trailer was a large, heavy-looking metal canister. An unmarked car followed.

Two men stepped from the van and another came from the car. The man who'd driven the van said, "Sheriff O'Connor?"

"Here."

"Sergeant Dave Gorman." Tall, tanned, early thirties, buzz cut, good shape.

They shook hands. He introduced his colleagues, Sergeant Rich Klish and Sergeant Greg Searson.

"Where is it?" Gorman asked.

"Down the street. Two-sixteen Gooseberry Lane. The Bronco in the drive with the hood up."

Gorman nodded. "So what did you see?"

"A white PVC pipe, three inches in diameter, maybe fifteen inches in length, capped at both ends."

"A timing device? Clock, watch?"

"I didn't see one."

"Where was the explosive placed?"

"On the engine block, near the battery."

"Wires?"

"Yes."

"Did you see where they connected?"

"To the battery."

"The battery?" Gorman glanced at the men who'd come with him. "You're sure?"

"With alligator clips."

"Was there a clothespin glued to the pipe?"

"Yes."

"Did you notice any fishing line?"

"Fishing line? I don't recall."

Gorman puzzled over that. Cork felt that he was letting the bomb technician down. He should have checked more thoroughly, but he'd been worried about getting his family and his neighbors out of harm's way.

"Okay. You're sure about the clothespin?"

"Yes."

Gorman went to the van, came back with a pair of binoculars. He looked for a minute toward Cork's house.

"The Bronco, huh?"

"Yeah."

He looked some more. "You like it?"

"I beg your pardon?"

"I'm thinking of getting one. I just wondered if it's been a good vehicle for you."

"Good enough that I'd hate to see it end up in little pieces."

"Well, we'll see what we can do about keeping that from happening." He turned to his companions. "Let's take the van in, Greg. Rich," he said to the man who'd driven the unmarked car, "you stay with the sheriff, keep him apprised."

Gorman and Searson got back into the van. Cork's people moved the barricade aside and let them pass. They drove to the end of the block and stopped a good five hundred feet short of Cork's house.

"They're parked in the cold zone, a safe distance from the explosive," Sergeant Klish said. He was much shorter than Gorman, and older. He had a square face that seemed oddly unconcerned about the danger his colleagues might be facing.

"You go out on a lot of these calls?" Ed Larson asked.

"Sometimes two or three a day. Not usually this far north, though. A Bronco, you said, Sheriff?"

"That's right."

Klish nodded. "Probably too high for the camera on the robot. I'm guessing Dave'll suit up and go in for a look-see."

They watched as Gorman laboriously donned a heavily padded green suit with a high collar and large helmet. Slowly, he began to walk toward the Bronco down the street.

"Looks like he's taking it pretty careful," Cy Borkmann said.

"He's wearing eighty pounds of Kevlar plates," Klish replied. "He doesn't have any choice but to go slow."

Gorman reached Cork's drive and approached the Bronco. He stood for a while peering under the hood.

"He seemed interested in fishing line," Cork said. "What was that about?"

"You said wires were connected directly to the battery?"

"Yes."

"Every explosive needs a power source. In this case, that's the battery. With power already supplied, the only thing that's needed to detonate is to complete the electrical circuit. That's where the clothespin comes in. On this type of device, the electrical contacts are often thumbtacks pushed into the legs of the clothespin. What keeps them from connecting and completing the circuit is a thin piece of plastic or maybe cardboard that's been slipped between. The question is, how does the plastic or cardboard get removed so the tacks can make contact, complete the circuit, and detonate the explosive? The answer: fishing line. Secure one end of the line to the cardboard, the other to the hood. When the car doesn't start, the victim lifts the hood to see what the problem is, the fishing line gets pulled up, the cardboard gets yanked out, the thumbtacks connect, the circuit is completed, and . . . boom." He gave Cork a wistful look.

"You're a very lucky man, Sheriff. All I can think is that the fishing line broke."

Cork nearly staggered under the thought of what almost happened, thinking less about himself than the fact that Jenny had been with him.

"What's in the pipe?" Larson asked.

"Could be anything," Klish said. "Black powder, dynamite, even C-4, I suppose. They'll check that out next." He shook his head. "You know, the hell of all this is that it's a very destructive device, but simple to make. Instructions for it and bombs a lot more sophisticated are all over the Internet. Go figure."

Gorman backed away from the Bronco and, when he was a safe distance, turned and walked to the van. He returned to the Bronco with what Klish described as a portable X-ray machine. Fifteen minutes later, with Gorman at the van, Searson began assembling a tall stand with what looked like a rifle barrel on the end.

"They're going to shoot," Klish said.

"My Bronco?"

"Relax, Sheriff. They'll probably shoot just the battery, or one of the cables, to remove the power source. Then they'll probably shoot the device to break it open so they can take a look inside. What Greg's constructing is called a PAN disrupter. It's basically a remote gun. It has a laser beam for aiming, a barrel that'll fire anything from shot to a slug to plain water."

Half an hour and two PAN shots later, they sent the robot in to lift the explosive from the Bronco. Searson guided the small wheeled device back to the van where Gorman waited, still suited.

"Dave's going to remove the detonator, then he'll

drop the explosive into the trailer for transport and disposal. You wouldn't happen to have a gravel pit around here, would you?" Klish inquired.

"Just west of town," Cork replied.

When Gorman was finished and the explosive was safely in the transport canister, he removed his suit and walked to where Cork and the others waited. He was drenched with sweat and looked beat. He carried a liter bottle of water, from which he frequently drank.

"What was inside?" Klish asked.

"Trenchrite. Four packs."

"That's a very common explosive," Klish explained. "That gravel pit of yours probably uses it. What about the fishing line, Dave?"

"It was there. Broken."

"I explained to the sheriff his good fortune."

"You were lucky on two counts," Gorman said to Cork. "The line broke, yes. But also whoever made the bomb inserted a dead blasting cap. It had already been used. Even if the line hadn't broken, there's no way that bomb would have gone off. That was one really stupid perp."

Within twenty minutes, the bomb team cleared out, heading with Cy Borkmann to the gravel pit, where they intended to dispose of the explosive. The barricades were removed, the pumpers went back to the firehouse, and the crowd dispersed. Cork told Larson and Rutledge that he'd meet them in his office in half an hour.

He walked his family home and checked his Bronco. The cable to the positive battery terminal had been severed and there were white PVC fragments everywhere, but the damage seemed minimal. Inside the house, everything felt different, as if they'd been gone a very long time.

"Everybody out of the kitchen," Jo said. "I'm going to make us something to eat."

The children mutely drifted toward the living room.

When they were alone, Jo said, "Why, Cork?"

"I don't know. But one thing is certain. I don't want you or the kids around until we've nailed this guy."

"I agree. I've been thinking. Jenny wants to see Northwestern and Annie's dying to have a look at Notre Dame. Why don't I call Rose, see if we can stay with her and Mal in Evanston?"

"That's a good idea."

"I don't suppose you'd come, too."

"You know I can't."

She accepted it with an unhappy nod.

"I'm sorry, Jo. Sorry about all this."

"Not your fault, sweetheart." She tried to smile.

23

CORK WAS SURPRISED to find Dina Willner with Larson and Rutledge in his office. He'd seen her among the crowd on Gooseberry Lane, but they hadn't spoken. She wore black jeans, a white turtleneck sweater, sneakers. She held a disposable cup from the Gas Pump Grill, an old gas station on Oak Street that had been redone as a gourmet coffee shop. Larson and Rutledge had cups, too. Several cream cheese *kolaches* lay on a paper plate on Cork's desk, next to another cup from the Gas Pump Grill. The aromas of the coffee and the pastries were wonderful, the first good thing that whole morning.

"Do you mind if I sit in?" she asked.

Cork glanced at Larson and Rutledge. "Any objections?"

"Fine by me," Rutledge said. Ed Larson nodded his agreement.

"I brought you some coffee," Dina said. "French roast, black, but there's cream and sugar if you'd like."

"Thanks." Cork sat down, took the coffee, put in half-and-half from a tiny container and a couple of packets of sugar lying next to the *kolaches*.

"What do you think?" he said.

"A dead blasting cap. My first guess would be somebody who doesn't know what they're doing," Larson said.

Rutledge pursed his lips skeptically. "They got everything else right. Maybe it was a bomb never meant to go off."

Cork put his coffee down. "Why try so hard to kill me at the Tibodeau cabin, only to give me some kind of bullshit scare now?"

They were quiet a moment. Then Larson said, "A stupid prank?"

Rutledge scratched the back of his neck and didn't look happy with that possibility. "If it was, it's one that could land the prankster in jail for a good long time. He'd have to be way off the impulsive scale. Way too risky. There's substance here."

Dina sat forward, just a little, but the men's eyes turned to her. She spoke quietly. "Remember, you have two major investigations under way. Is it possible this incident has nothing to do with what happened on the reservation?"

"Are you saying it's related to the Jacoby murder?" Larson inched his wire-rimmed glasses higher on the bridge of his nose.

"I don't know. I'm just suggesting it's a possibility."

"Somebody warning me off the investigation?" Cork sat back, considering.

"You said yesterday that there are people on the reservation who might have been blackmailed by Jacoby. Maybe one of them is afraid of what you might discover. They don't want to kill you—maybe they're not that kind, or maybe because of your blood connection, I don't know—but they're trying to dissuade you from looking too closely."

"If it was meant as a warning, why no note?" Rutledge said.

"To whoever planted it, maybe what it related to was obvious. They're not seeing any of this from Cork's perspective, which is much broader." She lifted her cup but paused before sipping. "On the other hand, I suppose it could just be somebody who really wanted you dead but doesn't have the brains God gave a caterpillar."

"Who has access to that kind of explosive?" Rutledge said.

"Up here, lots of folks," Larson replied. "Mining, logging, and we've got a hell of a lot of construction going on, new roads. It wouldn't be difficult to steal."

Rutledge looked at Cork. "Maybe you should think about getting your family out of Aurora for a while."

"I've already taken care of that. Jo and the kids are going to Chicago to stay with her sister and husband."

"Good. So what now? Any ideas?" Rutledge took a bite of his *kolache* and chewed quietly.

Cork said, "I'll hit the reservation, talk to some people out there. If Dina's right—if it's somebody trying to scare me off the Jacoby investigation—maybe I can get a handle on that."

Larson nodded. "We'll do a complete canvass of your neighbors, find out if anybody saw anything helpful. While that's going on, I'm going to do a couple interviews related to the Jacoby murder."

"Who?"

"The night clerk at the Four Seasons. He's been gone camping the last couple of days, but I understand he's back. I'm hoping he might be able to shed some light on Jacoby's comings and goings the night he was killed. And we're still looking for Arlo."

"Arlo?" Dina said.

"Arlo Knuth," Cork explained. "A local character, lives out of his truck and sometimes sleeps in the county parks. He was at Mercy Falls earlier on the night Jacoby was killed. One of my deputies ran him off, but we should talk to him. Good luck tracking him down, Ed."

"I'll find him."

There was a knock at the door. Deputy Duane Pender stepped in. "Here's the information you asked for, Cork." Pender handed over a sheet of paper. "And we've got a gaggle of reporters gathering out there."

"Thanks, Duane. Keep them at bay awhile, and then I'll talk to them."

Pender left and Cork glanced at the sheet he'd delivered.

"I asked Duane to run a DMV check on Harmon LaRusse."

"Moose LaRusse?" Larson said. "Why?"

"He followed me yesterday when I was on the rez."

"Moose? I didn't know he was back in these parts."

"Neither did I. According to the Department of Motor Vehicles, he isn't. He's got a Minneapolis address."

"Tell me about this Moose," Rutledge said.

"A Shinnob from the rez. Big guy, big trouble-maker," Cork said. "Five, six years ago, we busted him for a series of burglaries in the county. Judge gave him five years in Stillwater."

"Why would he be following you?"

"I have no idea, but I'm going to make a few inquiries today, see if I can find out. But the first thing, Simon, you and I should talk to the media. We'll need to cover both investigations. Then what I'm going to do is see if I can get to the bottom of those bruises on Lizzie Fineday's face, find out if Eddie Jacoby had anything to do with it."

Dina put her coffee down. "You said I could be there when you talked to her."

"I haven't forgotten."

Rutledge stood up. "I'm going to try to have that talk with Lydell Cramer's sister this afternoon, see if anything shakes loose there."

"Everyone stay in touch," Cork said.

24

THEY HEADED TOWARD the North Star Bar, driving between stands of aspen with leaves yellow as the sun. They turned onto Waagikomaan Road, a shortcut across the rez paved with oil and crushed stone. Cork drove into marshland where cattails bent under the weight of idle red-winged blackbirds.

"Waagikomaan?" Dina said.

"Not wag like a dog's tail. It's a soft *a*. Like in father."

She tried again, more successfully.

"It means crooked knife," Cork said. "See how the road cuts back and forth, trying to keep to dry, solid ground."

They moved out of the marsh and into a series of low, rocky hills covered with red sumac, balsam, and more aspen.

"Interesting country," Dina said.

"You don't know the half of it."

He could have told her. How the Canadian Shield, the stone mass that underlay everything there and broke through the thin topsoil in jagged outcroppings, was the oldest exposed rock on earth. How the glaciers two miles thick had crept across this land over the centuries, scraping everything down to that obdurate rock and leaving, as they receded, lakes as numerous and glittering as the stars in the night sky. How the land was still lifting itself up, released from the weight of that continent of ice, rebounding, a living thing unimaginably patient and enduring.

"It's pretty," Dina said. "If you like trees."

"You don't?"

"A city girl. I spent a lot of summers at Camp Wah-kee-shah, though. That's Wah with a soft *a*."

The windows were open, and the wind ruffled her hair, loose strands drumming her cheeks like tanned, restless fingers. Cork thought again what a remarkably pretty woman she was.

"Me and a bunch of kids like me, Jewish mostly, sent to camp to be out of our parents' hair."

"You didn't come away with an appreciation of nature?" he asked.

"Not at all. But I can braid a pretty mean lanyard. You were a Chicago cop for a while. What brought you back here?"

"This is my home."

"A lot of people leave home at the first opportunity and never look back."

"You, for one?"

He waited but she never replied. The wind smelled of pine sap and of the yellow dust the Pathfinder kicked up. The road cut through an open area blanketed with purple fireweed, the first thing to grow after a burn. Ahead of them, the sky filled in the gaps between the trees like blue water. Except for the road, the land felt untouched.

"There are problems in a small town, sure," Cork said. "You can't have a thought without everybody knowing it. If your family doesn't go back a few generations, you can spend your whole life here and still feel like an outsider. The nearest foreign film is five hours away. And yeah, the kids leave as soon as they can, go to college, into the service, whatever. But a lot of them come back eventually. Why? It's a good place to raise a family, a good place for kids to grow up."

"And that's important?"

"Are you married?"

"I was. At the moment, no."

"Any kids?"

"Just little old me."

"It might be tough for you to understand."

Dina was quiet for a bit, then said, "I understand."

They came out on County 33, half a mile south of the North Star Bar. Cork turned onto the asphalt road.

"I'm going to stay with the car," Dina said. "I'd just as soon keep our relationship out of the limelight. Out here anyway."

"Don't want to kill the potential of the push-up bra?"

"Or any of my other tricks," she said.

"Other tricks?"

"Don't ask." It sounded like a wisecrack, but she didn't smile. "If Lizzie's there, let me know. Maybe I'll come in anyway."

Cork pulled into the dirt lot and parked away from the half dozen vehicles already there, dusty in the morning sunlight. Inside, it felt like a dark cave. Johnny Cash was on the jukebox. Cork didn't see Lizzie Fineday or her father. Leonard Trueur was tending bar. He was a heavy man, slow, with fat hands and fingers, a shuffle for a walk. It was still early in the day and the bar wasn't crowded. A couple of Shinnobs Cork didn't recognize sat at a table under an old neon sign that said *Hamm's*. They weren't talking. Maybe they fell silent when Cork came in, but they also had the look of men who didn't say much anyway. Three others played pool in the corner, ball caps shading their faces. They glanced at Cork. He knew them. They went on with their game.

"*Boozhoo*, Leonard," Cork said, stepping up to the bar.

Leonard wiped the bar, a needless thing because at the moment no one sat there. In fact, the rag looked more in need of a good cleaning than the bar top.

"I'm looking for Will."

Leonard watched his fat hand moving the dirty rag and shrugged.

"Is he around?"

"Nope."

"Where is he?"

"Dunno."

"Lizzie here?"

"Dunno."

"Think I'll go up and knock," Cork said.

Leonard didn't offer an objection, and Cork headed toward a door to the left of the bar that opened onto a steep stairway leading to the second story. At the top of the stairs was a small landing and another door, this one closed. Behind it were the rooms where Will Fineday lived with his daughter. Cork knocked, put his ear to the wood, knocked once more, very hard. Finally he turned away and went back down.

The music had stopped. The men under the Hamm's sign hadn't moved. At the pool table, two men held their cues while the third hunched and lined up a shot.

"You guys seen Will or Lizzie?" Cork asked.

"Ain't seen shit, cousin," said Dennis Finn, the one bent over the green felt.

"How about Moose LaRusse?"

"The Moose? Thought you had him doing a stretch in Stillwater."

"He was here yesterday."

"News to me, cousin."

Cork looked to the other men, but no one met his gaze.

"*Migwech,*" Cork said to Leonard, who was still working the rag over the bar. *Thanks.* He walked back out into the sun.

He stood with his back to the bar, thinking. A couple of crows hopped around the Dumpster at the side of the building, looking for a way to an easy meal. A moment later, the door behind him opened, and Ernie Champoux, one of the men at the pool table, stepped out. He lit a cigarette, blew the smoke into the windless air. Champoux was a hard man, but his dealings with Cork had always been reasonable.

"Stone," Champoux said. Then he said, "Moose, him I ain't seen."

That was all. He went back inside.

Cork walked to his vehicle and got in.

"Lizzie not there?" Dina said.

"No."

"You find out where?"

"Maybe." Cork started the car and pulled away from the bar. "We're going to see Stone."

They drove awhile before Dina asked, "Why are you doing this?"

"Doing what?"

"An investigation on the reservation."

"I do most of the law enforcement work on the rez myself."

"Why?"

"My grandmother was true-blood Iron Lake Ojibwe. Things tend to go a little smoother because of that."

"What I mean is, I thought reservations were under federal jurisdiction."

He explained about Public Law 280.

"Lucky they have a sheriff who's part Ojibwe."

"Not everybody thinks it's such a good idea."

He turned north onto County Road 17.

"This Stone," Dina said. "What's he like?"

"Smart like a wolf. Balls of a grizzly bear."

"I don't know about bear balls. Is that good?"

"He's stripped himself of most everything you think of as common goodness. A lot of men like him are just plain stupid, and they're also afraid, which limits their impact. Stone's sharp, and if there's something he's afraid of, I don't know what it is. On the rez, there's the legitimate authority, the tribal council. If you want something that's less than legitimate, Stone is who you go to."

"I like a man who's a challenge."

"This guy's a land mine."

"As in 'Watch your step'?"

"Exactly."

"What about the noble red man?"

"Stone's real father was a decent guy. A Shinnob poet, actually. Got himself killed in a car accident on his way back from the Twin Cities when Stone was just learning to walk. His mother remarried, a white man named Chester Dorset, owned a string of Dairy Queens, had money. He was also a drunk, a brutal drunk, and I mean to tell you, Stone had it tough as a kid. One night, Dorset's loaded, lays into Stone's mother. Stone splits his stepfather's head with an ax."

"Sounds justified to me."

"Problem was, he waited to do it until his step-father had gone to sleep. He was sixteen and certified to stand trial as an adult. Convicted of manslaughter one. Got eighty-six months and served every day of it in the prison at St. Cloud. That's where he got his name: Stone. His real name is Byron St. Onge, but his papers got screwed up. Somehow they dropped the *g* from his name and missed the period after Saint. He went in as Byron Stone instead of St. Onge. Stone stuck." Cork swerved to avoid hitting a red squirrel that scampered across the road. "While he was in prison, his mother died, destitute, because Chester Dorset's kids from his first marriage got all his money. Stone's had a clean record since he got out of prison, but I'm certain he's been involved in an enormous amount of illegal activity. Smuggling for sure. Drugs, arms, cigarettes."

"Cigarettes?"

"Back in the nineties. The Canadian tax on ciga-rettes was high and Canucks were paying through the nose for a smoke. They could buy smuggled cigarettes for a song. A lot of evidence suggested the tobacco companies were complicit in the smuggling. I worked with ATF for months trying to get something on Stone. Nothing. Same with DEA and Customs. Stone was way too smart to get himself caught. Knows the woods along the border better than any man I can think of. And he intimidates the hell out of anyone who might be inclined to testify against him."

They'd been driving half an hour and were

approaching the northern edge of the Iron Lake Reservation where it butted against the Boundary Waters Canoe Area Wilderness. Cork turned off onto a road that was barely wide enough for the Pathfinder. A few hundred yards farther, the road skirted a long narrow lake that ended at the base of a ridge covered with jack pine. A ragged thread of wood smoke climbed the face of the ridge.

"Stone built his cabin himself, where he could see anyone approaching from a good distance away," Cork said. "The land on either side is mostly marsh, so it's almost impossible to come at it on foot. And directly beyond that ridge is the Boundary Waters. He's got himself a decent stronghold."

"Boundary Waters?"

"The Boundary Waters Canoe Area Wilderness. Over a million acres of forest along the Canadian border. On the other side is the Quetico, another wilderness just as large. Easy place for a man to lose himself, on purpose or not."

Cork pulled into the clearing where Stone's cabin stood, and he saw Will Fineday's old Dodge pickup parked behind Stone's new Land Rover. Both vehicles were covered with a thick coat of red dust.

The two men faced each other in the open in front of the cabin. Fineday gripped a tire iron in his huge hands. Stone, shirtless, held an ax. Fineday didn't look when Cork pulled up, but Stone's dark eyes flicked away for an instant.

Stone was smaller, but where Fineday had gone to fat, Stone was smooth rock under taut flesh. He wore his hair long, tied back with a folded red bandanna that ran across his forehead. He was handsome, and there was a certainty in his face, particularly his eyes, that most men found intimidating and women, Cork had heard, found exciting.

Near Stone was a flat-topped stump that he used as a chopping block, and around the stump lay sections of split birch waiting to be gathered and stacked. Stone's chest glistened, and the bandanna was stained dark with sweat. It looked as if Fineday had interrupted preparation for a winter supply of wood.

Cork walked to the men slowly.

"Will, Stone, what's going on?"

"None of your business, O'Connor," Fineday said.

"Looks to me like you're both ready to let a little blood, and that *is* my business. This have anything to do with Lizzie?"

Fineday didn't answer, but he said to Stone, "Let her go, or I swear I'll kill you."

"You think I'm keeping her here against her will, Will?" Stone laughed at that, the ax held easy in his hands, the split wood on the ground around him like killed things. "Why don't I just call her out here, then, and let's see." He yelled her name over his shoulder.

They all waited. The sun was high and unusually hot. The drone of blackflies, an oddity for so late in the season, filled the quiet. The insects lit on Stone's bare, salty skin and crawled over his hairless chest and shoulders. He seemed not to notice, although blackflies were vicious biting insects, one of the worst scourges of the north country.

"Lizzie," he called again, more harshly this time. "Get your ass out here, girl."

The door opened slowly and Lizzie Fineday stepped out. She wore a bright blue knit sweater and wrinkled khakis. Her hair snaked across her face, wild. She hung back in the shadow of the cabin, smoking a cigarette. She stared at her father, then at Cork, as if she didn't quite understand their presence.

"Lizzie, you come on over here. I'm taking you home," Fineday hollered.

He took a step toward his daughter, but Stone moved to block his way.

"Ask her, Will," Stone said. "Stay right where you are and ask her if she wants to leave."

Fineday gave him a killing look. "Lizzie, you come home with me. You come home now. You hear?"

"You want to go home with him, Lizzie?" Stone asked.

The young woman smoked her cigarette, finally shook her head.

"See?" Stone said to Fineday. "If that's what you needed, you have it. You, too, O'Connor. She's not a minor. She makes up her own mind. She wants to stay, she stays." He finally shifted his gaze from Fineday and spoke to Cork directly. "Unless you have a warrant of some kind, it's my right to ask you to leave."

"Lizzie," Cork called to her, "I'd like you to step out into the sunlight so we can see you clearly. Do you understand?"

She didn't react immediately, but eventually she took a step forward into the light.

"Are you feeling all right?" Cork said.

She carefully drew the hair away from her eyes and nodded slowly.

"You see?" Stone said.

"If you come with us, I promise nobody's going to hurt you."

"Nobody's going to hurt her here," Stone said, then called out, "Lizzie, you want to go with these folks, you go."

She blinked in the bright sunlight but she did not move.

Fineday gripped the tire iron and cocked his arms like a batter in the box. "Stone, you fucking son of a bitch."

"Will Fineday," Cork said, "you've been asked to vacate this man's property. You'll do that or I'll arrest you for trespassing."

"He's got my daughter, goddamn it."

"Your daughter is here of her own volition. You heard her as clear as I did. Let it go, Will. Leave her be."

"Lizzie," he tried one last time, but his daughter turned away and went back into the cabin.

"Come on, Will," Cork said. "You need to leave. We all do."

Fineday stormed to his truck and sped down the narrow lane.

"I'm looking for a way to come back, Stone," Cork said.

"You find it, I'll be here." Stone lifted his ax and went back to chopping wood.

In the Pathfinder, Dina said, "Prison tattoos?"

She was speaking of the designs on Stone's upper arms and chest.

"Yeah," Cork said. "Inked them himself. The feather on each arm recalls the eagle feathers on a warrior's shield. The bear over his heart is because he's Makwa, a member of the bear clan."

"I'm sure I saw a thunderbird, too."

"You did. Bineshii. Thunderbird was one of the six original beings that came out of the sea to live with the Anishinaabeg. Unfortunately, every Shinnob that Bineshii looked at died, so Thunderbird was sent back to the sea."

"A Shinnob-killer. Interesting choice for a tattoo."

"Isn't it?"

Fineday was waiting for them where the road met the county highway. He stood with his legs spread, the long scar that cleaved his sandstone-colored face white as jagged lightning.

"He hurts her, and he's not the only one I'll come after," he said as Cork got out of the Pathfinder.

"At the moment, Will, the law's on his side."

"The white man's law. When did it work for me?"

"What's she running from? What's she afraid of? Help me with that and I can take her away from Stone."

"She's running from nothing."

"She just likes Stone's company, is that it?"

"I'll get her myself."

"He'll be watching for you. And think about this. You try something, it's not only Stone you'll have to deal with, it'll be me as well. Wouldn't you rather have me on your side?"

"Fuck you, *chimook*."

Fineday spun away, climbed into his truck, and slammed the door.

"I'll be around to talk to you again, Will, you can bank on it. In the meantime, stay away from Stone."

Fineday sped off, kicking up a tail of dust and gravel.

"Did he call you a schmuck?"

"*Chi-mook*," Cork said, enunciating each syllable. "Ojibwe slang for white man. Not complimentary."

"But you're part Ojibwe. Doesn't that count?"

"When people are pissed at me, I'm not Ojibwe enough for the Ojibwes, and not white enough for the whites," Cork said.

25

Jo HAD SPENT the day calling clients, judges, re-arranging court dates, appointments. Everyone understood, she told Cork. She'd washed clothes, packed, helped the girls and Stevie get ready to travel. Cork promised to call the high school and Stevie's teacher and explain the children's absence.

Dinner was a subdued affair: ham and cheese sandwiches, Campbell's tomato soup, chips. They talked quietly about Chicago, seeing Rose and Mal, visiting Northwestern and maybe Notre Dame. No one said a word about the dynamite in the Bronco. Afterward, they played a game of Clue. Stevie won, although Cork and probably everyone else knew a couple of turns earlier that it was Mrs. White in the study with the candlestick.

Cork read to Stevie, something he enjoyed doing. The book was *Hatchet,* about a boy lost in the wilderness who uses his own wiles and strength of character to make his way back to safety. Stevie's dark brown Ojibwe eyes locked on the ceiling as he imagined the scenes painted by the words, saw the story playing out in his mind. Eventually, his eyelids began to flicker, and when they'd closed for good, Cork kissed him good night on his forehead and turned out the light.

As he came downstairs, there was a knock at the front door. Cy Borkmann.

"Just wanted to let you know that we'll have someone posted out on the street all night," Cy told him.

"I never authorized that," Cork said.

"Nothing needs authorization. We're all off-duty. Just wanted to make sure everything here is secure until your family's off safe and sound."

Jo came to Cork's side and said, "Thank you, Cy. And please thank the others for us."

He smiled a little shyly. "Sure. Look, you all sleep well, okay?" He tipped his ball cap and lumbered down the front steps toward the curb where his truck was parked.

With Stevie in bed, the girls probed Cork for information on the dynamite and the rez shooting. He wished he could offer them something substantial—anything—but he admitted he had nothing.

It was after ten when he got the call from Simon Rutledge.

"I'm at the sheriff's office in Carlton. I've been down here all day. I think I might have something. My cohort in St. Paul called me, and guess who just happened to visit Lydell Cramer at the hospital yesterday. His sister. It seemed a big coincidence that each of her last visits preceded a threat to your safety, so I decided to reconnoiter her farmhouse. There's a good-sized barn, but there aren't any animals around. I watched a couple of guys go in and out of that barn all day long, one of them always sporting what appeared to be an assault rifle. I did some checking with the police in Moose Lake and found out Lydell's sister lives with a guy name of Harmon LaRusse."

"Son of a bitch."

"Exactly. Turns out the Carlton County Sheriff's Department has a big file on him. On Cramer's sister, too, and the other guy out there whose name is Carl Berger, an ex-con with a pretty long history of drugs and violence. Sheriff's investigators have had them under surveillance for a while, after a neighbor complained he'd been threatened. An IR thermal scan of the barn showed a lot of heat. Which might have been understandable if there'd been livestock inside."

"An indoor marijuana operation."

"Bingo. A big one. That's why I'm at the Carlton County sheriff's office right now. For the last couple of months, they've been putting together everything they need for a good bust. They've been holding off, thinking they might be able to intercept a sale. When I explained my concern about a possible connection with your incident on the rez, they agreed to go ahead ASAP. They're hoping for a no-knock first thing in the morning, if you'd care to be here."

"Got a go time yet?"

"Not until they're sure they've secured the warrant. Want me to call?"

"Yeah. Thanks, Simon. Good work."

"That's why I get the big bucks."

Cork hung up and turned to find Jo watching him. "What's up?"

He told her.

"You think this woman and Moose LaRusse might be responsible for the shooting and the bomb?"

"It's certainly a possibility we can't ignore."

"Oh God, I hope it's them and that you get them."

"I still want you away from here until we're sure. Besides, the girls are looking forward to visiting college campuses."

She put her arms around him, pressed her cheek to his chest. "I hate leaving, thinking you might still be in danger."

"I'll be fine. I *am* fine."

He locked the doors, checked the windows, turned out the downstairs lights, and briefly moved aside a curtain. Out front, Cy Borkmann sat in his truck drinking coffee from his big silver thermos. Upstairs, Cork looked in on his daughters, who were in their rooms, in bed but not yet asleep. He talked with each of them awhile, kissed them good night, then went to his own room, where quietly and rather gently he and Jo made love. For a long time after that, he lay with his wife in his arms. They'd never finished their talk about her past with Ben Jacoby, but at the moment it didn't matter. Cork knew that despite every threatening thing, past and present, he was the luckiest man on earth.

26

IN THE EARLY morning shortly before sunrise, Jo drove toward a blood-red streak of sky, carrying away in her Camry everything that was most important to Cork.

After they'd gone, he approached Howard Morgan's Explorer, parked at the curb where Borkmann's truck had been the night before.

Morgan stepped out and stretched. "So they're off," he said.

"Thanks, Howard."

"No problem. Good to see them go. Safer, I mean."

"I know what you mean. Be glad to fix you some breakfast."

"Thanks, but I've been thinking for the last couple hours about a stack of blueberry pancakes at the Broiler. Then I got a bed that's calling my name."

Cork went back inside, pulled down a bowl from the cupboard, shook in some raisin bran. He was just about to pour in some milk when Rutledge called.

They waited in an oak grove a quarter mile north of the farmhouse. Four cruisers, an unmarked Suburban, twelve deputies, two DEA agents, Undersheriff Jeff McGruder, and Sheriff Roy Killen. Cork and Rutledge were there, too. The sheriff's people wore midnight blue Kevlar vests and camouflage outfits. A couple of the deputies smoked. They all watched the sheriff as he held the field glasses level on the farmhouse. They should have gone in before this—they all knew it—but Killen had decided to wait. The problem was the mist.

The farmhouse was an old white structure with paint flaking off in leprous patches, a sagging front porch, and a satellite dish on the roof. Across the yard stood the barn, in far better shape than the house and painted a new dark red. Cork had been told that there were empty animal pens, but he couldn't see them because of the mist.

The buildings stood a quarter mile off the road, in a field long fallow, full of thistle and timothy gone yellow in the dry of late autumn. The mist did not quite touch the ground and reached only a couple of dozen feet into the air, so that everything about the scene seemed to exist in colored layers. Far away were the yellow grass, the gray mist, the blue sky. Nearer, the russet oak leaves, the midnight blue vests, the camouflage outfits. Enclosing it all was the waiting.

Killen didn't like the idea of going in with the mist still thick. He couldn't see the farmhouse yard at all. Someone looking out a second-floor window could spot the cruisers coming and take up a hidden position in the yard. He didn't want to risk his people. Better, he'd decided, to let the mist burn off. So they waited.

Traffic picked up on the rural highway that ran past the oak grove, many of the cars heading to a small white church built among Norway pines just visible in the distance. Around the church, the mist had already vanished, but it still hung thick over the fields and the farmhouse and the red barn.

After a while, Killen spoke to McGruder and the two DEA agents, then approached Cork and Rutledge.

Killen was near sixty, with freckles across his forehead and age spots on the back of his hands, retirement not many years away. "I don't know what it is with this fog but we wait much longer and the whole damn world's going to know we're here," he said. "We're going in. You two stay back. This is our business."

He went to his deputies, who'd stopped talking and had thrown down their cigarettes when they heard what Killen had said to Cork and Rutledge.

"All right, let's do it. Just like we talked about, boys. Quick and simple. Everybody do their job."

They moved to the cruisers, and as the doors shut, popping like muted gunfire, Cork heard the bell in the little church steeple to the north begin to ring, clear notes that carried far in the morning air.

An unmarked Suburban went first. It stopped at the chained gate that blocked the access to the farmhouse. A deputy leaped out, split the chain with a bolt cutter, swung the gate wide. A couple of seconds later the cruisers sped through, hauling ass down the dirt lane, disappearing into the gray mist.

The dogs had already given the bust away. They began to bark as soon as the cruisers turned off the highway. Cork and Rutledge, staying far back on the lane as they'd been instructed, heard the dogs going crazy as the mist ate the cars. A few moments later, gunfire erupted. From the rapid crack of the first weapon, Cork knew it was a heavy automatic of some kind. Shotgun blasts boomed from a second-floor window, something Cork and Rutledge could see above the top of the mist, and immediately the boards around the window frame exploded in chips and splinters as the deputies returned fire.

Rutledge drew his sidearm. "I can't just stand here and do nothing."

"If you're thinking of going into that mist, Simon, I've got to tell you it's a bad idea. Way too confusing. Your Glock'll be no good at a distance, anyway."

"I have to do something," Rutledge said. He swung out of the vehicle and ran.

Cork jumped out, too, calling after him, "Simon!" but the BCA agent had already vanished into the mist. "Shit," he said. He popped the tailgate open and pulled his Remington from its cradle. He grabbed several slugs, jacked five into the chamber, stuffed a few more into the pocket of his windbreaker. He stood by the Pathfinder, resisting the temptation to move forward, although every impulse pushed him in that direction. He waited, as Killen had told him to do, while the gunfire became sporadic and the sound of the automatic weapon ceased.

The mist had begun to lift, ragged white fingers reaching toward the sky, then evaporating. The long grass of the fields became clearer by the moment. Cork glimpsed a slender figure sprinting from the farmhouse, a figure with long, dark hair, wearing a yellow sweatshirt, carrying a rifle, and making hard for the south end of the field.

He got on the radio, tried to raise Killen or McGruder, got no answer. He left the Pathfinder and gave chase.

The mist was spotty, heavy in some places, almost gone in others. The long grass was still wet with dew and slapped at the cuffs of his khakis. He cut at an angle he calculated would bring him to the fleeing figure somewhere near the fence at the end of the field. Behind him, the gunfire had ceased completely.

Barbed wire edged the field. When Cork reached the fence, he saw that the figure had stopped. The rifle lay against the wire as the figure bent and spread the strands to slip through. Thirty yards back, Cork went prone in the tall grass, put the stock of his shotgun to his shoulder, and sighted. The mist still lingered between Cork and the fence, but the yellow sweatshirt made an easy target.

"Police," Cork shouted. "Raise your hands."

The figure let go of the strands, surprised. A hand shot toward the rifle.

Cork hollered, "Don't touch the weapon."

The figure ignored him, swung back, and pulled off a round that went high and wide.

"O'Connor," Rutledge shouted from somewhere behind Cork.

The figure at the fence corrected its aim, pointed the barrel above the place where Cork lay, and sighted toward Rutledge's voice.

Cork fired. The figure took half a step back into the fence, then crumpled to the ground, leaving an arm snagged on the wire, raised as if in surrender.

Lydell Cramer's sister and Harmon LaRusse were killed in the exchange of gunfire at the farmhouse. The dogs, too. The man in the mist whom Cork had shot, Carl Berger, was taken to the hospital in Moose Lake, where he was listed in serious condition and in no shape to be questioned. Rutledge had no doubt that these people were involved in the rez shooting because, in addition to the marijuana operation in the barn and nearly a kilo of cocaine and a sizable stash of crystal meth in one of the farmhouse bedrooms, the sheriff's people found a cache of weapons that included a Savage 110GXP3 fitted with a Leupold scope. Rutledge sent the firearm to the BCA for a ballistics comparison.

It was going on two o'clock when Cork rolled into his parking space at the Tamarack County Sheriff's Department in Aurora. A little more than eight hours had passed since he'd said good-bye to Jo and the children, but it felt like days. He was bone tired, and the relief that came with finding the rifle that had probably been used in the shooting at the Tibodeau cabin was tempered by the memory of two bodies lying together in the front hallway of the farmhouse in a pool of their mixed blood. They'd made the choices that had brought them to that end, but always in the stillness after violent killing there was a hollowness inside Cork that held no sense of victory or justice or right, only the empty absolute of death.

Ed Larson joined him in his office, along with Dina Willner. The windows were open to a quiet Sunday afternoon. A slight breeze out of the southwest kept the skies fair and the temperature pleasant. Beyond the little park that Cork could see through his window, the bell tower of Zion Lutheran was etched like a white tattoo against the body of the town.

"When will we know for sure?" Larson asked.

"Simon said he'd pull strings to get the ballistics done ASAP, so maybe tomorrow or the next day." Cork sat forward, rubbed his lower back. He opened the top right drawer of his desk, pulled out a bottle of ibuprofen, and tapped out four tablets.

"Let me get you some water for that," Dina said. She went out and came back with a paper cup filled from the cooler in the common area.

"Thanks." Cork popped the tablets in his mouth and swallowed them down with the cold water.

"Headache?" Larson asked.

"Back," Cork said. "Wrenched it when I dropped to a firing position out there in the field."

Larson glanced at Dina. "We might have something that'll make you feel better. Something on the Jacoby killing."

"Yeah? What?"

"Tell him your part first, Dina."

Willner wore a tight black sweater and formfitting black jeans that Cork figured she had to grease herself down to slide into. She looked good and fresh, as if she'd had plenty of sleep, something Cork envied.

"I went to the North Star Bar last night," she began.

"Another session with the push-up bra?" Cork broke in.

She ignored him. "I talked with a dumpy guy behind the bar, name was Leonard. He told me that on the night Jacoby was murdered, Lizzie Fineday was out but came back in around midnight beat up bad. Her father took her upstairs, then came down a short time later and went out, moving like a man on a mission. He wasn't back for closing, so Leonard had to do it by himself, which he says is unusual. Fineday always insists on closing."

"You got all this with a push-up bra? I may have to start wearing one."

Larson piped in. "I finally caught up with the night clerk at the Four Seasons. He told me that around eight or nine on the evening Jacoby was killed, Lizzie Fineday came into the hotel looking for him. He wasn't there, so she left a note."

"He didn't happen to see what the note said?"

"No such luck. But Jacoby comes in around eleven, gets the note, heads right back out."

"Think it's enough to bring her in?"

"It's thin," Larson said. "Especially since we'll have to go through Stone to get to her. But that's not all."

He nodded to Willner, who brought from her purse a little Baggie containing several cigarette butts.

"I did some Dumpster diving late last night," she said. "When I was in the bar the other night, I'd noticed that Lizzie chain-smokes. In the Dumpster, I found a bag of trash that had some mail with her name on it, and these cigarette butts. Doesn't absolutely mean they're Lizzie's, but her father doesn't smoke, and even if he did I doubt he'd be wearing lipstick, so it's a good bet they're hers. We're sending one of these and one of the hair samples taken from Jacoby's SUV for a DNA match."

"That'll take time."

Dina shook her head. "We're not sending it to your BCA lab. We're using a private lab in Chicago. Flying it out this afternoon. We can have the comparison in forty-eight hours."

Cork looked at Larson. "You okay with this, Ed?"

"It might not stand up in court, but if it is a match, it'll give us plenty for a probable cause pickup and hold. It'll get us past Stone."

"Lou Jacoby'll foot the bill?"

"Of course. And he's supplying the transport.

Tony's already in the air on his way here. ETA in about an hour."

"Jacoby's private jet? We'll have to get down to Duluth for that."

Dina shook her head. "He's going to land at the local landing strip."

"The jet?"

"A small plane."

"All right," Cork said. Then to Larson: "You ever connect with Arlo Knuth?"

"Not yet. Every briefing I ask the watch to keep their eyes peeled for him, check all the usual places. Nothing so far."

"You know Arlo. He can make himself scarce when he wants to."

"But why would he want to? That's what I'm wondering."

"You don't really think he had anything to do with Jacoby's murder, do you?"

"No, but I'm thinking he might have seen something that scared him into hiding. I'd like to know what."

"Stay on it."

"You know I will."

With the cigarette butt and the hair sample in an evidence envelope that had been sealed and signed by Ed Larson, Cork drove Dina toward the county airfield, which was located in the little community of Flax on Lake Margery, three miles south of Aurora.

Flax consisted of a few private cabins, a combination restaurant and gift store called the Cozy Caribou Café, and a small gas station with a garage and mechanic, all situated within hailing distance of the lake and the airstrip. Cork parked near the café, and they got out and wandered toward the airfield. It was a simple affair, a single landing strip, a small control tower, several corrugated buildings that housed the local planes. The sky was blue and almost cloudless— a perfect sky for flying, Cork thought.

"So, you think Lizzie Fineday was with Eddie at Mercy Falls?" Dina said.

"Sure looks that way."

"Do you think she killed him?"

"If she was doped up and freaked out, I suppose I could see it."

"Know what I think? It was her old man. He went ballistic when he saw what Eddie had done, went to Mercy Falls, and killed him."

"Couple of things about that bother me. Why did Eddie hang around Mercy Falls after she left? And why didn't he put up a fight?" He gave a single shake of his head. "I'm laying odds it was someone who surprised him, someone he didn't expect, or at least didn't expect to have a knife."

"So you're back to Lizzie."

"Not necessarily. I think there was someone else out there, someone with a colder heart than Lizzie has. I just don't know who or why yet."

Dina checked her watch just as the drone of an engine came out of the sky to the southeast. "Right on time."

A plane appeared above the treetops, circled, and made its approach from the north. It touched down, and as it rolled off the runway onto an apron near Cork and Dina, the prop ceased to spin and the engine fell silent. Tony Salguero stepped out. "Sheriff O'Connor. Dina. I hope I haven't kept you waiting. You have the freight?" he asked.

"Here." Cork handed over the sealed envelope. He looked at the plane while Salguero signed the receipt. "The Jacobys own a fleet?"

"The jet is Lou's," Salguero said. "This baby is all mine. I built her myself."

"How's Lou doing?" Dina asked.

Salguero inspected the envelope. "We buried his favorite child this morning, but you know Lou. A mule could kick him and he wouldn't grunt. He simply takes it out on everyone around him." Tony looked toward the Cozy Caribou Café. "I need something to eat before I head back. How is the food here?"

"Reasonably priced and mostly deep-fried," Cork said.

"Perfect." Salguero began long strides in that direction.

They sat on the deck in the cool air of early October, the only ones outside. The waitress was reluctant to seat them there, but Salguero insisted.

"I have been cooped up for hours," he explained with a stunning smile and Spanish accent.

Cork never drank on duty, but he decided that, having handed off the evidence envelope, he was done for the day. He ordered a beer. So did Dina.

"A hamburger, bloody," Salguero told the waitress.

"We don't serve them rare anymore. Health reasons."

Tony closed the menu and held it out. "I will sign an agreement. If I get poisoned, it's my own fault." The waitress didn't take the menu or put anything down on her pad. Salguero finally tossed his hands up. "All right, cook it any way you please, just make sure the beer is cold."

"Beer?" Cork said. He looked toward the plane Salguero had to fly back to Chicago. "Should you be drinking?"

"I have flown hundreds of thousands of miles, Sheriff, without a single incident. But tell you what. If I crash I will make certain it is into an empty field." He smiled pleasantly.

"Have you flown long?"

"My father had his own planes. He flew himself everywhere, to the pampas, the rain forest, wherever he had investments. From the time I was a young boy, I dreamed of flying."

"The pampas?"

"I am from Argentina. Buenos Aires."

Cork said, "How long have you worked for the Jacobys?"

"Five years. But I've known them most of my life. My father and Lou Jacoby are old friends."

"So you know them well?"

Salguero grinned, showing beautiful white teeth. "What do you want to know?"

"Everybody keeps referring to Eddie as Lou's favorite child. Near as I can figure, he was mostly a son of a bitch."

"No, Sheriff. He was a bastard. Born out of wedlock. That is no secret. But I also think he was born out of love. Eddie's mother was the true treasure of Lou's life, and I think that when he looked at their son, what he really saw was Eddie's mother. Would you not agree?" he said to Dina.

She shrugged. "That's one explanation. I'm more inclined toward the sick-puppy theory myself."

"What's that?" Cork said.

"Lou's other children have done just fine in their

lives, become responsible adults. If Lou died tomorrow, they'd probably grieve but they'd be fine. Eddie was like a sick puppy, always needing Lou. But I think in his way Lou needed Eddie just as bad. Maybe, in fact, that's why Eddie never really grew up, never learned how to be a responsible man. Lou never gave him the chance to be one."

The waitress delivered the beers.

"I think I will have that burger to go," Tony said. "And do you have a men's room?"

"Inside."

Salguero followed her in.

Dina sipped her beer. "This is good."

"Leinenkugel's. Local favorite." He took a swallow from his bottle and looked where Salguero had gone. "So. Argentina. A story there?"

"Tony's family had money," Dina replied. "When the Argentine economy collapsed, they lost it all. Pretty simple."

Salguero returned just as the burger was delivered in a paper sack, along with a tab for the food and the beers. He threw money on the table.

"Your beer is on Lou," he said. Then to the waitress: "Sorry if I gave you a hard time, miss. I have a long trip still ahead of me."

She smiled into his handsome face. "You were no problem at all."

He picked up the evidence envelope and the burger sack and started toward his plane.

"Need to gas up?" Cork asked.

"There is an airport in Wisconsin midway that I use for that purpose." He opened the plane door, tossed the envelope and the sack inside, then looked back at Cork. "I don't know what it is that I'm taking back, but I hope it helps to find the person who killed Eddie."

"I'm sure it will."

Cork stepped away as the engine kicked over and the prop began to spin. Salguero swung the plane around and took off into the wind. He circled back, tilting his wings in salute as he flew over.

Cork said, "Lost a fortune and now he flies for the Jacobys. He seems to take it well."

"Doesn't he," Dina said, watching as the plane disappeared into the southeast.

27

HE DROPPED DINA at her car in the Sheriff's Department lot, then went home.

He couldn't remember the last time the house had been so empty. The air felt close, smelled stale, and he realized that he'd left without opening the curtains or lifting the windows. He spent a few minutes going through the rooms doing just that. On the desk in Jo's office, he found notes she'd scribbled to herself as she'd scrambled to rearrange her schedule. He sat in her chair and felt the slight indentation that over time she'd left in the cushion, and he thought how small her hips were and how good they felt pressed against him in bed. On the floor in Stevie's room lay a sheet of paper, crayons, and a pair of scissors. Stevie had drawn a crude face on the paper and colored it green. For Halloween, he wanted to be the Hulk and he'd been trying to make a mask, but his work had been interrupted. In the living room, lying open on an end table next to the sofa, was a book Jenny had been reading, *The Beet Queen,* her place marked with a tarot card that held the image of a skeleton. In the kitchen, as he passed Annie's softball glove hanging on a hook by the back door, he leaned to it and breathed in the smell of oiled leather. His family had been gone less than a day, but they'd left behind silence and a deep, painful loneliness that Cork was glad he would not have to endure for long. Every man's life ought to be about something, he believed, and he was comfortable with the knowledge that his was about family.

But so was Lou Jacoby's, apparently, a man Cork didn't admire in the least and with whom he felt he had little in common.

He didn't know what to do with that, so he let it go. He was exhausted, hungry, and couldn't get out of his mind the image of Carl Berger's right arm hung up on barbed wire. He went upstairs to shower, hoping it might refresh him a little. He thought that afterward he would go to the Broiler for dinner.

Half an hour later, as he was coming downstairs, the doorbell rang. When he opened the door, he found Dina Willner standing on his front porch, a grocery bag in one hand and a twelve-pack of Leinenkugel's in the other.

"I figured after the kind of day you've had, you might need a little company," she said. "So I brought dinner. Hope you like New York strip."

Cork's surprise probably showed on his face. "I don't know, Dina."

"Look, you just relax." She squeezed past him into the house. "I'll do the cooking. Just show me to the kitchen."

She twisted the caps off two beers, handed a bottle to Cork, and drank the other as she worked. She started charcoal going in the backyard grill and wrapped garlic bread in foil so she could heat it over the coals while she grilled the steaks. Then she began to prepare a salad of assorted greens, red onion, and avocado. She talked the whole while, pleasantly.

"People around here think a lot of your family." She took a long draw on her beer and tore up lettuce. "They tell me your father was the youngest sheriff ever elected in Tamarack County. That true?" She glanced at him, her brows lifted questioningly above her attractive green eyes.

"True," he said.

"I also heard that the hands on the clock tower of your county courthouse have been stopped for thirty-five years, frozen at the moment of his death. Is that true, too?"

"More or less." He told her the story. The escapees from Stillwater, the shoot-out in front of the bank during which his father stepped between a bullet and an innocent bystander. How the clock was hit about the same time by an errant round and the hands had never moved since. How the town viewed it as a kind of memorial to his father's selfless act.

"Board of Commissioners periodically discusses getting the clock fixed, but they never do anything. They say it's out of respect. I think they just don't want to spend the money."

"I think it's a wonderful tribute." Over her shoulder, she threw him a lovely smile.

The steaks sizzled when she laid them on the hot grill, and the good smell made Cork's mouth water. He realized how hungry he was, and how happy that Dina had come.

It was dark outside by the time they sat down at the kitchen table to eat. The steak was excellent: rare, tender, juicy. She'd dressed the salad with her own balsamic-vinegar-and-oil preparation that tasted of garlic, lemon, and pepper. It was accompanied by the garlic bread and more beer.

"How are you feeling now?" she asked.

"Better. Thanks."

She eyed him as she lifted her beer bottle to her lips. "Mind if I ask you a question? About this morning?"

He paused in cutting his steak. "All right."

"A shooting, that's a hard thing, I know. Still, I find it interesting that you didn't kill Carl Berger."

"It was a lousy shot."

"Is that so? With a rifle at thirty yards? People around here seem to think you're an excellent shot. Been hunting all your life." She put her hands on the table and almost imperceptibly leaned toward him, narrowing the distance between them. "I've been wondering if you really meant to kill him."

"Of course I meant to kill him. You never shoot unless you mean to kill. He was drawing a bead on Rutledge."

"You've killed two men. People here talk about that. Respectfully. Men, I gather, who were better off dead. I'm guessing it wasn't easy, but you did it. So I'm wondering what was different about this shooting."

"I'd rather not talk about it."

"I managed to get a copy of your statement, and I've gone over it. Stay with me for just a minute. The mist. A figure not clear to you. Panicked, afraid, finally cornered. A slender figure with long, dark hair. I think you might have been wondering if it was Lydell Cramer's sister, a woman you were about to shoot. Could that have made a difference?"

"It shouldn't have mattered."

"But it did." She reached across the table and laid her hand against his cheek. "It did, didn't it?"

"Like I said, I'd rather not think about it."

"I understand." She pulled her hand back slowly. "How about another beer?"

After dinner, they sat in the quiet of the living room. It was late—later than Cork had imagined he'd be up. He was tired, what with the beer and the weight of all that had occurred that day. He wanted to be alone, and at the same time he didn't.

"How's your back?" Dina asked. "You said you wrenched it this morning during the raid."

"Stiff. Hurts. A lot of it's probably stress."

"I can help that." She put her beer on the end table and moved toward the easy chair where Cork sat. "Lie down on the floor. Come on. I won't hurt you, I promise. That's right. On your stomach." She took her shoes off. "Now, close your eyes."

The next thing Cork knew, she'd stepped onto his back. She was surprisingly light or knew exactly how to distribute her weight, because she was anything but oppressive. With her toes and the balls of her feet, she started to knead his muscles, beginning with the small of his back.

"Oh my God. Where did you learn that?"

"Picked it up along the way."

"You know, this could be very effective in getting suspects to cooperate."

"There's something I'd like to tell you."

"Go ahead. I'll try to listen, but this is distracting."

"I was wrong about you."

"How?"

"I've worked with a lot of rural law officers. More often than not they're pigheaded, defensive, and incompetent."

"I hope I'm only pigheaded."

"I don't work well with just anyone, but I feel like we're working well together."

"That's interesting. I'm not sure I feel the same way."

He could sense her reaction in the momentary pause of her feet.

"What do you mean?" she asked.

"I can't help thinking that there are things about Eddie Jacoby you know but aren't telling."

"I can't. Client confidentiality."

"His? Or his family's?"

She didn't reply.

"Would you tell me if I wore a push-up bra?"

She laughed. "There is one thing I'll tell you about Eddie that might give you an additional glimpse of the man. When he was twenty-five, he received the distribution from a trust fund his grandfather had set up for him. Several million. Eddie always wanted to be a hotshot movie producer, so he invested in a production company in California, proudly told everyone he was in the movie business. You know what kind of movies he was making? The kind that show pretty young girls doing pretty ugly things. And he was proud of that. His partners ended up taking him, stole most of the fortune, though legally. His father refused to bail him out of that one. But he still has business cards with his Hollywood logo, and I know he doles them out and when he hits on women he uses some line about making them a star."

"Do they ever buy it?"

"I'm thinking Lizzie Fineday might have. I can't imagine any other reason she'd be with Eddie."

"Anything else you'd care to share?"

"I'm helping you all I can, trust me."

She stepped off him. He couldn't move, didn't want to.

"Better?"

Slowly he rolled over and looked up at her. She seemed taller from that perspective, even prettier, if that were possible. He did want to trust her, and felt himself inclined. But he also knew his thinking was being filtered through exhaustion and alcohol. And he couldn't forget the fact that, in the end, Dina worked for the Jacobys.

"I think it's good night now," he said.

"Don't get up. I'll see myself out."

While she put on her shoes, he gradually pulled himself off the floor and followed her to the door.

"We're closing in on the end, Cork," she said in the doorway. "Coming toward the home stretch. Once we bring Lizzie in, I think it will be over, one way or another."

She hesitated a long moment before heading into the night, as if there was something more she wanted to do or to say. Whatever it was, she thought better of it, and the last moment of their evening together was left empty. She went down the porch steps and walked through the light of the street lamp to her car.

He flipped the dead bolt, checked the other doors and windows, began turning out the lights, thinking all the while that if he loved Jo so much, why did he feel a small disappointment in the emptiness of that last moment with Dina.

He headed toward the stairs, but before he took the

first step, the telephone rang. It was almost eleven o'clock. It was either the office or Jo, he figured.

"O'Connor," he said into the phone.

"You think it's over?" the voice at the other end said. "Think again. You're dead, O'Connor. You're so dead."

28

*I*T WAS THE quiet that woke her. That and Stevie's elbow burrowing into her hip. The elbow didn't surprise her: her son was a restless sleeper. But the quiet was an odd thing. Not quiet exactly because there were the usual city noises. Traffic early and heavy on Green Bay Road two blocks east, the rattle of suspension, the screech of brakes, the warning beeper on a truck backing up, probably collecting garbage. Like Stevie's elbow, these were expected things. What was unexpected was the silence of the birds. Spring, summer, and fall in Aurora, the birds began their songs and arguments long before dawn. Jo had grown so used to their chirp and chatter that she didn't even notice anymore. Except when it was missing. In Evanston, Illinois, that morning there seemed to be no birds at all.

It was the West Nile virus. Rose had told her the night before how the mosquito-borne disease had devastated the avian population all along the north shore of Lake Michigan, leaving birds on the ground under trees like fallen, rotting fruit. It was an awful image to spring to mind first thing in the morning, and the silence in the wake of all that death was disturbing.

She hadn't slept well, and not just because of Stevie's restless jerking. She missed Cork. She was relieved when he'd called the evening before and told her about the raid on the farmhouse in Carlton County, relieved that it ended the danger to him. She wanted so much to be with him then, to hold him. But he was safe, and that was the important thing.

Her nose lifted at the smell of coffee brewing, and she pulled back the covers and slipped from the bed, careful not to wake her small son. She threw on her robe and left the guest room of her sister's home. Rose lived with her husband, Mal, in the upper level of a duplex in a nice neighborhood at the north end of Evanston. The building was long and narrow, what Rose called a railroad car design. In front was the living room, connected by a long hallway to the kitchen in back. Off the hallway on either side were the bedrooms and the bath. Jo found Rose in the kitchen rolling dough on a cutting board while coffee trickled into a pot on the counter.

"Cinnamon rolls," Jo said. "The kids will love you. They've missed your cooking."

"And I miss their appetites. Mal appreciates my cooking, but eating's never been that important to him. All those years of self-denial, I suppose. Coffee's just about ready. Want some?"

"I'll get it," Jo said.

"Sit down, relax. This is my kitchen," she said proudly. She wiped her hands on her apron and went to the cupboard.

Jo watched her sister with amazement and pleasure. There was so much different about Rose now.

She'd been plain and heavy all her life, but in the past few months she'd dropped weight, and a lovely color flushed her cheeks. There was a lively snap to all her movements, a joyous energy. This, Jo suspected, was due to love.

"Mal likes his job?"

"It's perfect. Basically the same thing he did before he came to Aurora, but he doesn't have to be celibate now." She laughed sweetly.

For seventeen years, Rose had lived with the O'Connors, most of that time in a cozy attic room, taking care of the household while Jo and Cork both worked the law from different angles. Near the end, Mal Thorne had come to Aurora. Father Mal Thorne, then. For nearly two years, he'd served the parish of St. Agnes. During that time, he began to question significantly his commitment to the Church, and in the fertile ground of that doubt, his love for Rose had grown until he could not deny it. She'd felt the same. Yet, it had taken the actions of a madman to put her into Mal's willing arms and to convince him it was time to divest himself of his collar and cassock. They'd been married in a civil ceremony and had moved to Chicago, where Mal, as a priest, had once headed a homeless shelter run by the Chicago Archdiocese. He did the same now for a publicly funded shelter.

As Rose turned to bring the coffeepot to the table, Mal walked into the kitchen in his drawstring pajamas. He was medium height. His hair was light brown, thin, and cut close enough to see the tan of his scalp. In his youth, he'd been a champion boxer, middleweight—he still had scar tissue over his left eye and a nose that was crooked from having been broken several times—and carried himself in a way that suggested both power and grace. He smiled often and broadly and did so now.

"Good morning, ladies." He swept Rose into his arms and kissed her lavishly.

Rose held the hot coffeepot at a safe distance. When Mal stepped back, she said, "I was going to offer you coffee to wake up, but I see you don't need it."

"A beautiful day," he said, and opened his arms toward the window and the sunlight beyond. "Family here and Cork out of danger, blessings both. Where are the kids?"

"Sleeping," Jo said. "Even Stevie. It's been hard on them lately. They could use the rest."

"I'm sure." Mal sat down at the table, opposite Jo. "What's the plan for today?"

Jo hid a yawn behind her hand. The coffee was good, but rest would have been better. "I'm thinking that Jenny and I will take a look at Northwestern, since that's one of the reasons we're here."

"Good. Then tomorrow or maybe the next day we might drive to South Bend so Annie can have a look at my alma mater."

"She'd love that, Mal. She talked nothing but Notre Dame the whole way down."

"Is she still hoping for a softball scholarship?"

"She's determined."

Rose, who was forming dough strips into tight spirals for the cinnamon rolls, said, "She's like you. When she sets her mind to something, she makes it happen."

The phone in the hallway rang. Mal got up.

"Sit down, I'll answer it," Rose said.

Mal kept moving. "You'll get the phone all sticky." In the hallway, he answered with a cheery "Good morning." Then: "Yes, she is. Just a moment." He put the receiver to his chest. "For you, Jo."

"Is it Cork?"

"No, but it's a man." He handed her the phone and went back to the kitchen.

It was Ben Jacoby. His voice sounded showered and shaved and sparkling. Jo still had sleep in her eyes.

"Ben? How did you know I was here?"

"Dina Willner."

Dina. The woman working with Cork to solve the murder of Ben's brother. It made sense.

"I'm sorry about the bomb scare, but I understand they got the bastards."

"Yes."

"That's wonderful. Look, I'm sorry to be calling so early. I have some good news. I talked with a friend of mine in the admissions office at Northwestern. If you and Jenny are available today, he can arrange a private tour of the campus."

"Today?" she said.

"Unless you have other plans. I'm sure he'd be willing to schedule anytime. I just wasn't certain how long you'd be staying."

"Today would be fine. Thank you, Ben."

"Also, I was wondering if you might be free for a drink tonight."

"I don't think so."

"A glass of wine and half an hour of your time."

"It's not a good idea, Ben."

"I understand, but . . ." He fell silent, and Jo didn't know if he was gathering himself for another attempt or had given up. "Look, there are things I need to say to you."

She moved into the front room, distant from the kitchen.

"Like what?"

"Give me half an hour."

"You'll have to do better than that."

"I want to tell you why I left."

"That's not important to me now."

"It might be, if you knew. One drink. One glass of wine. One last time. Please."

She considered a long time before replying. "All right."

"I'll pick you up. Seven?"

"Seven is fine, but I'll meet you there."

"Deal."

He gave her the name of a restaurant on Green Bay Road, and he gave her his cell phone number, just in case.

"Ben?" Rose said when Jo came back to the table.

"Jacoby. I told you about him last night. The brother of the man who was killed."

"That's right. Your old law school buddy."

Although they'd shared many confidences, Jo had never told her sister about Ben Jacoby, and as far as Rose and Mal knew, they'd simply been acquainted in law school. At some point, Jo intended to tell Rose the whole story, but not at the moment.

"He's pulled some strings to get Jenny a tour of Northwestern today."

"That's great," Rose said.

"He also asked me out for a drink."

"We'll be glad to watch the children," Mal offered.

"Thanks."

She reached for her coffee. Although she'd put Ben

Jacoby behind her long ago, his sudden departure from her life had been a nagging mystery for twenty years. She cradled her cup in both palms and carefully sipped the strong French roast amid the deep quiet of the dead birds.

29

*T*HEY ALL SAT in Cork's office and for a long time said nothing, just drank the good coffee Dina Willner had brought, and sifted through their own, silent thoughts.

"We won't know for a while if the rifle we found at the farmhouse is the same one that fired the rounds at the Tibodeau cabin," Simon Rutledge finally said. "So we need to assume this isn't just some goofball who wants to scare you and is using the situation."

"Anybody ever tell you, Simon, that you've got a real knack for stating the bleeding obvious," Ed Larson said.

Cork knew the tension in the room was the result of tired people once again having to step into the front lines feeling as if they'd gained no ground.

"The phone records will tell us where the call came from," he said.

"It came from nowhere that'll be of any help to us, I can tell you that right now," Larson said.

He took off his gold wire-rims and massaged the bridge of his long nose. Rutledge tapped the desktop with his fingertips as if sending out Morse code. Dina

Willner stirred a white plastic spoon in her coffee. Cork, who'd hardly slept, sat with a notepad in his lap and read over and over again what he'd written about the voice on the phone the night before.

Low. Muffled, but precise. Male. Dispassionate.

Several manila folders lay open on the desk, all containing documents related to the investigation of the attempts on Cork's life. They'd been gone over a dozen times and no one saw anything new there.

He got up and walked to the window, watched a man in the park let his small dog off a leash to run free. Ralph Grunke and his terrier, Sparks. Cork watched Sparks begin to sniff every tree.

"I've been thinking about this guy who called. He wasn't angry. He didn't seem emotional at all. I keep replaying what he said, how he said it. It was very calculated."

"Calculated for what effect? Just to scare?" Rutledge said.

"No, I think he meant it. But it was as if the personal element was missing."

"Like a hit?" Dina asked.

Cork thought a moment. "I don't know what a hit's like, but maybe."

"It's interesting," Dina said. "If it is a hit, why let you know it's coming? In my experience, that's pretty unprofessional."

Cork turned to her. "What exactly is your experience?"

She took the spoon from her coffee and tapped it clean against the side of her cup. She set it on Cork's desk. "I dealt with a number of contract killings when I was with the Organized Crime Section. It's seen as an expeditious way to cover tracks, silence a witness."

"Cover what tracks here? And if Cork was a witness, a witness to what?" Rutledge said.

"Got me." Cork headed back to his chair.

"Maybe it *is* a hit," Larson said. "But not by a professional. Whoever it is sure bungled the first attempt."

"And the bomb," Rutledge said.

"And now this announcement of further intent," Dina added. "I think Ed's onto something."

Cork sat down. A dull throb had begun in his head. Too little sleep. "Could it still be related to Lydell Cramer?"

"The connection with Moose LaRusse and the rez would sure point in that direction." Larson hooked the wire-rims over his ears. "He certainly could have supplied the information needed for the location of the hit."

"Was there someone we missed who was connected to the farmhouse?" Dina asked.

Rutledge shook his head. "Lydell's sister, LaRusse, and Berger. Those were the only ones the Carlton County sheriff's people observed out there."

"Does Cramer have any other relatives?"

"I've already put someone on checking that out," Rutledge said. "We'll follow up on the phone records as soon as we have them. You never know what might turn up."

"What about the Jacoby investigation?" Cork asked. "Anything new, Ed?"

"I've got the record of the calls Jacoby made and received on his cell phone. I'll be looking those over."

"I'd like a copy, too."

"Sure. And we're waiting to see if there's a DNA match with Lizzie Fineday and the evidence we got from Jacoby's SUV." He glanced at Dina. "Any idea when we might hear?"

"I don't expect anything until tomorrow."

"If it's a match, we go after Lizzie and I'll bet something will break." Larson sounded truly hopeful.

"All right. Let's see what shakes," Cork said.

As the others filed out, Dina stayed behind and closed the door. She crossed the room and sat on the edge of his desk. She smelled of herbal soap, a clean, fresh scent. "You get any sleep at all last night?"

"Barely."

"It might be a good idea to stay somewhere else until this is over. Anywhere other than home."

"I've thought about that."

"You could stay at my hotel, take the room next to mine. Among other things, I'm an excellent bodyguard." She waited, gauging his response, which was simply to stare at her. "The other alternative is I could stay at your place."

To that he shook his head. "Small town. Big talk."

"I'd sleep on the sofa." She drilled him with her wonderful green eyes. "Unless you wanted otherwise."

"I think I'll put a cot in here."

She gave a diffident shrug, slid off his desk, and headed toward the door. "Just keep it in mind."

He watched her leave, but not without a little stab of regret.

30

JENNY WORE A plaid wool skirt and a rust-colored turtleneck. Her blond hair was carefully brushed. She appeared, Jo thought, very collegiate, probably a look she would abandon once she was actually attending college. It was just fine for her meeting at Northwestern with Marty Goldman.

His office was on the second floor of a three-story brick building with white colonnades, a block off the main campus. He looked like he'd been an athlete in his youth, but over the years a lot of his muscle had gone to fat and spilled over his belt. He wore a light blue Oxford with a yellow tie, and he rose from his desk to greet them, the skin of his face pink and shiny.

"I understand we're your first choice," he said after they'd finished with the pleasantries. "We're always glad to hear that. Have you taken your SATs or the ACTs yet?"

"SATs."

"Do you recall your scores?"

Jenny told him.

"Very impressive," he said, with a lift of his brow.

"What kind of extracurricular activities have you been involved in?"

"I'm the editor of the school paper, *The Beacon*. I've been on the yearbook staff for the past two years. I'm a member of National Honor Society, president of the Debate Club. I can go on," she said.

"That's just fine," he laughed. "What is it about Northwestern that attracts you?"

"The Medill School," Jenny said.

"Journalism," Goldman said with an approving nod.

"I want to be a writer."

"Well, we certainly have some fine authors among our alumni. And we have several writing programs in conjunction with Medill that might interest you."

The talk was interrupted by a knock at the open door. A wiry young man a little over six feet tall with neatly groomed dark hair and a brooding look in his eyes stood just inside the threshold. He wore pressed jeans, a navy sweater over a white shirt, penny loafers. He stood stiffly, as if waiting for an invitation.

"Phillip. Come on in," Goldman said, rising.

Phillip came forward with a stiff, military stride.

"Jenny, Jo, this is Phillip. I've asked him to give you a tour of the campus this morning. He's a senior. I'm sure he'll be able to answer any questions you might have. I've scheduled you for about ninety minutes. That should be plenty of time to see almost everything of interest and for a Coke or cup of coffee in the bargain." He looked at his watch. "I'll see you back here at twelve-thirty and we can talk a bit more. Phillip?"

"This way." The young man led them out.

Jo hung back as they headed toward campus, letting Jenny and Phillip walk side by side in front. She was proud of her daughter, of Jenny's confidence and goals, proud of the woman her daughter was and proud of who she was becoming. She relaxed and listened as the two young people talked. Jenny had a million questions. Phillip answered them all. He was polite, informative, but there was something in his voice that hinted at irritation, as if this were a small ordeal.

The Northwestern campus was beautiful, deep in colorful fall. The collegiate structures, the flow of students along the sidewalks, the energy of freedom that was a part of college—Jo remembered the feel of it from her own undergraduate years long ago. For her, college had been an escape. It wouldn't have mattered where she'd gone. Anywhere, just to get away. She'd ended up with a full scholarship to the University of Illinois in Champaign, a campus that rose out of cornfields. She'd come well prepared to stand on her own, having spent her life standing up to her mother. There'd been nothing about college that intimidated her. The academics had been routine. Sex, drugs, and books she juggled easily and graduated magna cum laude.

After that had come law school at the University of Chicago, her first great challenge. She'd put aside the drugs and she'd also put aside men. Then came Ben Jacoby. When he stepped into her life, she was ready for something permanent, and until he said good-bye, she'd thought he was offering it.

Watching Jenny ahead of her, she hoped her daughter would have a different experience. Someone who would care about her the way Cork cared about Jo. Not that a man was necessary, because she remem-

bered only too well how alone she'd often felt even
when she was with a man. Ben Jacoby had changed
that. For the first time in her life, she wanted to be
with someone forever. She'd never let a man hurt her
before, but Jacoby had hurt her deeply.

Maybe everyone needed their heart broken once.
Maybe it had been that kind of hurt that helped her
appreciate Cork from the beginning. From their very
first meeting in Chicago.

It was spring. She still lived on South Harper
Avenue in Hyde Park in the apartment where several
months before she'd shared her nights with Ben. She
came home from working late in the D'Angelo Law
Library to find that her place had been broken into
and she'd been robbed of her stereo and television.
She called the police. A uniformed patrolman
responded. Officer Corcoran O'Connor.

He filled out an incident report, then he spent a
while looking over her apartment inside and out.
Finally he sat down with her.

"I've got to be honest with you. There's very little
chance of recovering your stolen property. No serial
numbers, almost impossible to trace. But I'd like to
make some recommendations for the future. First of
all, I'd get a better lock on your front door."

"He didn't come in the front door. He came
through the window."

"I understand. But almost anybody could break in
through the front door if they were so inclined, so I'd
get a good dead bolt. Now, about the windows. I think
you should put bars on them."

"I don't relish the idea of living in a jail," she said.

"Ever been in jail?"

"No."

"It won't feel like a jail, I promise. I understand you object to having to barricade yourself, but that's the reality of your situation. In a way, you're lucky. This time, they only stole from you. Next time, they might be after something different."

"As in rape."

"Yes, ma'am."

"I don't know that I can afford bars on the windows," she said.

"You don't need them on all your windows. I've checked around back. You're on the second floor, so you're fine there. But in front, with the porch and that elm, you're vulnerable. Really, your landlord ought to be the one who puts them on. If you get flack from him, I know where you can get them at a reasonable price." He cleared his throat. "And I'd be glad to install them."

"You?"

"Yes, ma'am."

"Please stop calling me ma'am. And why would you do that?"

"I know you volunteer your time helping people who can't afford a lawyer. I've seen you in the store-front office on Calumet."

"Yes."

"You do it, I'd guess, because you believe it's the right thing to do. Considering your situation here, I just think it's the right thing to do."

She studied him. He looked a little older than she, maybe twenty-six or twenty-seven. His hair was red-brown, shorter than she preferred on a man, but that was probably a dictate of the job. He wasn't hand-some, not like Ben Jacoby or many of the others she'd been with, but there was a sincerity in his face, in his words, in the sound of his voice, that was attractive.

"That's it?" she asked with a sharp edge of skepticism. "You'd do that without expecting something in return?"

He capped his pen and scratched his nose with it. "You cook?"

Halfway through the ninety minutes that Marty Goldman had allotted for the tour, Phillip took them out to a long, grassy point on which nothing had been built. Lake Michigan lay to the east, a stretch of blue that looked as enormous as an ocean. Several miles south, clear in the crisp air of late morning, rose the Chicago skyline, as beautiful as any city Jo had ever seen.

Jenny stared at it for a long time. "Now I know what Dorothy felt like when she saw Oz."

"This is where I come when I need to get away," Phillip said.

"You like it here?" Jenny asked.

"It's my favorite spot."

"No, I mean do you like Northwestern?"

There was a breeze off the lake with a slight chill to it. Jenny hugged herself, and Phillip, without making anything of it, moved to block the wind.

"I wanted to go to school in Boulder," he said. "I love to ski."

"Why didn't you?"

"This was my father's preference."

"That's the only reason? I'd never go somewhere just because my father wanted me to."

"Lucky you," he said coldly, and turned back toward campus. "We should be going."

They stopped at the student union. Jo ordered a latte. Phillip did the same. Jenny didn't usually drink coffee, but she ordered a latte as well. They sat at a table for a few minutes.

"What's your major?" Jenny asked.

"Pre-law."

"You want to be a lawyer?"

"My father wants me to be a lawyer."

"What do you want to be?"

"It doesn't matter."

"Because you're going to be a lawyer like your father wants."

"He pays the bills."

"I don't know," Jenny said. "To me, that sounds like a recipe for an unhappy life."

"You're a lawyer," Phillip said to Jo. "Do you like it?"

She didn't remember telling him that she was an attorney, but maybe it had come up in his conversation with Jenny and she'd just missed it.

"Yes, I do," she replied.

"I've never known a happy lawyer," he said. "We should be getting back."

At the door to the admissions office, he stopped. "This is as far as I go. I have a class to get to."

"Thank you, Phillip," Jenny said. "We really appreciate your time." She shook his hand.

"Look," he said, "I apologize if I seemed rude. I'm a little stressed these days."

"You were great," Jenny said.

"Yeah, well, good luck. If Northwestern is really what you want, I hope you get it. Nice to meet you," he said to Jo.

Inside, Marty Goldman's secretary asked them to

wait a few minutes. Mr. Goldman was still with someone.

"How did you like the campus?" she asked. She was a small black woman who spoke with a slight Jamaican accent.

"It's beautiful," Jenny said.

"Isn't it? And your guide?"

"He was fine."

"Good. He's not one of our usual group. He was a special request, as I understand it. His father, I believe. You must be friends of the family."

"And what family would that be?" Jo asked.

"Why, the Jacobys, of course."

31

CORK PASSED MUCH of the morning going over the record of the calls made to and from Eddie Jacoby's cell phone in the days before his death, and also the record of his hotel phone. Jacoby spent a lot of time with a receiver pressed to his ear. It fit the image Cork had of the man, the kind who drove his SUV with one hand and constantly worked his cell phone with the other.

In the afternoon, he attacked the paperwork that had piled up. The budget was a huge concern. The investigations, which required an uncomfortable amount of overtime, were eating up officer hours and resources. He knew he was going to have to go to the Board of Commissioners, explain the deficit that was developing, and ask for additional money. Christ, he'd always hated that part of the job.

Shortly after the three o'clock shift change, Ed Larson came into his office. Like everyone these days, he looked tired. Behind his wire-rims, his eyes rode puffy bags of skin and seemed to be sinking gradually deeper into his face. He still dressed neatly and held himself erect.

"Got a minute?" he asked.

Cork looked at his watch. "Not much more than that. I have a session with Faith Gray this afternoon. I've already missed one appointment. She's threatened that if I miss another, she'll require a temporary suspension. The regs, you know."

"I was just wondering if you've had a chance to look over Jacoby's phone records."

"Yeah." Cork picked up the document. "Several interesting items."

"I thought so, too. Particularly that call from the pay phone at the North Star Bar on the night he was murdered."

"You're thinking Lizzie?"

"That's what I'm thinking."

Cork arched his spine and worked his fists into the tight muscles in his lower back. He wouldn't have minded another session with Dina and her magic feet. "We need to be careful," he said, grimacing. "We know Jacoby visited the North Star, but we don't have anything that connects him solidly to the girl."

"She was certainly looking for him."

"We don't know that she found him."

"The bruises."

"Fineday says she fell."

"And he went charging out of the bar after she came home from that 'fall.' I'm betting he wasn't headed to a movie. It had to do with Jacoby. We both know that."

"We can speculate, but we don't really know." Cork settled back with a sigh. "They're afraid of something, it's clear. I'd love to know what she was running from when she ran to Stone."

"From her father?"

"Maybe. But why? He's a hard man, sure, but he'd never lay a finger on her."

From beyond Cork's door came the squawk of the radio in Dispatch and Patsy's voice responding.

"Another thing about these phone records," Cork said. "Not a single call to his wife or from her."

"So?"

"If you were gone from Alice for a week, wouldn't you call?"

"Sure."

"So why didn't Jacoby? And why didn't she call him? I'm just wondering if we ought to look at that marriage. It's an old adage but a good one that murder begins at home."

"I'll see what I can find out." Larson adjusted his glasses and tapped the phone records in his hand. "He may not have talked to his wife, but Jacoby sure talked to a lot of other people. His office in Elmhurst. New York. Las Vegas. And where exactly is Kenosha, Wisconsin?"

"South of Milwaukee, on Lake Michigan. May be a casino there."

"Makes sense," Larson said. "He also made a lot of calls to members of the Reservation Business Committee. Have you had a chance to talk to them?"

"Nobody at length. But I will. I know Lizzie looks good for this right now, but we need to keep checking all the possibilities. Have you been able to get anything on Eddie Jacoby's background?"

Larson took a notepad from his pocket. "I spoke with his boss at Starlight, a guy named Clayton. He said Jacoby'd been with them less than a year. I had the sense he wasn't going to be with them much longer."

"Why's that?"

"He wasn't representing Starlight well. Securing a contract with the Iron Lake Ojibwe was important for his career with the company."

"If he was dealing with Stone, he had to be desperate."

"Clayton said he hired him as a favor to Jacoby's brother. I asked about his employment record. He worked a string of jobs before Starlight, none very long."

"Dina told me he was into moviemaking for a while. Porn."

"Doesn't surprise me. Was he still into it when he was murdered?"

Cork shook his head. "Lost all his money, apparently."

"I spoke at length with his family before they left. Jacoby was married, two kids. Lived in Lake Forest not far from his father. He wasn't an easy son or sibling, I gather."

"Anything specific?"

"According to them, only minor scrapes with the law, nothing serious."

"You ask them about substance abuse?"

"Considering what we found in the glove box of his SUV, it was one of the first questions I asked. They claimed it was a surprise to them."

"A surprise? I doubt he was just experimenting."

"So did I. I checked for any criminal record. Nothing in Illinois. I called the Lake Forest police. They gave me nothing. But I can't help thinking that for a guy with an appetite for drugs and beating up prostitutes, he seems to have a suspiciously clean record."

"Maybe the Jacoby money has something to do

with that. And maybe we need to check on him through a less official channel. I have a friend, a guy named Boomer Grabowski. We worked out of the same division when we were cops in Chicago. Boomer's a private investigator now, a good one. I think I ought to give him a call, see what he can dig up on Eddie Jacoby. Hell, on all the Jacobys. It'll cost us, but the budget's already shot."

"If you think it'll help. And you're the one who has to beg the Board of Commissioners for more money."

There was a knock at the open door. It was Patsy.

"Call for Ed."

"Put it through in here," Larson said.

A moment later, Cork's phone rang.

"Captain Larson," Ed said. He listened. "I see." He glanced at Cork, and something flared in his usual cool blue eyes. He took a pen from the desktop and jotted a couple of notes on the back of the top sheet of Jacoby's phone record. "You're certain?" He nodded at the answer. "I appreciate it. Thank you very much." He hung up.

"What is it?" Cork said.

"BCA's been helping us run the prints we took from the inside of Jacoby's SUV. Got an interesting match on one of them."

"No kidding. Who?"

"Lizzie Fineday."

They rendezvoused at the opening to the narrow dirt road off County 17 that led to Stone's cabin. Cork and Larson had come in the same vehicle, the Pathfinder. Morgan and Pender had been patrolling the eastern roads of Tamarack County and had been dispatched to accompany. Dina Willner was there, too.

"Stone's going to see us coming a long way off. That's all right. We have a suspect, and so a lawful reason to be here. He shouldn't give us any resistance," Cork said. "If he does, we take him down right away, cuff him, book him for interfering with the execution of a lawful order. Morgan, Pender, that'll be your responsibility. Ed and I will conduct the search and apprehension of Lizzie Fineday. And, Dina, you're here by invitation, and I'd like you to stay well back." He lifted the back door of the Pathfinder and brought out a dark blue Kevlar vest with SHERIFF'S DEPT. printed in white letters across the back. He tossed it to her. "Wear this."

She caught it and put it on.

"Everybody else armored up? Then let's roll," he said.

It was late afternoon, the air still, the woods quiet. They drove through a thick stand of aspen that smelled of leaves fallen, dried, crumbling to dust. Breaking from the trees, they followed the shoreline of the narrow lake. Sun glinted off the water in piercing arrows of light. At the far end, wood smoke rose from Stone's cabin, straight and white as a feather. Behind it, like a prison wall, stood the gray ridge. Cork led the procession, his window down. There was no way to move quickly enough to surprise Stone. Cork couldn't help thinking of the raid on the farmhouse in Carlton County, how badly things had ended. You never knew. That was the hell of it: even with routine procedures, things could go wrong. You tried to be careful, to consider all the options, choose the best approach, but so much was out of your hands, beyond your control. In the end, you made your choice and went in hoping. Praying never hurt, either.

"Movement in front of the cabin," Larson said. He lifted a pair of Leitz binoculars to his eyes. "Stone."

"What's he doing?"

"Waving, it looks like."

"At who?"

"Nobody I can see. Toward the ridge. Now he's stopped. He's looking this way. Son of a gun. He's waving at us."

"Us?"

"Looks that way. Wait."

They kept moving, getting closer. Larson finally lowered the field glasses and laughed quietly.

"What?" Cork said.

"He's not waving. He's casting. He's got a fly rod in his hand."

They rounded the north end of the lake and climbed a rise to the cabin. Stone stood in front of his place, fifteen yards from the chopping block. He held the rod in his right hand and, with a deft snap of his wrist, flicked the line out again and again toward the chopping block. At his feet lay a zippered canvas bag long enough and wide enough to accommodate several rods fitted with reels. He paid no attention to the approaching vehicles.

Cork pulled up behind Stone's Land Rover, which was parked in the shade of a paper birch. He got out and Larson did, too. The deputies halted farther back and exited their cruisers. Dina stayed in her Accord as Cork had asked.

"Afternoon, Byron," Cork said.

"Sheriff." Stone watched the thread of fishing line sail out. The end touched almost dead center on top of the chopping block. He wore olive jeans, a long-sleeved wool shirt also green but of a lighter shade, with the sleeves rolled up to reveal his powerful muscles. His black hair was tied back with a folded bandanna of gold and green. "Looks like D-day. What's with all the troops?"

"We're here for Lizzie."

"Too late. She's already gone."

"Where?"

"Search me. I went into Allouette after lunch. When I came back, she was gone."

"Did someone come to get her?"

"I don't know."

"Why did she leave?"

"Same reason she came, I suppose. It suited her."

Stone whipped his arm back and the line arced through the air, catching the sunlight along its whole length so that for an instant it appeared to glow as if electric.

"Byron, I have an order authorizing me to pick up and detain Elizabeth Fineday for questioning in connection with the murder of Edward Jacoby. That order authorizes me to search your property for Lizzie."

"Be my guest. Mind if I keep working on my technique?"

"Morgan, Pender," Cork said. "Keep him company while Captain Larson and I have a look inside."

"Sure thing, Sheriff," Morgan replied.

Cork saw that Dina had left her car and was making her way to the back of the deputies' cruisers, keeping them between herself and any threat Stone might pose. He wondered what she was up to.

He held the screen door open for Larson, who went into the cabin first. Cork had been inside twice before, once with ATF and a couple years later with DEA. The place looked as spotless now as it had on the other two occasions. Once the casino allotments began to be distributed to the enrolled members of the band, some Iron Lake Ojibwe had gone a little crazy, packing their homes to the rafters with all manner of junk, feeding appetites generated by the sudden wealth. Stone continued to live simply. The Land Rover outside was his only obvious extravagance.

He'd built the cabin himself, a simple square divided into four rooms: a main living area, a kitchen, a bathroom, and a small bedroom. The wide window in the living area looked toward the lake. Cork suspected the beautiful view wasn't the only reason for its location. Through that window, Stone could see anything approaching along the road. The walls were bare logs, no paneling to hide insulation. Stone had cut the trees, planed and notched the logs so that they fit perfectly. The winter wind could not penetrate. He'd drilled his own well, put in his own septic system, had done all the wiring and plumbing himself. The electricity came from his own generator. He probably had ignored codes, but no inspector ever bothered to check. When dealing with Stone, most people didn't sweat the small things.

They went through the cabin, found no sign of Lizzie, not even any evidence that she'd been there. They stepped back outside.

Stone hadn't moved. With the canvas bag of rods on the ground at his feet, he still cast his line at the chopping block. Morgan and Pender watched him closely, and no one uttered a word. Dina was lurking behind Stone's Land Rover.

"She cleaned up after herself pretty well," Cork said.

"Didn't she?" Stone replied.

"Morgan, you got a cell phone?"

"In my cruiser."

"Call the North Star Bar, find out if Lizzie Fineday is there."

Morgan started to turn.

"Cell phones don't work here," Stone said. He nodded toward the gray ridge at his back. "It's the iron in the rock. Interferes with the signal."

"Try it anyway," Cork said to Morgan. "If he's right, relay the request to dispatch and have Patsy make the call."

Morgan hopped to it.

"I'd like you to come with us into town, Byron, answer a few questions about Lizzie."

"Got a warrant? No? Then you know I don't have to go. I'm content here."

"All right. While she was here, did Lizzie say anything to you about Edward Jacoby?"

"Most of the time she slept. She needed the rest."

"You didn't answer my question."

"No. The answer is no."

"Her face was bruised. Did she tell you how that happened?"

"I believe she fell."

"She told you that?"

"That's what she said."

From behind Stone's Land Rover, Dina called, "What time did you get back from Allouette today?"

Stone turned his attention away from the fishing line to the woman. His eyebrows arched as if he were surprised, only just now aware of her presence. Histrionics, Cork knew, because Stone didn't miss a thing.

"I heard you were pretty," he said. "And that you like to flash your breasts around."

"When *did* you get back from Allouette?" Cork said.

"Couple of hours ago."

"Engine's still warm," Dina said to Cork.

Stone went back to his casting. "I left again and came back again."

"Where?" Cork said.

"Brandywine. Had business at the mill there. You can check. But what difference does it make? Am I a suspect?"

"Sheriff," Morgan hollered from his cruiser. "Patsy says Lizzie's not at the North Star. Will Fineday claims he hasn't seen her since he was out here the other day."

"If I wanted to protect my daughter, I'd claim the same thing," Stone said. "On the other hand, Lizzie's lived on the rez her whole life. She's got friends, other relatives. Seems to me you've got a lot of checking to do, Sheriff. I'd get started if I were you."

Cork looked back at the empty cabin. He thought about warning Stone that if he was hiding Lizzie he'd be in trouble, but he knew Stone didn't care. "Pack it up," he said to the others. "Let's get out of here."

Under Stone's intransigent eye, they turned their vehicles and headed back the way they'd come. This time Dina Willner led the way. At the junction with the county road, she pulled over and got out. The two cruisers rolled past and braked to a halt ahead of her. Cork drew alongside and leaned out his window.

"What is it?"

"The cast of the tire tracks out at the Tibodeau cabin. What kind of tires did you say those were?"

"Goodyear Wranglers. MT/Rs, I think. Why?"

"Stone's got Goodyear Wranglers on his Land Rover. MT/Rs, and they're new."

Cork looked over at Larson.

Larson said, "You think?"

Dina said, "At the Tibodeau cabin, you had two people, probably a man and a woman, involved in the shooting. They knew the reservation well enough to know the Tibodeaus would be gone. At least one of them understood how to plan an ambush. And they escaped in a vehicle sporting Goodyear MT/Rs. You told me Lizzie wants to be an actress. Could she do a pretty good imitation of Lucy Tibodeau, do you think?"

"I imagine," Cork said.

"And is Stone a decent shot?"

"Stone's an excellent shot. Been hunting all his life."

"I don't know why they'd do it, but they certainly seem to me like prime suspects in that shooting," Dina concluded.

"Why didn't you say something back at the cabin?" Larson asked.

"Did you see the canvas bag at his feet?"

"For his rods?"

"He never moved a foot from that bag. I'm betting it wasn't fishing rods he had in there."

"A rifle?" Cork said.

"It seemed like a possibility to me. And if he is the shooter, it's likely that he's using armor-piercing ammunition. It didn't seem prudent to challenge him at that point. People could have been hurt."

"Let's go back now," Larson said.

Dina shook her head. "I wouldn't if I were you. He saw me looking at the tires. He pretended not to, but he did."

"Would he know about the tracks he left?" Larson said.

"Our people have been all over the county asking about those tires." Cork thought it over. "Let's see if we can get a warrant and go in after dark."

32

*B*EN JACOBY POINTED toward a bright pinpoint of light in the sky just above the horizon.

"First star on the left," he said, "and straight on till morning."

They were seated in a booth at Lord Jim's, a restaurant at the exclusive North Lake Marina near Evanston, looking east over the inky evening blue of Lake Michigan.

"Neverland," Jo said.

"That's where I'd love to be headed." Jacoby sat back. "Rough day." He wore a gray suit, white shirt, blue tie. He'd come from the office, he said, although he looked freshly shaved. "But it's better now. And thanks."

"For what?"

"Agreeing to have a drink with me. How did it go at Northwestern? Did you like your guide?"

"He was quite a surprise."

"A pleasant one, I hope. He did it as a favor for his old man. A good son."

Jo noted that he spoke of Phillip with more enthusiasm than Phillip had shown when speaking of him.

"Did Jenny like the campus?" he asked.

"She was thrilled."

"Great. Look, if she needs anything, a recommendation, help with her acceptance—"

"She doesn't."

"I'm just saying that a word from me wouldn't hurt. And I'd be happy to."

"Jenny will get in or not on her own merit."

"Just like her mother."

He'd ordered Scotch for himself and for Jo a chardonnay. He drank and looked melancholy.

"Halston," Jo said, noting the scent of his cologne. "You still wear it."

"You bought me Halston on my twenty-seventh birthday. It's all I wear. Like Proust says, smells transport us in time." He sipped from his drink. "You ever miss Chicago?"

"Some things."

"Like what?"

"The blues bars."

"Blues bars? We never went to the blues bars."

"Cork and I," she said.

"Oh. Sure."

"Ben, my life in Aurora is good and I don't regret leaving anything behind."

He looked hard at her face, searched her eyes. Finally he said, "I'm happy for you, then."

A passenger jet flew overhead, banked south, circled back toward O'Hare, high enough that it caught the rays of the sun, which was already below the horizon, and for a few moments it glowed like a giant ember.

"I never told you why I left you," he said.

"No, you never did."

He shifted uncomfortably, watched the plane slide out of sight. "When I met you I was already promised to someone else."

"You were engaged?"

"Not exactly. It was an arranged marriage. There are still such things. I knew from the time I was very young that I would marry Miriam. My father had arranged it, an agreement with his business partner, Miriam's father. It was conceived as a union of great fortunes, and it was. Her family, my family, everyone wanted it."

"So, was I a complication or simply a diversion?" The acid in her tone surprised her, and she saw Jacoby flinch.

"You were love," he said. "I wanted to tell you, to explain everything, but there never seemed a right time. I always thought that in the end I might make a different decision. When I walked out that night, I knew I was turning my back on happiness. I told you I didn't have a choice, but I did. I chose family." He breathed deeply, his broad shoulders rising. "Sometimes when my father stood up for Eddie, protecting him after the schmuck had done another stupid or cruel thing, I'd shake my head and wonder. I have a son now, and I understand. People fall out of love, but family is different.

"You told me about your mother, the Captain, about how awful you had it growing up, all the moving and the drinking and the fighting. That was your experience. Mine was different. My father isn't perfect, but I grew up knowing he loved me, knowing my family loved me. The idea of turning my back on them . . ." He shrugged. "I just couldn't do it. So I gave you up. I gave up love."

"You could have told me all this then instead of just walking out."

"Would it have made a difference? Would it have hurt you any less? Would it have made me any less a bastard in your eyes? I'd seen you argue on behalf of your storefront clients. I didn't want you to dissuade me from what I believed to be the right thing. And you found happiness. You met Cork. Me, my whole life I've loved one woman, and I didn't marry her."

"People fall out of love, you said. But love also fades, Ben, especially if it isn't nurtured."

"That's not been my experience." He finished his drink and signaled for another. "I have a confession. When I found out that Eddie was dealing with you in Aurora, I imagined for a little while that I might be able to step back into your life, still somehow create everything we might have had together. Then I saw your family and Cork and how happy you are, and I knew it was stupid and impossible." He looked out the window, stared into the distance above the cold lake water. "In the end everything fades but family, doesn't it?"

His cell phone bleated and he answered it, listened, and smiled. "I'm at a bar, actually. You'll never guess who with. Nancy Jo McKenzie." He laughed. "No, really. Would you like to talk to her?" He glanced at Jo with a welcome humor in his eyes. "I'll ask but my guess would be no." He said to Jo, "It's my sister Rae. You remember her?"

"Of course."

"She's at my father's house. We're sitting shivah tonight for Eddie. Rae wants you to drop by so that she can say hello in person."

"I don't think so, Ben."

"We're just fifteen minutes away. Stay fifteen minutes and leave. It would be less than an hour out of your life."

"I'm not dressed—"

"You look fine. It would thrill Rae no end. Please."

Jo thought it over. "All right. Fifteen minutes."

Along Lake Drive in Lake Forest, the homes became palatial. Jacoby pulled through a gate and into a circular drive that was lined with cars. Jo, who'd followed in her Toyota, parked behind his Mercedes, got out, and joined him.

"Very rococo," she said, looking at the house.

"My grandfather had it built to remind him of Italy, where he studied as a young man. The happiest time of his life, he used to say. He came to America to seek his fortune, something that didn't make him very happy, I can vouch for that."

"Looks like he succeeded in making the fortune."

"He was a harsh man in a lot of ways, but he knew how to handle money." He took her arm and gave her a brave smile. "You ready for this?"

As they neared the front door, a Jeep Cherokee pulled into the drive and parked behind Jo's Toyota. A six-footer got out, attractive, with long dark hair, thirtyish.

"Just arriving, Ben?" There was a Spanish roll to his r's.

"Good evening, Tony."

Tony looked long and appreciatively at Jo.

"Tony, this is Jo O'Connor. Jo, Tony Salguero."

He wrapped Jo's hand very warmly in his own. "You're here because of Eddie? Did you know him well?"

"Not well."

"A pity, his death." Tony turned his attention to Ben. "By the way, that package I flew back from Aurora. Any word?"

"Aurora?" Jo said. "Minnesota?"

"That's right."

Ben said, "Tony flew some samples back yesterday for DNA testing."

"My husband is Sheriff O'Connor," Jo told him.

"Your husband?" He looked to Ben, then back to Jo, and smiled wickedly. "A long way from home, are you not?"

"What about the DNA?" Jo said.

"They were hairs taken from Eddie's SUV," Ben explained. "And a cigarette that had been smoked by a woman in Aurora. There's a lab here that's doing a match. Your husband thinks the woman might have been with Eddie the night he was murdered."

"What woman?"

"Her name is Fineday."

"Lizzie?"

"You know her?"

"I know who she is. Is she a suspect?"

"Dina reports that she's the focus of the investigation at the moment."

She was thinking like a defense attorney, thinking that Lizzie's presence in the SUV meant nothing in itself. There had to be more to tie her to Jacoby's murder.

Jacoby said to Tony, "Why don't we go inside. Gabriella is there, I'm sure."

A cadaverous white-haired man in a black suit opened the door for them all.

"Good evening, Evers," Jacoby said.

"Mr. Jacoby," Evers replied with a trace of a bow. "Mr. Salguero."

"Everyone here?" Ben asked.

"They come and go, sir. May I take your wrap?" he asked Jo.

"We won't be long," Jo said.

"Safer to surrender it," Ben advised her.

Tony left them as Jo removed her coat and handed it to Evers.

Beyond the expansive foyer, the house opened left and right onto huge rooms filled with people. Some of the guests wore black, but many—the family members, like Ben—had only a torn black ribbon pinned to a lapel or bodice. They didn't appear necessarily to be dressed for mourning, but all were dressed elegantly.

Ben led her into a room dominated by a Steinway baby grand. There were two mirrors in the room, both completely covered by fabric to block any reflection, a custom of sitting shivah, Jo figured. Seeing them arrive, a woman separated herself from a small group on the far side of the Steinway.

"Ben," she said, languorously drawing out the word. She took both his hands and kissed him on the cheek. Her hair, dark red and expensively cut, brushed against her shoulders. Her face, tight skin over wonderfully sculptured bones, was so skillfully made up, Jo guessed it had been done professionally. She carried herself with finishing-school panache. Although her dress was the appropriate color for the occasion, it was cut low enough to show off substantial cleavage with freckles like splashes of rusty water. She looked forty, although Jo had the feeling that she was much older. "I'm so sorry."

"Thank you, Rachel."

Rachel seemed to notice Jo as an afterthought. "I don't believe I've had the pleasure."

"This is Jo O'Connor. An old friend. Jo, Rachel Herschel."

"How do you do?" Rachel's eyes cut into Jo, but she forced a smile, then looked back at Jacoby in a knowing way. "Lovely," she said, with an edge of ice.

"Have you seen my father?"

"It seems to me he was heading toward the veranda. For a cigar, no doubt." She still hadn't let go of Jacoby's hands. "I'd love to have a moment to talk with you. It's been . . . a while."

"Call me," he said, extracting his hands and looking past her toward a set of French doors on the far side of the room.

"Of course." She gave Jo another lengthy appraisal, pursed her pomegranate-red lips, and turned abruptly back to the piano.

They made their way through groups that were like floating islands on the soft white sea of carpet. Everywhere it was the same. Jacoby was greeted heartily, sometimes greedily, and Jo was addressed through a veil of civility that barely hid the looks of appraisal and approval, as if she were something that had been bought at auction for a good price.

Jacoby finally reached the French doors and opened them for Jo to pass through ahead of him. Outside on the veranda, the air was cool. Jo could see the back of the estate stretching to the lake, the long expanse of lawn turned nearly charcoal in the fading light. The water of an unlit swimming pool flashed now and again with a reflection from the windows of the big house. In a corner of the veranda sat a man in a great chair of white wicker, the glow of a cigar reddening his pinched, narrow face, lighting a dull fire in his eyes as he stared at Jo and Ben Jacoby.

"Escaping, Dad?" Ben said.

"What needs taking care of is being seen to. Has there been any more word from Minnesota?"

"Nothing from Dina."

"What about that yokel sheriff?"

"There's someone here you should meet," Jacoby said.

"I don't want to meet anyone right now."

"This is Jo O'Connor. She's the wife of Sheriff Corcoran O'Connor in Aurora."

The cigar reddened considerably. "When your husband has the murderer of my son in jail, Ms. O'Connor, I'll gladly take back the *yokel*."

"I'm sure my husband is doing everything possible to make that happen."

"Why are you here?"

"I asked her, Dad. Her daughter's applying to Northwestern. They came to see the campus."

Lou Jacoby took the cigar from his mouth and studied the long ash beyond the ember. "You know each other?"

"I told you," Jacoby said. "We went to law school together."

"That's right." He seemed to be putting it together now. "You were Eddie's attorney in that town."

"Not exactly," Jo said. "I represent the Iron Lake Ojibwe. Your son was trying to negotiate a management contract with their casino."

"That have anything to do with his murder?"

"I can't imagine that it did, but that's really a question my husband should answer."

"Does he confide in you?"

"Sometimes. In this, he's told me nothing that you probably don't already know."

He slipped the cigar back into his mouth, took a long draw, and sent out enough smoke to temporarily obscure his face. "Then I don't really want to talk to you right now, Ms. O'Connor. You either, Ben boy. I'd rather just be alone."

"All right," Jacoby said dutifully. He opened the French doors and waited for Jo.

"Grief can be blinding," Jo said, standing her ground. "But at some point, you're going to have to take a good long look at the man Eddie was."

"You think I don't know? Hell, I know all about my son."

"And loved him anyway," Ben said bitterly.

"I told you, I want to be alone."

Without another word, Jacoby strode back into the house. In the corner of the veranda, the cigar flared and little points of fire lit the old man's eyes as he glared at Jo.

"He's got himself a little blond shiksa this time," he said. "A shiksa with spine."

Jo turned and followed Jacoby.

She caught up with him in another room where he'd stopped under a chandelier to speak with a black-haired beauty who had two young boys at her side. As Jo neared them, the woman looked her way.

"Jo," Jacoby said, "this is Gabriella. Eddie's widow."

"How do you do?" Gabriella spoke softly and, like Tony Salguero, with a Spanish accent. She offered a tanned hand with nails red as rose petals. A diamond tennis bracelet sparkled on her wrist.

"I'm sorry about your husband," Jo said.

"Ben told me you worked with Eddie in Minnesota."

"Not significantly."

"Mommy," one of the boys said. He was perhaps five years old, with his mother's black hair and fine face, his father's insolent eyes. "I'm *tired*. I wanna *go*."

"Find your cousin Mark, play with him."

"Mark's a dork," the other boy said. Similar features, older by maybe a year, bored out of his skull.

Gabriella smiled, leaned down, and kissed her son's black hair. *"Pobrecito,"* she said. "Find your uncle George, then. He will entertain you."

The two boys wandered off, defeated.

Gabriella turned back to Jo. "I'm sorry. Eddie kept business to himself, so I don't know anything about what he was doing in Minnesota. I hope his death . . ." She hesitated. "I hope his death does not inconvenience you."

Inconvenience? Jo thought.

"Excuse me, please." Gabriella went in the direction her sons had gone.

"She's from Argentina," Ben explained. "Her family have been clients for years, but the economy there is shot to hell. My father and her father made the arrangements for the marriage. Eddie sure got the better end of that deal. Poor Gabriella, she had no idea what she was getting herself into."

"Jo!"

She turned as a woman swept toward her across the room. There was a bit of gray in her hair, a few lines at the edges of her mouth and eyes. Unlike so many of the other women Jo had seen that evening, she didn't seem especially concerned about fighting time and age. She was smallish, a little round, and had a wry smile on her face. Although two decades had passed, Jo had no trouble recognizing Ben's sister, Rae.

"This is wonderful." Rae threw her arms around Jo. "I can't believe I'm seeing you again after all these years. How are you?"

"Good. And you?"

"Marvelous. Couldn't be better." She looked Jo over and shook her head as if in disbelief. "Twenty years and you're still gorgeous. Come on, let's go somewhere and sit down. I want to hear all about you."

"What about me?" Ben said.

"Go have a drink, Benny. I'll fetch you when I'm done with her."

Before they could move, from outside came the crunch of metal and the shatter of glass. People crowded the front windows, and someone called, "Ben, you better get out there."

Jacoby moved quickly. Jo and Rae followed.

Outside, they found Phillip Jacoby standing beside a Jaguar that had plowed into one of the brick pillars that flanked the entrance to the drive. He was staggering a little but seemed unhurt. A woman, also unharmed, stood near him, her arms crossed as if she were cold.

Phillip pointed at the pillar. "That damn thing's been out to get me for years."

"You've been drinking," his father said.

"I'm still drinking." He reached into the Jag and hauled out a bottle of Cuervo Gold. He put his arm around the waist of the woman, several years his senior, with brassy gold hair and dressed in a tight midnight-blue dress that was too skimpy for the cool evening, though it did advertise very nicely her wares.

"This your place?" she said to Ben with a slur.

Jacoby extended his hand. "Give me your keys, Phillip."

"Like hell."

"Give me your car keys. You're in no condition to drive."

"My fucking car," Phillip said.

"My fucking insurance," Jacoby shot back.

"Come on, Phil baby," the woman in the blue dress said. "This is a drag."

"Don't worry, baby, we're getting out of here."

He turned toward the Jag. Ben caught his arm, spun him, and used his son's drunken disequilibrium to throw him to the ground, where he pinned him quickly with his knee against his chest. The young man struggled briefly, then gave in.

"I'll take those keys." Jacoby reached into the pocket of his son's pants and extracted a plastic Baggie and a key ring. He studied the Baggie.

"Ecstasy? A parting gift from Uncle Eddie?"

Phillip glared up at him, his eyes bloodshot, his nostrils wet with mucus. "Fuck you."

Ben stood up, taking his weight off his son. "Get up. I'm driving you back to campus. We'll drop your friend wherever she wants."

Phillip picked himself up. He kicked at the bottle of tequila, which had fallen from his hand when his father tackled him. "I'll walk." He spun away and staggered from the drive into the street.

His woman companion watched him go, then said in a quiet voice, "I don't want to walk."

"I'll call you a cab," Ben told her.

She seemed to realize how alone and out of place she was. She folded her arms across her thin body.

"Why don't you come inside and wait," Rae said. She turned to Jo. "I'd love to talk, but this probably isn't the best time. Maybe lunch tomorrow?"

"I'm at the zoo with the kids."

"What if I met you there?"

"All right."

"What time?"

"Eleven. At the sea lion pool."

"I'll be there."

Rae turned her attention to the woman, who'd made no move yet to go inside. "Come with me," she said gently. "It'll be all right."

Most of those who'd come out had, by now, returned to the house. The others followed Rae inside.

Jo walked to Ben, who was inspecting the damage to the Jaguar.

"I'll give him a few minutes to cool down and sober up, then I'll go after him." He shook his head. "I'm sorry. I didn't imagine this was the way the evening would end. I guess I've never been very good at endings, huh?"

"Good night, Ben."

She kissed his cheek softly and left him standing beside the ruined car, looking toward the dark that had swallowed his son.

33

*T*HEY MOVED ON Stone's cabin after nightfall, before the moon rose. Cork, Larson, Rutledge, Willner, and a dozen deputies. They went silently, on foot, in armor, and carrying assault rifles, semiautomatic AR-15s. In the trees that crowded the dirt road, the black was almost impenetrable, but as they filed along the lake with the open sky above them, the ambient light of the stars lit their way. Ahead, the ridge behind Stone's cabin cut a jagged silhouette against the star-dusted sky. Several of the men, including Cork and Larson, had night vision goggles. They crept single file up the rise that led to the cabin, which was completely dark. Cork put on his goggles.

"His Land Rover's there," he whispered to Larson, who was donning his own goggles.

Cork scanned the yard, empty except for the chopping block. He signaled and four deputies, with Morgan in charge, slipped along the edge of the trees outlining the yard and took up positions behind the cabin. Four others, led by Larson, spread themselves out in front undercover or in prone positions with a good line of sight. Rutledge and Willner stayed well back. Cork and the remaining deputies cautiously approached the front door.

Unlike many Ojibwe on the rez and the rural people of Tamarack County in general, Stone kept no dog to bark a warning. This may have been because he was gone for long periods of time, disappearing into the Boundary Waters, and a dog would be neglected. Cork thought it might also have been that Stone was a man for whom companionship, even that of a dog, was not only unnecessary, it was unwanted. Whatever the reason, Cork was grateful for the absence of any animal that might sound an alarm.

The curtains across the front window were drawn shut. There was no porch. He walked the hard ground silently and put his ear to the front door, listened for a full minute, then stepped back. Schilling and Pender readied the battering ram. On his signal, the two deputies splintered the pine boards.

"Police," Cork shouted and rushed in. He glanced left, right. The room, luminescent green through the goggles, was vacant. The bathroom door was open, showing only empty space. "The bedroom," he said to the others, and motioned his deputies to flank the closed door.

He stood off to the side. "Stone, this is Sheriff O'Connor. I have a warrant for your arrest. Come out now with your hands in the air."

They waited. Cork's heart hammered in his chest. He wanted this to be over quickly and cleanly, without shooting, without blood.

"Lizzie, are you in there?" he called.

Still no response. Cork tried the knob. Although it turned, the door didn't open. Latched from the inside. Pender and Schilling had come into the cabin. He motioned them into position to use the ram. On his signal, they swung it forward and sent the door tumbling off its hinges. Immediately, they fell back, out of the line of fire through the doorway. Cork waited again, ready for gunshots, but heard only the heavy breathing of his own men. He waved the deputies to follow and swung into Stone's bedroom.

The room was empty, the bed made, everything left in neat order like a hotel room awaiting the next guest.

Cork unclipped the walkie-talkie from his belt. "All clear. Repeat, all clear. The chicken has flown the coop."

They drove the vehicles up from the county road and parked with the lights shining on the cabin. Cork and those in charge stood outside the glare. The moon wasn't visible yet, but there was a strong glow coming from behind the eastern hills. It washed out the stars on the horizon.

"Morgan's certain no one came or left between our visit this afternoon and the raid," Larson said. "The Land Rover's still here. Wherever Stone's gone, he's on foot."

"Into the Boundary Waters," Cork said. "I can almost guarantee it. He knows those woods."

"He can't hide there forever," Rutledge said.

Cork shook his head. "Stone's one of the few people who probably could."

"Maybe he's trying to make it across the border into Canada." Larson waved vaguely to the north. "Or slip out of the woods somewhere far away."

"And what? Start over?" Cork didn't hide his skepticism.

"What do you think, then?"

"I'm not sure. None of this has made a lot of sense so far."

Dina Willner spoke up. "What about Lizzie Fineday?"

Earlier, they'd checked with relatives and friends. No one admitted having any knowledge of her whereabouts. Cork believed Stone had lied that afternoon when he said she was gone.

"I think we can assume he has her," Cork said.

"Why would he take her?" Rutledge asked.

"I can think of at least three reasons. The best face to put on it would be that he's trying to protect her. Or that he's got a hostage if he's cornered."

"You said three reasons," Willner pointed out.

"He might be thinking she's the only witness against him in the shooting at the Tibodeau cabin and he'd rather not have her found. Period." Cork turned to Larson. "Any word from Borkmann?"

As soon as they were certain the area was secure, Cork had directed his chief deputy to drive to the North Star Bar, apprise Will Fineday of what was going on, and escort him to Stone's place.

"He's on his way with Fineday. ETA fifteen minutes," Larson said.

The cough of a gas engine turning over hit the quiet of the night, and a moment later, the engine settled into a steady thrum.

"Good," Cork said. "Schilling's got the generator going. Let's get some lights on inside."

Larson started in that direction with Cork right behind him, but Morgan called to him from a cruiser, "Cork, it's Bos on the radio for you," and the sheriff turned back.

"This is Cork. Go ahead."

"Sorry to take you away, Cork, but Jo just called. She's been trying to get hold of you. She sounded worried."

An hour before hard dark, he'd tried to call her. He didn't know what he might be walking into at Stone's cabin, and he wanted to hear Jo's voice, hear that the children were having a good time, that everyone was safe. Rose told him that Jo had gone out for the evening. A drink with Ben Jacoby. He'd chatted with his sister-in-law, then talked with each of his children. Jenny told him about her tour of Northwestern. Mr. Jacoby had arranged it, she said, had pulled strings. Cork told her that was a nice thing for him to have done. He told them all that he loved them, and at the end he thanked Rose for taking them in. "Should I have Jo call back?" she'd asked. "No," Cork had replied. "Not necessary. Just tell her I love her."

Afterward, he'd thought darkly, *Jacoby*.

"Any message, Bos?" Cork said over the radio.

"She just asked that you call her back as soon as you can."

"Did you tell her anything about what's going on up here?"

"Not a word. Didn't want her to worry. I told her you were on a late call. Routine."

"Thanks, Bos. Out."

Cork headed to the cabin where Dina Willner stood looking through the door as Larson moved about carefully inside, trying not to disturb the scene any more than Cork and his men already had.

"No sign she was ever here," Larson said, adjusting his wire-rims. "Was she hiding, you think, when we came this afternoon?"

It was a question with a hidden implication: that maybe Stone had already taken care of her for good, hidden the body somewhere, and cleaned away all trace of her presence.

"I don't know," Cork said.

He heard the cruiser coming up the road and headed down to meet it. Before Borkmann or Pender could exit the vehicle, Will Fineday was out and charging at Cork like an angry moose.

"You found her?" he said.

"Not yet, Will."

"I'll kill him," Fineday said. "I should have killed him the other day."

"When she ran, Will, why did she come here to Stone?"

"She was scared, not thinking. Stone, he's a son of a bitch, but everybody's afraid of him. She thought he could protect her."

"From what?"

"You guys. She didn't want to talk to cops."

"We know she was in the SUV with Jacoby the night he was killed. Was it Jacoby who bruised her face?"

"The son of a bitch. When I found out, I wanted to kill him."

"Did you?"

It was clear Fineday understood the direction this was going. Cork could see the struggle in the man's head and his heart. The truth might land him a view cut by iron bars, but it might also save his daughter.

"You went to Mercy Falls that night, didn't you, Will?" Cork said it quietly, and not as an accusation.

The threads—fear, distrust, prejudice—that had held him from speaking finally snapped and he nodded. "He was already dead when I got there, lying on the ground, blood everywhere. Somebody had cut his balls off, too. Shame. I wanted to do that myself."

"Did Lizzie kill Edward Jacoby?"

"No, but I'd've understood if she did. The asshole beat her and raped her."

"She told you she didn't kill Jacoby?"

"Until I came back from Mercy Falls, she didn't even know he was dead."

"You believed her?"

"Yeah, I believed her."

"Did you do anything at Mercy Falls?"

"Like what?"

"Interfere with the scene."

Fineday studied the sky. "Maybe I wiped the door handles clean."

"'Maybe'?"

"I didn't want Lizzie's fingerprints there, okay? I picked up some beer bottles that might have had her prints on them."

"Nothing else?"

"Nothing, I swear."

"If you'd told me all this before, it might've saved a lot of trouble, Will."

Fineday's hard brown eyes leveled on him. "If you were full-blood or at least not a cop, maybe you'd understand." He looked toward the cabin. "Where are they?"

"We think Stone went north, into the woods."

"He knows the Boundary Waters better than anyone." Fineday's eyes traveled over the ridge that lay between the cabin and everything beyond. "He took her with him, didn't he?"

"Maybe."

"When I find him, I'll tear out his goddamned heart."

"Cork," Larson called from the cabin. "Something here you've got to see."

Cork walked to where Larson and Dina Willner awaited him at the door. "What is it?"

"Follow me."

Larson led the way to the bedroom and stepped over the door that lay on the floor, torn off its hinges. He leaned over the bed and pointed toward an indentation in the pillow.

Cork took a step and saw what Larson meant. A large-caliber rifle bullet had been carefully placed in the center of the pillow.

"Jacketed round," Cork said. "Just like the ones fired at the Tibodeau cabin."

"It didn't get there by accident," Dina said.

Larson glanced at Cork. "What do you think it means?"

Cork crossed to the back window, pulled aside the curtain, shielded the glass so that he could see beyond the reflection of the room light. He stared out at the black silhouette of the ridge.

"It means we've got a long night ahead."

34

MAL AND THE children had gone to bed, but Rose was waiting up when Jo got home. There was a low fire under the kettle on the stove and two mugs on the kitchen table, each with a bag of Sleepytime tea hung over the lip.

Rose turned up the flame under the kettle. "Have a good evening?"

"A weird evening."

"You can tell me all about it in a minute. First you need to call Cork."

"He called?"

"Yes. Not long after you left."

"What did you tell him?"

Rose looked a little puzzled by Jo's concern. "That you went out for a drink with Ben Jacoby. What is it, Jo?"

"Let me call Cork, then we'll talk."

She tried him at home and got voice mail. She called the sheriff's office and Bos told her Cork was on a call. Routine.

"Routine?" Jo said. "It's almost ten o'clock, Bos."

"I can radio and let him know you called. Want a call back?"

"Yes. Please. As soon as he can."

"Sure thing. Miss him, do you?"

"Like crazy."

"I'll let him know."

When Jo returned to the kitchen, the kettle was just starting to whistle. Rose poured hot water into the mugs and sat down at the table with her sister. All their lives, long before Jo met Cork, before Rose fell in love with Mal, it had been like this, the two sisters and tea. In the places their mother, an army nurse whom they called the Captain, had dragged them, the desolate bases, the bleak military housing. None of that mattered because they'd had the comfort of their love for each other, embodied in late night cups of tea and talk.

"All right," Rose said. "What don't I know about Ben Jacoby?"

Jo told her the whole story.

"And I thought I knew everything about you." Rose sipped her tea. "But your relationship with him was a long time ago."

"I thought so, too. Then I saw him in Aurora, Rose, and for just a little while all the old feelings, I don't know, tried to come back."

"And?"

"I let myself feel them. And I realized absolutely there was room only for Cork in my life."

"So what's the problem?"

"For Ben it's been different, all these years."

"He's carried a torch?"

"That's what he says. I need to talk to Cork as soon as possible. God only knows what he must be thinking."

Stevie wandered into the kitchen looking half asleep. "I had a bad dream."

"Well, come on, big guy, let's get you back into bed." Jo took his hand. "Thanks for the company, Rose. You know I miss you in Aurora."

"I miss you, too. If Cork calls . . . ?"

"Wake me."

She led Stevie back to bed, got ready herself, and slipped under the covers. She tried to stay awake, waiting for Cork's call. Finally, sleep overtook her.

The call she was waiting for never came.

35

AT FIRST LIGHT, the tracking dogs began sniffing the area around Stone's cabin. Stone's scent was everywhere, but the scent of Lizzie Fineday led straight through the trees, over the ridge that backed the cabin, to Bruno Lake. It was the first in a series of lakes that led deep into the Boundary Waters Canoe Area Wilderness.

The dogs halted briefly at a large dock on the southeastern shore of the lake, deep in the shadow of the ridge. Cork and the others stood at the end of the dock, breathing hard from the fast hike over the ridge, puffing out clouds of vapor into the cold, damp air above Bruno Lake while the dogs went on, working the ground along the shoreline.

"What do you make of it?" Rutledge asked.

"Big dock," Cork said. "There's no access to Bruno except on foot or by canoe. Not the kind of traffic that would require a dock. I think this is for floatplanes."

"For trafficking?" Larson said.

"That would sure be my guess." Cork briefed Rutledge on the investigations his department had conducted earlier with the ATF and the DEA. "We never saw any sign of smuggling, probably because this ridge provides perfect cover. You can't see the lake except from the air, and I'll bet the ridge blocks the sound of a plane engine."

The sun had risen enough to fire the far shoreline, and the mist on the water there looked like steam coming from a cauldron. In a stand of gnarled cedars fifty yards down the shore, one of the dogs began barking furiously.

Rutledge looked toward the cedars. "What's all that ruckus about?"

As if in answer, Deputy Schilling called from the trees, "Cork, something here you ought to see."

"What?"

"Looks like a grave."

A faint trail had already been broken through the brush along the shore. Cork followed and near the end climbed over a fallen and rotting pine. He stepped into the cedars whose smell was sharp in the morning air. Orville Gratz, who'd brought the dogs, had pulled his hound back. The animal sat on its haunches, tongue hanging out, looking where Schilling looked, at a mound of rocks that had been piled in the middle of the cedars. The mound was two feet wide and five feet long, and looked as if it hadn't been there very long.

"Lancelot followed the girl's scent here," Gratz said. He didn't sound thrilled with the discovery.

Cork said to Schilling, "Get Cy over here with the Polaroid."

For a minute, no one spoke. The other dogs were still moving along the shoreline, their barks punctuating the silence in the cedars. Then Rutledge said quietly, "The son of a bitch."

Schilling brought Borkmann and the Polaroid.

"We need shots of that rock pile, Cy," Cork said.

Borkmann was still sweating from the exertion of the climb over the ridge, but he positioned himself and shot from several angles.

"All right, let's see what's under there," Cork said.

He approached the stones, bent, and began removing them carefully, piling them behind him. Rutledge joined him. Within a few minutes, they'd cleared the rocks away and had exposed a small area of newly dug earth. It was only a few feet long, however, much too small to accommodate a body fully laid out. Cork and Rutledge dug in the dirt with their hands, slowly clearing a shallow basin. A flash of blue appeared. Cork remembered that the last time he'd seen Lizzie Fineday in front of Stone's cabin, blinking in the sun, she'd been wearing a sweater that same shade of blue. As they removed the soil, the sweater was revealed, but that was all. It quickly became clear that the indentation had been scooped only deep enough to hold Lizzie's sweater. Below that, the ground was undisturbed. Rutledge stood up, the cardigan sweater hanging from his hand, rumpled and dirty.

"I don't get it," he said.

"There's something in the pocket," Cork said.

"Anybody got a glove?"

"Here." Schilling handed him one, leather.

Rutledge put it on and removed a folded slip of paper from the sweater pocket. He opened it. Cork looked over his shoulder and saw what was written.

48 hours.

"Mean anything?" Rutledge asked.

Cork wiped his palms on his khakis and looked at his nails, which were packed with black dirt. He pulled his walkie-talkie from his belt and called to Howard Morgan, who was at Stone's cabin, and told him to send Will Fineday down to the lake. He turned to Gratz. "Did you bring Pook?"

"You betcha. Nestor's got him." He waved toward the sound of the other dogs.

"Bring her to the dock. You know what we need to do."

"Yah," Gratz said. "Come on, Lancelot."

Rutledge watched the man and dog trot away. "What now?"

"Pook's an air scent dog," Cork said. He turned and started out of the cedars. "Gratz'll take him onto the lake. If Stone dumped Lizzie's body in the water, Pook might be able to locate her."

"And if he didn't dump her there?"

"We keep looking."

The mist vanished. Where sunlight struck the lake the clear water turned gold. Under the dock, the lake bottom was a jumble of dark stones; nearer the surface a school of minnows darted, moving together like a shadow creature.

For two hours, Orville Gratz had crisscrossed the lake in a canoe with Pook, but the dog hadn't caught Lizzie's scent. The other two dogs had sniffed the entire shoreline of Bruno Lake without success. Cork stood on the dock looking north where the Cutthroat River fed toward Sugar Bowl Lake and the other lakes beyond. He chewed on a ham sandwich, one of a couple dozen he'd ordered brought out to feed the searchers, along with coffee and water. Everything had to be carted over the ridge.

"I don't get it," Rutledge said. He sat on the dock,

running his hand through the crystal clear water. "This place is so remote, how could Stone manage a serious smuggling operation? The planes fly everything in fine, but it has to be moved out of here on foot or by canoe."

"For a hundred years, the Voyageurs moved millions of dollars of goods through here that way. Helped build a few fortunes," Cork said.

"Why did Stone do it?" Dina Willner asked. She stood near him, sipping coffee from a Styrofoam cup. "From what I understand, he has plenty of money coming from the distribution of the casino profits."

"It's not about the money," Will Fineday said.

"No?" Rutledge said. "What, then?"

"Fuck you," Fineday said.

Rutledge looked surprised by the response.

"No," Fineday said. "That's what it's about. Everything he does is just a way of saying fuck you. To me, to you, to his people. He doesn't need anybody, doesn't want anybody. To him, we're all weak, like sick animals to be preyed on." Fineday strode to the end of the dock and stood between Cork and Dina. "On the rez, some people call him *majimanidoo*. A bad spirit. A devil." He followed Cork's gaze north toward the mouth of the Cutthroat. "They're right."

Larson came down the trail from the ridge.

"What's the word from the plane?" Cork asked.

He'd arranged for a Forest Service DeHavilland to fly over the area and look for anyone in a canoe on the lakes or along the Cutthroat. The nearest official access to the wilderness was ten miles west. It was late in the season and few permits were being issued, so anyone in a canoe would be suspect.

"Nothing. They didn't see a blessed soul."

"Got the map, Ed?"

"Right here."

Larson unfolded a topographical map of the region for four hundred square miles. "The dogs are getting nowhere. The search plane's a bust. What do you think?"

"He moved fast," Cork said.

"Does he still have the girl?"

"If he'd left her at the bottom of the lake, Pook would probably have picked that up. I think Stone's still got her," Cork said.

Rutledge ran his hand through the water, making ripples that were edged with gold. He eyed Fineday. "Did she go willingly?"

Fineday didn't look at him. His own eyes were glued to the north. "You don't say no to Stone." He rubbed the long scar on his face as if the old wound still hurt him. "Why would he take her? He doesn't care about her. She'd only get in his way."

"He has reason," Cork said. "Somehow it goes back to that cartridge on the pillow and the sweater in the ground."

Rutledge glanced up. "Why wouldn't he just make a beeline to Canada? He could be there by tomorrow."

"When he gets to Canada, where is he?" Cork said. "No better off, and he knows it."

"We could wait him out. Put a watch on every wilderness access. Make sure every police and sheriff's department's on the lookout. I know what you said about him being able to stay in there forever, but that was before he took the girl."

"Maybe that's why he took Lizzie," Cork said. "With the girl, he can't stay in there long, and he knows we know it."

"I don't get it," Dina said.

"She's a liability. He can't afford to keep her. It's like that hourglass in *The Wizard of Oz*. As soon as the sand runs out, Dorothy dies. I think that's what the note in her pocket was about. Forty-eight hours. He'll keep her for forty-eight hours. He knows we won't wait him out. He knows we have to try to find Lizzie before her time's up."

"He wants us to go after him?" Rutledge said.

"I think that's why he left the cartridge. He wanted it clear that he was the one who'd fired the shots at the Tibodeau cabin. Maybe he figured we were already on the road to figuring that out for ourselves. But he makes the declaration, he maintains control. I don't think he's trying to escape. I think he wants us to follow him into his territory. It's like Will says. 'Fuck you.'"

"Seems a stretch to me," Rutledge said.

"It's the kind of man Stone is. He'd get off pitting his power against ours."

"What are you going to do?"

Cork tossed the crust of his sandwich into the lake, and a moment later the bread disappeared in a flash of shiny green scales and a splash of silver water. "I'm going to give him what he wants. I'm going in after him."

Rutledge scratched the top of his head. His face looked puzzled and he spent a minute fishing through his hair. He studied something he'd pinched between his fingers. "Damn. I thought tick season was over." He flicked the critter into the lake and shook himself. "Feels like they're crawling all over me now. Look, I don't like the idea of anyone going in, Cork."

"I don't like it either, Simon, but I don't see any

way around it." Cork pulled the walkie-talkie from its holster on his belt. "Morgan. Over."

"Morgan here."

"Howard, I want you to get some gear together for a trip into the woods. Enough for three men for two days."

"One canoe?"

Fineday said, "I'm going with you."

Cork started to shake his head, but he could see the determination on the man's face. He understood how he'd feel if it was his daughter out there.

"Make it two canoes and four men. I want everything ready to go by"—he looked at his watch—"oh four hundred."

"Ten-four. I'm on it."

"You're really going in?" Dina said.

"Yeah. But I think Simon has a good idea. We should put a watch on all the nearest accesses and float Stone's photo everywhere. Contact the provincial police in Ontario, too. Let them know Stone may be headed their way."

Rutledge still looked skeptical. "You think you can find him?"

"No." Cork turned away from the lake and started for the ridge. "But I know a man who can."

36

Jo's FIRST OFFICIAL date with Cork had begun at the Lincoln Park Zoo. It had ended at Rocky's on the lakeshore, where Cork picked up a sack of fried shrimp and french fries, which they ate while sipping beer and watching Lake Michigan slide into the deep blue ink of evening. In between, she found a man who was funny, gentle, smart, who came from a small town in Minnesota and had somehow managed, despite the awful things he'd seen as a cop on the South Side, to retain a belief in simple human dignity.

"You're a good cop?" she'd asked in jest.

"Depends on the situation. I try to be a good man first. Sometimes that might make me look like a bad cop, but I don't think of myself that way. You don't have to be a hard-ass to be in control of a tough situation. Connection, that's what I try for. Maybe it's because I'm part Ojibwe. Connection is very important."

"Ojibwe?" It sounded exotic, exciting.

"Or Anishinaabe. Some people call us Chippewa, but that's really the white man's bastardization of Ojibwe. Most Shinnobs I know aren't fond of the name."

"Connection," she said. "Are we connecting?"

"I think we are."

"Then why haven't you kissed me?"

He smiled, as if amused by her boldness. "When I was twelve and my father sat me down to talk about the birds and the bees, one of the things he said to me was, 'Cork, always let the woman make the first move.'"

"Was it a good piece of advice?"

"Do you want me to kiss you?"

"Very much."

"Then it was excellent advice."

Through all the years, the hardships, even when they both stood at the painful edge of abandoning their marriage, she'd never forgotten that kiss or the promise it held for her.

As arranged, Rae Bly was waiting for Jo at the sea lion pool near the zoo entrance. She was so engrossed in watching the animals cavort that she didn't notice Jo, who finally touched her on the shoulder.

"Here you are," Rae exclaimed with a broad smile. "And these are your children?"

Jo introduced them and Rose, then sent them along saying she would meet them at the primate house in an hour.

Ben's sister wore sunglasses and a white cap with a bill that shaded her face. She carried a purse and also a long canister that hung by a strap over her shoulder. "A lovely family, Jo."

"Thanks."

Rae waved toward a bench in the shade of a tree. "Shall we sit down?" When they were seated, she put down the canister, reached into her purse, and pulled out a silver cigarette case. She held it open toward Jo.

"I don't smoke."

"You used to. Pretty heavily, as I recall."

"I quit when I became pregnant with Jenny."

"I don't have children, so I'm still looking for that compelling reason. Unfortunately, smoking and painting are tied together in my thinking. Paint a little, smoke a little, paint a little. The truth is, I'm afraid to give it up. Maybe the art wouldn't come without it."

Jo settled back so that she was out of the sun. "You're famous, Ben tells me."

"Famous? I sell well, but 'famous' is something else entirely. I enjoy what I do, and that's what's important for me." She sent out a cloud of smoke, and waved it away from Jo. "I was so pleased to see you last night. You and Ben. It reminded me of that wonderful summer."

"That was a long time ago. A lot has changed."

"Some things. Ben still loves you. He always has."

"Twenty years ago he left me, Rae. Without a word of explanation."

"I know." She looked up at the blue sky, squinting through her dark glasses. "When I left for school at the end of that summer, I prayed Ben would marry you. I'd talked to him about it. I know he hadn't told you about Miriam, and he made me promise not to say anything. He was so torn between love and duty. For a little while I thought he would choose love. But Lou's a formidable obstacle for us all, and in the end, fate seemed to be on his side. In September, our mother was diagnosed with pancreatic cancer. She went quickly."

"He never said a word to me."

"How could he? Her dying wish was for him to marry Miriam, and he couldn't say no. If it's any consolation, he was miserable his whole marriage."

"What was she like?"

"Miriam? A horrible JAP. I'm Jewish, so I can say that. She was spoiled, self-centered, vain. What was important to her was the big house, the country club, the glittery life. She didn't love Ben any more than he loved her, but the life she had seemed to give her everything she wanted. Ben walked through that marriage with his eyes and his mouth closed. And his heart. God, it was painful to see."

"How did he endure it?"

"By doing what the Jacoby men have always done. Poured himself into the business, made money to support his family, found his pleasure in other women." She looked deeply into Jo's eyes. "When I saw how Ben looked at you last night, I thought about how everything might have been different."

In the silence that followed, she took a long drag off her cigarette.

"I brought you something," she said, brightening.

She lifted the canister, unscrewed a cap at one end, and pulled out a rolled canvas, which she gave to Jo.

"Open it," she said.

Jo spread the canvas and recognized the painting immediately. It was her, Jo, in the white dress, in Grant Park, twenty years ago.

"Ben asked me to do it for him before I left for school that fall. He wanted to give it to you as a gift. Then he ended things and gave it back to me and told me to get rid of it. He couldn't bear to look at it. I've kept it all these years. I'd love for you to have it."

"It's beautiful, Rae, but I can't."

"Please. It was always meant for you. It would give me great pleasure knowing that you finally have it." She put a hand on Jo's arm. "And honestly, if you decide you can't keep it, you have my blessing to sell it. Believe me, you could get enough for that canvas to send Jenny to Northwestern for a year. Take it, Jo, please. For me."

She didn't feel comfortable accepting, but she also felt that to decline, particularly in the face of Rae's strong insistence, was not right, either.

"All right. Thank you." She rolled it again and slipped it back into the canister. "So you've become the artist you always wanted to be."

"No thanks to my father." Rae laughed. "He disinherited me."

"Because you became an artist?"

"That and because I didn't marry the man he'd chosen for me." She dropped her cigarette and crushed it on the pavement. "My parents' marriage was arranged and was a dismal affair. Ben married the woman my parents chose for him, and I saw how miserable he was. I decided, come hell or high water, I was going to marry for love. And I did. George Bly, a wonderful man. It was George who urged me to follow my heart and to paint. He's an artist, too. Stained glass. My father cut me off financially and cut me out of his will. Big deal. George and I do fine financially. The important thing is that we love what we do and we love each other. Believe me, that's not typical for the Jacobys."

"What about Eddie and his wife? How was that marriage?"

Rae shook her head sadly. "That may have been the greatest travesty of all. You knew Eddie well?"

"Well enough to wonder about the woman who would agree to marry him. Ben told me she's Argentine."

"Yes. From one of the best families. She's beautiful, well educated, cultured, and broke. When the Argentine economy collapsed, her family lost everything. Once again, Jews became the target of old hatred and prejudice. Many of those who were able to emigrated—to Israel, Spain, the States.

"My father and Gabriella's father had been financial associates for years. The situation in Argentina developed about the same time Eddie hit marriageable age. No woman who knew him would marry him. My father understood that. He'd seen Gabriella and knew the plight of her family, and he arranged to marry the poor girl to Eddie. It got her out of Argentina, and Lou promised to help the rest of the family emigrate. Her parents chose to go to Israel. Her brother came here."

"I was impressed with her last night."

"She is impressive. She proved to be a dutiful wife, good mother, doting daughter-in-law. Lou absolutely adores her."

Jo detected a note of bitterness in that last statement. "Is that a problem?"

Rae pulled another cigarette from her silver case and lit up. "In his business dealings, my father's a powerful and perceptive man. In his personal life, he's clueless. He has no idea about real love. He mistakes subservience for affection. My mother didn't put up with his tyranny, and he ignored her. Ben tried to break free of his control, and Lou has never completely forgiven him. I defied him, and he all but banished me. See, my father's great weakness is this. He'll deny it with a vengeance but he needs desperately to feel loved, and feeling loved means two things to him. That you need him and that you obey him. Eddie's mother, Gwen, understood this perfectly. She played to it flawlessly. Dad loved her and gave her whatever she wanted. Eddie grew up doing the same thing, the little toady, and became the apple of Lou's eye. Gabriella's no slouch. She understood immediately which way the wind blows." She shot out a puff of smoke. "If I sound bitter it's only because, despite everything, I still love my father. And I pity his blindness and I miss his affection. So maybe, in the end, I'm just as screwed up as all the other Jacobys." She looked away as a tear crawled down her cheek from behind one of her dark lenses. "I'm sorry, I didn't mean for that to happen."

"That's okay," Jo said.

"You"—Rae laughed gently—"you would have made a great sister-in-law. Tell me about your life now. Everything."

They talked for an hour, then Jo looked at her watch and said it was time to meet Rose and the children. She stood up, slung the canister strap over her shoulder, and gave Rae a parting hug. As she walked away, heading toward the primate house, Jo couldn't help thinking that there were a lot of cages in the world, and not all of them had bars.

37

No ONE KNEW the true age of Henry Meloux. He was already old when Cork was a boy. Meloux was one of the Midewiwin, a Mide, a member of the Grand Medicine Society. He lived on a rocky, isolated finger of land called Crow Point that jutted into Iron Lake at the northern edge of the reservation.

Cork parked the Pathfinder on the gravel at the side of the county road, locked up, and followed a trail that began at a double-trunk birch and led deep into the woods. For a while, the way lay through national forest land, but at some unmarked boundary it crossed onto the reservation. Cork walked for half an hour through woods where the only sounds were the chatter of squirrels, the squawk of crows, and the occasional crack of a fallen branch under his boots. When he broke from the pine trees, he could see Meloux's cabin on the point, an old one-room log structure with a cedar plank roof shingled over with birch bark.

"Henry," he called, not wanting to surprise the old man, though surprising Meloux would be a rare thing. The Mide had a remarkable knack for anticipating visitors. If that failed, the barking of Walleye, Meloux's yellow dog, was usually warning enough. Meloux did not respond, and Walleye was nowhere to be seen. Cork approached the door, which stood open, and looked inside.

The interior of the cabin was always clean, though full of a hodgepodge of items that recalled other eras. On the walls hung snowshoes made of steam-curved birch with deer hide bindings, a deer-prong pipe, a bow strung with sinew from a snapping turtle. There was a Skelly gas station calendar forty years out of date, but the old man kept it because he admitted appreciating the young woman in the cheesecake photo whose breasts were big and round as pink balloons ready to burst. Resting on two tenpenny nails hammered into the wall was an old long-barreled Remington with a walnut stock. There was a sink but no running water, a hickory table and two chairs, a potbellied stove, and a small bunk. These were practically all the material goods Meloux possessed, but he was the most contented man Cork had ever known.

The open door didn't bother Cork. In good weather, Meloux often left the door ajar for fresh air to circulate inside. It also allowed Shinnobs to bring and leave for the old Mide offerings of respect and gratitude. Cork could tell from the sacks on the table that the recent offerings had been *manomin,* wild rice. In the Ojibwe language, August was Manomingizis, the Month of Rice. In the final days of August and into early fall, the Anishinaabeg poled through the fields in the lakes, knocking the ripe kernels loose and filling their boats. After the rice was prepared, some would be eaten, some sold, and some given as a gift, as it had been to Meloux.

A distant bark brought Cork around. He gazed toward the trail he had followed, and in a moment he spotted Walleye bounding from the pine trees, his yellow coat full of burrs. Meloux was not far behind. He walked slowly but erect, his hair like white smoke drifting about his shoulders. He wore bib overalls, a faded blue denim shirt, deer hide moccasins that he'd made himself. In his hand was an ironwood staff ornamented with an eagle feather, and over his shoulder hung a beaded leather bag. He smiled when he saw Cork but didn't change his pace. Walleye, however, ran ahead. When Cork knelt to greet him, the old dog eagerly nuzzled his palm.

"Anin, Corcoran O'Connor," the old man said in formal greeting.

"Anin, Henry." Cork eyed the bag hanging from Meloux's shoulder. "Let me guess: mushroom hunting."

"I have gathered a feast. I will make a fine soup with rice and mushrooms. Will you join me?" Meloux said.

"I have to decline."

The sun was directly overhead, beating down out of a cloudless sky. Meloux shaded his eyes with a wrinkled hand and studied Cork's face.

"You always come like a hungry dog, wanting something, but it's never food."

"Sorry, Henry."

The old man lifted his hand in pardon. "It's all right. Like a dog, you're always grateful for even a scrap."

"It's more than a scrap I need this time."

Meloux nodded. "Let me put away my harvest, then we will smoke and talk."

*   *   *

They sat at a stone circle that enclosed the ashes of many fires. Down the slope a few feet away lay the water of Iron Lake, crystal clear along the shore, blue and solid as a china plate in the distance. The old man had listened to Cork's story and now he smoked a cigarette hand-rolled from tobacco Cork had brought as a gift. Although he'd given up smoking more than two years before, Cork held a cigarette, too. The ritual he shared with Meloux had nothing to do with addiction.

"Stone," Meloux said. "Like a Windigo, that one."

In Anishinaabe myth, the Windigo was a cannibal giant with a heart of ice. The only way to kill a Windigo was to become one. Once you had succeeded in destroying the terrible creature, you had to drink hot wax so that you would melt back down to the size of other men. If that didn't happen, you were doomed to remain a Windigo forever. Thinking of how Stone had killed his monster of a stepfather, Cork believed he understood what Meloux was saying. Myths were simple things, but they cut to the heart of brutal truths.

"What do you want of me?" the old Mide asked.

"You've lived in *Noopiming* all your life." *Noopiming,* the Ojibwe name for the north country. "You know the woods better than anyone alive. Since I was a boy, I've heard stories of your prowess as a hunter. Henry, I need someone who knows the Boundary Waters and who can track the Windigo."

The old man smoked awhile. Indian time. Never hurried.

"That was when I was a young man. It has been too many years to count since I was on a hunt, and this kind of animal I have never hunted. Stone, he will be dangerous."

"Will you do it?"

Meloux finished his cigarette. He threw the butt into the ash inside the stone circle. "I'm old. Death and me, we've been eyeing one another for a while now. There's not much left that scares me. One last hunt, that would not be a bad thing, especially to hunt the Windigo." He used his staff to help himself stand. "When do we leave?"

38

WHEN THEY RETURNED from the zoo, Jo told the kids it was time to concentrate on schoolwork. Stevie was in the first grade and had no homework, so Jo gave him the book she'd brought along for just this occasion, *Johnny Tremaine*. Luckily, all the reading his parents had done at bedtime was paying off. Stevie loved to read. He took the book and settled onto the sofa without an argument.

Rose was down the hallway, in the kitchen.

"Did Cork call?" Jo asked as soon as she walked in.

"No. Worried?" Rose was washing her hands at the sink.

"He hasn't returned any of my calls."

"Try him again."

Jo looked at the clock. Two-thirty. He should be at the office, but she was hoping maybe he was home, resting. God knew he needed it. And if he was, should she disturb him? She decided to.

The phone rang five times, then voice mail kicked in.

"You've reached the O'Connors. We can't come to the phone right now, but if you'd leave a message, we'll get back to you as quick as we can."

It was Cork's voice. Not him, but the illusion of him. Still, she liked what she heard, his words warm with easy hospitality, a genuine goodness in his tone. Or maybe she only heard it because that's how she thought of him.

She'd left messages already and didn't leave another.

"Still no answer?" Rose said. "Maybe you should try his office."

"They won't tell me anything."

"They certainly won't tell you if you don't try."

Jo called the Tamarack County Sheriff's Department. Bos answered.

"No," she told Jo. "He's not in."

There was something in her voice, a hesitancy, Jo thought.

"What's wrong, Bos?"

"Nothing's wrong, Jo. Cork's been working hard on two investigations, you know. He's just out a lot."

"I've left him messages asking him to call me. He hasn't. That's not like him."

Bos didn't reply.

"Is Ed Larson in?"

"He's out in the field, too."

"Is anybody there but you?"

"We're a little shorthanded."

"Look, Bos, I've heard that Lizzie Fineday is a suspect in Edward Jacoby's murder. Is that true?"

"You know I can't talk about an ongoing investigation."

She went hot with anger. "Goddamn it, Bos. What can you tell me?"

"Not much, and you know it."

It was useless to strike out at Bos, who was just following Cork's instructions. Jo breathed deeply, let go.

"Will you have him call me?"

"Of course. Just as soon as he can. And, Jo"—Bos sounded like a soothing grandmother now—"if there's anything you need to know, I'll make sure you know it right away, okay?"

Rose went to the refrigerator and pulled out a pound of raw hamburger and a package of sausage. She was about to start making a meat loaf for dinner. "So what's going on?"

"I don't know. Bos is keeping something back, but I have no idea what."Jo's whole body felt stiff, and she rubbed the tense muscles on the back of her neck. "It's not like Cork not to call. Is he angry, do you think?"

"About what?"

"He knows that Ben and I have a past together. He knows that we were out last night."

"I think you should give him more credit."

"I know, but I feel like I'm stumbling around in the dark."

Stevie wandered in to ask about a word in his book. He saw Rose working at the kitchen counter. "Whatcha making?"

"Meat loaf, for dinner."

"Meat loaf! Sweet! You make the best meat loaf in the whole entire world." He ran back down the hallway to share the good news with his sisters.

Rose said, "Can you call someone else—not one of Cork's people?"

Jo leaned on the counter watching her sister shape the loaf. "I suppose I could call Ben."

"Why him?"

"He hired someone to consult on the investigation of Eddie's murder. He gets regular updates."

"Seems worth a try. You'll certainly be no worse off."

Jo tried Jacoby's cell phone, but got only his voice mail. She called his office and was told he was in meetings all afternoon. She left a message.

"What's in the canister?" Rose asked.

The children had asked, too, but Jo had put them off. Now she unscrewed the cap, took out the canvas, and showed it to Rose.

"It's beautiful," Rose said.

Jo told her the history and that Rae had insisted she accept the gift.

"What are you going to do with it?" Rose asked. "Given your history with Ben Jacoby, I can't imagine Cork would be thrilled to see that hanging in your home."

"I know. I've been thinking. What if I gave it to Ben?"

"That might be the best thing, if he wanted it."

"I'll ask him."

It was three hours before Ben called back, just as Jo had begun to set the table for dinner. The whole house smelled of savory meat loaf.

"I'm in traffic right now, Jo, and I'd rather talk in person anyway. What if I dropped by your sister's place?"

His tone sounded a little ominous, and if it was bad news he was going to deliver, she wanted to be somewhere the kids couldn't hear.

"Or," he went on, "if you'd rather, we could meet at my house. It's only about ten minutes from where you are now. I'll be there in half an hour."

Jo agreed and Ben gave her the address and directions. The house was on Sheridan Road, easy to find. She hung up.

"That didn't sound good," Rose said. She was at the stove, checking the potatoes. "What did he say?"

"It's what he didn't say, and how he didn't say it."

"Until you know the worst, anticipate the best."

Jo said, "It's already pretty bad because I have to leave in a few minutes, which means I'm going to miss the best meat loaf in the whole entire world."

39

"WHY MORGAN?" Schilling asked.

They were gathered at the dock on Bruno Lake. The gear had been loaded into the canoes, and Cork was looking over the map one last time with Ed Larson and Simon Rutledge. Meloux already sat in the bow of the lead canoe, and Will Fineday had settled into the bow of the second.

Deputy Howard Morgan looked up from where he knelt on the dock, retying the lace of his hiking boot. "Because I do the Boundary Waters a lot. Because I have a sharpshooter rating. Because I don't whine about assignments. And," he added, standing up, "because I'm a bachelor." He gave Schilling a light, friendly jab in the stomach.

"I just meant that I'd be willing to go."

"I know," Cork said, glancing from the map. He could have added one more reason it was Morgan who was going. That in a tight situation he'd prefer Morgan at his back.

"The chopper and the critical response team will be standing by," Larson said. "Give the word and they'll be there in no time."

"Sure you don't want a few more men along?" Rutledge asked.

Cork shook his head. "If I'm wrong about all this, we'd be taking deputies from where they're needed. If I'm right, we've got the CRT for backup."

"By the way," Rutledge said, "Dina asked me to give you this."

He handed Cork a gold medallion the size of a silver dollar.

"A Saint Christopher's medal?" It seemed an odd gift, because Cork knew Dina was Jewish. "Where is she?"

"She left right after you headed off to recruit Meloux."

Cork slipped the medallion in his pocket. "We'll check in hourly with our location," he told Larson.

"I wish I felt better about this." Rutledge eyed Meloux with a look Cork interpreted as skepticism of the old man's ability to be of any help.

"I wish I felt better about everything, Simon. And if you've got another idea for saving Lizzie Fineday, I'm still open to suggestions."

Rutledge only offered his hand. "Good luck."

Cork stepped into the stern of the lead canoe, and Morgan took the stern of the other. They pushed away from the dock and into the lake, paddling toward the Cutthroat River, which would take them north into the Boundary Waters Canoe Area Wilderness. Halfway across the lake, a great bird appeared in front of them, high up, the tips of its wings like fingers scraping against the hard blue ceiling of the sky. Meloux watched the bird closely.

"An eagle?" he asked.

"A turkey vulture," Cork replied.

"Too bad," the old man said, sounding disappointed.

"What's it mean, Henry?" Thinking that for some reason the turkey vulture was not a good sign.

Meloux squinted at the bird and said with a note of sadness, "That my eyes aren't what they used to be."

Cork knew that Meloux's physical senses weren't those of a young man, but it was a different sense he'd hoped for from the old Mide, something that came from a lifetime not just of hunting but of understanding the nature of human beings. He prayed that this sense was still sharp.

The Cutthroat took them to Sugar Bowl Lake a mile north of Bruno. It was a round lake ringed by high hills, hence its name. The sun was at their backs. Their shadows moved ahead of them across the water, and behind followed a deep, rippling wake. Cork watched the slopes carefully. On top of his pack, which was situated directly in front of him, was a pair of Leitz binoculars. Beside the pack rested a Remington Model 700 police rifle. Morgan had brought an M40A1 sniper rifle and scope, and Fineday, who'd hunted all his life, had brought his own Winchester. Before embarking, they'd held a conference regarding the wearing of the Kevlar vests each man had been issued. Meloux and Fineday, neither of whom had ever worn body armor, were clearly not thrilled with the prospect of the stiff armature. Morgan commented that the vests were generally uncomfortable and would be particularly so during the kind of prolonged physical activity that the canoeing and portaging would demand. He also pointed out that they had every reason to believe that Stone, if he fired at them, would use armor-piercing rounds. Cork told them he'd prefer it if they wore the armor, but he understood their objections and drew up shy of insisting. They were, however, to keep the armor handy at all times and not hesitate if he gave the order to suit up.

The afternoon was still, the only sound the burble of water that swirled with each dip of the paddle.

"Should we be concerned yet, Henry?" Cork said.

The old Mide scratched his head and thought an unusually long time. "Not here. Not yet."

The Cutthroat left Sugar Bowl via a series of rapids too shallow for the canoes. One followed the Cutthroat, the other veered west toward a little lake called Snail.

"Which way, Henry?" Cork said.

Meloux walked the trail along the Cutthroat, came back, and followed the other portage for a distance. He studied the rocky soil carefully, shaking his head with uncertainty. "Hard ground, no tracks," he said.

Morgan spoke quietly. "Up here, it's all hard ground and no tracks."

Meloux stood where the trails diverged, looking west, north. Finally he pointed along the Cutthroat. "I think Stone would go this way."

"You're sure?"

"He would go quickly and far enough so that you would not bring the dogs. So north."

"How far, Henry?"

Meloux shrugged. "We will see."

Morgan gave Cork a look of concern, but held his tongue. The men hefted their canoes and began to walk.

Sunset found them at Lamb Lake, hitting the end of a short thirty-rod portage as the light turned blazing orange and ignited a wildfire of color that swept over the aspen on the hills. Cork and the others stood in the shadow of tamaracks on the western shore of the lake, the water dark at their feet. Already they could sense the cold that would descend with the fall of night.

The afternoon had not gone well. At every juncture, every point where a decision about direction had to be made, Meloux seemed uncertain. He spent a long time studying each trail. He knelt, his old bones cracking, and peered at the ground. He rubbed his eyes with his gnarled knuckles and afterward seemed to have a bewildered look. Each time he finally pointed the way, Cork wanted to ask, "Are you sure?" But what would have been the use?

In Morgan's face, the concern was obvious. Had they put their faith in a man too old? He said nothing. Fineday, too, held his tongue, but Cork could imagine his worry. Were they losing his daughter?

Still, none of them had been able to say that Meloux was wrong, that Stone had gone a different way. But were they, Cork wondered, the blind following the blind?

Beyond Lamb Lake, their way would lie to the east, along a narrow flow called Carson Creek that fed out of the far shoreline. It would take them to Hornby, a huge lake with dozens of inlets. The most direct route across Lamb was through a channel between two small islands. Although it was difficult from a distance to judge their size, Cork recalled from the map that both islands were shaped roughly like bread loaves, the larger approximately one hundred yards long, the other half that size. It appeared that at one time they'd been connected, but the natural bridge had collapsed, its ruin apparent in the great stone slabs that broke the surface in the channel. On the larger island, a few jack pines had managed to put down roots, but they were ragged-looking trees, like beggars huddled against a cold night. The southern end of the island was dominated by a sharp rise thick with blood-red sumac.

"Do we go on?" Morgan asked.

"Hell yes, we go on," Fineday said. "We haven't found Lizzie yet."

"Henry?" Cork turned to Meloux.

"I would like to sit and smoke," the old man said.

Fineday spoke urgently, but not without respect. "We don't have time. She's still with him out there somewhere."

"Stone knows we're coming," Meloux said. "He will be patient now. We should be patient, too."

"I'll go on alone if I have to."

"If you have to. But consider how much more eight eyes can see than two. And there's one more thing." Meloux settled his bony rump on the trunk of a fallen tamarack. "I am tired."

"We'll break for a while," Cork said. "Then decide."

Not far off the trail, in a stand of quaking aspen, was an official Boundary Waters campsite. While Meloux smoked and ruminated, Cork checked the camp. When he came back, he sat beside Meloux on the fallen tamarack, rolled a cigarette, and smoked with the old man in silence. Morgan lay with his back propped against an overturned canoe, his eyes closed. Fineday paced the shoreline.

"How're you doing, Henry?" Cork asked.

"When I was a young man, I could read a trail

across a face of rock. Now . . ." He took a deep, ragged breath.

Cork was concerned. It was obvious the day had taken a heavy toll on Meloux. He looked ready to buckle.

What had he been thinking, bringing an old man, a man of parchment skin and matchstick bones, on such a difficult journey, such a dangerous mission? Had he put the others at risk, and Lizzie Fineday as well? Should he have mounted an army of deputies and volunteers, swept into the woods hoping to catch Stone in a huge net? Would anything he tried have worked?

Meloux finally said, "We are near the end, I think."

"How do you know, Henry?"

"He knows he has gone beyond the dogs. The next lake is Asabikeshiinh."

Spider. The Anishinaabe name for the lake. Because of all the inlets like legs, Cork knew.

"It is a big lake, easy to lose someone who follows him," Meloux said. "But he does not want to lose us."

"What do you think he'll do?"

"He will set a trap. Or he will circle."

"Come up on us from behind?" Morgan's eyes were open now.

"It is a trick of bears, a good trick. So maybe that is what he will do." He spoke to Fineday. "Put your restless walking to use. Look carefully along the shoreline, in the soft dirt, for boot prints. Go that way." He pointed to his right. "You, Corcoran, go the other way."

"What about me?" Morgan asked.

"Go back down the trail and look for signs of his turning there."

Fifteen minutes later, they regrouped at the over-turned canoes. None of them had found any indication that Stone had ever been that way. Another disappointment.

"It's getting dark," Fineday said. "We should keep moving. We can make Lake Hornby before nightfall."

"If he is behind us," Meloux said, "moving ahead will take us away from him. If he is ahead, he is waiting, and dark is not a good time to walk into his trap."

"We should stay here?" Cork said.

The old man said, "Yes."

There was no way to know for sure what Stone had up his sleeve. Ahead, behind, watching them from somewhere even now, perhaps. When Fineday didn't argue, Cork figured that he'd accepted Meloux's advice. It sounded good to Cork, too.

"Maybe I should park myself out of sight near the last landing, see if anybody's following," Morgan said.

"Not a bad idea, Howard."

"It's almost time for a radio check," Morgan reminded him.

"I'll do it," Cork said.

When he raised Larson on the radio, Ed's first question was "What's your twenty?"

"Lamb Lake."

"Any sign of Stone or the Fineday girl?"

"Nothing."

"Have you seen anything, anything at all, that would confirm you're on the right track?"

"That's a negative."

"Cork, you could be on a wild-goose chase. Or, worse, walking right into Stone's gun sight."

"I'm still open to suggestions." Cork waited for a reply, then said, "In the meantime, have the DeHavilland make one more pass over the area before it's too dark."

There was a grill at the campsite, but it was too risky to build a fire. Morgan returned having seen nothing, and they sat down to a meal of peanut butter sandwiches, dried apricots, and Hershey bars with almonds. Once the sun had set fully, the chill of the autumn night rolled in quickly. Although it had taken precious space in the Duluth pack, Morgan had brought a one-burner Coleman stove and a small propane tank. He boiled lake water and made instant coffee, which the men drank eagerly.

The sky was amethyst and still without stars. "You said he would circle or he would set a trap." Fineday spoke out of the growing dark under the aspens. His form was clear, but his face was almost lost. "What kind of trap?"

"Why does he have your daughter?" Meloux said.

"Because he's a son of a bitch."

"That," the old man agreed. "But if our sheriff is right, Stone has her for the same reason a hunter puts fish and honey in a bear trap. Have you ever built a bear trap in the old way?"

Fineday said no.

"You build it of brush. It does not need to be sturdy, so long as there is only one way for the bear to get in. Even a hungry bear will look for the easiest way. The hunter puts the fish and honey far back in the trap, and he sets a heavy log over the opening. When *makwa* walks in," Meloux said, using the Ojibwe word for bear, "the hunter springs the trap, the log falls, *makwa*'s back is broken. It is the fish and honey that are his undoing."

"Stone is counting on us wanting the girl," Morgan said.

Meloux sipped his coffee. "Would we be here if he did not have her?"

They heard the drone of the DeHavilland as it approached and flew low overhead. It circled Lamb Lake, then headed north into the darkening sky.

A few minutes later, Larson radioed from base. The floatplane had nothing to report.

Cork stood up and said, "Going to see a man about a horse."

He started in the direction of the pit toilet. Although he took a flashlight, he didn't turn it on. He'd gone less than a dozen steps when he froze and listened. From the portage came the snap of twigs and the crack of dry leaves underfoot. Quickly he riffled through the possibilities. An innocent canoeist? But the floatplane had spotted no one on the lake behind them. An animal? A moose might make that kind of noise, so maybe. Stone? No, Stone would never give himself away so easily. Unless he was up to something.

Cork was too far from his weapon, but in the thin light he saw Morgan in a kneeling position with his rifle stock snugged against his shoulder. Fineday quickly brought his own rifle to the ready. Meloux was invisible, already part of the woods somehow. Cork dropped to the ground and kept his eyes on the portage, visible through the trees twenty yards away. The ground was littered with golden aspen leaves, and the scent of their desiccation should have been strong, but all he could smell was the coffee Morgan had made. He wondered how far that good smell had traveled. Had Stone picked it up?

From the lake came the cry of a loon and, nearer to Cork, the buzzing of a night insect the cold had not yet killed. He heard the approaching footfalls, the scrape of something huge pushing against the brush at the side of the trail, something that seemed to let out a small growl now and then as it came. Both Morgan and Fineday had their cheeks laid against the rifle stocks, sighting.

The black shape that appeared, rattling the under-brush, was like nothing Cork had ever seen. Nearly as tall and long as a moose, it lumbered along the portage toward Lamb Lake. Cork couldn't help thinking of the cannibal ogre, the Windigo.

The creature stumbled and let out a cry. Then it spoke.

"Shit."

Cork recognized the voice.

"Dina?"

He realized the truth of what he was seeing. No creature, but Dina Willner, portaging what looked to be an inflatable kayak, which was sometimes called a duckie.

She set the kayak on the ground, and as she did so, the heavy rubber siding scraped the underbrush, resulting in what sounded like a growl.

"I was surprised you stopped," she said, a little breathless. "There was still daylight."

Morgan and Fineday lowered their rifles. Cork made his way across the campsite.

"What the hell are you doing here?" he said.

"What I'm paid to do. Consulting."

On her back she carried a pack, and slung over her right shoulder was a scoped rifle.

"Jesus Christ, we almost shot you."

"With all that noise? You might not have known it was me, but I know you didn't think it was Stone."

"A visitor?" Meloux asked. He'd materialized from nowhere.

"Not for long, Henry. She's going back," Cork said.

Meloux shook his head. "Not tonight. Not with Stone in these woods."

Dina walked to him and gave her hand. "I'm Dina Willner."

"Henry Meloux." The old man appraised her, top to bottom, and nodded appreciatively. "You are small but you have the look of a hunter. Are you hungry?"

"Henry," Dina replied with a huge smile, "I'm absolutely famished."

"It was the last inflatable the sporting goods store had. Not the best, but I figured that for a couple of days, it would do." She'd eaten a sandwich and a handful of the apricots, and now she was sipping coffee Morgan had offered. "I stashed it on the other side of Bruno Lake before you all got started."

"You haven't answered my question," Cork said.

"You mean, why am I here?"

"That would be the one."

"Because I'm not one of your people and have to stay back. Because you wouldn't have let me come if I'd asked. Because this is the kind of thing I'm good at."

"How did you find us?" Fineday said.

"I'm an excellent tracker," she said. "Also, I bugged Sheriff O'Connor."

Cork thought a moment, then dug in his pants and pulled out the medallion she had passed to him through Simon Rutledge.

"Good old Saint Christopher," Dina said. "He never lets me down."

"The DeHavilland didn't spot you," Cork said.

"I have a radio tuned to your frequency. I made sure I was under cover whenever the plane was due to fly over."

"We need to let base know the situation." Cork turned to the radio.

He explained everything to Larson, said that Dina would stay until morning, then would be sent back. To which she shook her head with a definite no. Larson gave him the latest weather forecast—clear skies, cold temperatures—and then gave him the difficult news.

"Faith Gray says you have one more chance to keep your appointment with her before she orders your suspension."

"Christ, doesn't she understand the circumstances?"

"The circumstances don't matter, Cork. The language of the rule is clear. You ought to know. Your rule."

Cork signed off feeling tired, feeling as if there was too much on his shoulders at the moment.

With hard dark, the stars came out by the millions and the sky through the branches above the campsite looked as if it were full of a thin frost.

"At least the weather's holding," Morgan noted.

"A little snow would be good," Meloux said.

"Snow?" Dina sounded surprised.

"Just enough," Meloux said.

"We call it a hunter's snow," Cork explained.

"I get it. The tracks."

Fineday had been quiet. Meloux said, "Worry will not save her."

For the first time, Fineday spoke to Meloux harshly. "Sitting here won't either. We haven't seen a single sign of them. How do we know they came this way? They could be miles from here."

Meloux replied calmly, "If they are, what can we do? Better to believe that we have been guided well."

"By an old man with failing eyes?"

"By the spirits of these woods."

"That's what's been leading us? Spirits?"

"We have not failed yet," Meloux said. "There's no reason to distrust or despair."

Despite the old Mide's encouraging words, Cork wondered if he saw uncertainty in Meloux's dark eyes.

"So in the morning the plan is that we cut between those two islands, hit Carson Creek, and see what happens from there?" Morgan said. "Sounds a lot like the plan we followed today."

His tone was not accusatory, but his point was clear. All the evidence so far seemed to indicate that they'd spent their time in a fruitless hunt that had netted them nothing except tired muscles and the prospect of a long night on cold ground. Cork understood that as a working plan for the next day it lacked appeal.

"Until Henry says different, we stay on the trail," he said.

"You're the boss. Anybody want more coffee?" Morgan got up from where he sat on his sleeping bag and took the pan to the lake to fill it with water. It was dark and he carried a flashlight. A minute later he hollered, "Hey, look at this."

Cork and the others hurried to Morgan, who stood on the lakeshore near the overturned canoes. He pointed the beam of his flashlight at the water a few feet out. Something gold glinted in the light.

"It looks like a watch," Dina said.

Cork used his own flashlight to locate a stick, then he fished the watch from the lake bottom.

Fineday grabbed it from him. "It's Lizzie's. I gave it to her when she turned sixteen."

"Do you think she dropped it on purpose, to let us know?"

Meloux said, "She would drop nothing that Stone did not know about."

"Stone left it?" Morgan asked.

Meloux looked across the dark water of the lake. "Fish and honey," he said.

40

IT WAS SOFT twilight when Jo pulled off Sheridan Road onto a long drive that cut through a hundred yards of dark lawn. The tires growled over dun-colored bricks that had been used for paving. She pulled up to a house big as a convent, with a red tile roof and stucco walls. In every way, it rivaled the home of Lou Jacoby.

Ben met her at the door. "Come in. I just got home." He was still dressed in his three-piece pin-striped suit, looking handsome, distinguished.

She stepped inside.

"It's a little dark," Ben said. "I can turn on some lights if you prefer."

"No, I'm fine."

They were in a large entryway that opened left and right onto huge rooms.

"Where would you like to talk? In the parlor?"

"You have a parlor?"

"And a billiard room, a library, a study. With a candlestick and a lead pipe we could be a game of Clue. It's way too big, but it's what Miriam wanted.

How about we sit in the kitchen? It's really the coziest room in the house."

He led the way through a large dining room with French doors that opened onto a wide veranda. Jo could see a long stretch of lawn, green and tidy as an ironed tablecloth, with a turquoise swimming pool as a centerpiece. A tall hedge marked the rear boundary, and beyond that lay Lake Michigan, dark silver in the evening light.

The kitchen, which Ben had called cozy, was larger than any room in Jo's house on Gooseberry Lane. The floor was black-and-white tile. There were long counters, a dozen cupboards, and a butcher-block island. A round table with chairs was set near a sliding door that, like the dining room French doors, opened onto the veranda.

"You must eat well," Jo said.

"Miriam hired fine cooks." Ben indicated the table. "Have a chair. Would you like a glass of wine?"

"Thank you."

"Red? You used to love a good red."

"I don't drink red anymore. It gives me a headache."

"Things change, don't they? How about a chardonnay?"

He took a bottle from the refrigerator and opened it. From a rack above one of the counters, he took two glasses that hung upside down by their stems.

Several books lay stacked on one of the chairs at the table. They appeared to be college textbooks.

"What are these?" Jo asked.

Jacoby carried the wineglasses to the table and sat down. "They're Phillip's. He's around the house somewhere. He got expelled from his fraternity, and he's staying here for a while until he can arrange for other housing."

Jo had no idea what transgression might result in expulsion from a fraternity, but her sense, given the *Animal House* image she held, was that it had to be significant.

"All right," Ben said. "Let's talk. What do you want to know?"

"You get reports from a woman who's helping with the investigation of Eddie's murder, is that right?"

"Dina Willner."

"So what's going on out there?"

He settled back and folded his hands, a movement that seemed designed to give him a moment to think. "How much do you know?"

"Not much. When I call the department, they're evasive. I'm sure they're just following Cork's instructions. My guess is that it's because he's involved in something that I'm not supposed to worry about." When she said it, she heard a flutter of anger in her voice, and realized how strongly she felt.

"If they don't want you to know, why hit on me?"

"Because you're not one of his people. You can do what you like."

He sipped his wine and thought it over. "They've identified the man they believe was responsible for the shooting on the reservation."

"I know that. Lydell Cramer. He was burned during the meth lab bust a few weeks ago."

"Seems they were wrong in suspecting him. They're pretty sure now that it was a man named Stone."

"Stone? You mean Byron St. Onge?"

"I believe that's his name."

"Why? Why in the world would Stone want to shoot Cork?"

"As I understand it, that's still unclear."

"They could have told me that. There must be more."

"There is. When this Stone realized they were onto him, he ran, disappeared into the woods with the woman they suspect in Eddie's murder."

"Lizzie Fineday?"

"That's right. Your husband's gone into the woods after them."

"Alone?"

"No, the girl's father went with him. Also an old man who's a guide of some kind, and one deputy."

"Oh, Jesus. No wonder they wouldn't tell me. God-damn him." She looked away a moment. "You know, he loves this. He's in his glory."

"Dina indicated she was going to try to accompany them, officially or otherwise. If it's any consolation, if I had to go after a man like Stone, I'd want Dina there with me. She's very good at what she does."

"Tell me about what she does."

"We use her as a consultant on all kinds of security issues. Protective services, investigations. She's a crack shot, holds a black belt in some kind of martial art, has significant law enforcement experience. Really, Cork couldn't ask for better backup."

"So Stone ambushed Cork. And Lizzie may have killed Eddie."

"And once they're caught, it's all over." He held up his hands as if it were as simple as two plus two.

They heard coughing in the dining room, and a few moments later Phillip walked in. He wore a black terry cloth bathrobe and sandals and carried a big white towel. He seemed surprised to find Jo and Ben in the kitchen.

"Hello, Phillip," Jo said.

He glanced from her to his father, and a dark, knowing look came into his eyes. "Don't let me interrupt," he said. "Just passing through on my way to swim."

"Have you eaten?" Ben asked.

"Lasagna. Mrs. McGruder made a shitload. It's in the refrigerator if you're hungry. Nice seeing you again," he said to Jo as he slid a glass door open and went outside.

"Isn't it cold for swimming?" she asked Ben.

"I keep the pool filled and heated until the end of October. I swim every morning, and prefer to do it outside. The first of November I start swimming at my health club."

The light in the sky was thinning, and the kitchen had grown dark, but Jacoby made no move to turn on a lamp. He swirled the wine slowly in his glass.

"Rae told me she had a good long talk with you this morning."

"Did she tell you what she gave me?"

"No."

"A painting that you'd asked her to do twenty years ago."

"Grant Park? White dress?"

"That would be the one."

"I thought she got rid of that. God, I'd love to see it."

"I considered bringing it."

He looked genuinely disappointed. "There's something you ought to see, something I feel a little guilty about."

He led her from the kitchen through the house, down a long hallway past big empty rooms. The thick carpet seemed to suck all the sound from their feet as they walked.

"You and Phillip, you're here by yourselves?"

"When Phillip's gone, it's just me."

She followed him to a study that smelled faintly of cigars. He turned on a light switch and revealed a study with shelves of books, an enormous polished desk, an antique couch upholstered in leather, a fireplace. He went to the desk and, beckoning her to look, turned a framed photograph so that she could see the image. It was Jo, standing on the shore of Iron Lake, the water at her back shiny and blue as new steel. Jenny had taken the snapshot a year before for her high school photography class. She had framed it and given it to Jo as a Christmas present.

"That was in my office in Aurora," Jo said. "I couldn't imagine what had happened to it."

He lifted the frame and cradled it in his hands. "Eddie snatched it on one of his visits. I should have returned it, but I couldn't bring myself to do that."

"Did you ask him to take it?"

"No. He thought of it as a gift to me." His face turned pensive. "Jo, I have a confession. When I found out someone had tried to kill Cork, I thought for a while Eddie might have been behind it. For God knows what reason, Eddie wanted desperately for us to be as close as true brothers. I wondered if, in his thinking, killing Cork would open the way for me to have you. A kind of gift from him to me. I know it sounds crazy, but that's exactly the kind of guy Eddie was."

"What would you have done if that had been the case?"

"Honestly, I don't know."

He held out the photograph toward her reluctantly, and she saw the sense of loss in his eyes as she took it.

"I'd like you to have Rae's painting, Ben."

He looked stunned.

"If you'd like it."

"It was meant for you, Jo."

"Twenty years ago it was meant for me. My life is different now. Honestly, Ben, I wouldn't feel comfortable with it hanging in my home in Aurora. Do you understand?"

"I suppose."

"Would you like it?"

"Very much."

"Would you accept it?"

"I'm sure it's a valuable painting. What if I paid you for it?"

"I'd rather it remained a gift."

"Thank you, Jo," he said.

"What if I brought it by tomorrow? About the same time? Say, six?"

"I could pick it up at your sister's place on my way home from the office."

"I'm not sure what will be happening there tomorrow night. I'd rather the kids didn't ask a lot of questions. It would be best for me to come here."

"All right, then. Six."

There was a splash outside and Ben drifted to the window. Jo could see Phillip swimming laps with strong, even strokes, his body a long, lean silhouette against the glaring lights in the pool.

"He loves to swim," Ben said. "He says when he's swimming, all his problems go away for a while."

"Problems?"

"He has more than his share. His mother's dead, he hates his father."

"How do you know?"

"Because I was the kind of father my father was."

"And you hate Lou?"

"Why wouldn't I? He's arrogant, rude, demanding. He cheated on my mother, disinherited my sister, loved Eddie beyond all reason." He gave a small, derisive laugh and shook his head in futility. "You know, I can still remember when I was a kid how even one word of praise from him was the best thing imaginable."

He moved nearer the window and watched his son glide through the turquoise water to the end of the pool, climb out, and quickly grab the towel to dry himself. Then Phillip slipped his robe and sandals on and headed back toward the veranda.

"I should go," Jo said.

Ben nodded and led her back through the vastness of a house that seemed to hold nothing but a silence waiting to be shattered.

The children and Mal had gone to a movie. The teakettle had just started to whistle on the stove when Jo walked in. Rose poured boiling water over the herbal tea bags in the cups on the kitchen table, then sat down with Jo, who told her what she'd learned from Jacoby.

Jo didn't touch her tea, but the aroma, the soothing scent of apple and spice, registered in her senses. She wished she could give in to the pull of that smell, which seemed to come from a place of calm, of placid domesticity that was out of her reach at the moment. All she felt was irritation and worry.

"No wonder they wouldn't tell me anything. He's done it again, Rose. It's that damned cowboy mentality of his. That's the part of him I hate."

"If you were to ask me, I'd say it's also part of what you love about him," Rose said. "He's certainly come to your rescue on occasion. And mine."

"I know, I know." She lifted her cup, sighed into her tea.

"You're worried, Jo, and that's understandable. Why don't you call Aurora again. Now that you know what's going on, maybe they'll be more forthcoming. It's worth a try, don't you think?"

She was right, of course. Jo used the phone in the kitchen.

Bos was on duty. Jo told her what she understood of the situation and pressed Bos for more details.

At the other end of the line, Bos hesitated, then seemed to come to a decision. She told Jo that the search party consisted of Cork, Morgan, Meloux, Fineday, and now Dina Willner. They hadn't had any contact with Stone or Lizzie. Last check-in was at twenty-two hundred hours, ten o'clock, and everything was fine.

"Why did he do it, Bos? Why didn't he just wait for Stone to come out?"

"He was concerned about the Fineday girl. He believed that if he didn't locate her quickly, Stone might kill her."

"Did it have to be him?" She hated herself for the question, for the whining way it came out. Of course Cork felt it had to be him, and that was all that mattered. "Bos, you call me with anything, good or bad, you hear?"

"I hear, Jo."

She hung up, closed her eyes, breathed deeply. The whole kitchen was suffused with the smell of the tea.

"Sometimes," she said, "I wish . . ." She let it drop.

Rose stood up and put her freckled arms around her sister, offered a comforting embrace. "I know, but would you have him be less than he is?"

"Of course not."

They sat at the table again. Jo sipped her tea. "Morgan. He's a good officer, and Cork trusts him. And Meloux as a guide, that's a godsend. He's old, but he's tough."

"There you go. God has sent good people along with Cork."

They heard Mal returning with the children. "I don't want the kids to know, Rose. Tomorrow, when you go to South Bend, I'm going to stay here and wait for word on Cork."

"A good idea."

That night, after Stevie had gone to bed, Jo stood for a few minutes at the window, listening, thinking of the unnatural quiet that came with the mornings since the birds were dead. West Nile virus was a merciless killer.

A breeze rose up, and outside the leaves of the trees murmured softly, as if to remind her that there were those things, like the wind, that moved swiftly and could not be killed.

Jo thought of Cork and the others with him. "Dear Lord," she prayed, "let them be the wind."

41

THE MOON, before it rose, put a glow in the sky above the trees, as if a lost city lay blazing somewhere in the distant forest. Under the aspens on Lamb Lake, Cork and the others prepared for sleep.

"What about Stone?" Dina asked. "Will he sleep?"

"It has been a long day for him, too," Meloux said. "He will sleep."

"To be on the safe side," Cork said, "we'll stand watches, two hours each. Howard, Will, Dina, and me, in that order."

Meloux said, "I don't sleep so good anymore. I can watch, too."

"If you're up, you can help whoever's on watch stay awake."

Morgan took his rifle and walked to the shoreline as the moon began to push up out of the trees. Cork and the others settled into their bags. Cork didn't think Stone would try anything that night, but who really knew? It would have been comforting to have more deputies there, but Stone could probably elude an army if he wanted. It was best this way, to try to draw him out. Someone had to do it. Still, he couldn't help feeling the weight of the responsibility like an anchor on his chest. He was glad Jo didn't know what he was up to. Or the children.

He was surprised when Dina shook him awake.

"Your watch," she said.

He rolled out of his bag, his body stiff from the hard ground. Moonlight lit the woods, casting a net of silver and shadow all around. The air was cold, and he unrolled his fleece-lined jean jacket, which he'd used as a pillow, and put it on.

"Anything?" he asked.

"Only a beautiful night," Dina replied. "I'm not ready to sleep yet. Mind a little company?"

Cork arched his back, working out a kink that felt as though a horse had kicked him. He sat down beside Dina on the fallen trunk where earlier Meloux had smoked. On the lake, the silhouettes of the two islands were clear, the water in the channel between them sparkling like a swatch of black velvet sewn with a million sequins. Occasionally a soft breeze came out of the west and the aspen leaves rustled with a sound like the running of fast water.

"I never have nights like this," Dina said. "All my nights echo off concrete."

"But you like being a city girl. Or so you said."

"I could get used to this."

"Why are you here, Dina?"

She stared at the lake, then at the sky, and finally turned her face to Cork. Her skin was milk white in the moonlight and flawless. "People around your town tell me that even when you weren't sheriff you helped take care of some pretty troubling situations. Not because the responsibility was yours officially, but because that's who you are. I understand that."

"Nature of the beast?"

"Something like that. Also, I thought that when you found Lizzie, having a woman around might help."

"If you like this kind of thing so much, why did you leave the FBI?"

"Men and money. Too many of the first, too little of the second. By men, I mean flaming assholes with enormous egos. Now I only do what I want to do."

"And you do this kind of thing a lot?"

"I hunt people, yeah. Usually I find them. That's something I'm good at. I also protect people. I'm good at that, too."

Cork realized that his breath had started coming out in faint clouds. Soon, he knew, the frost would start to form, the leaves becoming brittle.

"What aren't you telling me?" he said.

She looked surprised, perhaps a little too theatrically so. "What do you mean?"

"Your story makes sense up to a point."

"What point?"

"That you're here out of the goodness of your heart, some protective sentiment about Lizzie. You're smart, you're tough, and you're not about public service and goodwill toward people. So why are you here?"

She smiled coquettishly. "Maybe I'm worried about you."

"Right," Cork said.

"Stranger things, Horatio . . ." She leaned over and kissed him lightly on the cheek. "See you in a couple of hours." She stood up, but when she turned, she let out a small, startled cry. "Henry."

Cork swung around and saw that Meloux stood very near, his dark eyes fixed on the lake.

"What is it, Henry?"

"I have been thinking about the bear trap." Meloux walked forward and waved toward the two islands. "Only one way in."

Cork followed his gesture and saw how the moon lit the water in the channel, a glittering path between the two black formations. He thought about it. The most direct way to the portage on the other side of the lake. The stone slabs breaking the water, requiring a slow, careful passage. He understood that whatever moved between the islands would be an easy target.

"You think he's on one of the islands, waiting for us to pass?"

"If his heart is set on killing, it would be a good place."

"How can we be sure?" Dina asked.

"Somebody needs to check it out," Cork said.

Dina shook her head. "Even if you headed there now, you'd be a sitting duck in all that moonlight."

"If he's awake and watching." Cork studied the island. "But if he's awake and if he's watching, he'll be looking this way and not watching his back."

Meloux laughed quietly. "You are thinking like the bear now."

"You're going to circle around behind him?" Dina said.

"It seems to me like the best approach."

"Not alone."

"I'm not risking anybody else." Cork scanned the eastern sky, still heavy with night. "How long before first light, Henry?"

"An hour," the old man said. "Maybe less."

"Then we should get started." He woke Fineday and Morgan and explained to them what was up.

"I'll go," Fineday said.

"It's already decided, Will."

"I'm not going to just sit here and see what happens."

"That wasn't what I had in mind." Cork looked toward the sky. "It'll be light soon, and if Stone's waiting for us, he's sure to be watching. We need to make certain his attention stays focused here."

"How?" Morgan asked.

"I think someone should cook breakfast. The wind's blowing toward the island and the smell ought to get his attention. There should appear to be a lot of activity going on."

"I don't want to sound pessimistic," Dina said, "but what if he shoots you, slips off the island, and gets away?"

"We need to close the back door, make sure he stays there. That's where Will comes in. And you, Howard. As soon as you can see enough to make your way through the woods, I want each of you to circle the lake from a different direction, post yourselves about two-thirds of the way around on either side, someplace where you have a clear view, a clear shot if Stone tries to leave. Dina, you'll be seeing to the same thing from this side. That way, you'll each have a third of the lake covered. As soon as we confirm that Stone's on the island or as soon as any shooting starts, you'll be responsible for radioing base, Dina, to get the critical response team out here right away."

"What about you?" Dina said.

"I'll be leaving very soon to paddle to the back side of the island."

"I already told you, in the moonlight you'll be a sitting duck."

"The moon's low enough that it casts a shadow of the trees onto the lake, see?" He pointed toward a black, ragged lip of deep shade that lay over the water all along the western shore. "If I stay in the dark there, keep to the shoreline, and circle carefully, Stone shouldn't be able to see me."

"You hope," she said.

"Whatever we do, there's risk. You and Meloux, you'll have to make it look good, like we're all still one happy family here at the campsite."

Meloux nodded thoughtfully. "It is a good plan, Corcoran O'Connor. Worthy of a good hunter."

"Thanks for the vote of confidence, Henry. Let's roll."

The first thing he did was to contact base, explain the situation, and make sure that Larson had the CRT standing by. There were only three walkie-talkies. Cork took one and gave the other two to Morgan and Fineday. He tuned the radio to the same frequency so that initially Dina could communicate with the others, then change frequency when she needed to communicate with base. He checked his rifle, stuffed extra cartridges into his jacket pockets, and with Morgan's help quietly set one of the canoes on the water.

"Half an hour to first light," he said to Dina. "As soon as Howard and Will take off, get a fire going, start something cooking, anything."

"How does peanut butter and jerky sound?"

"Awful. But see what you can do to make it smell good, okay?"

Meloux said, "I can think of a few tricks."

"Thanks, Henry."

"Good luck." For the second time that morning, Dina gave his cheek a kiss.

Morgan said, "I wish you good luck, too, but don't expect a kiss from me."

Fineday offered his hand. "Thank you, Cork. I owe you."

"All right, then."

He stepped into the canoe, shoved off, and dipped the paddle. A few strokes out, he glanced back. In the dark among the trees, his companions had become nearly invisible. He glanced toward the islands and hoped the same was true of him.

Lamb Lake was an oval with a circumference that Cork roughly calculated to be about two miles. If he didn't care about noise, he could easily make the trip to the backside of the islands in twenty minutes, but paddling quietly took more time. He was painfully conscious of the gurgle of water that accompanied each paddle stroke. Once, because he couldn't see clearly in the shadow of the trees, the canoe bow scraped a rock with a disquieting rumble.

In a while the birds, those that had yet to migrate and those that never would, began to sing, to call, to argue, to declare territory. Cork hoped the noise would help mask his own sound and he bent harder to the paddle.

By the time he slid around the southern end of the lake, out of the protective shadow of the tree line into moonlight, a faint evanescence had crept into the eastern sky, the promise of morning. The Northwoods began to take shape like a photo tediously developing. Cork glanced toward the campsite. A yellow tongue of flame licked among the trees there, and he knew that Morgan and Fineday had begun their mission. They were spreading a net across Lamb Lake, and if they were lucky they would snag Stone in it. If they were very lucky, no one would be hurt. But Stone was well named, and Cork was a realist. He would be satisfied if Lizzie and all those who'd come with him to look for her made it out of the Boundary Waters safely. He tried not to think of himself beyond the point of his own mission, which was simply to find out if Stone was on one of the islands, waiting. The possibility that they might have anticipated correctly and actually surprise him fueled Cork's tired body and brain. He felt remarkably ready.

A rat-gray light seeped over the lake. When Cork reached the shoreline almost directly opposite the campsite, the whole woods had emerged in particulars. Individual trees stood out, irregularities of the shoreline became obvious, distant hills were distinct. And everything had color. The green pine boughs over red-brown trunks, yellow meadow grass, silver reeds in the shallows. A breeze barely strong enough to ripple the water touched Cork's face, and he smelled a campfire. Along with it came the aroma of frying fish. Meloux, he knew. God bless him.

He slipped his walkie-talkie from the holder on his belt. He had set the volume low so any noise that might slip out wouldn't announce his presence. He spoke into it quietly.

"O'Connor, here. I'm in position on the eastern shore and just about to head to the big island. As soon as I know anything, I'll report. Out."

Cork had cautioned the others not to respond, not to risk any sound that might jeopardize him unless it was absolutely necessary.

Three hundred yards of water lay between him and the islands. Once he started toward them, he was, as Dina so aptly described it, a sitting duck, an easy target for even a lousy hunter, and Stone was a dead shot. But there was nothing else to be done now, and he dug his paddle into the water and shot forward.

Far across the lake, the first direct sunlight touched the tops of the aspens that enclosed the campsite, and the leaves glowed as if they were molten. Fish fed in the water all around Cork's canoe, flashes of scale and fin that left rings spreading on the still surface.

Cork headed for the larger island, toward a small indentation surrounded by pines. The shoreline there appeared to be free of rocks, and he hoped he could land without bumping the canoe against anything that would cause a sound. The part of the island dominated by the jack pines was to his right, and the hill covered with sumac rose to his left. As he approached, he saw no sign of Stone or of a canoe that would have brought him there.

Ravens flapped about in the crowns of the pines, their caws grating harshly against the quiet that lay over the lake. As Cork neared them, the birds seemed to grow more agitated, hopping along the branches, shrilly protesting. He drew up to the island and back-paddled to slow his approach. The bow kissed land and he stowed his paddle. Lifting his rifle, he disembarked and eased the canoe farther onto solid ground to anchor it. He hunkered down and listened. In the treetops, the ravens had fallen suddenly and ominously silent, but they still followed him with their black eyes as he slipped along the edge of the tree line. He saw no indication of Stone or Lizzie, no evidence that any human had ever set foot there. The ground under the pines was thick with brush and he knew there was no way to move through silently.

Instead, he hugged the shoreline, edging toward the rise where the blood-red sumac grew.

He'd half circled the island when the walkie-talkie on his belt crackled to life.

"I see her. I see Lizzie."

Although Cork had turned the volume low, in the silence on the island Fineday's voice exploded like a firecracker.

"She's on the shore. Christ, I think she's dancing."

Cork fumbled with the knob and turned the walkie-talkie off completely. He did a quick calculation. If Fineday had set himself up as planned and could see her, it meant that Lizzie must be on the far side of the sumac-covered hill. That she was on the island didn't necessarily mean that Stone was with her, but probably it did, so Cork no longer had a purpose in staying there. His mission had been accomplished. He could leave, make a judicious exit, but he couldn't bring himself to do that.

Lizzie dancing? What was that all about? What did Stone have up his sleeve?

He bent to the ground and began to crawl up the slope on all fours, snaking his way among the woody stalks of the sumac. The leaves hid him, but they also blinded him. As he neared the top of the hill, Lizzie's voice came to him, singing. Something about sunny days, clouds. Then he realized it was the *Sesame Street* song, the opening ditty his own children had grown up singing. Lizzie's voice was sweet, almost innocent, a little distracted. Cork took a risk and stood a moment, lifting his head and shoulders above the sumac branches.

There she was, dancing in a large patch of dry grass that grew between the sumac and the pines. It was less a dance than a simple swaying as she sang. Her eyes were closed and she seemed to be moving inside her own small, safe world.

Safe? Cork wondered. Where the hell was Stone?

The rifle barrel that kissed the back of his neck was cold. Stone, in his coming, had been absolutely silent.

"If you move, O'Connor, if you even twitch, your head is gone."

Cork felt a tug on the rifle in his hand.

"Let go nice and easy," Stone said. "That's right."

The rifle slid from Cork's grasp and he heard a soft rustle as Stone laid the barrel against a sumac bush.

Stone said, "You had me confused. I couldn't figure why you'd stop for breakfast or risk tipping me off with a fire. So I put Lizzie out there, thinking you'd come for her. I didn't realize you were already here until I heard that squawk box on your belt. By the way, I'll take that, too."

Cork handed it over his shoulder. "I've got people all around the lake, Stone. There's no way you're getting off this island."

"I'll take my chances."

Lizzie looked up from her patch of yellow grass and smiled. The sun was not high enough yet to strike her face, but there was a kind of light dancing there nevertheless. She lifted her hand dreamily and waved.

"What's she on?" Cork asked.

"What isn't she? That girl's a walking pharmacy."

"You brought her along just to use her?"

"That's what happens to the weak. They get used, preyed on, eaten. Basic law of nature."

"So what now?"

"Now you die."

"Why?"

"Are you afraid to die?" The question had a sneer to it.

"It might help if I knew why."

"Why? Stupidest question you can ask. Never gets answered. Nobody ever told me why that son-of-a-bitch stepfather of mine beat me like a dirty rug. When they locked me up for killing him, nobody ever told me why. When my mother died alone and dirt-poor, nobody ever gave me a reason why. So I stopped asking a long time ago, and the question became how. How to survive."

"What did I do to you?"

"You personally? Nothing."

"But this is personal."

"It is now."

Now, Cork thought. But not at first?

"You have me," he said. "You have what you want. Why not let Lizzie go?"

"So that your death will have meaning and purpose? I don't think so. I like the idea of you dying for no good reason at all."

"You want to know the only thing I regret, Stone? That I won't see them shoot you down."

"You mean like I'm going to shoot you? You think that's what I'm going to do? Hey, man, I tried that once. I'm glad it didn't work. Too removed from the kill."

The rifle no longer pressed its deadly agenda into Cork's neck. Behind him, he heard the ruffling of cloth. A moment later, Stone said, "Turn around."

A sharp, blinding edge of sun now cut into the blue above the trees, and Cork blinked against the glare. Stone had removed his shirt and stood bare chested, his prison tattoos dark green on his tawny flesh. They reminded Cork of parasitic worms that grow unseen inside a man but eventually reveal themselves through the skin. In the grip of Stone's right hand was a hunting knife, its seven-inch blade glinting with an icy light.

"When I was in Stillwater, I dreamed of the day I'd feel the twist of a blade in a cop's heart. I'm going to like this. I'm going to like the look on your face when you feel it, too."

He lunged. It was a feint, really, not a killing thrust. He was testing Cork's reaction. Perhaps he had expected Cork to retreat, jump back. If so, he was surprised. Cork met Stone's outstretched arm with a quick knife-hand blow that drove the weapon down and away and made Stone stumble. Cork followed with a kick to the man's knee. Stone bent but he didn't topple. It was enough for Cork. He turned and fled through the sumac, a desperate swimmer in a crimson sea. He heard Stone huffing at his back, crashing through the brush behind him. Cork raced across the grass where Lizzie danced and he headed for the lake. With a long arcing dive that took him beyond the rocks of the shoreline, he split the surface. The shallows dropped away quickly to a jumble of stone slabs that littered the lake bottom ten feet down. Cork swam deep, planted his feet on the gray stone, and turned to meet his adversary.

He'd done all this without thinking, but somewhere in his brain was the knowledge that water would equalize them, slow Stone's hand as it wielded the knife, handicap them both equally in their need for air.

Stone came with a splash, trailing a wake of bubbles

and white water. He swam straight for Cork, using both arms to propel himself. Cork watched the knife hand, and when it was drawn back at the end of a stroke, he thrust himself from the bottom and caught Stone before he could bring the blade into striking position. Without hesitation, he went for the man's eyes, driving the fingers of his right hand into a socket. Even in the muffle of deep water, Stone's bellow was a roar. He curled, kicked out, landed a boot in Cork's ribs.

Once more, Cork used the opening to retreat. He clawed to the surface and stroked hard to shore. Hauling himself onto the island, he sprinted past Lizzie, who watched him fly by with her eyes wide, as if he were some mythic creature or spirit, a *manidoo* that had sprung from the lake. He hit the sumac and made for the hilltop and the rifles there. He didn't look back to see if Stone was at his heels, but put all his energy into the race for a weapon. When he grabbed his rifle, he spun around.

Stone had not bothered to pursue him. He'd stopped where Lizzie, in her clouded state, had watched the struggle. His big bare left arm pinned her to him with an iron grip, and in his right hand the blade of the knife pressed against her throat. Her eyes were no longer dreamy but full of terror as she comprehended that her death was no farther away than a twitch of Stone's hand.

"She'll go first, O'Connor. You know I'll do it. Drop the rifle."

Cork did.

"Come down here. We still have business, you and me."

Cork descended, brushing aside the blood-red sumac leaves. He stepped onto the grass.

Stone's left eye socket was a raging red and already

swollen nearly shut. "You try to run again, I'll kill her."

Anger like acid pulsed through Cork, rage that Stone would use the girl this way. The hell with all the reasons Stone was the man he was. He would be a better man dead.

"Turn her loose and let's get to it, you son of a bitch," Cork said.

Stone flung Lizzie aside. She tumbled to the ground with a small cry. Stone set his mouth in a line that showed teeth—a grin or grimace, Cork couldn't say. Stone's hard body tensed and the muscles swelled under his taut skin. His good right eye, the pupil dark as an empty grave, regarded Cork intensely. Cork readied himself. Stone let out a scream, a kind of war cry, and charged, galloping across the grass, his knife lifted high, gleaming in the morning sun as if white-hot.

Then his chest opened, a portal that spouted blood, and he fell, collapsing far short of where Cork stood. At the same instant, the crack of a rifle shot broke over the island. Cork looked toward the lake. In the bow of a canoe, paused midway between the campsite and the big island, sat Henry Meloux. In the stern knelt Dina Willner, cradling a rifle and still squinting through the scope. In the heat of the battle, neither Cork nor Stone had seen them coming.

Blood wormed from the entry wound dead center between Stone's shoulder blades. Cork turned him over. The exit wound in his chest was the size of a man's fist, the edges ragged with fragments of white bone. His mouth hung open and his eyes looked stunned. It was illusion, for Stone felt nothing now, not surprise or bitterness or betrayal. He was dead. Simply dead.

Cork sat down, suddenly too weak to stand. He watched Meloux and Dina Willner paddle toward the island. Lizzie lay in the grass, crying softly. Cork thought he should go to her, offer comfort, but he couldn't move. The canoe touched shore. Meloux climbed out and after him came Dina. The old Mide went to the girl and spoke to her in a low, gentle voice.

Dina sat down beside Cork.

"Thanks," he said.

"I told you. It's what I'm good at."

The *whack-whack-whack* of chopper blades came from the distance. The critical response team.

Meloux left Lizzie, who'd ceased her weeping. He walked to the body, sat cross-legged beside it, and in his ancient, cracked voice began to sing, guiding Stone along the Path of Souls.

Cork was soaked and shivering now.

"Cold?" Dina asked.

"Freezing."

"Here. Let me help."

She put her arms around him, offering her warmth, for which he was grateful. He was even more grateful for the gift she'd already given him. His life.

42

FIRST THING, Cork called Jo.

"Hey, gorgeous."

"Cork!" she said, her voice full of joyous relief.

"Bos told me you'd talked to her."

"Oh, Cork. Thank God. I was worried."

"I knew you would be. That's why I didn't tell you I was going."

"Did you get Lizzie?"

"She's fine."

"And Stone?"

"We brought him in. Not alive."

"Does that mean it's over?"

"Not entirely. I still think someone hired Stone to kill me, and I still don't know who."

She was quiet. "So they may try again?"

"It's certainly a possibility." He wanted to give her more, an absolute reassurance, but that wasn't something he could offer. "How are the kids?"

"Fine. Rose and Mal took them all to South Bend today to visit Notre Dame. I stayed. I didn't want to miss this call."

"You mean if it came."

"I knew it would. Cork, when can we come home?"

"Soon, I hope. We'll be interviewing Lizzie shortly. Maybe we'll know more after that. I have to go, sweetheart. Things still to do."

"I know. I love you, cowboy."

"I love you, too."

Lizzie Fineday had been fed a decent meal and coffee, and was coherent. Although she distrusted cops, she was grateful for what Cork and the others had done and was willing to talk. She waived her right to counsel but asked that her father stay with her during the questioning.

Stone, she said, had enlisted her help to play a joke on the local cops, something she didn't mind doing. He told her that afterward they'd do a little Ecstasy. The afternoon of the shooting, they'd parked his Land Rover at the bridge over Tick Creek. He got out and told her to wait five minutes, then follow him on foot to the Tibodeau cabin. She'd wondered about the rifle he took with him, but not much. On the Iron Range, everyone seemed to have a rifle. Just as she started for the cabin, she heard two shots. She didn't know what that was about.

"The dogs," Cork said. "He shot the Tibodeau dogs."

She started crying, and they waited to go on until she'd calmed down.

She made the call from the Tibodeaus', imitating Lucy's voice, not a difficult thing. Almost anyone could do a decent impersonation of Lucy. After that, Stone had her climb the hill with him and they waited. She'd asked about the Ecstasy. He told her to be patient, gave her some grass to smoke in the meantime. She lay down on the top of the hill. It was evening by then, and she remembered staring up and thinking how soft the sky looked, like a big bed with dark blue silk sheets. She was tired and was almost asleep, when she heard the car from the Sheriff's Department coming down the road. She got up and saw that Stone had the rifle to his shoulder and was sighting. He started shooting. She freaked and ran. She barely remembered stumbling down the backside of the hill, and then she was standing in the dry bed of Tick Creek, crying uncontrollably, with no idea where to go. Stone came charging down the hill, grabbed her arm, yanked her after him, and they ran for the Land Rover. After they drove away, he told her if she said anything to anybody, she'd go to jail for sure. She was confused and scared.

"Did he tell you why he shot at the sheriff and deputy?" Simon Rutledge asked.

He'd said a guy paid him.

"He didn't tell you the guy's name?"

He hadn't.

"Did he say anything at all about him?"

Nothing she could remember.

Rutledge asked a few more questions about Stone, then Ed Larson said, "Tell us about your relationship with Eddie Jacoby."

She met him in her father's bar when he went there to see Stone. Jacoby made passes at her, the usual kind, and she didn't pay much attention. He gave her a business card, one with a Hollywood logo, and told her he could get her into movies. She still didn't want to have anything to do with him. She got weird vibes from him, creepy.

"But the night he was murdered, you went looking for him at his hotel. Why?"

Because after the shooting at the Tibodeaus', she was scared. She'd decided it was best to get out of town, and she thought maybe Jacoby was being straight with her and could get her to Hollywood. She left him a note saying if he was interested in partying to meet her at Mercy Falls.

"Why Mercy Falls?"

It was isolated and easy to find. She didn't want anyone to know she was seeing Jacoby, didn't want it to get back to Stone. When he showed up, she got into his SUV. They snorted a little coke. He gave her a beer. They drank, talked. He touched her. She didn't like it, but she wanted to get out of Tamarack County and she thought he might be her ticket. She felt trapped in the SUV, so she got out and went to the overlook. She was feeling woozy, light-headed. Jacoby joined her, began going at her again with his hands. She got tired of it and tried to push him off. He seemed to like that and began getting rough. He hit her, then he hit her again. She tried to make him stop, begged him. He pushed her down, fumbled with her jeans, worked at pulling them down. She fought him, and then he really laid into her. She remembered the blows, but she didn't remember any pain. Everything seemed to go kind of distant.

She stopped talking, and Cork and the others waited. Will Fineday's eyes were hard as agates, and deep hollows ran beneath his cheekbones. The scar on his face had turned bone white.

"Did he assault you sexually?" Larson asked gently.

She cried again, huge sobs that wracked her body, but she managed to say yes.

They took a break from the questioning. Cork

asked if she'd like something to drink, a Coke maybe. He got one from the machine in the waiting area. She drank a little, and when she seemed calmer, they continued.

She didn't remember him leaving, but she remembered being alone at the overlook, hearing the water of the falls, feeling the ground very cold under her. Then a strange thing happened. An angel spoke to her.

"An angel?"

That's what it had seemed like because of her voice. Gentle, kind.

"*Her* voice? It was a woman?"

Yes.

"What did she look like?"

She didn't know. The night was dark, the moon gone, and she wasn't thinking clearly.

"But a woman, you're sure?"

She thought so.

"What did she say?"

It sounded like "Poor vaceeto."

"'Poor vaceeto'? Vaceeto, is that a name?"

She didn't know.

Larson looked at the others. "Vaceeto?"

They shook their heads.

"What happened after the angel spoke to you?"

After a little while, she roused herself. Her pants were down and she pulled them up. She could see Jacoby's SUV still parked in the lot. She was afraid, so she ran like crazy to her own car, locked the doors, and got out of there fast. She drove straight home.

"Edward Jacoby was stabbed to death. Do you know anything about his murder?"

She said she didn't.

"Did you see him again before you left the parking lot?"

No.

"When we tried to locate you for questioning, you'd gone to Stone's place. Why did you run to him?"

She'd gone to Stone because she didn't want to talk to the police, and Stone promised he'd keep them away. He also promised to keep her high. That was something she very much wanted. To be high and to forget.

She broke down again. This time she couldn't stop crying.

Cork said, "Let's call it a day."

"An angel?" Rutledge said.

They sat in Cork's office. Larson, Rutledge, Willner, and Cork. It was almost noon. Cork had changed into his spare uniform, and he'd eaten a ham-and-cheese sandwich and had drunk some coffee. He was tired. The food and the coffee helped a little, but sleep was what he needed most. Days of uninterrupted sleep.

"'Poor vaceeto.' Mean anything to anybody?" Larson asked.

"A name? An endearment?" Rutledge said.

"Not a personal endearment, apparently. It didn't mean anything to Lizzie."

"It was a woman, yes?" Rutledge said.

Larson cleaned his glasses with a small soft cloth he kept in his wallet for that purpose. "Between the beating and the drugs, Lizzie was pretty far gone, so who knows. Think Jacoby slipped a little Rohypnol into her beer?"

"That would be my guess. It's what you found in the glove box of his SUV."

"A woman," Larson said. "A passerby?"

"Who just happened to be there at midnight, and who just sympathized and left her?" Rutledge shook his head. "I don't think so."

"How about a prostitute, then? Maybe beating and raping Lizzie Fineday wasn't enough and Jacoby brought in some extra entertainment."

"That's a possibility. And maybe it was the prostitute who killed Jacoby, defended herself with a knife."

"There's another possibility," Dina Willner said quietly.

The men waited for her to go on.

"Stone." She looked every bit as tired as Cork felt, but her brain still clicked along magnificently. "He's the thread that ties together Lizzie Fineday and Edward Jacoby. We know he had a personal relationship with Lizzie, and Cork believes he had a business relationship with Jacoby. He was certainly a man capable of a brutal killing."

"Why would he kill Jacoby?"

"He seemed like a man who didn't need a lot of reason. It could be that his relationship with Jacoby had soured. Or maybe he didn't like what Jacoby had done to Lizzie."

"She said the angel was a woman," Rutledge pointed out.

"She was drugged and beaten. I'm just saying it might be worth checking out."

Larson said, "I'll have my people go over Jacoby's SUV again, looking for any evidence that might link Stone to that vehicle."

"I think we should also have another talk with the working girls," Rutledge suggested.

Dina eyed Cork. "We still don't know who asked Stone to do the hit. A favor for a friend, Lizzie said. Moose LaRusse?"

"How's Carl Berger doing?"

"Alive, but not able to talk yet," Rutledge said.

For a lot of reasons, Cork was glad that the slug he'd fired into the man on the farm in Carlton County hadn't killed him. "When he can talk, let's squeeze him for answers."

Cork had listened to most of the discussion without comment. Partly because he wanted to take in carefully what was being said. Partly because he didn't have anything to add. And partly because he was so tired, his brain felt like a chunk of cement.

Larson said, "Cork, you need some sleep."

"I'm thinking about that. First, I'm going to take Meloux home. Then I'm going to take a bath. Then I'll take a nap."

"Don't forget, you've got a mandatory meeting with Faith Gray this afternoon at four. This one you can't miss."

"I'll be there."

"What about Lizzie Fineday?" Rutledge asked.

"Release her into her father's custody," Cork said.

"You don't think she'll run?"

"Look where it got her the first time. We should make it clear to Will that he's responsible for her until the county attorney decides if he wants to charge her with anything."

They filed out of his office, but Dina stayed behind.

"After that nap you say you're going to take, I'd

love to buy you a drink. Maybe even a steak," she said.

"I'll do the buying. I owe you big-time."

"I won't quibble with that."

"I think we should put the drink and steak on hold for today. You look like you could use a good rest, too."

"Me? I'm just getting my second wind." She laughed lightly. "If you change your mind, just whistle." She winked, turned, and sauntered from the room.

Henry Meloux was waiting in the common area. His statement had been taken, he'd eaten, and now he was sitting in an office chair, his head lowered, his chin resting on his chest, sleeping. Cork touched his shoulder gently.

"Henry, I'm taking you home."

Meloux blinked, then was wide awake and smiling. "Good," he said. "I need to lay these old bones down for a while." He got up from the chair.

Cork said to Patsy, who was on Dispatch, "After I get Meloux back to his cabin, I'm going home. No calls unless it's urgent, okay?"

"Sure, Cork. Get some rest."

They'd managed to keep the media in the dark about the operation in the Boundary Waters. Larson and Rutledge were preparing an official statement that would be released that afternoon. There were still a lot of unanswered questions in Tamarack County, foremost among them who killed Eddie Jacoby, but for a little while Cork thought he could step back and take a rest. He was looking very much forward to closing his eyes for a few hours.

* * *

Meloux nodded most of the way. When Cork pulled to the side of the road where the double-trunk birch marked the path to Crow Point, the old man roused himself and prepared to take his leave.

"Let me walk with you a bit, Henry."

The woods were quiet that day, the air warm and full of the musty smell of fall. For a while, they walked without speaking, the only sound the dry rustle of fallen leaves under their feet. Meloux moved slowly and Cork couldn't decide if it was weariness or simply that for Meloux there was almost never any need to hurry.

"Stone," Meloux finally said. "He was of the People in blood only. He did not understand the Anishinaabe spirit." He shook his head. "He might have been a great warrior, but a warrior fights for honor and for others. Stone's heart was too small. There was room only for him."

They reached Wine Creek, which was little more than a reddish iron-rich thread of water so late in the dry season. Meloux paused before crossing.

"Stone is on the Path of Souls, but I think he still weighs on you, Corcoran O'Connor. Or is it something else?"

"I can't help thinking, Henry, that maybe if we'd all done something different, stepped in a long time ago, Stone might have ended up a different man."

"Probably. But better? He spent much time in *Noopiming*," Meloux said. "This land can guide a man, young or old, to a peaceful place. Stone was like his name, blind, deaf, hard to the good he was offered here." The old man took a long look at Cork. "I think there is something else."

"It's not finished, Henry. Stone wasn't at the heart

of what's been going on. There's still so much I don't know, don't understand."

"I think you will," the old man said. "You are like a snapping turtle that does not let go. It also helps that you have a thick shell." He reached out and with his knuckles gave Cork a playful rap on his head.

Cork smiled. *"Migwech,* Henry," he said in thanks.

"No," the old man responded. "Thank *you.* You have given me one last good hunt to remember."

Meloux turned away, crossed the creek, and headed toward his sanctuary on Crow Point; to Walleye, who would be patiently waiting and would greet him eagerly; to a meal of wild rice and wild mushrooms; and finally to bed. That last part sounded so good, Cork wished he were going with the old Mide.

But he knew he still had miles to go before he slept.

Fucking miles.

43

MARSHA DROSS LIVED on Lomax Street, in a little white house with flower boxes on the front porch and green shutters on the windows. There was a For Sale sign on the lawn. Marsha and Charlie were planning to buy a home when they married, to start their life together in a new place large enough for a family. As soon as he returned to Aurora, Cork stopped by Marsha's house. She'd been released while he was in the Boundary Waters, and he wanted to tell her firsthand where the situation stood.

Her father opened the door. He wore a plain white shirt with gray slacks and black suspenders. He had on black socks, no shoes. A pair of black-rimmed reading glasses were nestled on the bridge of his broad nose. A folded paper, the *Duluth News Tribune,* was in his left hand. With his big free right hand, he waved Cork inside.

"Thanks, Frank," Cork said. "They told me at the department that Marsha had been released from the hospital. Is she here?"

"In her bedroom. Heard you had a little excitement."

"A little. All right if I talk to her?"

"Just let me make sure she's awake and decent."

Frank went down the hallway.

To anyone who knew Marsha, her house was a pretty fair reflection of the woman. Neat, uncluttered. Needlework hung framed on the walls, an art form that had been a favorite of her mother. A few lush plants, just enough to make the rooms comfortable. Finished floors with hand-loomed rugs. It was a nice place, but given her upcoming marriage, Cork could understand why she'd sell.

"Go on back," Frank said when he returned. "She'd love to see you."

Marsha's room was full of sunlight that made her face bright. Her hair was brushed, and she appeared to have put on a bit of makeup. She wore a clean white T-shirt and had the covers tucked around her below that. She was sitting up, her back propped against a pillow. She smiled when Cork walked in.

"You're looking better," he said.

"I wish I could say the same for you."

"Last couple of days have been a little rough."

A small white wicker chair had been placed next to the bed for visitors, and Cork sat down.

"We got him," he said.

"I know. Patsy called. What she couldn't tell me was why he did it."

"He died without saying directly, but I'm almost certain it began as a hit."

"Who hired him?"

"We're working on that."

She registered no emotion. She was in bed, recovering from a wound that had nearly killed her, that had jeopardized her hope of ever giving birth to a child; yet, here she was, accepting with a simple nod that Cork still had no idea who had ordered the attack or why. He wondered if it was because she understood that knowing wouldn't change her situation, or because she believed that eventually what was hidden would be revealed, that Cork would find the answers. Maybe it was both, because Marsha was strong and she believed in her work and in her colleagues.

"Doctor says in six weeks I can be back on duty."

"What's Charlie think of that?"

"Charlie's decided that he'd rather have a wife who's in a different profession. We've called off the wedding."

"I'm sorry, Marsha."

"It would have been an issue eventually. Better to deal with it now. You look beat. You should go home, Sheriff."

"I'll keep you in the loop, I promise."

He stood up and Marsha put her hand over his on the bedspread. "Going into the Boundary Waters after Stone, that was a stand-up thing to do."

"Thanks."

Frank was waiting at the front door to let him out.

"She told me about Charlie," Cork said.

"She's strong," Frank replied. "In every way. She'll be fine. And Charlie? Truth is, I never thought he was the right guy for her anyway. Thanks for stopping by."

Cork shook Frank's hand, then headed out into the sunshine of that fine fall day. The screen door creaked on its hinges, and a moment later he heard the soft slap of wood on wood as it closed behind him.

He finally went home. Upstairs, he tugged off his clothes, stepped into the shower, and stood for a long time hoping the hot water would melt all the tension in his muscles. While the water ran, he considered the situation as it now stood, sifting through what he knew for an understanding of what he didn't.

The shooting at the Tibodeau cabin was a hit, arranged by some guy. According to Lizzie Fineday, Stone hadn't been any more specific than that. Some guy. Moose LaRusse? Who was doing it for Lydell Cramer or Cramer's sister? Then why hadn't Stone referred to LaRusse as a Shinnob, more common among the Ojibwe? And so far, was there any substantial evidence linking Moose LaRusse or Lydell Cramer directly to Stone? The connection was certainly possible but yet to be proven.

Who else had a connection with Stone?

Eddie Jacoby.

Okay, Cork thought as the water started to parch his skin, suppose it was Jacoby behind the hit. Why? Generally speaking, murder, when it was planned, was either for vengeance or gain. Had he done something to Jacoby to warrant his hatred? He barely knew the man. So what about gain? Was there something in Cork's death that would benefit Jacoby? Did Cork stand in the way of Jacoby's scheming to get a contract for Starlight? He couldn't think how. What could Jacoby possibly gain by killing him? Cork had nothing. Jacoby came from a family that had everything.

He stepped out of the shower and toweled off, then went to the sink, intending to lather up and shave his two-day bristle. He opened the medicine cabinet and a jar tumbled out, which he managed to catch before it hit the floor. It was the Noxzema Jo used every night to cleanse her face, a simple object, but as he held it in

the palm of his hand he felt a solid and profound connection with the woman he loved. He seemed to be at
the bottom of a deep emptiness and wanted nothing
more at that moment than to have Jo there beside him.
He took a deep breath and put the Noxzema back.

He reached for his razor but stopped.

He realized there was something he had that one of
the Jacobys wanted, but it wasn't Eddie.

Ben Jacoby wanted Jo.

Hadn't he felt it the night Jacoby sat at his kitchen
table? Hadn't he seen it in Jacoby's eyes whenever he
looked at her?

Cork hesitated. Was this crazy thinking? Was this
lonely, jealous, tired, crazy thinking?

He tried to slow himself, to consider it carefully,
step by step. Stone had been hired to kill him. Eddie
Jacoby had a relationship with Stone that included
dealings of a potentially criminal nature, so arranging
a hit was not out of the question. Ben Jacoby was
responsible for getting his half brother hired by
Starlight. Had he been planning this for some time,
plotting to use Eddie's presence in Aurora to set up
the hit? Was he capable of such a cold, calculated act?
Hell, who exactly were these Jacobys?

"Grabowski Confidential Investigations."

Boomer Grabowski spoke words the way a rock
crusher spit out gravel.

"Boomer, it's Cork O'Connor."

"Again?"

After Boomer and Cork worked together as cops in
Chicago, Cork left the force to move to Aurora. A few
years later, Boomer had taken an early medical retirement because of an accident that left him with a leg

that was next to useless, and he had opened his own private cop firm. A lot of time had lapsed without the two men talking, then a few months ago Cork had called Boomer for some help with a situation that was tied to Chicago. Now he was calling again.

"What kind of mess you in this time?" Boomer said.

"I need you to check on some Chicago people for me, Boomer."

"It's what I do."

"It's a family. Jacoby's the name. I'm most interested in Benjamin Jacoby and his half brother Edward Jacoby. Eddie was murdered here a few days ago. We still don't know who the perp is or the motive." Cork filled him in on the details, then gave him the addresses for all the Jacobys, including the father, Lou.

"Money," Grabowski said when he heard where they lived. "What do you want to know?"

"Anything and everything. Where'd the money come from, where does it go. Connections. These are people used to manipulating the world to their advantage, Boomer."

"They think they're bad dudes, huh? So I should be careful?" He gave a callous laugh. "You want dirt?"

"If that's what comes up."

"Always comes up with money. When do you need it?"

"An hour ago."

"Done."

Boomer hung up without a good-bye.

Cork looked at the clock on the stand beside the bed. 1:15 P.M. More than three hours before his appointment with Faith Gray. He decided to lie down for a while, close his eyes, nap if he could. He set the alarm for four and stretched out on the bed.

An instant later, the telephone woke him. Cork rolled over, groped around on the nightstand.

It was Boomer on the line.

"You hit the jackpot, buddy."

"What are you talking about?"

"Those Jacobys you're interested in."

"You have something already? I just called."

"Four hours ago."

Cork looked at the clock. It was ten after five. "What have you got?"

"I called Adam Gabriel. Remember him?"

"Sure. Nice guy, worked out of Central, last I heard."

"He's in the north burbs now, with Highland Park. Currently assigned to work with NORTAF."

"Never heard of it."

"Northern Illinois Major Crimes Task Force. Provides investigators for a number of northern communities. Gabriel says Eddie's pretty well known to the local constabulary, although if you talk to them, they'll swear his record is clean. He's never been formally charged with anything, and the feeling Gabriel has is that it took a lot of family money to keep him out of trouble. Fat envelopes under the table to a badge in the right position. You know how that goes. Appears to be a family tradition with these Jacobys."

"How so?"

"American branch began in the late teens. Guy name of Albert Jacoby comes over from somewhere in Europe, ends up in Chicago, associated with Jake Guzik."

"Greasy Thumb Guzik? Capone's financial wizard?"

"The same. He never gets his hands soiled with the dirty work because he's got a knack for handling finances. And not just for Capone. Made a lot of money for the mobsters, and made himself rich in the process. His only son, Lou, continues the family business but distances himself from the underworld, or so it appears. Does millions in legit transactions, but a lot of people in the know think he never completely severed those early, dirty ties. You know how it is. Even if a rat dresses in Armani, the stink of the sewer is still all over him. Cork, these Jacobys reek."

"What about his son Ben?"

"I don't get the sense of the old man's ruthlessness, but they're in business together and I can't believe he's not complicit. Does the apple ever fall far from the tree, buddy?"

"Any active investigations?"

"There have been from time to time but nothing at the moment, according to Gabriel."

"Good work, Boomer."

"All in knowing who to ask."

"There's someone else I want you to check on."

"Your dime."

"A security consultant out of Chicago. Her name's Dina Willner."

The sound at the other end may have been a cough or a quick, harsh laugh, or just a catch in Boomer's gravelly voice. Then he said, "What's Willner got to do with this?"

"The Jacobys brought her in to be sure Tamarack County's bumbling law enforcement didn't blow the investigation into Eddie's murder. You sound like you know her."

"Oh, yeah. I know Dina."

"So tell me."

"I'll tell you what's official, then I'll tell you what I think, what a lot of us security consultants think.

"She's good. And expensive. A thoroughbred background as far as law enforcement goes. Great record with the Bureau. Her client list probably reads like a who's who of Chicago's richest and most powerful families. Does very personal business for them."

"*Personal* meaning?"

"Now we get into speculation. You had a chance to observe her in action?"

"I have."

"Note anything unusual?"

"Like what?"

"That she could probably hold her own against a platoon of Navy SEALs."

"I've seen enough to be glad she's on our side."

"Is she?"

"Cut to the chase, Boomer."

"A lot of us in the business don't even carry a piece. Word is, Dina Willner travels with an arsenal. I'm saying that *consulting* is a delicate word for what Dina does."

"Which is?"

"Among other things, she's probably not above doing a hit."

"You know that for a fact?"

"I told you, speculation. She's good, she's discreet, and she works for only the best-positioned people, so she's also protected. Ask a cop, and she's clean as a whistle. Ask me, I'd say watch your back."

"She saved my life, Boomer."

"Bully for you. I don't know what happened, but if

I were you, I'd take a good look at the circumstance, make sure that it is what it seems."

"You've been a big help, buddy."

"Bill's already in the mail. You need anything else, just holler."

Cork swung his legs off the bed and stood up. He walked to the window. It was late afternoon. He'd missed his appointment with Faith Gray. That meant a mandatory suspension until Faith agreed to recommend he be permitted to resume his duties as sheriff, and in the meantime Ed Larson would be in charge of the department. Cork knew he'd fucked up, fucked up pretty major, but he had other concerns on his mind. So when, a few minutes later, he received a call from Larson informing him that, in accordance with departmental regulations, he had been relieved of duty pending psychological evaluation and a recommendation for reinstatement, he was not alarmed.

"Faith said she'd be willing to work you in tomorrow, Cork. Considering the circumstances, she's been very understanding, but her hands are tied. It's the regs."

"I know, Ed. I'm okay with it."

"Well, hell, there's nothing to be done about it now. You might as well go back to sleep," Larson advised. "Let me know what you arrange with Faith."

"Anything new on the Jacoby murder?"

"Nothing so far."

When he hung up, Cork had no intention of going back to sleep. He paced his room for a few minutes, going over questions in his mind. Then he reached for the phone.

"Dina? It's Cork O'Connor."

"I thought you were out for the count."

She sounded a little groggy herself, as if he'd awakened her.

"I napped some. Got my second wind. Thought if you were still interested, I'd love to buy you that drink and steak I promised."

"When?"

"Say, six-thirty? I'll meet you in the bar there at the Quetico Inn."

"It's a date." She sounded awake, and she sounded pleased.

44

THE DAY, which began so well with Cork's call that he was safe, was destined to end in a nightmare.

When she hung up the phone, Jo felt an enormous weight lifted from her, felt as if she were floating. Cork was out of the Boundary Waters, tired but alive. She gave a prayer of thanks, then called Mal's cell phone. Rose answered, said that they were on the interstate halfway to South Bend. Jo told her the good news, declared that she felt like getting drunk, like celebrating, and proposed that she whip up a gourmet Italian dinner that night—spaghetti and meatballs, the one thing she knew for certain how to make. Rose sounded skeptical but agreed, and said to expect them between six and seven.

Most days in Aurora, she found an hour to slip away from her office and work out at the YMCA, but she hadn't exercised at all since she'd come to Evanston. She knew she needed an outlet for all the energy that filled her now, so she put on a sports bra, a T-shirt, and her Reeboks, and stretched in the living room for fifteen minutes. After that, she doffed her blue warm-up suit and drove along Green

Bay Road to Kenilworth, then east to Sheridan Road. She parked on a side street in front of a house decorated with jack-o'-lanterns and ghosts and witches in anticipation of Halloween. She locked her car and began a relaxing jog on the sidewalk heading north. The homes on the eastern side of Sheridan, huge affairs with vast grounds, sat with their backs against Lake Michigan. Those on the opposite side were still grand, but all the windows seemed like jealous eyes glaring at the greater splendor across the road. She passed Ben Jacoby's house and kept running.

A long time ago, Jo had dreamed of being a part of this kind of wealth. Her desire had had little to do with money, but was instead a desperation to rise above the drab, unhappy existence that had been her adolescence. She'd driven herself to be the best at everything, to get into a first-rate law school, and for a while to be on the partner track of one of the top law firms in Chicago. It had been her great fortune, she believed, to marry a man of a different ambition, whose life had been rooted in a small town buried deep in the remarkable beauty of the Minnesota Northwoods. She'd never regretted abandoning the chance for a splendid estate on Sheridan Road in favor of the cozy house on Gooseberry Lane.

As she ran through the glorious morning light, through the deep shadows of trees on fire with autumn color, with the lake silver-blue in the distance, she knew absolutely that her life with Cork couldn't have been more satisfying or full.

She spent the afternoon napping, catching up on the sleep she'd missed the night before worrying

about Cork. At five-ten, she took the cylinder with
Rae's painting rolled inside and headed out. She
stopped at a grocery store and picked up a few items
she needed to make the spaghetti dinner, then went to
Ben Jacoby's home. She rang the bell, waited, and
rang the bell again.

Phillip Jacoby opened the door. He smelled of alcohol.

"Ah, Ms. O'Connor. I was told to expect you."

"Your father's not here?"

"He's been delayed. He asked me to play host until
he arrives." He stood back and welcomed her inside
with a deep bow and a sweep of his hand. "Would
you like to wait on the veranda? That's where I've
been hanging out. It's a lovely afternoon, warm for
this time of year, don't you think?"

He led her through the large dining room to the
French doors that opened onto the veranda. The view
was stunning, the long carpet of grass set with the
blue swimming pool, the low hedge at the back of the
property, the lake beyond. He offered her a chair at a
white wicker table and she sat down. "May I get you
something to drink? Myself, I'm having a martini.
Several, actually."

"No, thank you."

"Oh, come on. How about a martini?"

"Nothing, thank you."

"A Coke at the very least. Dad would never forgive
me if he thought I'd neglected you."

"A Coke, then. Diet, if you have it."

"Coming right up." He walked a bit unsteadily
toward the sliding door that opened onto the kitchen.

She took in the view, checked her watch, wondered how long Ben would be. A notebook lay open

on the table, and on top of it a book facedown. A bookmark had been slipped between the pages near the end. She turned it so that she could read the spine. *The Great Gatsby*.

"For my American lit class," Phillip said, returning from the kitchen. "A big bore, if you ask me." He held a tumbler in one hand and a martini glass in the other. "Here you go. Diet, just as you asked." He handed her the glass and sat down in a wicker chair. "Did you have a good time the other night?"

"Last night?"

"No, at my grandfather's house, the night the stone pillar attacked my Jag."

"I'm sorry. That must have been difficult for you."

"If by *difficult* you mean humiliating, then yes, it was."

She thought about pointing out that Ben had simply been worried about Phillip's safety but decided it wasn't her place to defend or explain the father to the son. She drank her Coke.

"You know, I have to give my old man credit. He knows how to choose his women."

"I'm an old friend of your father, nothing more."

"Is that why he has a picture of you on the desk in his study?" He held up his hand in surrender. "Sorry. None of my business."

She looked again at her watch.

"Somewhere you have to be?"

"I'm just wondering what's keeping Ben."

"Oh, it could be anything. He's a very important man, my father. You'd be surprised, all the excuses he's found over the years not to come home." He sipped his martini. "How's the Coke?"

"Fine, thank you."

"So. Your daughter—what's her name?"

"Jenny."

"That's right. Jenny. Is she, like, all in love with Northwestern?"

"At the moment, it's her first choice."

"But you'd let her go anywhere she wanted?"

"Within reason. A lot depends on financial aid."

"It must be a bitch being poor." He shrugged. "Me, I could afford to go anywhere. But here I am, stuck in my own backyard because it's where my old man went to school. You think I look like him?"

"Yes."

"Everybody tells me that, as if it's a compliment."

"You don't think it is?" She was suddenly feeling a little ill. Where was Ben?

"I don't want to be him," Phillip said with venom.

Jo put her hand to her head, feeling dizzy.

Phillip said, "You don't look so good."

"I don't feel well. I think I need to lie down."

"Sure. Let me help."

He took her arm and eased her up. She could barely stand. He walked her inside.

"Oh, my," she said, and her legs gave out.

Phillip caught her in his arms and lifted her.

The room seemed out of focus. She tried to gather herself, but everything was swimming. She was aware of stairs, of rising, then a soft bed beneath her and Phillip looming into view near her face.

"You think my father is an important man," he said, his voice distant. "Sure you do. All his women think that."

She wanted to tell him once and for all that she was not one of Ben Jacoby's women, but she couldn't make her mouth form the right words.

"By the way, my father called and canceled your rendezvous. He asked me to look after you, to give you anything you need."

She felt his hand on her breast and she wanted to scream, to fight him off, but she could not move.

"That's what I'm going to do," he said. "I'm going to give you exactly what a woman like you needs."

45

CORK ARRIVED AT the Quetico Inn well in advance of six-thirty and spent a while talking to Dick Granger, the desk clerk on duty. After that, he sat down at a table with a good view of the lake and the marina. The sun had just set and, reflecting the fiery afterglow in the sky, Iron Lake was a vast expanse of burning water.

Dina walked in a couple of minutes later, dressed in a black knit top and black slacks, flashes of gold at her ears, and a chain with a small diamond at her throat. Her clothing was simple but displayed nicely every slope and curve. Cork stood up and pulled the chair out for her.

"I can't remember the last time a man did that for me," she said. "So you changed your mind about dinner."

"The house felt too big and too empty." Cork took his own seat.

"I know that feeling well."

"I decided I needed company."

"And it was mine you wanted." She sounded flattered.

The cocktail waitress came.

"What'll you have?" Cork asked.

"Cutty," Dina said. "On the rocks."

"Two," Cork told the waitress.

Dina put her purse, a small black beaded thing, on the table, then folded her hands and gazed at Cork. "Out in the Boundary Waters, there were moments when the thought of good Scotch and a thick, rare steak was just about all that kept me going. I didn't imagine I'd be sharing it with you."

"A nice surprise, I hope."

"Very nice."

"It was quite a surprise for me," Cork said. "You showing up out there like that. And certainly lucky."

There was a candle on the table, a small votive in a glass jar. The reflection of the flame danced in Dina's eyes.

"Lucky for both of us. If Stone had killed you, I'd . . ." She gave a slight shrug. "I'm just glad he didn't." She gazed out the window at the lake. "I'm beginning to understand what it is you love about this country. It's beautiful and it's dangerous. That's an attractive combination."

"The land is just the land. It is what it is. The danger comes from people who go into it with the wrong attitude. Good people without a proper respect for what the Boundary Waters demands. And not-so-good people whose reasons for being there are at odds with the spirit of the place. I've seen both end in disaster."

The drinks came. Cork lifted his glass. "To friends," he said.

"Friends," she echoed, and sipped her Scotch. She glanced at him curiously, maybe a little shyly. "I've been wondering about your change of heart this evening. Was it only the empty house?"

For a moment he didn't answer. "In the Boundary Waters my way of looking at things changed."

"Changed how?"

He studied his hands. "Out there on Lamb Lake, I started to see life as a fuse getting shorter by the minute."

"And?"

He finally looked at her directly, looked into her dancing eyes. "I liked the feel of your arms around me."

She'd been drinking her Scotch. Her hand slowly descended as if it had taken hold of a heavy weight. "I liked how that felt, too."

Cork said, "We could take our drinks up to your room."

"My, that's quite a change."

"It was just an idea."

"Not a bad one, if you ask me."

Cork left plenty of money on the table for the Scotch and a good tip. They walked from the bar together, past the front desk, to the elevator, which opened the moment Cork pressed the button.

Inside, after the doors had closed, he said, "I don't know what you're wearing, but it's a wonderful fragrance."

"It's called Black Cashmere."

She reached out, touched his cheek, started to lean toward his lips just as the elevator stopped.

Halfway down the hall, she slipped her card into the key slot, opened the door, and stepped inside.

"Nice room," Cork said as he followed her in.

He crossed to the window. Outside, evening had descended fully, and the fire on the lake was gone. The water had become nickel colored in the dusk. When he turned back, Dina had put her glass on the stand beside the bed. She hadn't bothered to turn on a lamp, and in the dim light of the room she eyed him intently.

"I don't do this as a rule," she said.

She came toward him carefully, as if walking the dangerous edge of a high cliff. Her eyes never left his face.

When she was very near she said, "I told you that men don't interest me much. But when I find one that does, I'll let him do anything." Her smell, partly the Black Cashmere but also something else, better than perfume, profoundly human and female, enveloped him. "Anything."

He put his glass on the windowsill, reached out and took her. She pressed herself to him, breasts and stomach and hips and thighs, and her arms went around him like soft rope binding them together. She lifted her face hungrily toward his lips. He bent, felt her hot, Scotch-scented breath break against his face.

And the phone rang.

"Ignore it," she said in a hoarse whisper, and arched more tightly against him.

"It might be important."

"Nothing's more important right now than this."

Cork slowly drew away. "Answer it. I'll still be here."

She relaxed, let out an exasperated sigh, and released her hold. At the nightstand, she grabbed the phone from its cradle. "What?" she said, with great aggravation. She listened. "Thank you. I'll take care of it later." She listened a bit more, rolled her eyes. "All right, all right. I'll be down in a minute." She hung up. "There's some sort of problem with my credit card. Apparently it can't wait."

"Go ahead," Cork said. "I'll make myself comfortable."

She returned to him, cupped his face with her hands, and kissed him. "This won't take long, I promise."

As soon as she was out the door, Cork hit the closet, found her suitcase, and opened it. Empty. He checked the shelf, the floor. He went to the bureau, yanked the drawers open one by one, riffled through her clothing. Kneeling, he looked under the bed, then stood up and headed to the bathroom.

When Dina came back a few minutes later, he was standing at the window again. The sky outside was almost dark and Iron Lake was the color of an ash pit.

"False alarm," she said. "You Minnesotans are very nice, but what you don't know about doing business would fill an encyclopedia." She sauntered toward him. "Where were we?"

She was still a few feet distant when Cork brought from behind his back the black ski mask. She stopped abruptly and considered first the mask, then Cork.

"I found it in the bottom of your cosmetics case," he said.

"In this country, you can never be sure about the weather," she replied in a leaden voice.

"It's the one you wore the night you planted the explosives in my Bronco."

"Were you looking for that, or just on a fishing expedition?"

"*Why?*" Cork spit the word. "Why bring my family into it?"

"Take your clothes off."

"What?"

"Take your clothes off. I want to see if you're wearing a wire."

He didn't move.

"Do you want to talk or not?"

He undressed. Sport coat, shoes, socks, shirt, pants. He laid everything on a chair. When he was down to his boxers, Dina said, "That'll do."

"Now tell me why," he said.

"I don't know why you think I can answer that question, but maybe I can help your thinking a little, provide a dispassionate perspective. For example, it might be productive to think about the explosive itself. If I recall, it was made with a blasting cap that was dead, yes?"

"You know it was."

"So it couldn't possibly have detonated. Now, it might be that the person who put it in your Bronco was simply stupid. On the other hand, it might be that it was never intended to hurt anyone."

"Then why was it put there?"

Dina picked up her glass from the nightstand and finished the Scotch with a clink of ice against the empty glass.

"All right," Cork said, addressing her silence, "let me do a little speculation. Let's say the device wasn't intended to kill anyone. What did it accomplish? It caused me to lose a lot of sleep. It certainly confused the situation. Were either of those the point? Or was it to separate me from my family, send them scurrying to Chicago? I'm thinking this because the night before the bomb was planted, Jacoby was at my house. He learned all about my family. Jenny and Northwestern, Rose and Mal in Evanston. He even knew Jenny was planning on using my Bronco the next morning. I'm thinking that a man like Jacoby believes he can manipulate anything and anyone to get what he wants. So he has someone—someone, let's say, like you—plant a bomb—or a nonbomb—to scare me into sending my family his way so that he can be with them, comfort them when word of my demise reaches them. Tell me I'm wrong."

"I enjoy seeing a fanciful mind at work. Go on."

"That's what the hit was about, I think. To get me out of the way because another man coveted what I have. It wasn't Lydell Cramer who wanted me dead. It was Ben Jacoby. And he used his brother Eddie to broker the deal. Now, your part in all this is still a little uncertain. What were you supposed to do? In the event that Stone couldn't complete the hit, were you instructed to kill him, make sure he didn't talk?"

"I was hired to make sure the investigation into Eddie's death wasn't mishandled. Period. When I came here, I didn't know anything about Stone."

"Then why this?" He shook the ski mask at her.

"You've overlooked something obvious. It could be that the point of the bomb—or nonbomb, as you appropriately call it—was to ensure that your family was out of harm's way."

"Is that what Jacoby told you? Or did you even care, so long as he paid you enough? Out of harm's way, sure. And my wife right into his waiting arms."

"Not every outcome of an action can be predicted. It seems to me that whether Jo stepped into someone's waiting arms was entirely up to her, wasn't it? And as for killing Stone, when I pulled that trigger, I pulled it for only one reason."

In the little illumination that still fell through the window, he saw anger in her face, and perhaps hurt. He almost believed her.

"Tell me I'm wrong about Ben Jacoby," he said.

"It's an interesting speculation. Do you have any substantiating evidence?"

"He's a thorough man, but I'm sure he's slipped up somewhere. I'll find out where."

He went to the chair and began to dress.

Dina watched him. "What are you going to do?"

"Let Jo know who Ben Jacoby is. Then I'm going to figure how to nail him."

"Be careful, Cork."

He pulled on his shoes, tied them, and stood up. "You're worried about me?"

"Your family's safe. You need to think about yourself."

It took a moment for him to weigh her words and her tone. Then he understood. "He offered you the contract on me, didn't he?"

"If I wanted you dead, I'd have let Stone finish the job on Lamb Lake."

He still held the ski mask. He threw it to Dina.

"I should have it checked for explosive residue, and I should have your luggage and your car checked, too. If I were a betting man, I'd bet we'd come up with something. But you saved my life. Consider my debt paid."

As soon as he returned home, Cork called Evanston. Rose answered. Her "Hello?" sounded anxious, and when she knew who it was, her voice took a serious nosedive to a bleak octave.

"What is it?" Cork asked.

"I was hoping you were Jo."

"Why?"

"Well," Rose said hesitantly, "she seems to be missing."

46

ROSE EXPLAINED THAT they'd come back from their day in South Bend to an empty house. Jo had left a note on the kitchen table saying she was going out to buy some wine, had an errand to run, and would be back before six. On the note, she'd put the time she left, five-ten. She still hadn't returned. There was also a message waiting on Rose's voice mail, from Ben Jacoby, left at five-fifteen, apologizing to Jo for having to cancel out. Something important had come up. He was sorry and promised to be in touch.

Jacoby again, Cork thought.

"Cancel out on what?" he asked.

"I don't know, Cork."

"Was she going to meet Jacoby?" he asked.

"She didn't say a word to me about it."

"Did you try her cell phone?"

"Yes. She doesn't answer."

"How about Jacoby? Did you call him?"

"We don't have his number," Rose said. "It was blocked on our caller ID, and when we tried directory assistance, they told us it's unlisted."

"I have it," Cork told her. "I'll call."

"Oh, good. Let me know what you find out."

In his wallet, he had the card Jacoby had given him when the man came to Aurora after Eddie's murder. Only his business number was printed on it, but on the back Jacoby had written the number for his cell phone. Cork punched it in.

The phone rang at the other end. Jacoby didn't answer. The recorded voice said the customer was not answering calls at this time but a message could be left. Cork left one telling Jacoby to call, it was urgent, and he gave his cell phone number.

After a minute or two of hard, desperate thinking, he called the Quetico Inn and asked to be connected with Dina Willner. She didn't answer. He called the front desk.

Dick Granger told him Dina had just gone into the dining room. Should he page her?

"No. Just make sure she doesn't leave before I get there."

He called Rose and told her he'd had no luck with Jacoby, but he knew someone who might have a better idea how to get in touch with him. He'd let Rose know.

"How're the kids?" he asked before he hung up.

"Mal and I are downplaying this, but if we don't find her soon they'll know something's wrong."

"Do what you can, Rose. And thanks."

He found Dina seated near the fireplace, a glass of red wine in front of her, a thick New York strip bleeding onto her plate.

"This is a pretty good steak," she said, "and if you don't mind, I'd just as soon enjoy it alone."

"You told me my family's safe. You lied."

"Oh?"

"My wife's missing. She went to meet Jacoby and hasn't come back."

"Does she have a cell phone?"

"She's not answering it."

"What about Ben?"

"No answer there, either."

"Did you try his townhouse?"

"I don't have that number."

With an exaggerated effort, she reached into her purse and brought out a pen and a small notepad on which she wrote two phone numbers. "The first number is his townhouse, the second is his home in Winnetka."

"Thank you."

Cork stepped away from the table and tried the numbers. He didn't get an answer at either of them, but he left messages saying basically "Where the hell is Jo?" He turned back and found Dina watching him. Her steak was getting cold.

"What now?" she asked.

"I'm going down there."

"How?"

"Driving, I guess."

"Long drive alone."

"At this point, it'll be just as fast as trying to get a flight out of Duluth or the Twin Cities."

"How much sleep have you had?"

"Thanks for your help," he said grudgingly, and turned to leave.

"Wait." She wiped her mouth carefully with her napkin. "I'll go with you."

"I don't need—"

"You try driving to Chicago alone right now and you'll be a danger to yourself and everyone else on the road." She stood up. "You know what I'm saying is true. If you want to get to Chicago in one piece, let me help."

The weight on him felt enormous. Worry, sleeplessness, a long drive in the night with only his fear and uncertainty for company. He knew she was right, but didn't trust her motives.

"Look," she said. "Whether you believe it or not, I've always been on your side. And think about it. If I'm riding shotgun, am I going to shoot you while you're going seventy?"

He gave in because her logic was sound, and he knew he needed help to get to Chicago.

"Give me a few minutes to change and I'll meet you in the lobby," she said.

While she was gone, he called Rose and told her he was coming. She didn't try to argue him out of it. He instructed her to call the area hospitals in the meantime.

He phoned Ed Larson at home and filled him in.

"You really think there's reason to be concerned, Cork?"

On a normal day, maybe not, but Cork couldn't remember the last day his life felt normal.

"I'm going, Ed. That's all there is to it."

"We'll hold down the fort here. Keep me posted."

Dina came down dressed for business—black jeans, black sweater, black sneakers, and a black windbreaker. A large black purse hung over one shoulder.

"Let's do it," she said, and hit the door ahead of him.

Cork glanced at his watch. It was almost nine o'clock. He figured if the roads stayed dry, if a cop didn't pull him over for speeding, if he didn't hit a deer, he'd be in Evanston in just under eight hours.

A lot of ifs.

They didn't talk much at first. Cork kept hoping his cell phone would chirp any minute and it would be Rose with word that Jo was fine and there was a good explanation for her disappearance. What that explanation would be, he couldn't imagine. Maybe her cell phone battery had died, although that was not like her. Why didn't Jacoby answer his phones?

"You have connections on the Evanston police force?" he asked Dina.

They were outside Duluth, heading over the bridge on the interstate into Superior, Wisconsin.

"I have connections on every police force."

"How about calling to check out accidents with injuries." He waited a beat, then added, "Or fatalities."

She talked to a guy she called Red, shot the breeze for a minute, then ran her request past him. She gave him Jo's name, the car make and license plate number, which Cork fed to her. It didn't take but a minute for Red to respond. Nothing involving Jo or even an unidentified victim. So far, it had been a quiet night in Evanston.

"How about Winnetka?" Cork said when she'd completed the call. "You know the cops there?"

"Couple."

"Think you can get them to send a patrol to Ben Jacoby's place?"

"What'll I tell them?"

"That some fuckhead rich bastard thinks he owns the universe and everyone in it."

"What'll I tell them?"

Cork let out a breath that momentarily fogged the windshield in front of him. "That there's an emergency, and Ms. O'Connor needs to be contacted and we believe she's at the Jacobys', who aren't answering their phone. You can embellish as you see fit."

She did a nice job of embellishing and got a promise that a patrol car would swing by. It was, apparently, a quiet night in Winnetka, too.

"Today, after we came out of the Boundary Waters, did you give Jacoby an update?" Cork asked.

"That's part of what he pays me for."

"So at this point, he knows everything?"

"Everything we know."

"Is there anything you know that I don't?"

"Nothing that would help right now."

"Do you think Jacoby knows anything that would help right now?"

"Ben Jacoby always knows more than he tells."

She was quiet, staring out the window as the empty streets of Superior slid by. It was an old port town on the harbor, and its glory days were a memory. In the daylight, everything about the place seemed gray. At night, it looked even worse.

"When I told him about the Fineday girl's recollection of the night Eddie was murdered, something happened. I could hear it in his voice." Dina seemed to be addressing the door window, or her own faint reflection in it.

"What did you hear?"

"Like lock tumblers clicking into place. I think he put something together."

"What?"

"I don't know. But he told me I was done in Aurora."

"Except for killing me, if you wanted the contract?"

In her seat, she pivoted toward him angrily. "Just who the hell have you been talking to about me?"

"A reliable source."

"Let me guess. One of my colleagues in the security business."

"Someone I trust."

"Who repeated shit he knows nothing about."

Cork swerved to miss a black cat with glowing green eyes that had frozen in the headlights. "So that was nothing but a lucky shot on Lamb Lake?"

"I train for that kind of shot. That doesn't mean I enjoy it."

"And Jacoby didn't offer you a contract on me?"

"Go fuck yourself."

They took US 53 south out of Superior and in a while were skirting the Brule River State Forest. There wasn't much traffic and the road seemed to tunnel through the trees into endless black.

On the seat beside him, Cork's cell phone bleated. He picked it up. Rose was calling.

"We've tried all the hospitals anywhere near here, Cork, but nobody will tell us anything. They say legally they can't. But they're also saying that if Jo had been admitted and they were looking for nearest relatives, you'd have been notified. So I guess that's one way of saying she's not there."

"Okay, Rose. That's good. Evanston Police Department said they have no report of her being involved in an accident. And we've got someone checking out Ben Jacoby's house in Winnetka right now."

"What if she's not there?"

"Then we'll keep looking."

"The kids are scared, Cork."

"I don't blame them."

"Shouldn't we notify the police that she's missing?"

"They won't do anything, Rose. Not for at least twenty-four hours. Adults disappear all the time for their own private reasons." It was a line he'd delivered many times as a cop to a worried husband or wife. The truth was, most people showed up, came back after they'd had time to think things over. "Do what you can for the kids, okay, Rose? And thanks. If you hear anything—"

"I know."

Cork put the phone down beside him.

"Nothing?" Dina asked.

"Nothing." Cork swung around a slow-moving Voyager, the speedometer at eighty when he pulled back into the lane. The broken white lines came at him like tracer bullets from a machine gun. "You think I'm wrong about Jacoby wanting my wife?"

"I've never met your wife." She laid her head against the seat back. "But I know that people kill for less compelling reasons than love."

"A man like Jacoby, does he even understand love?"

"We most desire what we can't have."

"Desire's not love."

"No," she said. "It isn't."

Her phone rang. She answered and listened. She said thank you and hung up.

"Winnetka PD. A couple of uniforms stopped by the Jacoby residence on Sheridan Avenue. Phillip Jacoby answered the door. That's Ben's son."

"I know," Cork said.

"He told them Jo wasn't there, that he hasn't seen her at all and he's been home all evening."

"Was Ben Jacoby there?"

"The cops talked to Phillip, that's all I know."

"Does he lie?"

"I don't know anyone who doesn't. Do you?"

In Eau Claire, they stopped for gas and Cork drove through a McDonald's because he hadn't eaten all day. Dina took the wheel and guided them to I-94, which would take them to Chicago. Cork ate, barely tasting the food. All he could think of was Jo. Where the hell was she, and was she safe?

And when that became almost unbearable, he thought about Jacoby and wondered what Dina had said that made him want her off the investigation.

47

THEY TOOK TURNS driving, nodding off briefly when they weren't behind the wheel. Once, Cork jerked awake with a terrified suck of air.

"Bad dream?" Dina said, shifting her attention momentarily from the road ahead. "You have a lot of those?"

"Tell me someone who doesn't." Cork rubbed his eyes and directed her to pull off at the next exit. He was ready to drive.

He wondered what was true about Dina Willner. How much of her had Jacoby bought? Was she really along to keep him from sleeping at the wheel or mostly to keep him in her sight for Jacoby? He was tired, knew that his judgment was off, and decided if he couldn't trust himself it was best to trust nothing.

They hit Evanston around five-thirty and fifteen minutes later pulled up in front of Mal and Rose's duplex. There was a faint glow in the eastern sky, but under the trees on the street where Cork parked, night still held solid. Most of the homes were dark. Upstairs in the duplex, a light shone behind the curtains.

Mal opened the door and hugged Cork in welcome. Rose was right behind him.

"Anything?" he asked. He'd checked in by phone only an hour earlier, but he still hoped that good news might have arrived.

"Nothing," Mal said.

"This is Dina Willner." Cork stepped aside. "She's been helping with the investigation in Aurora. She offered to come along and make sure I didn't fall asleep at the wheel."

"Won't you come in?" Rose said to her warmly. "I've got coffee."

"Thanks. I could use a cup."

Inside, Cork asked, "The kids?"

"Asleep," Mal said. "The girls have been up most of the night but they finally conked out a couple of hours ago."

"Let them sleep," Cork said.

They sat around the kitchen table, hunched over the coffee Rose poured. Jo's note lay in front of Cork. He could almost hear her voice in her carefully hand-written script.

"I feel so helpless," Rose confessed. "I don't know what to do."

"Let's start with what we know," Cork said. "She left to meet Ben Jacoby, but before he called to cancel. Did you save Jacoby's message?"

"Yes."

"Let me hear it."

Rose brought him the phone and punched in the number for voice mail. She tapped in a security code, then a code to replay the message, and handed the phone to Cork.

"Jo, it's Ben. I apologize, but something extremely

important has come up that I have to take care of right away. I won't be able to meet you. I'm hoping you haven't left yet, but just in case you have, I'm going to call Phillip and let him know to expect you. You can certainly leave the painting, but I'd much rather you gave it to me personally. Again, I'm sorry to bail on you at the last minute. Honestly, this is business that can't wait. I'll be in touch."

Cork handed the phone back to Rose.

"Time on the message is five-fourteen. And the note Jo wrote said she left at five-ten."

"Yes," Rose said.

"So he just missed her." He looked at Dina. "You said you updated Jacoby about Stone. When did you talk to him?"

"As soon as we came out of the Boundary Waters. Later I gave him a full update on what we learned from Lizzie Fineday."

"About Eddie's murder?"

"That's right."

"What time?"

"I don't know. Around five, I'd guess."

"And when you talked to him, you had the feeling things seemed to fall into place for him, right?"

"That's the feeling I got, yes."

"A few minutes later, he calls Jo, cancels their meeting, and rushes off to take care of something that can't wait. Something that had to do with Eddie's murder?"

Dina nodded thoughtfully. "If I were you, that's the first question I'd ask when I see him."

"Second," Cork said. "The first thing I'm going to ask is 'Where the hell is Jo?'"

He stood up and took his mug to the coffeepot on the counter.

"Okay," he said, pouring himself a refill. "She was headed to Jacoby's place. He has two residences. A townhouse near downtown Chicago and a home on Sheridan Avenue in Winnetka. Her note says she'll be gone less than an hour. I'd say that eliminates the townhouse. During rush hour, it would take at least that long just to get there. So I'm betting it was the house on Sheridan."

"The uniforms who talked to Phillip said she hadn't been there."

"Maybe Phillip lied."

"Why?"

"I don't know, but it's the only solid lead we have, so that's where I'm starting." He grabbed his yellow windbreaker from where he'd draped it over the chair back.

"What are you going to do?" Dina asked.

"Pound on the door, or on the kid, until I get some answers."

When Cork pulled off Sheridan onto the private brick drive that led to Ben Jacoby's palatial home, the sky along the horizon above Lake Michigan burned with a warm orange glow that was dawn. The trees of the estate, a mix of yews and Catawba and maples, were eerily quiet, and Cork, as he stepped from the Pathfinder, realized that there were no birds in them and wondered where they'd all gone.

Curtains were drawn across the windows. The panes reflected an empty sky. At the end of the drive, which circled a small fountain edged with dewy grass, Cork spotted the garage doors, three of them, each with a row of glass panes roughly at eye level. He walked to the doors, Dina a step behind him, and peered in. It was an area large enough to accommodate four vehicles. Currently it was full. There was a Mercedes, a Jaguar with a smashed front headlight, a Lincoln Navigator, and a blue Toyota Camry with Minnesota plates.

"She's here."

"And that's Ben's Mercedes," Dina said.

He went back to the Pathfinder, opened the glove box, and took out his Smith & Wesson .38 Police Special and a box of cartridges. He filled the cylinder and snapped it shut.

Dina watched him. "You're not going in shooting."

"If this isn't a kidnapping, I don't know what is."

She put a hand on his arm. "Cork, what if she's here because she wants to be?"

"If that were true, she would have called. She wouldn't want Rose or the children to worry. Or me."

He approached the front door under the portico and tried the knob. Locked. He stepped back, looked left and right, turned toward the south corner of the house.

"I'm going around in back, see if I can find an open door," he said in a low voice.

"Why don't we just ring the doorbell?"

"You wait here," he said. "And don't ring the doorbell. Not yet."

He started across the lawn, the heavy dew soaking his shoes and the cuffs of his pants. He tried to move carefully, to keep his breathing steady while he battled fear and a mounting rage. Though his brain was fried from exhaustion and worry, he kept focused on the one thing he knew absolutely: Jo was somewhere inside this house, and she was not there because she wanted to be.

He turned the corner and lost sight of Dina. Trimmed bushes grew against the length of the house and Catawba branches reached above him. It seemed as though he'd entered a long, dim hallway that opened at the end onto the back lawn.

He'd gone less than halfway when shots rang out, two of them. Without thinking, Cork dove for the cover of the bushes and lay in the dirt, gripping his .38. He scanned what he could see of the estate, which wasn't much. In his mind, he replayed the sound of the shots. They'd come from ahead, from somewhere behind the house, out of his line of vision. He decided that they were probably not meant for him.

The quiet had returned immediately, pressing so heavily on Cork that he felt as if he were underwater. He forced himself to move and in a crouch went forward. At the back corner, he peered around the edge of the house. The yard was empty. He saw a pool, a small pool house, stairs that led up to a veranda. A black robe hung over the back of a lounge chair beside the pool.

He hugged the wall, edging his way toward the stairs. He finally pushed from the house and swung his revolver toward the veranda, which proved to be as empty as the yard. He looked at the pool, at the rose-colored stain spreading across the water. He crept nearer and bent over the edge. The body lay on the bottom, eyes closed, two dark plumes rising from somewhere underneath, near the middle of the back.

He didn't hear her but felt her presence. He turned his head and there she was, gripping a white robe closed over her breast, her hair a tangle, her feet bare, her blue eyes wide with astonishment.

"Oh, Cork, no," she whispered.

He was so happy to see her, he wanted to cry.

"Jo," he said, "I came to bring you home."

48

"HEY, CORK. Long time no see."

Adam Gabriel closed the door and offered Cork his hand. He stood six feet tall and was slender, with curly blond hair and a serious look in his face.

"What are you doing here, Adam? I thought you were with Highland Park."

They were in an interview room of the Winnetka Village Police.

"I'm also assigned to NORTAF. We float all over."

"That's right. I remember Boomer saying that."

"Good old Boomer." Gabriel allowed himself a brief smile, then sat down across the table from Cork.

"Good to see a familiar face," Cork said.

"They've been rough on you?"

"Just doing their jobs. You've got yours, too. They send you in to play good cop?"

Gabriel gestured toward the Styrofoam cup that held coffee, which was cold now. "Want something besides that?"

"I'm fine."

"You look like you could use sleep. I understand you drove all night."

"A lot of ground between me and Jo to cover. I'd love to be with her right now."

"She's in good hands, Cork. With someone from SANE. Sexual Assault Nurse Examiner program."

"I know what it is."

"Sure."

"How's Lucille?"

"Back in school. Almost fifty and she's finally finishing her degree. Never too late, huh?" He folded his hands on the table. "So this is what I understand. You came down here because Jo disappeared. You went to Jacoby's because of the message on Rose's phone. By the way, I didn't know she'd moved back down here. Happy to hear she's found a good man."

"We all are."

"So you and Willner head to Jacoby's. You see Jo's car in the garage, ring the bell—"

"We didn't ring the bell."

"Did you knock?"

"No. I tried the door."

"Which was locked?"

"Yes."

"So you started looking for another way in. You were on the south side of the house when you heard the shots and dove for cover in the shrubbery. Because you thought you were being shot at?"

"That's right."

He nodded in an understanding way. "Skittish. After that business on the reservation in Minnesota, it makes sense. How's the ear?"

"Doesn't bother me anymore. Stitches'll be coming out pretty soon."

"How long did you stay there in the shrubs?"

"Couple minutes."

"No more shots?"

"No."

"Then you continued to the backyard, which was empty."

"Except for Jacoby on the bottom of the pool."

"You saw no one leaving the scene?"

"No one."

"You told the other detectives that you thought Jacoby was dead. You think about pulling him out, checking for a pulse?"

"No."

Gabriel seemed a little troubled with that. "You know dead when you see it?"

"Jo came from the house at the same time. I was more concerned with her."

"And besides, you figured it was Jacoby who'd kidnapped her, right?"

"I didn't want him dead. I just wanted Jo back safely."

"But things got out of hand. I can understand how that might happen."

"Look, Adam, I know you have to do this. I didn't shoot Jacoby."

"But you did have a gun."

"Which I didn't fire. Winnetka Police can easily confirm that. They swabbed my hands for residue. They decide to have it analyzed, it'll show negative. But I'm sure they told you all this already."

"Cork, they're searching for gloves."

"Gloves?" He thought about it a few seconds and understood. "They found the gun that killed him. Let me guess. A throw-down?"

"That's right."

"Adam, you know me. You know I'm not a dirty cop."

"I told them that. But they don't know you, Cork. They're looking at a guy who believed his wife had been kidnapped, who believed Jacoby was responsible, and who charged in on his own, thinking he'd save her. On top of that, he's a guy who's currently suspended from his duties as sheriff pending psychological evaluation."

Cork sat back, weary to the bone.

"It would have helped if you'd told them about that last part."

"They ready to charge me?"

Gabriel shook his head. "Timing and motive are strong, but they don't have any physical connection between you and the throw-down. Plus, you've been extremely cooperative."

"Are they going to hold me?"

"No. But they want you to stick around for a while. You know the drill." Gabriel breathed a deep sigh. "There's something else, Cork. Phillip Jacoby came in a while ago with his lawyer, Lawrence Blumenthal. He's admitted that he had sex with Jo, but says it was consensual."

"Consensual?" Cork almost leaped from his chair.

"That's his statement. He says his father came home, found them together. Jo had had too much to drink and had passed out. Jacoby was extremely upset and sent Phillip to stay with an old friend who just happened to be Lawrence Blumenthal, one of Chicago's best defense attorneys. Blumenthal insists that Phillip was at his home when Ben Jacoby was murdered."

"Money makes everything so much easier, doesn't it?" Cork said bitterly.

"When Boomer called me yesterday, I wish I'd

known what all this was about. I'd have been happy to help."

"That was yesterday, Adam." He reached across the table and shook Gabriel's hand. "And you *have* helped."

Dina Willner was waiting for him.

"You look like the walking dead," she said. "Why don't I give you a ride back to your Pathfinder. We need to talk."

While the police were questioning Dina, one of her operatives had delivered her car to the village police station. It was a red Ferrari, and she fit into it as if she'd been born in the driver's seat.

"I saw Phillip at the police station, but they wouldn't let me talk to him," she said.

Cork told her what he'd learned from Gabriel.

"Consensual? That's ludicrous." Her voice was pitched with anger.

"Adam says his attorney's one of the best in Chicago."

"Blumenthal's good, but Phillip's got a history of date rape. The Jacobys hired me last year to make a Rohypnol situation go away."

"Do the police know that?"

"The police know all about the Jacobys, but money's an enormous protective moat."

She stopped at a light. The Ferrari purred under her like a contented lion.

"There are things I haven't told you, but now that Ben's dead, I think I should."

The light changed. She shifted and accelerated with a roar of the powerful engine.

"I can understand why you thought it was Ben

who was responsible for Stone trying to kill you, but you're wrong. He didn't know anything about it. Eddie was mostly all about Eddie, except where Ben was concerned. He looked up to Ben, desperately wanted his approval, wanted to feel like they were true brothers. The trouble was, he was the kind of guy who fucked up everything he did.

"Eddie knew about Ben and Jo. When he turned up dead and Ben went to Aurora and heard about the ambush on the reservation, he didn't believe it was just a coincidence that Eddie was there when it happened. He was afraid Eddie might have done something stupid, like arrange the hit. I wasn't hired just to make sure the investigation was handled correctly. I was hired to find out if what Ben feared was true."

"And if it was?"

"My first priority was to make sure you and your family were safe. Then, if Eddie was responsible, identify the person he hired for the hit and intervene discreetly. Dissuade that person any way I could and keep the Jacoby name out of it."

"Tall order."

"I'm well paid."

"So I was wrong about Ben Jacoby wanting my wife?"

"I don't know about that. Ben always struck me as a man who never had a handle on happiness. If Jo made him happy once, maybe he would have given almost anything to get her back. He might even have been just fine if it had to be over your dead body, so long as he wasn't responsible, but he wasn't the kind of man who'd have had you killed for it."

"You seem to know Jacoby pretty well."

"In my business, people tell me their secrets."

"You're paid to keep those secrets. Why are you telling me this?"

"Call it a moral imperative. Anyone who'd care is dead. Ben, Eddie, Stone. And with everything that's happened to you and your family, I think you deserve to know the truth. But if you ask me to testify in court, I'll refuse. You understand?"

"Sure."

"However, I can give you the name of the girl and her family in the date rape incident. I'd bet it wouldn't take anything at all to make them turn on the Jacobys."

They were on Sheridan, not far from Ben's place.

"So who killed him?" Cork said.

"Until you told me about Blumenthal, I'd thought it might have been Phillip. An argument, maybe."

"If Blumenthal's telling the truth, Phillip's off the hook. From what I've gathered, Jacoby was probably shot with a throw-down, so that would indicate a planned killing."

"Ben was a powerful man. I'm sure he had enemies. Maybe his murder didn't have anything to do with the rest of this business."

Cork shook his head. "Think about it. After you called him with your report on Lizzie's interview, he canceled his meeting with Jo and went somewhere. You said it yourself, that he put something together. What was it he figured out? That might be clear if we knew who he went to see."

"You think his death had something to do with Eddie's murder?"

"It's the only connection I can see at the moment. It's all too closely related to be just coincidence."

Dina pulled onto the brick drive that led to

Jacoby's home. The crime scene team was still there, but the media vans were gone and the neighbors had all retreated back into their own big houses. She pulled up to the Pathfinder, still parked where he'd left it earlier that morning.

"Cork, I'm not on the Jacoby payroll anymore. Eddie, Ben, they're not my worry now. But you are." She reached into the glove box, pulled out a business card, and gave it to him. "If you need me for anything, call."

"Listen," he said. "That was a lousy thing I pulled in Aurora. I'm sorry."

"Done in a good cause," she replied, then smiled wistfully. "'Of all sad words of tongue or pen, the saddest are these, it might have been.'"

She leaned over, kissed his cheek, watched him get out, then growled away in her Ferrari, a car that cleaning up the messes made by people like the Jacobys had paid for.

By the time he arrived at the clinic, Jo's examination was over and she'd gone home with Rose.

At the duplex, he found the women gathered around the kitchen table—where else?—drinking tea. The long night of despair had left them with puffy, dark-circled eyes and faces still pinched with worry. Jo was safe, but Cork suspected that for Jenny and Annie the ordeal was not over. It was clear they knew what she'd been through, were probably even now imagining it, living it in their own minds, feeling the filth of it on their own bodies. What had happened to their mother had been the kind of thing that happened to other women, other families, in other places, but here it was at their table, the monster of all fears, and Cork understood that for a while it would shadow their world.

He kissed Jo and held her.

"They kept me a long time," he said. "I would have been there."

"It was fine. Rose was with me."

"Thank you." He spoke over Jo's shoulder to his sister-in-law. "Where's Stevie?"

Rose said, "Mal took him to the park. He doesn't really know what's happened."

"Good. Hi, guys." He kissed both his daughters as he circled the table toward an empty chair.

They smiled bleakly.

"Would you like some tea?" Rose offered.

"Sure, what the hell. Wouldn't happen to have a cookie to go with it?"

"Chocolate chip."

"Rose, you are an angel."

He looked at the two most dour faces at the table and he spoke especially to them. "You know, in the last week I've been shot at, threatened with a bomb, attacked with a knife. Your mother's gone through her own terrible hell. But here we are together around this table, and I can't remember a time when I've felt so lucky. Rose," he called, "cookies all around. And don't stint on the chocolate chips."

Smiles like small bright caterpillars crawled across his daughters' lips.

Later, in the privacy of the room Jo had shared with Stevie, Cork held her for a long time.

"I'm sorry," he whispered into her hair.

She spoke, her breath soft against his cheek. "The truth is, I don't remember anything. I only have vague impressions, like a bad dream. I suppose that's lucky."

"It may hit you later."

"Probably."

"I have to see Faith Gray when I get back to Aurora. Maybe you should, too."

"All right."

"I wish I could have kept it from happening."

She drew back just enough to look into his eyes. "How could you? It was such a predatory act, who could have predicted it?"

"It's not the first time Phillip's done something like this, Jo. I'm going to do everything I can to make certain he doesn't prey on anybody else."

"Do they have any idea about Ben? Who killed him?"

"Not yet. I get the feeling they'd like to pin it on me."

"They can't possibly suspect you."

"If I were them, I'd consider me a pretty good suspect. Jo, Dina told me some things I think you ought to know."

They sat on the bed in the room she had shared with Stevie, and he told her everything he knew.

"All this," she said, "because Eddie Jacoby thought he could make a gift of me."

"It's a possibility."

"All this death."

He touched her cheek, felt her heat, her life flowing into his fingers. "We're not dead, you and me."

"But Ben is. Why him?"

"I don't know."

"I want to leave here, Cork. I want to go home."

"The Winnetka police would like us to stay awhile.

They'll have more questions when they're finished with the crime scene and start looking at the evidence."

"I've told them everything I know."

"So have I, several times. They'll ask again. Before we talk to them we should have a lawyer. And there's something else, Jo."

He told her about Phillip Jacoby's assertion that she had consented to the things he'd done.

"That little son of a bitch," she gasped.

"So for a while, we sit tight and see what develops and make sure that we're prepared to face the worst."

She felt the tears welling, her throat closing. "Shit doesn't just happen, does it, Cork. It happens and happens and happens."

"Here," he said. He kissed her hands, lifted them, and waved them gently over their heads.

"What was that?" she asked.

"A shit shield."

She was laughing quietly when the knock came at the door.

"Cork?" Rose called. "There's a call for you."

Jo followed him to the kitchen, where he took the phone and said, "Yes?" He listened, looked concerned. "I'll be right there." He hung up.

"What is it?" Jo asked.

"That was Lou Jacoby. He wants to see me."

49

CORK PARKED ON the drive that circled in front of
Lou Jacoby's Lake Forest estate home.

"I swear to God," he said, killing the engine, "the
North Shore has more castles than the Rhine."

He'd tried to convince Jo not to come, but she'd
insisted, telling him that now that they were
together, she'd be damned if she'd let anything separate them.

Evers, Jacoby's houseman, answered the bell. He
looked tired but still maintained the rigid formality
his position required.

"The O'Connors," Cork said. "Mr. Jacoby is
expecting us."

Evers led them down a long hallway to the rear of
the house, where a small, lovely woman with black
hair and a Latin look awaited them. She seemed familiar, but Cork couldn't recall where he'd seen her
before.

"I'll take it from here," she said to Evers.

"Of course." The houseman vanished back into the
vast silence of the place.

"It is a pleasure to see you again," she said to Jo.

Then to Cork: "We have not met. I am Gabriella Jacoby, Eddie's widow."

She spoke a foreign accent he'd recently heard, and he realized where he'd seen her before. In the face of a pilot.

"Do you have a brother?"

"Yes."

"Tony Salguero?"

"Do you know Antonio?"

"I've met him."

"He is a good brother." She smiled briefly, then lapsed into a somber tone. "I told Lou this was not a good idea, but he insisted. I warn you, he is out of his head with grief. He will probably say things that will sound crazy. You may leave now, and I will explain it to him."

"If he wants to see me," Cork said, "let him see me."

She reached for the knob, hesitated as if she were going to speak again, perhaps argue the wisdom of proceeding, then she opened the door and stepped ahead of them inside.

The room was mostly dark and smelled of an old man and his cigars. The only illumination came through the slits of partially opened blinds over the long windows. In the far corner, bars of light like the rungs of a ladder fell across a stuffed chair and its occupant. Jo's eyes climbed each rung until they encountered the red eyes of Lou Jacoby staring back. He wore a dressing gown that hung open over his chest, showing a white undershirt. His legs were bare, his feet slippered. His hair was a wild spray of white. He seemed smaller than the last time she'd seen him, as if Ben's death had taken away something physical from his own form. He held a glass that contained ice and a hickory-colored liquid. A smoking cigar sat in a standing brass ashtray to his right.

"I knew you were trouble the moment I saw you with him." The voice came from the darkness beneath his red eyes, from the mouth Jo still couldn't quite make out.

"I'm sorry about your son," she said.

For a moment, he didn't reply. Then: "The sons should bury the father. That's how it's supposed to be."

Gabriella crossed to him and stood at his side, her hand protectively on his shoulder. In the slatted light, her shadow fell over the old man and swallowed him.

"You wanted to see me," Cork said.

"If I were a younger man, I'd stand up and beat you to death with my own hands."

"I didn't kill your son."

"Lou has been told about the police investigation," Gabriella said. "He knows about the gun they found. What they call a throw-down, I believe. They told him it is something policemen have been known to do to get away with murder."

"Not this cop. Have you talked to Dina Willner?"

"She has been mysteriously silent to our inquiries," Gabriella replied.

"It's not enough you kill my son," Jacoby spat out. "You slander my grandson, too, with your lies."

"I understand your grief," Cork said. "But don't let it blind you to the truth."

With difficulty, Jacoby rose from his chair. "I'm not a man of idle threats. An eye for an eye. You hear me?"

"Mercy," Jo said, speaking softly into the dark of the room. "It falls like the gentle rain from heaven, Mr. Jacoby."

"Not in this house, woman." He said to Gabriella, "Get them out."

Gabriella came forward and placed herself between the O'Connors and the old man. "It's time for you to go."

"We've done nothing to you," Jo said.

"You've done everything short of killing me. Get out."

Jo turned away, then Cork. Gabriella followed them out and led them toward the front door.

"I warned you," she said.

"Have you even tried to help him understand?" Cork said.

"You saw him. When he's ready to listen to reason, I will reason."

As they neared the door, they saw Evers blocking the way, arguing with someone standing just outside.

"What is it?" Gabriella said.

Evers stepped aside, and Jo saw Rae Bly framed in the doorway.

"I was trying to explain that I have my instructions."

"To keep me out?" Rae's voice was a sharp blade of indignation. "I don't believe it."

"That's all right. I will take care of it," Gabriella said.

Evers stepped back, turned, and walked away, stiff as a zombie.

Gabriella addressed her sister-in-law. "It is true. He does not want to see you."

"Does he even know I'm here?"

"I told him that you called. He won't see you. If you try to talk to him now, you will only be hurt by him. When he is ready, I will let you know."

"I'm his daughter, Gabby."

"As am I now. And we must think of him. Later he will see you. It will be all right, I promise, *pobrecito*. Now, good day to you all."

Cork and Jo stepped outside.

Rae stared at the door that had closed against her. She wilted and then she wept. "Ben, Ben. Oh, Benny."

Jo put her arms around her. After a minute, Rae pulled herself together.

"I'm sorry," she said.

"That's all right."

"I didn't get all the details, but enough to say I'm sorry for what happened to you, Jo. It's shameful, but that's the Jacobys. Did Lou see you?"

"Only long enough to threaten us," Jo said.

"Don't take him lightly."

"This is Cork, my husband."

"I figured."

"Rae is Ben's sister."

"I was sure he'd see me. We're all we have now, each other."

"Apparently, he thinks he has Gabriella, too," Cork said.

"Will you be all right?" Jo asked.

"No, but that's not your concern. You have your own problems. And the Jacobys," she said bitterly, "we take care of our own affairs."

They left her, a small figure standing alone in the shadow of her father's great house.

50

FROM ROSE AND Mal's duplex, he called the number on the card Dina Willner had given him.

"I just came from Lou Jacoby's," he told her.

"And you're still alive?"

"Not for long, from the way he's talking."

"Cork, Lou doesn't just talk."

"Gabriella Jacoby says you've been silent on what happened at Ben's place."

"Silent? I've been trying to reach Lou but Gabriella is screening everything. I can't get through to him."

Cork heard the frustration in her voice, a rare emotion in his experience. He realized how tired she must be, too.

"How's Jo?" she asked.

"Doing remarkably well, considering."

"Strong woman. How about you? Are you all right?"

"Jo's safe. I can handle everything else."

"I'll get to Lou somehow, explain things, Cork. That's a promise."

He was exhausted, but he spent the afternoon at a park on the lake with his family, pushing Stevie on the swings, talking with his daughters about North-western and Notre Dame, watching Jo—who seemed, in spite of what she'd been through, calm as the water on the lake that day. Twenty years before, he had pro-posed to her on Lake Michigan, on a dinner cruise, an evening that had changed his life and taken it in the best of directions.

He sent Jenny and Annie off to play with their brother while he sat on a blanket with Jo.

"I've been thinking about Gabriella," he said. "And her brother. And about an angel who spoke to Lizzie Fineday."

"An angel?"

"In Lizzie's confused recollection anyway. What was it that Gabriella called Rae this morning? *Pobrecito*? What does that mean?"

"If I recall my college Spanish, it means something like 'poor little one.'"

"Lizzie said her angel called her 'poor vaceeto.' Could it be that the angel spoke Spanish and what she really said was *pobrecito*?"

"You think Gabriella was Lizzie's angel?"

"When I called Edward Jacoby's home the morning after he was murdered, his housekeeper told me that Mrs. Jacoby wasn't there. She was on a boat. Tony Salguero told me he was sailing on Lake Michigan. Because I didn't know there was a connection between them, I didn't put it together at the time, but what do you want to bet they were on the same boat? How dif-ficult would it be to anchor somewhere not far from an airfield, fly to Aurora, take care of some pretty gruesome business, and get back to the boat in time for Lou Jacoby's call the morning after Eddie was murdered?"

"I don't know. How would you prove something like that?"

"They had to leave a trail. Dock somewhere, file a flight plan, gas up, land and park a plane. If they tailed Eddie out to Mercy Falls, they had to have a vehicle of some kind. A rental, maybe? There's got to be documentation for some of this somewhere. It should just be a question of tracking it down."

He stood up and called to the children. He hated to end the picnic, but there was work to be done.

First he called Ed Larson, who had already spoken with the Winnetka police and knew about what had happened to Jo.

"Christ, Cork. I'm so sorry."

"Yeah."

"I'd love to get that Jacoby kid alone somewhere."

"Won't happen, Ed."

"How's Jo doing?"

"Holding her own."

"Look, I do have two pieces of good news."

"I could use some about now," Cork said.

"First, Simon Rutledge was finally able to talk to Carl Berger. Looks like we'll be amending the complaint against Lydell Cramer to include conspiracy to commit murder. Berger says that Cramer used his sister and LaRusse to arrange to have Stone do the hit at the Tibodeau cabin. The motive was revenge, pure and simple.

"Now for the second piece of good news. We finally found Arlo Knuth. He'd gone on a bender and wound up in the drunk tank in Hibbing. I talked to him. He says that after Schilling ran him off, he parked behind the blockhouse on the lower level at

Mercy Falls. Around midnight, he saw two vehicles head to the upper lot near the overlook. Right behind them came a third vehicle that parked in the lower lot. Two people got out and hiked up the stairs toward the overlook. They came back down half an hour later and left. Arlo says he left right after that. The place was getting too busy."

"Was he able to give you a description?"

"No, but he did give us something very interesting. Whoever those two people were, they spoke Spanish."

"*Pobrecito,* Ed."

"What?"

Cork told him about Gabriella Jacoby and Antonio Salguero, and explained his thinking about Eddie's murder.

"The Salgueros lost everything in Argentina. Marrying Eddie Jacoby gave Gabriella a handle on another fortune. With her husband dead, she probably stands to get her hands on a significant chunk of change. Insurance, at the very least. Maybe she even moves up a notch in the old man's will."

"They'd been married for years. Why kill Eddie now?" Larson asked.

"Maybe she waited until she was solid with his father. She's given Lou grandchildren, weaseled her way next to his heart. I'd bet she and Tony have been thinking about it for a while. Could be that Aurora's isolation seemed to offer the opportunity they'd been hoping for."

"And the hick cops they figured would do the investigating."

"Probably that, too. Look, it's a lot of speculation, I know."

"Makes sense, though."

"When Dina gave Ben her report on our questioning of Lizzie Fineday, Jacoby must have known what 'poor vaceeto' was really all about. He took Dina off the case in the hope of keeping her ignorant, and I'll bet he canceled his rendezvous with Jo because he went to see Gabriella or Salguero, to confront them."

"Didn't want the police involved?"

"Exactly. A family matter. The family name at stake. Something like that. There's a lot of digging to do, Ed."

"I'm on it, Cork," Larson said. "I'll keep you posted."

The next call was to Dina Willner's cell phone.

"Tell me what you know about Tony Salguero," he said when she answered.

"Handsome. Educated. Refined. Daring."

"Daring? What do you mean?"

"He flies. He sails. Like his father, he's a world-class big-game hunter. He was in the Argentine military for a long time, an officer."

"Special training?"

"I could find out. Why?"

"I want to know if he's the kind of man who'd know where to thrust a knife to kill somebody instantly."

Dina's end of the line went silent a long moment. "As in Eddie Jacoby."

"Exactly."

He told her what he knew and what he suspected.

"Gabriella and Tony together." She was quiet, probably rolling the idea around in her thinking. "Gabriella was a better woman in almost every way than Eddie could have hoped for. Murder might not have been on her mind at first, but I imagine anybody married to Eddie would, over time, begin to think about it seriously."

"There's something else," Cork said. "I think Ben suspected. I think that's why he took you off the case. 'Poor vaceeto.' He put it togther right away."

"God, why didn't I?"

"It had been a hard day, remember?"

"Still . . ."

"Look, with your connections, any way you could find out quickly who Ben called after he talked to you yesterday afternoon?"

"You're thinking he called Gabriella or Tony?"

"And then went to see them."

"That's why he canceled on Jo. Cork, do you think they killed him?"

"Not necessarily themselves. They may have had it done. Ed Larson's working on the connection with Eddie Jacoby's murder. Once we have that, Winnetka PD might be persuaded to look at them for Ben's murder as well. Given the ties between the Jacobys and local law enforcement, it might be best not to tip our hand too early."

The silence again. Then: "It feels so cold, Cork."

He thought about Gabriella, the shadow she'd cast over Lou Jacoby that morning, her control. It may all have started as a way to rid herself of a man no woman in her right mind would want, but it was different now, huge and malevolent. It had probably taken the life of Ben Jacoby, and Cork could feel the menace at his own back, in Lou Jacoby's ignorant vow, "An eye for an eye."

"Watch yourself, Cork."

"You, too."

He put the phone down. He'd made the calls in the front room of the duplex, away from the rest of the family who were all gathered in the kitchen around the table talking and laughing. He could hear Mal and Rose, each of the children, and Jo. He thought about the Jacobys, the various reasons they had married—money, position, beauty, prestige, duty. For all its pain, all its uncertainty, all the terror of the power it wielded, love was still, in Cork's book, the best reason.

He started toward the kitchen, toward the laughter that was a song, toward the love that was everything.

51

*H*E HEARD THE phone ring, looked at the clock beside the bed, wondered who would be calling at two in the morning. In the hallway, the floorboards creaked, and Mal Thorne said, "Hello?"

He didn't say anything else. A minute later, a cupboard door squeaked open in the kitchen, followed shortly by the rattle of glass in the refrigerator.

Cork threw back the covers, pulled on his pants, and slipped from the room where Jo lay sleeping.

The kitchen light was on. Mal stood at the counter near the sink, a glass of milk in one hand, a cold chicken leg in the other. He held up the leg. "There's more in the fridge if you're hungry."

"No, thanks."

Mal wore a white T-shirt, red gym shorts, white socks. "Trouble sleeping?"

"Can't get my eyes to close. My brain won't stop working. Who was on the phone?"

"Nobody there. Second time tonight. Would it help you to talk?"

"Maybe."

Mal used the chicken leg to point toward the kitchen table. "Confessional's open."

Cork sat down. His feet were bare and cold on the linoleum.

"I've been thinking about everything that's happened recently," he said. "A lot of what's occurred I understand now, but I'm having trouble understanding my place in all this."

"How so?"

"Jo's a wonderful woman."

"You won't get an argument from me on that."

"She didn't want me to take the job as sheriff, Mal."

"Did she tell you that?"

"No, but I knew. She's always been afraid of the effect it's had on our family."

"Cork, if you're going to start blaming yourself for what's happened—"

"It's not that, Mal. It's a realization. I was doing fine running Sam's Place. It's a pretty location there on Iron Lake. I grilled good burgers. I set my own hours, closed up at night, went home, and what did I have to worry about except making sure there were enough potato chips for the next day? Now I lie awake worrying about everything. The department budget, county politics, the safety of my people." He glanced toward the hallway. "The safety of my family."

"Why did you take the job?"

"I told myself there were good reasons, but in the end it was pride, plain and simple."

"I suspect there was more to it than that, but I understand what you're saying. So what are you going to do?"

The fridge kicked on, and the hum grabbed Cork's

attention. He looked at the refrigerator door, which was decorated with photos, mostly ones Jo had sent of the children and her and Cork.

"I'm going to quit. When I get back to Aurora, I'm going to tender my resignation."

Mal took a bite from the chicken leg and didn't seem inclined to argue.

The phone rang in the hallway.

"There it is again," Mal said. "The caller who isn't there." He got up to answer. "Hello?" He paused. "Yes, he is. Just a minute." He brought the cordless into the kitchen. "It's Dina Willner, for you."

"Dina, what's up?"

"Make sure the lights are out, then carefully look out the front window."

Cork said, "Kill the lights, Mal."

Mal did as Cork asked and followed him to the front room. Cork parted the curtains a crack.

"What am I looking for, Dina?"

"Black Malibu two houses down, far side of the street."

He located it parked in a place where the street-lights didn't quite reach. "I don't see anything. Wait." Inside the Malibu, a match flared, lighting a cigarette perhaps. "Okay, I make 'em."

"They've been watching for a while."

"Who are they?"

"Lou threatened you this morning. I'd say he's making good on that threat."

"A hit?" Cork eyed the Malibu fiercely. "Where are you?"

"In the alley back of the duplex. Get dressed and get out here. You have a firearm, bring it."

"Winnetka PD took it."

"Then just get out here."

Cork handed the phone to Mal.

"What is it?"

"See the black Malibu? Dina thinks there's someone in it who's been paid to kill me."

"Jesus, Mary, and Joseph. Let's call the police."

"Wait, Mal. There's not much they could do at this point but roust the guy. If it *is* a hit, that would only delay the inevitable."

"What are you going to do?"

"Dina's out back. I'll talk to her. Maybe we can come up with something. Don't wake anybody."

Cork went to the bedroom, dressed quietly, put on his windbreaker, and paused a moment before he walked out. Jo lay on her side, the top sheet half covering her face. She looked peaceful, and he wanted her to stay that way. He closed the door silently as he left.

In the kitchen, Mal said, "Take the back stairs. I'm going to keep an eye on the guy out front. You know Dina's cell phone number?"

Cork gave it to him.

"He moves, I'll let you know."

"Thanks, Mal."

Outside was a small landing with a flight of wooden stairs that led down to the backyard. Cork descended, crossed the yard, and went out a gate near the garage. Dina was parked in the alley, in a dark blue Honda Civic.

"What happened to the Ferrari?" Cork asked when he got in.

"This car doesn't shout when I'm on surveillance." Her eyes shifted to the mirror, then back to the alley in front of her. "Among the calls I made after we talked this afternoon were a few discreet inquiries about Lou and those threats he made. Couple hours ago I got a call back. Lou got things going fast. There's a contract on you. Half a million is what I was told."

"He wants me dead pretty bad."

"Half a million is nothing to Lou. It gets worse, because it's not just a hit, Cork. It's a bounty. It's open season on you. Whoever gets to you first."

"If I'm hit, Lou Jacoby's the guy the cops will look at."

"He's old. He's lost everything. Probably in his thinking, his life's over. He goes to jail or even to death row, big deal. I know Lou. He won't hesitate to do what he feels he has to. That includes collateral damage, Cork."

"My family?"

"Or whoever happens to be with you at the time. Half a million dollars is a lot of incentive not to be neat."

"What if we brought in the police, Adam Gabriel, say, and NORTAF?"

"What can they do until somebody actually tries something? You know how that goes. Even if they wanted to help, they can't watch your back twenty-four/seven. And we both know there are badges up here on the Jacoby payroll. You deal with them and everything gets funneled right back to Lou.

"I worked a case in New Jersey. We had a witness sequestered in a farmhouse outside Passaic. Somebody—a badge, we suspected—leaked the location. The place got hit with three rocket-propelled grenades. Killed the witness and two federal agents. You don't want that to happen to your family." She looked grim and sorry. "You need to find a safe place to disappear for a couple of days."

A flare of anger shot through Cork, seemed to explode in his brain. He slammed his fist into the dashboard. "I'm not running, Dina. I'll talk to Lou Jacoby, pound a little sense into that old man if necessary."

"You barge in, you really think he'd back down? Hell, he'd probably shoot you himself." She put a hand gently on his arm and spoke calmly. "Right now you need to back off. Let us gather enough evidence to convince Lou to listen to reason. With Ed Larson working his end and me here, we'll have what we need in a couple of days, I promise."

"A lot of homicides never get solved."

"A lot of homicides don't have me working the case."

He knew she was right, knew that an irrational act in response to another irrational act usually spelled tragedy.

"A couple of days, Cork, that's all."

In the dark inside the Civic, he stared into her eyes.

"Trust me," she said.

Her cell phone chirped. She looked at the display. "It's coming from the duplex." She answered. "Yeah?" A few seconds and she said, "Thanks," and broke the connection. "Shit."

"What?"

"The Malibu's on the move."

Behind them, a car screamed into the alley. Its headlights blasted over them. Dina jammed the Civic into gear and shot off with a squeal. The car was far more powerful than it looked, and Cork figured she had customized the engine, added muscle. She hit the street at the other end, took a hard right. Cork looked back as the black Malibu fishtailed into sight. Dina cut up side streets and blazed down alleyways. She worked gradually east, putting distance between them and the car in pursuit. Finally she skidded to a stop in a driveway behind a high hedge. She killed the engine and the headlights. They sat a moment and the Malibu shot past, roaring into the dark at the far end of the street.

"You need to disappear and you need to do it now," she said.

"Where?"

"Pick a direction and go. Do you have any money?"

"Not much."

"Here." She reached under the dash and something clicked. A small compartment popped open next to the glove box. She reached in and pulled out a stack of bills. "There's twelve hundred. I keep it for emergencies. Take it. And take this, too." She reached down, pulled up the cuff of her pants, removed her .32 Beretta from the ankle holster, and handed it to Cork.

"I can't even say good-bye to my family?"

"The choice is yours, but I think it's risky. Obviously the guys in the Malibu weren't alone. Somebody tipped them off that you were in the alley. No telling how many people are on you or where they are. I'll let Jo know what's going on."

He gave a nod and they were both quiet.

Dina sat back with a tired sigh. "Lou, Eddie, Phillip, Gabriella, Tony. My God, what you must think of us Jews."

"It's got nothing to do with religion or culture. It's just a screwed-up family. You find those everywhere. Irish Catholics, Ojibwe—hell, probably even among the Bushmen of the Kalahari."

At the end of the block, the black Malibu crept into view like a panther stalking its prey.

"I'll lead them on a merry chase," Dina said. "You make yourself scarce."

"Once again you come to my rescue."

"I'm a sucker for a pretty face. Get going."

He opened the door, slid out.

"You have my number. Let me know where you end up. Good luck, Cork."

Dina backed from the drive and turned on the headlights. As soon as the Malibu squealed in her direction, she shot off. Cork hunkered in the dark of the hedge while the Malibu sped past. He waited until the sound of the two engines had faded into the distance before he walked to the street.

Dawn seemed far away. At that moment, everything did.

EPILOGUE

A SOLITARY TWO-LANE highway splits the marsh. To the right and left, brittle reeds disappear into a dingy, low-hanging mist. A fragile light falls over the scene, the day almost breaking. The marsh is silent. The birds have fled south or been killed by the virus, or perhaps it's something about the place itself that inhibits their song, for there is the feel of abandonment here, of death, like an old battlefield or a cemetery.

Far to the west rises the dark square of a barn wall and the slope of a roof. It seems like an ark floating on a dun-colored sea. East there is nothing but the empty slate sky and the reluctant dawn.

He walks in his windbreaker with his shoulders hunched, each breath of cold air a reminder that autumn is making its last stand. He knows what will follow is a killing season.

He hears the rattle long before the mist around him begins to glow from the headlights, and then the truck passes, an old pickup, the bed fitted with rickety slat-board sides. Thirty yards beyond him the brake lights flash. The truck slows, stops. As he approaches, he sees that the bed is filled with feed sacks stacked half a dozen high in neat rows, and a contraption of wood and metal with gears and a long handle whose purpose is unknown to him. He opens the door. The smell of manure greets him.

"Hop in." The man at the wheel beckons. He's in overalls and his boots are caked. "Where you going?"

"North," he says as he climbs in and slams the door.

"Whereabouts?"

"Just north."

"Big place, that." The man grins in a friendly way and gears into the mist.

In a moment, the truck is lost, heading north, which is indeed a big place, but not big enough.

ATRIA BOOKS
PROUDLY PRESENTS

COPPER RIVER

WILLIAM KENT KRUEGER

Available from Atria Books in hardcover

Turn the page for a preview of
Copper River. . . .

1

HENRY MELOUX, the old Ojibwe Mide, might tell the story this way.

He might begin by saying that the earth is alive, that all things on it—water, air, plants, rocks, even dead trees—have spirit. In the absence of wind, the grass still trembles. On days when the clouds are dense as gray wool, flowers still understand how to track the sun. Trees, when they bend, whisper to one another. In such a community of spirits, nothing goes unnoticed. Would not the forest, therefore, know that a child is about to die?

She is fourteen years, nine months, twenty-seven days old. She has never had a period, never had a boyfriend, never even had a real date. She has never eaten in a restaurant more formal than McDonald's. She has never seen a city larger than Marquette, Michigan.

She cannot remember a night when she wasn't awakened by nightmares, some dreamed, many horribly real. She cannot remember a day she was happy, although she has always been hopeful that she might find happiness, discover it like a diamond in the dust at her feet. Through all the horror of her life, she has, miraculously, held to that hope.

Until now.

Now, though she is only fourteen, she is about to die. And she knows it.

Somewhere among the trees below her, the man she calls Scorpio is coming for her.

She cringes behind a pile of brush in the middle of a clear-cut hillside studded with stumps like gravestones. The morning sun has just climbed above the tops of the poplar trees that outline the clearing. The chill bite of autumn is in the air. From where she crouches high on the hill, she can see the gleam of Lake Superior miles to the north. The great inland sea beckons, and she imagines sailing away on all that empty blue, alone on a boat taking her toward a place where someone waits for her and worries, a place she has never been.

She shivers violently. Before fleeing, she grabbed a thin brown blanket, which she wrapped around her shoulders. Her feet are bare, gone numb in the long, cold night. They bleed, wounded during her flight through the woods, but she no longer feels any pain. They've become stones at the end of her ankles.

In the trees far below, a dog barks, cracking the morning calm. The girl focuses on a place two hundred yards distant where, half an hour earlier, she'd emerged from the forest and started to climb the logged-over hillside. An hour after dawn, Scorpio's dog had begun baying. When she heard the hungry sound, she knew he'd got hold of her scent. What little hope she'd held to melted instantly. After that, it was a frantic run trying to stay ahead.

Scorpio steps from the shadow of the trees. He's

like a whip, thin and cruel and electric in the sunlight. She can see the glint off the blue barrel of the rifle he cradles. Snatch, his black and tan German shepherd, pads before him, nose to the earth, tracking her through the graveyard of stumps. Scorpio scans the hillside above. She thinks she can see him smile, a gash of white.

There is no sense in hiding now. In a few minutes, Scorpio will be on her. Grasshopper quick, she pops from the blind of brush and sprints toward the hilltop. Her senseless feet thud against the hard earth. She lets the blanket fall to the ground, leaves it behind her. Starved for sunlight, the skin of her face and arms looks bleached. Beneath her thin, dirty T-shirt her breasts are barely formed, but the small, fleshy mounds rise and fall dramatically as she sucks air in desperate gasps. Behind her, the dog begins a furious barking. He has seen the prey.

She crests the hill and comes to a dead end. Before her the ground falls away, a sheer drop two hundred feet to a river that's a rush of white water between jagged rocks. There is no place left to run. She casts a frenzied eye back. Scorpio lopes toward her with Snatch in the lead. To her left and right, there is only the ragged lip of the cut across the hill.

Only one way for her to go now: down.

The face of the cliff below is a rugged profile offering handholds and small ledges. There are also tufts of brush that cling tenaciously to the stone, rooted in tiny fissures. She spies a shelf ten feet below, barely wider than her foot, but it is enough. She kneels and lowers herself over the edge. Clinging to the brush and the rough knobs of stone that punctuate the cliff, she begins her descent.

The rock scrapes her skin, leaves her arms bleeding. Her toes stretch for a foothold but, numbed, feel almost nothing. Weakened by an ordeal that has gone on longer than she can remember, her strength threatens to fail her, but she does not give up. She has never given up. Whatever the horror in front of her, she has always faced it and pushed ahead. This moment is no different. She wills a place to stand. Her feet find support, a few inches of flat rock on which she eases herself down.

"Come on, sweet thing. Come on back up."

Scorpio's voice is reasonable, almost comforting. She lifts her face. He's smiling, bone-white teeth between thin, bloodless lips. Beside him, the dog snarls and snaps, foam dripping from his purple gums.

"Hush!" Scorpio orders. "Sit."

Snatch obeys.

"Come on, now. Time to end this foolishness."

He lays down his rifle, bends low, and offers his hand.

In the quiet while she considers, she presses herself to the cliff where the stone still holds the cold of night. She can hear far below the hiss and roiling of the white water.

"We'll go back to the cabin," Scorpio says. "Have a little breakfast. Bet you're hungry. Now, doesn't that sound better than running over these woods, ruining those pretty little feet, freezing your ass off?"

He bends lower. His outstretched hand pushes nearer, a hand that has offered only humiliation and pain. On his wrist is a tattoo, a large black scorpion, the reason for the name she has given him in her thinking. She eyes his hairy knuckles, then looks into his face, which at the moment appears deceptively human.

"Think about it. You find a place to perch on that cliff, then what? It's not so bad out here right now. Sun's up, air's calm. But tonight it'll be close to freezing. That means you, too. You want to freeze to death? Hell, it doesn't matter anyway. I'll just leave old Snatch here to make sure you don't climb back up, go get me some rope, and come down there to get you. But I guarantee if I have to do that, I won't be in a forgiving mood. So what do you say?"

Not taking her eyes off him, she seeks a foothold farther down, somewhere out of his reach, but she cannot feel her toes. Finally, she risks a glance below her. In that instant, Scorpio's hand locks around her wrist.

"Got you."

He's strong, his grip powerful. He drags her kicking up the face of the rock. She struggles, screams as he wraps his arms around her. The dog dances back from the edge, barking crazily. Scorpio's breath smells of tobacco and coffee, but there's another smell coming off him, familiar and revolting. The musk odor of his sex.

"Oh, little darling," he croons, "am I going to make you pay."

She puts all her desperation, all her remaining strength, into one last effort, a violent twist that breaks her loose, sends her tumbling backward over the cliff.

The world spins. First there is blue sky, then white water, then blue sky again. She closes her eyes and spreads her arms. Suddenly she isn't falling but flying. The wind streams across her skin. Her held breath fills her like a smooth balloon. She is weightless.

For one glorious moment in her short, unhappy life, she is absolutely free.

* * *

Meloux would finish gently, pointing out, perhaps, that the fall of the smallest robin is known to the spirits of the earth, that no death goes unnoticed or unmourned, that the river has simply been waiting, and like a mother she has opened wide her arms.

2

Renoir DuBois kept his heart in his bedroom closet, hidden in a Nike shoe box.

There was an agate he'd found on the shore of Lake Superior when he was very young, the image of a wolf so clear on its smooth surface that it seemed etched by a purposeful hand. In the totemic system of the Anishinaabeg, Ren was Ma'iingan, Wolf Clan, and he believed the stone was a sign of some kind whose full meaning he would someday understand.

In the box there was also an eagle feather given to him by his great-grandfather, who told him this story: A certain man spent his whole life searching in vain for an eagle feather that would signify his great wisdom. He paid no heed to the needs of his family or relatives or other people. Finally he gave up and said to the Great Spirit, "I have wasted my life searching for the eagle feather. Now I will spend my time helping others." As soon as he said this, a beautiful eagle flew overhead and a feather gently drifted down.

There was a small figure of the Marvel Comics character Silver Surfer, one of Ren's all-time favorite superheroes. His best friend, Charlie, had spotted it at a swap meet in Marquette and had given it to him for Christmas.

There was the skull of a vole, small, delicate, perfect, that Ren had discovered in the meadow south of the cabins one summer afternoon. Only the skull, no other bones. So that it would not be crushed by his other treasures, he kept it in a tiny box that had once held one of his mother's necklaces. Sometimes he opened the necklace box and spent hours drawing the skull in minute detail, imagining as he did so what kind of world such a small brain and perspective would see.

There was a newspaper article, which his mother did not know he had, cut from the *Billings Gazette,* about the murder of his father, and also the long, celebratory obituary that had been printed in the *Marquette County Courier.*

The most precious item in the box was a drawing his father had given him, done on a plain sheet of notepad paper, the kind kept by the phone to write messages. It had been created on a good day, Ren recalled, an August day. They'd spent the morning putting a new toilet in one of the cabins, and his father had talked while he worked, offering Ren his understanding about Kitchimanidoo, the Great Spirit, about life, about art. He'd said, as he put the wax ring in the flush hole and settled the porcelain bowl on top, that life was a reflection of the Great Spirit, and that art was a reflection of life. All of them were simpler than people imagined. At lunch in the main cabin, which was called Thor's Lodge, he'd illustrated his point with a pen-and-ink drawing—two long arcs, a few easy loops. "What is it?" he'd asked Ren. Though nothing connected in a way that completed the image, Ren saw it was a bear. "There aren't many clear connections in life. God, Kitchimanidoo, they're pretty sketchy when you come right down to it. But you don't need everything spelled out for you, son. Here"—and he touched Ren's chest above his heart—"here is where it all comes together." A week later, his father was dead.

All the treasures in his box Ren loved and in loving them found the connections simple and unseen that ran from the outside world deep into the world of his heart, just as his father had promised.

That afternoon, fourteen-year-old Ren was at work on something that would eventually find its way into his box. He had no idea at the moment of the enormity of the events that would put it there.

"On your knees with your nose in the dirt. Dude, that's so lame, but so *you*."

Ren looked up from his work, startled. Charlie Miller stood above him, her face a narrow mask of disgust. Her real name was Charlene, but she preferred Charlie. A lot about her besides her name belied her gender. She looked like a boy, dressed like a boy, and was the fastest runner in the eighth grade at Bodine Area Middle School. Her hair was shaved close to her scalp and from a distance appeared to be no more than a dusting of charcoal. Her left nostril and her lower lip were pierced and sported small silver rings. She was taller than Ren, more slender, and moved with the quickness and grace of a forest animal. Also the wariness.

"Get bent," Ren said, and returned to his work.

Charlie knelt beside him. Ren could smell that she needed a bath.

"What's up?" she said.

"Cougar track."

"Bullshit."

Two nights before, rain had turned the ground around the cabins soft. Ren hadn't discovered the track until the next afternoon; as soon as he did, he set about preserving it. He was used to seeing tracks in the vicinity of the resort cabins. Raccoon, bear, even an occasional bobcat. They came nosing around the trash bins, which Ren's mother kept locked. At first he'd thought the track was a large bobcat, but when he got out his copy of Peterson's *A Field Guide to Animal Tracks,* he realized it was not. He'd heard stories of cougars still roaming the woods of the U.P., but he never thought he'd find the evidence. Using an old paintbrush with soft bristles, he'd gently cleaned debris from the imprint, then sprayed it with clear lacquer. When that dried, he mixed up a batch of plaster of Paris in an empty Folger's coffee can, and he'd been pouring this into the track when Charlie startled him.

"How do you know it's a cougar?" Charlie asked.

"I looked it up."

"I never heard of a cougar around here."

"They used to be all over the place, but people killed most of them and drove the others away. I heard there might not be more than twenty on the whole U.P."

"Dude, you're worse than *National Geographic.*"

She hit him hard on the arm and he dropped the coffee can.

"Goddamn it, Charlie, quit screwing around. This is important."

"Yeah? So's this." She hit him again.

Ren launched into her and they rolled over in the soft dirt. Charlie easily got the upper hand, straddled him, and pinned him to the ground.

"Say it," she commanded.

"Bite me."

She slapped the side of his head lightly. "Say it."

"You suck."

She lifted her butt and bounced hard on his stomach so that he grunted.

"Say it."

"All right. I give."

She sprang off him, raised her hands above her head, and did a victory dance. Ren got back on his knees and crawled to the cougar track.

Charlie knelt beside him again. "Cougar. No shit."

"No shit."

"Sweet," she said.

Ren heard the scrape of pine wood. He glanced up as the door to the nearest cabin opened.

The man with the wounded leg stood at the threshold, looking stunned, as if the beautiful afternoon, the evergreen-scented air, the blue autumn sky, the warm sunshine, were the most amazing things he'd ever seen. Or maybe it was just the fact that he was still alive. After a moment, he fell forward, tumbled down the steps, and lay sprawled facedown in the dirt.

"Jesus." Ren sprang to his feet and sprinted to the fallen man.

"What happened to him?"

"Somebody shot him yesterday."

The man's pants were bloodstained. The left leg had been cut off near the crotch, revealing two wounds, one on the outside of his thigh where the bullet had entered and another on the inside where it exited. The exit wound was larger and open, fitted with a tube and drainage bag that were held in place with surgical tape. The entrance wound had been stitched, but the stitches were broken and the wound was bleeding. The man's eyes were closed. His face had gone slack.

"Is he dead?" Charlie asked.

"God, I hope not. I was supposed to be watching him." Ren felt the man's neck. "He's got a pulse. We've got to get him back inside. You take his left arm, I'll take his right. Let's see if we can lift him."

"Unh-uh." Charlie backed away a step. "I've tried dragging my old man into bed when he was passed out. You might as well try lifting a dead horse."

"Come on, damn it, give me a hand."

"All right, but I'm telling you, you're better off just getting a blanket and letting him lie there."

She grasped his arm as Ren had instructed and they tried in vain to bring the man to his feet.

"Like a dead horse, I told you," Charlie grunted as she dropped the arm.

Ren pushed himself up. "Don't leave him."

"Where are you going?"

He bounded up the steps and ran inside Cabin 3. The bedding lay on the floor where the man had thrown it. Ren grabbed the blanket, then another from the closet, and raced back outside. Charlie was bent over, examining the man's wounds.

"He's been bleeding pretty bad," she said.

Ren spread out one of the blankets on the ground next to the man.

"Could he, like, bleed to death?"

"Mom says it looks worse than it is."

"She sewed him up?"

"Yeah. Help me here."

Together they rolled him so that he was on the blanket. Ren stood up.

"I'll be right back."

He made for Thor's Lodge, took the steps in a single bound, shoved open the door, and grabbed the telephone. He dialed the animal clinic where his mother worked. Dawn, the receptionist, told him she was out on a call. He tried her cell phone, got her after three rings. Her signal was breaking up, but not so badly she didn't understand. She told him what to do and that she'd be there as soon as she could.

After he hung up, he went to the closet in his mother's bedroom and took her medical bag from the shelf. He returned to where Charlie sat beside the man.

"You were gone a long time," she said.

"I talked to my mom. She'll get here as soon as she can."

He checked the tube and bag taped to the man's thigh.

"What *is* that?" Charlie asked.

"It's called a Penrose drain. It helps the wound stay clean while it heals." Ren dug into the medical bag, brought out a pair of latex gloves and Betadine scrub. He put on the gloves. "Hold his leg."

Ren cleaned the area around the second wound where the stitches were broken. The fast flow of blood had subsided into a steady ooze. He reached into the medical bag again and pulled out a sterile pad, a roll of gauze, tape, and a pair of scissors. He pressed the pad to the wound, bound it in place by wrapping the gauze tightly several times around the man's thigh, and secured it with the surgical tape.

Charlie watched in silent fascination. When Ren finished, she looked at him with admiration. "That was pretty sweet."

"Yeah, well."

"Who is he?"

"Family. My mom's cousin."

"Has he got a name?"

Charlie pulled off the gloves and began to put away the medical things. He considered a moment before answering her.

"Yeah," he said. "It's Cork."

Not sure what to read next?

Visit Pocket Books online at

www.simonsays.com

Reading suggestions for
you and your reading group
New release news
Author appearances
Online chats with your favorite writers
Special offers
Order books online
And much, much more!

13456